Somewhere

That's

Green

To those who have always been by my side. You are honored in small ways in this book.

Chapter 1

I've been many different people throughout my life. From Veruca Salt to Tinkerbell, I know that the moment the lights come up on stage that I am no longer Morgan Hathaway. I've loved theatre ever since I was a little girl. The feeling of adrenaline pumping through my veins, the audience's reactions, and the overall satisfaction I get from doing what I love.

Theatre has always been a passion of mine. I always loved the idea of transforming into a character, and soon you are lost in their world. My favorite were musicals because characters just broke out in song and got to sing about their feelings whenever they felt like it. Mostly, I liked it because of the love story and the happy endings. It was nice to escape into that world and forget reality.

Because reality wasn't presented to you with a shiny ribbon on top. The real world doesn't always give you what you want. Life isn't fair and for me, I had to learn that the hard way at a young age.

I inherited my love for theatre from my grandpa. He used to live in El Paso and worked at a movie theater. This movie theatre held big movie premieres and he saw famous actors like John Wayne. He loved movies and Western movies were his favorite. From then on, he loved theatre and began acting in some productions. He began studying acting from the big screen working at the theatre during the day and at night he would go and perform.

He taught me everything he knew about acting and showed me his love for musicals which I adopted. His favorite musical was *West Side Story*, and we would watch it every summer together. We did everything together and were inseparable. My grandma died at a young age from cancer, and I never got the chance to meet her. My grandpa was then alone, and my mom insisted to her father to come live with us. He refused, saying he was too young and in good health to go live with us.

He liked to be independent and free to do as he pleased. He was stubborn like that. Sure, he was lonely sometimes without my grandma, but he kept going on. He always took me out and we would spend the whole day together. We mostly bonded over theatre, but we could talk about anything. My parents were also into theatre, and they encouraged me to follow my dreams. They were really supportive of me as they followed their own dreams in life.

I remember kids in school always saying how I was rich, and I had big house. I never considered us rich or fancy, but I figured it out pretty quickly how we compared to others in town. We lived in a nice big house up in the hills and my grandpa lived a few blocks from us. I never had any friends because I was shy and timid. Most kids also didn't want to be friends with the weird girl who was into theatre.

Theatre was the only thing I cared about and the only way I could express myself. Once they felt I was old enough, I begged my parents to let me do theatre. So, I first started at the age of seven, when they put me in community theatre. My whole life from then on truly began, because that's how I met my best friend in the whole world. We were doing *Charlie and the Chocolate Factory*, and this boy came up on stage to audition for Charlie.

He had big brown eyes and honey hair. He had a great smile and acted like I never seen anyone act before. He was so confident, and he sang like an angel. I never thought someone my age could be as passionate as I was about theatre. He seemed to have it down with the singing and the acting. I wished I could be half as good as him.

I got the part of Veruca Salt, and soon me and the boy became fast friends. Sebastian Montgomery also went to the same school as me and lived on the next street from me, but we had never met until that moment. We both didn't have any friends because we were outcasts who only loved theatre. From then on, we became inseparable. We went on to do more plays together and we always landed the lead roles. He was my best friend and I admired him.

We would stay up late and talk in our treehouse, our families were great friends, and my grandpa grew to love him as well. He was happy I made a friend and that he loved theatre just as much as we did. Sebastian and I were always together. Everyone knew that there couldn't be one without the other. Kids in school always teased our closeness and would say we were boyfriend and girlfriend. Well... eventually those feeling developed.

I don't know exactly how it happened, but I always knew Sebastian was the one. He was not only my best friend, but he was the perfect guy. He was handsome, sweet, charming, and talented. He lit up the stage but illuminated everything with his presence. It was hard not to be around him and love him. I wasn't too sure, but I felt like he loved me too. We were just kids, but it felt like we were on the same path and the feeling was mutual.

My parents met young and had a great relationship. I would watch them and how they were still in love after so many years together. I always admired their relationship and couldn't help but want the same for me. I felt like that could be Sebastian and me. In middle school, I felt our bond getting closer and a potential relationship coming along.

In the eighth grade, we got cast as Peter Pan and Tinkerbell in the school play. There was a lot of rehearsal time together and late-night hang outs. It felt like we were gravitating to being more than friends. We went on and did the show and got standing ovations from my grandpa every night. My life was great back then. I had a great family, a great grandpa, a great theatre life, and a great best friend. And then.... the accident happened.

Shortly after we did *Peter Pan,* my grandpa got into a horrible accent and died. My perfect life came crashing down on me. The person I cared deeply about and loved was gone. My grandpa got taken away from me too soon. From that point on, I became isolated and shut down. He was my reason for getting into theatre and so I stopped doing what I loved.

There wasn't a point to continue with it if he wasn't around to watch me. I became depressed and never did anything anymore. My mom was devastated about her father dying but was more devastated that her daughter was gone too. Because I had a close bond with him that couldn't be replaced. He was gone and I couldn't be fixed. I became depressed and didn't enjoy the things I loved anymore. My parents tried everything they could with me.

They talked to me and took me to therapy, but nothing helped. My grandpa was gone, and I couldn't get him back. I shut everyone out and didn't talk to anyone anymore.... and that meant Sebastian. I couldn't face him and tell him the terrible truth about what happened to my grandpa. I didn't want to talk about it. I knew he would persist until he got answers.

Even if I didn't tell him the truth, Sebastian would try to fix it. He would try to fix and heal me because that's how Sebastian was. I became depressed and didn't want to drag him into it. He was my best friend, and I didn't want him to stop his whole life for me. Sebastian was a talented actor and he had to go off and do bigger and better things without me.

I felt like I didn't deserve a friend like him, and I didn't want to be the reason to hold him back. So, I stopped talking to him and ignored him. He knew about my grandpa's death but never knew the whole story. Every day he would try to talk to me, and I pushed him away. He would stop by my house, call me, and would try talking to me at school.

Over and over, he would beg me, but it was no use. Eventually he just gave up and moved on. I didn't blame him because I was unreachable. I gave up on life and decided to just be alone. That's how I was, and my plan worked. I sat alone at lunch and never talked to anyone in school. I didn't have any friends and I liked it that way. I wanted to be alone and not participate in anything. That was my routine for a while until I finally woke up.

Things started to slowly get better, and I was opening up more. I talked to my parents more and found joy in theatre again. I never lost my love for theatre, but I started to go to the movies again with my parents and not feel bad. I started to sing again and soon I felt like my true self. Time healed me and I became myself again. My parents slowly worked with me and helped me get back up again. Sadly, with this, I finally realized the pain I had caused Sebastian.

I realized what I did was wrong, and I shouldn't have shut him out. It had been two years since I had spoken to him and felt it was too late. I wanted to make things right and be his friend again, but I didn't know how. I would just watch him from afar and I always kept an eye on him. My lunch table would be close to his at lunch just so I could feel near him.

I would tell myself that I should just go up and talk to him, but I would always chicken out. What if he hated me? What if he rejected me after I rejected him so many times? What if he was mad that I waited this long to talk to him again? What if he didn't want to be my friend again?

So that was my life, just watching and seeing what I missed out on. Seeing what I lost. It had been two years and it was the start of junior year. We were sixteen and so much had changed. I would watch him from my lunch table like I did every day. Living his new life without me. And that's exactly what I was doing in the middle of September at the start of our junior year when everything was about to change.

Chapter 2

I got home from school exhausted and found my parents cooking in the kitchen. I threw my backpack down on the couch and walked over to the marble isle of our kitchen and took a seat.

"How was school?" My mom asked, her back faced toward me. "Did you talk to Sebastian?"

I shook my head in disappointment. "Sorry to hear that, kid." My dad responded.

"What happened this time?"

"Well, I was at lunch and I was really going to do it. I mustered up the courage and I was going to walk up to him....then the bell rang."

"Morgan, you have to stop making up these excuses. There's always something that stops you or gets in the way. You just have to go and talk to him. He will talk to you. After all, you are best friends."

"*Were* best friends." I corrected her. "It's just not the same anymore."

"I think you are over thinking this." My dad chimed in.

"And what am I supposed to say? Hey Sebastian, sorry I pushed you away and ignored you for two years, but will you let me back into your life, pretend like nothing ever happened, and go back to being best friends?"

My parents exchanged a concerned look. "Well, if you don't talk to Sebastian, then why don't you try making new friends?" My mom suggested.

"It would be helpful if people didn't see me as the girl who shut everyone out after her grandpa died."

Silence.

"I just wish I could meet someone that didn't know anything about me. Who would be my friend and not see me as the girl who's grandpa passed away and shut everyone out. I need a friend that won't judge me."

"Maybe you will one day. But I think we both know that person is Sebastian. He's your best bet. If you want your friendship back, then you really need to put in the effort."

I didn't say anything as my mom gave her motherly advice speech. My dad just nodded in agreement as he was preparing the food.

"I'm going upstairs." I said, defeated.

"Okay, we'll call you when dinner is ready."

Dinner that night started out in silence, but then we eventually talked about another topic other than my pathetic life and failed friendship with Sebastian.

****

I lived my life by a routine. I got up and got ready for school even though I always dreaded it. I'd rather be at home watching my favorite musicals than going to school and being the weird girl who had no friends. It got tiring to do the same thing at school. I would keep my eyes down, headphones in, and not talk to anyone. Still, it was something I had to do.

I put on a blue dress with my black flats and put my blonde hair into the same waterfall hairstyle I did every day. I put light makeup only to bring some sort of liveliness to my face, and neatly combed my bangs. I observed myself in the mirror. I wondered why I still put so much effort into looking nice for school, but if there was one thing that those self-help books taught me, it was that looking nice was feeling nice.

If there was one thing I loved as much as theatre, it was fashion. I always put a lot of thought into what I wore and wanted to look nice. It stopped when I was depressed, but soon came back again when I felt better. If I looked nice on the outside, then I felt good on the inside. Looking better instantly improved my mental state. It made me in a better mood, which I needed to be in these days. Dresses and light wear were my usual choices since the weather in Southern California was always nice and sunny. It never got too cold or rainy for a long time, which helped my fashion taste.

And lucky for me, it was the middle of September and still scorching hot. I stopped looking in the mirror and finally approved my look to make it to school. It was still the beginning of the new year, but I already hated being there. I looked at the signs all around for the new school play. Burwood High School had a great theatre production and this year they were doing *Little Shop of Horrors.* My stomach felt queasy.

It was half because it was one of my favorite musicals and half because I knew Sebastian was the lead. Sebastian was always the lead in the plays. I still kept tabs with the theatre department in school and sometimes I would sneak into the rehearsals just so I could watch and feel like I was a part of that world again. I missed being on stage, but it was two years, and I was out of the game. I also definitely couldn't audition as long as Sebastian was there.

Part of me wished I could have the guts to audition for something again in the hopes that I would get the part and rekindle our friendship. But that was too far-fetched. The bell rang and the sound broke away my inner thoughts. I was off to first period which was my improv class that I hated. I still wanted to be involved in theatre in some way, so I always picked my extracurricular classes to be a theatre one.

It was called Through the Artists Eyes and my teacher was Mr. Bryant. I was never any good at improv, but it was worse since I didn't have a solid partner to practice with. I didn't have any friends and every day I would ask different people if they wanted to partner up. I could tell Mr. Bryant didn't like me. It was the start of the school year, but he could tell I was already difficult by my reluctance and lack to work well with others. I just pulled through class like I had been the past few weeks and partnered up with anyone who didn't have a partner.

It was hard though, since everyone had friends and I was the only one without one. The dread of improv finally ended, and I went along the rest of the day to my other boring classes with my boring life. Lunch was the only thing I looked forward to. Even though it hurt me, it meant that I could see Sebastian. So, like I always did, I sat at my usual table and spied on him.

He never noticed because he wouldn't dare to look my way. I never made it obvious and would sneak glances when he wasn't looking. I only saw him from afar, but he always looked better than ever. It hurt me to see him older and better. A lot had changed with him in the last two years. It wasn't just his physical appearance, but I was sure with his personal life as well.

I watched as he settled in and because it was my daily routine, I memorized the scene well. He sat at his usual table with his smile, puffed up hair, and usual flannels he always wore. Beside him was Embry Peterson. Embry and Sebastian became best friends basically right after Sebastian finally gave up on me. They shared the same love for theatre as they would perform alongside each other on stage. Often times I would see Embry rehearse when I would sneak into rehearsals, and he was just as talented as Sebastian.

Embry was small and short. He was very nerdy, goofy, and the complete opposite of Sebastian. I guessed that's why they got along so well. Embry didn't have many friends before Sebastian, and Sebastian took him in. Sebastian was like that, and he loved to make friends with the underdog. I was the best example of that. Still, I could see he really liked and cared for him. It had always just been the two of them ever since I left.

I liked watching them every day at lunch talking animatedly about anything. I watched them with an aching sadness in my chest. How could I have lost my friendship with Sebastian? Guilt rose within me, and I knew I messed everything up. Not a day went by where I didn't feel guilt. I wanted our friendship back more than ever, but I couldn't see how. It was the start of junior year and the middle of September. I didn't want it to get to three years without us talking. Something had to change, and I knew I had to do something about it. I didn't know if had the strength to do it on my own.

After school I did my homework, ate dinner with my family, and then we all watched a movie. The typical routine of my life was still going but I didn't mind when I wasn't at school. My parents were always so great, and I loved spending time with them. I was the only child, so they always spoiled me. I felt comfort being at home with nothing to hide whereas at school, that's all I did. But I didn't have to hide with my parents.

They knew everything and helped me out of my depression. Through every step of me grieving my grandpa's death, they were by my side. I went to the cemetery once a week so I could talk to him. My parents always stayed behind since it was really hard on my mom to go, and my dad stayed behind to comfort her. I had finally made peace with it but the only thing in my life that was unfixed was my friendship with Sebastian. I didn't know how to mend it.

I was so deep in my thoughts that my mom looked up from the movie and turned to me.

"What's wrong, Morgan?" "Oh, nothing. I'm just really tired and had a long day. I think I'm just going to bed now." She nodded suspiciously. "Goodnight!" My dad called out as I headed up the stairs.

I looked around at my room with all the theatre posters, play bills, and theatre trophies. The only thing that was out of place was my personal photos. I used to have photos of Sebastian and I all throughout my room from when we were young until the eighth grade when we stopped talking. Most were from plays we did but some were from the summers of us hanging out in my old treehouse in my grandpa's back yard. I hid all the pictures of us in a box.

I couldn't bring myself to throw them away, but it was too painful to see them in my room. I put them all away in a safe place under my bed, never to be seen again. I couldn't even keep pictures of my grandpa and I in my room because it still hurt and reminded me of the accident. I plopped down on my bed and put my hands over my face.

I took a deep breath and shoved my bangs out of my eyes. I overplayed the conversation I had with my parents the night before. Sebastian was my best bet and if I wanted to talk to him again, then I had to take that first step and put in the work. I really did want us to be friends again, but part of me wished I made a new friend. A friend that knew nothing about me and wouldn't judge me. A friend who didn't see me as the girl who shut everyone out when her grandpa died.

The girl who everyone felt bad for because she lost herself. Who they used to know as lively and would light up the stage but now was just to herself. Who they remember as always being with her best friend but was now a loner. I needed a friend who would like me for me and didn't care about my past.

I would never have believed it then but strange enough, my wish at having that friend would come. But that night I shook my head because I knew it couldn't be true. I turned off the lights and tried to go to sleep. I tossed and turned thinking about how I could save my friendship with Sebastian. But this story isn't about him, it's about the girl who changed my life. And the next day, I would meet her for the first time.

14

Chapter 3

I was at my locker when I first saw her. The locker next to mine had been vacant up until that point. I put my things into my locker that morning and noticed a figure from the corner of my eye. The figure came to the locker next to mine. She had a paper in her hands and was trying to figure out the locker combination. She was tall and beautiful. Her short black hair sat on her shoulders and was hidden beneath a black stylish hat.

It was nice to see that someone else around school cared about fashion. She looked like a girl who you would see writing poetry at Starbucks. She had on an olive-green romper that looked fresh for the still hot weather that occurred in September and black combat boots. Burwood was a pretty big school so if there was a new person, then you wouldn't really know it.

I saw as she stared at her paper and fiddled with the locker combination. She finally got it open, and she glared at me with dark eyes. I immediately turned away, realizing that I was intensely staring at her. I didn't want her to think I was one of those people who was sizing her up because she was new. If only she knew that I was the outcast of the school. A lightbulb thought suddenly occurred to me.

She was new and had no idea who I was. She didn't know anything about me and my past. And she didn't have to know. Could she be the friend I've been looking for? Could she be my way out? If I couldn't be friends with Sebastian anymore then didn't I deserve to have at least one friend? A million thoughts ran through my head as I thought out all the possibilities.

Usually, I found myself to be irrational, but what else did I have to lose? I needed to put myself out there if I wanted to get anywhere in life. This wasn't going to be like when I met Sebastian. I was shy and he sought me out. He rescued me or else I would still be that weird theatre kid who had no friends.

He was always more likable and popular than me whereas I had no luck making friends. If it wasn't for him, I don't know where I would be. But now I was without him, and I needed to fend for myself. After all, he met Embry and now they were best friends. Maybe this girl could be mine. I continued to stare not so obviously at her. I was trying to convince myself to say something. Finally, I got my mouth to move, and I was able to speak.

"Hi." I said, my voice small and weak. I thought she didn't hear me as she kept putting things in her locker. "Hi." She said in a cold tone, not acknowledging me at all. Maybe she wasn't too friendly after all. I was going to give up but reminded myself to be friendly and persistent.

"You must be new here." I slapped myself mentally. Of course she was new here, idiot. "Looks like it." She replied in the same tone. I rocked back and forth on my heels. I wanted to crawl under a rock as this girl clearly didn't want anything to do with me. I figured she would be willing to make friends since she was new, but maybe I was wrong. I tried another approach and tried to be more confident.

"I'm Morgan." I said.

"Vienna." She replied.

"Wow, that's a pretty name."

Vienna didn't reply. I waited in silence.

"I could help you find your first class if you'd like." She finally looked up and handed me her schedule. I was so terrified and intimidated by her.

Seeing her fully face me, I saw her real beauty. She had the looks, the style, and I knew she was definitely too cool to hang out with me. I knew I had to be her friend before she realized I was a lost cause. I took a look at her schedule and my eyes went over her first period class. I stood there in shock. She looked at me annoyed while she waited.

"You have Through the Artists Eyes with Mr. Bryant?" She shook her head. "You have first period with me." She now looked at me, intrigued. I had this feeling inside of me when I knew what that could possibly mean. I didn't want to assume since she could have just taken the class as an elective, but I tested my luck.

"Do you like theatre?" I asked. She stared at me seriously. "Only in the way that's it's my whole life." She replied. I knew then that it was the beginning of a beautiful friendship.

Vienna and I walked into Mr. Bryant's class together. Everyone stared, not from a new girl walking in, but from seeing me walk in with someone. Pretty much everyone in the whole school knew about me. They knew the tragic story of my grandpa's death and how I was the weird girl who had no friends ever since. I was a loner and was constantly by myself. Everyone also knew how Sebastian and I used to be best friends and how I stopped being his friend after.

Nobody ever approached me because I was unapproachable. Seeing me walk in with someone must have blown their minds. They stared at me and then went to stare at Vienna. It was strange for Vienna to be a new student since it had already been weeks since school started. Everyone around was starting to whisper.

I felt bad for Vienna who looked around as she was the talk of the class. The new girl who was treated as a specimen. The whole school and class always judged everyone. I saw as they eyed her nice clothes and nice hat. Most girls at the school hated girls who cared about what they looked like and figured they were showing off. I looked at them as I figured they were just jealous of Vienna's beauty.

Vienna kept her eyes close to the ground and even though I didn't know her, I felt protective of her. I knew what she was going through and how hard it must be to be a new kid when school already started. Everyone stared and judged, and I knew what it was like because that's how it was for me every day. Everyone had their eyes on me, watching me, seeing what I would do, and judging me. Now I knew why Vienna had been so cold with me.

We took a seat in the back of the room where I usually sat. She looked relieved that we weren't up front and noticeable. "Good morning, everyone! We are going to jump into exercises today, but first, I see we have a new student. Joining us here at Burwood is Miss Vienna Chamberlain. Everyone, give her a warm welcome!" Mr. Bryant said enthusiastically.

Everyone gave their mumbled hellos and waved. Vienna waved awkwardly. "Okay, now let's get into it. Today we are doing a few exercises. We will be doing mirroring, a game, and ending with trust falls. So, everyone partner up!" I was relieved to actually have a partner, but I still didn't want to participate. To my luck, the worst thing happened.

"Vienna! Why don't you start us off?" Vienna's face was in shock, and she stayed frozen in her seat. "Don't be shy! Who's your partner?" Mr. Bryant asked. She turned to me skeptically. "Um.... Morgan?" Mr. Bryant looked shocked. "Great! Miss Hathaway and Miss Chamberlain come on up!" We slowly got up and made our way to the small stage.

"Okay, so in this exercise, you will simply just be mirroring each other." We began copying each other's movements and I was happy that it wasn't so bad. We usually did mirror exercises when I was in theatre, so I was used to it. Then we played a game called, What Were They Wearing? In the game, you had to look at your partner for a certain amount of time.

Then you had to close your eyes and try to remember what they were wearing. You got bonus points if you remember small things like accessories. Vienna and I were surprisingly really good at the game. I memorized her outfit well since I thought it was really nice. It turned out Vienna had memorized what I was wearing too.

"She has on a pink dress with white flowers on it. I think they are daisies." She recalled. "That's great, Vienna! Dig deeper! What does her hair look like?" Mr. Bryant asked enthusiastically. He was crazy about improv.

"She has blonde hair and it's pulled back." "Good! Now this is a hard one. What color are Morgan's eyes?" I stood there as I watched Vienna with her eyes shut. "Blue?" Mr. Bryant clapped. "That was a great way to start off class! You were the first ones, but you did fantastic. Great first time, Vienna!" Our classmates gave us their applause.

"Okay now, we end this in a trust fall." I hated doing trust falls and I always avoided them. Mr. Bryant was a huge fan of trust falls as he said it made us "a better actor." I didn't see how fake falling into a stranger's arms was going to help my acting. Usually when we did trust falls in class, we did them all together and my partner and I got away with hiding not doing them. My partners usually ignored me and didn't talk to me. I was nervous as Mr. Bryant was waiting.

I went first and held my arms out. Vienna was taller than me and I wondered how it would work out. I was a pretty small and short girl, and I hoped I wouldn't drop Vienna. She awkwardly turned and her back was faced toward me. She leaned back and fell, and I rushed over to catch her. I did horrible as I barely caught her, and she was too tall for me to pick up.

The whole class laughed. My face easily turned red against my pale skin. I watched as Mr. Bryant looked disappointed. It was my turn and I felt anxiety forming in my stomach. I turned around and stood there with my eyes closed. I stayed there as I was unable to move.

"Um, what are you doing?" Vienna asked.

"I can't do it." I said. I could hear the annoyance in her voice.

"Come on, just go. I won't let you fall." She said.

I didn't want to randomly trust fall into this strangers' arms that I barely knew. I kept my eyes closed and I awkwardly leaned back. I felt myself falling back and I got scared and fell on the ground. I saw as Vienna tried to help me and I fell flat on the ground on my butt.

The whole class erupted in laughter. In that moment I felt stupid and felt like crying. I was too shocked to cry though, but my face was burning with embarrassment. "Are you okay?" Vienna and Mr. Bryant both asked. "Yeah, I'm fine." I choked out.

Vienna helped me to my feet. "Are you sure? You can go outside to cool off if you like." He offered. I took the chance since I didn't want to endure the rest of class being humiliated by my peers. I nodded and got up. "I'll go with her." Vienna said. Mr. Bryant nodded, and we walked out the door.

I felt like such a wimp. I embarrassed myself not only in front of the class, but in front Vienna. I wanted to make a good impression and be cool, but it was clear I needed a lot of help. Sebastian had been my only friend and I hadn't spoken to him in two years, it was going to take a lot to make another friend. I just wanted Vienna to think I was cool. She seemed pretty moody, but I hoped we could be friends. She was pretty, stylish, and she loved theatre too. Where was I going to find another friend like that? And I just blew it.

I kept my head down as we walked out of the class and sat on a bench in the hallway. "Well, you just made me look good on my first day." She said sarcastically. I didn't reply. She stared at me and sighed. "Hey, I didn't mean that. I'm still new and I'm adjusting here. Don't worry about them. They will forget all about it by tomorrow." She reassured me.

I looked up and her big dark eyes seemed kind. I felt better now that she was being nicer to me. "Thanks." I replied. "So, you love theatre too?" I asked, trying to forget about my humiliation and to keep conversation. "Oh, yeah. I've been acting since I was a little kid." She said. "Yeah, me too!" I chimed. She seemed more comfortable and relaxed. I was glad I had her open up more. She seemed like a cool person, but it seemed like I would definitely be the one to have to try hard to get her to talk. I knew this was my chance.

"If you want, we could talk more about it a lunch." I said. I felt like I was asking someone out on a date. I didn't know how to make friends and I felt awkward asking her to have lunch with me. I figured she would say yes since she was new and probably didn't want to sit by herself at lunch.

Luckily, I was right. "Yeah, that would be great." That was the first time I saw her smile.

When lunch came around, I directed her around the cafeteria. "They have the best food on Tuesday's. You definitely have to try the muffins. The fruit cups are awful and on Friday's they serve pizza." I told her. She nodded as she filled up her plate. We got our trays, and I took her to my normal lunch spot. I tried to walk fast to my spot so I wouldn't draw too much attention to myself. We settled in and I saw as a few eyes turned to stare at Vienna sitting with me.

I tried not to look at Sebastian's table. I saw from the corner of my eye that he was staring at me. When I felt it was safe, I looked up and I only saw Embry staring at me. He quickly looked away and resumed to his conversation with Sebastian. I hoped Vienna didn't notice. Vienna began eating and I tried to think of friendly conversations.

"So, Vienna, where did you move from?" I asked.

"Not super far from here, but this is definitely a nicer area then where I used to live."

"That's good that you didn't have to move too far." She nodded while she chewed.

It got a little quiet. "You have a really nice name. Have you ever been to Vienna?" I didn't want to sound dumb, but I wanted to get to know her. She stayed quiet a little before she responded. "Yeah, I have actually. I've been there a few times."

"No way! That's so cool. I've gone on some nice vacations before, but I've never been out of the country." I admitted. "How is it like over there?"

"It's really beautiful. My family and I like to travel. We've been to a lot of different places all over the world." Yup, she was definitely cooler than me. I guess it was habit for me to make friends that were way out of my league. "We were traveling and that's why I started school late. We didn't make it back in time." She said.

I nodded as everything was coming together. "Wow, that sounds so cool. I would love to travel with my family more. I think the only cool thing I ever did was go on my dad's boat. We don't usually go anymore though. That was a long time ago." I recalled.

I hadn't thought about the memory in a while. Sometimes we would go on my dad's boat and Sebastian and his parents would come along too. We would have dinner and it was one of the best times I ever had before the accident, and everything changed. She stared at me, shocked. "Your dad has a boat?" She asked, surprised. I didn't think it was all that great since she said her and her family traveled a lot, but I guess she thought it was still impressive. I didn't want to seem like I was bragging though, so I played it off.

"Oh yeah, but we hardly go on there anymore." I said. We continued to make small talk. "So, when did you get into theatre?" I asked. "When I was eight. My first play I did was

Little Red Riding Hood, and I was the lead." She said proudly. I smiled wide as our stories were similar.

"Wow, that's so cool! We were about the same age when we both did theatre. I was seven and I did *Charlie in the Chocolate Factory*." She seemed excited to talk about theatre with me. "Wow, really? Who did you play?" She asked. I laughed as I wondered how her reaction would be. "I played Veruca Salt." "That's so cute!" She chuckled. We began talking more about theatre and I felt happy that we were starting to get along.

"Musicals are my absolute favorite!" I said. "Oh, me too! I love musicals so much. What are your favorites?" She asked. "So many! I can't even choose but a few I can name are *Les Miserables, In the Heights, West Side Story, and Newsies.*" She smiled in agreement. "I love all those too. Musicals are just the best."

I couldn't believe what was happening. I made a friend and a friend who loved theatre as much as I did. I couldn't believe that I got my wish. She was everything I could ever want in a friend. It was a nice to also make a friend with a girl since I was only ever friends with Sebastian.

"How did you get into theatre?" I asked curiously.

"Well, my mom has always been into theatre. She's done a few plays back in the day. I would always watch old musicals with her, and I fell in love. Once I was old enough, she put in theatre. I loved it ever since and been in multiple plays."

I felt touched by her story and how ours were not far off from each other. It was nice to hear of another person's story of how they got into theatre. "What about you?" She asked. I froze as I didn't want to bring up my grandpa or Sebastian. I went with the shortcut.

"My parents met in high school while doing theatre. It was always their passion. They landed the lead roles, and their onstage love became real offstage. They went off to college and studied theatre. I always saw how they pursued it and were so passionate about it. I just picked it up from them. They finally put me in community theatre when I was seven."

The whole story was true, but it just wasn't the story I told when anyone asked how I got into theatre. The real story was with my grandpa and later with Sebastian, but I knew it was too soon to talk about it to this girl I barely met. Still, it was nice that she was just obsessed with it as me. I saw as she attentively listened to my story. "Wow, that's amazing." "There's nothing like the theatre is there?" I replied. "There's this special feeling of being on stage. It's so exhilarating." She commented.

Vienna understood what it was like, and I couldn't have said it better myself. She had this gleam in her eyes when she talked about the theatre, and I saw the passion in there. The same passion and drive that I used to have. "Were you in any plays at your old school?" She looked sad as I mentioned her old school and I wondered if I had struck a nerve. She must have had a whole better life over there and had tons of friends. I hoped I didn't offend her, but I waited for her answer anyway.

"Yeah, the last one I did was *Hairspray*. I had just got the part for this new play but then..." she stopped and sighed. "But then we had to move." I felt an ache in my stomach for her. I didn't know the right words to say to comfort her. She stayed with sadness in her eyes. "Oh, I'm sorry to hear that. Why did you have to move?"

I wished I didn't say it and I knew I was being nosy. The words just came out and I couldn't stop them. I hoped she wouldn't get mad and go back to her attitude when we first started talking. If she was mad, I would understand. I looked at her and her expression was unreadable. "We just had to get out of there." She said blankly.

I felt bad that I brought up a sore subject, so I tried to sympathize. "Sorry to hear that. For personal reasons, I actually haven't done theatre in two years." I admitted. "Really?" She asked. I nodded and we both looked sadly at each other. The uncomfortableness hung between us until I heard a group of girls who used to do plays with Sebastian and I walk by our table. "So, Morgan, I guess you finally made another friend." One of the girls told me.

They all laughed and walked away. I put my head down to avoid Vienna seeing my face. I felt awful, not for myself, but for attention I had brought to Vienna. I didn't care about the comments people said about me, but I didn't want Vienna to be dragged into my mess. Vienna looked bewildered.

"What was that about?" She practically yelled. "It's nothing." I mumbled. "That was so rude though. I'll go over there and tell them something." She sat up. "No!" I urged her. "Don't worry about it. It's really nothing. Don't pay attention to them." I motioned for her to sit down.

She seemed heated, as if they were the ones who insulted her. I realized how the situation must have looked to her and knew she was only trying to help. It wasn't like I got bullied, but with Vienna around, someone was surely about to talk.

"Well, what happened?" She demanded. I tried to go around it. "It's just because you're new, I'm sure." I said. "The girls around here are like that. They make fun of girls who are pretty and fix themselves up." She didn't seem to buy it. "I mean, I don't see what that has to do with anything. Other then I'm glad someone in this school cares as much about fashion as I do." She motioned to my outfit. "Spill it." She said.

I didn't want to lie to her already, but I also didn't want to tell her the truth. "You barely know me, and we've only met today but haven't you noticed something?" I said. She looked oblivious. I motioned to our empty table. "I sit here alone, and I don't have any friends. This is what it's like for me every day. I'm a loner, I'm shy, and I'm timid. You are the first person to sit here with me. That gives people a reason to talk." I explained so she could get the hint.

She didn't seem sad for me or judged me. She just sat calmly in her seat. "To be honest, I don't have friends either. I was never good at making friends." She admitted. I was shocked and wondered if she made that up to comfort me. From her face, it didn't seem like she was lying. I watched as she adjusted her hat, embarrassed. I couldn't believe she didn't have friends either. It was weird how we just met but we already had so much in common.

She seemed like the coolest person already from barely talking to her, and I was lucky to be her only friend too. "Really?" I asked, unbelievingly. "Yup, I've heard it all. I'm too sarcastic, moody, and self-centered." For some reason I felt relieved. I didn't like how she dealt with the same issues I had, but I felt comfort in knowing I could relate.

"So, I just fly solo." She continued. "That makes two of us." I commented. "Well, I'm glad I met you then." She said genuinely. I smiled at her, and she returned it with her own warm smile. She got her juice and raised it up. "To new friendship." She stated. I got my juice and lightly tapped it with hers.

Chapter 4

I couldn't wait for school to be over so I could run home and tell my parents about the day I had in case it wasn't real. I held on to making friends with Vienna as if it were something intangible that would eventually fade away. School finally ended and I hurried home to tell them. I felt like I was keeping an amazing secret that was so precious that if I revealed it, it might get lost. When I opened the door with a huge smile on my face, my parents looked strangely at me. They probably didn't recognize me because I rarely smiled anymore.

"Morgan? What happened?" My mom asked. I walked over like I was a little kid excited to show them what I brought for show and tell.

"How was school today?" My dad asked, seeing my expression.

My mom gasped loudly. "Did you talk to Sebastian?"

"No, it's not that." I told her. She looked a little disappointed, but then curious.

"But I do have good news." I reassured her.

"Well, what is it?" She demanded.

"I made a friend today!" They both looked shocked and looked at each other. My mom put her hands on her face and squealed.

"Oh, honey! That's fantastic! Tell us all about it."

I put my backpack down to join them on the couch. As soon as I sat down, they both excitedly moved closer in their seats to get all the information. "She's a new girl who just moved here. Her name is Vienna. She's amazing and she loves theatre!" "Really?" My dad exclaimed.

So, I began talking about how we met, our awkward class experience, lunch time, and everything she told me about herself. "Wow, she seems like a great girl and she's into theatre!" My mom said. "Yeah, I couldn't believe it. She's so cool and her family likes to travel. She's even been to Vienna before." My parents looked impressed.

"That's so great, Morgan! You found another friend who's into theatre! Maybe you can get back into it." I rolled my eyes at my mother. "Mom, slow down. I'm not getting back into theatre. Just be happy I made a friend." She caught herself and nodded. "You're right. You made a new friend and that's all that matters. It's still too bad it didn't work out with Sebastian." My mom was so hung up on Sebastian and I ever since we stopped being friends.

She couldn't accept that our friendship was really over. Sometimes I felt like my mom held me back from moving on from him as well. I didn't want to move on from him, but it was never going to happen because I blew the chances of us ever being friends again. I met Vienna for a reason, and it was time for me make another new best friend. I would always love and care for Sebastian, but it hurt too much to hold on.

I wanted my life to be more than just to watch him from afar from the cafeteria and wonder what could have been. "Yeah, well this girl is my only chance at making a friend. Sebastian and I are just history now." I told my mother. It hurt to be so harsh with her, but I needed her to understand. She nodded and my dad put his hand on her shoulder. "Well, I'm happy for you. Vienna seems like a great girl." He said. "Thanks, dad."

A few days passed by, and everyone did eventually move on from Vienna and I being the talk of the school. The shock of me

28

finally having a friend and not being alone washed off on them and I was relieved. It was nice to be seen with Vienna though and to have a friend. After being alone for so long, it was nice to know that I had something to look forward to at school. Someone to meet up with at our lockers, be in class with, and have lunch with.

Vienna and I were getting along really well. Soon, we moved out of the awkward phase of getting to know each other into becoming good friends. We waited for each other at our lockers to go to first period and we would partner up and endure improv together. We both weren't fans of improv, but we now had each other to get through Mr. Bryant's weird exercises. Our trust falls were still bad, but they weren't as awful as the first one.

It was nice to have company and someone beside me. Soon, school didn't feel like something I just had to get through, but I actually had a friend to make it better. We mostly just talked about theatre, but that was just fine with me. I missed talking about theatre to someone. Even though I wasn't performing anymore, I was still involved in the theatre world. I still talked about it with my parents, seen all the musicals, and listened to the soundtracks constantly.

"So, what musical soundtrack do you have on repeat?" Vienna asked me. That's how lunch usually went for us. We would go back and forth asking each other questions about theatre. "The *Hamilton* soundtrack." I answered quickly. "Ever since I saw it live, I've been obsessed with the songs. The soundtrack has been on repeat ever since." She held onto the beret she was wearing as if it was going to fall off and stared at me with her wide dark eyes.

"You saw *Hamilton* live? Like, with the original cast?" She asked. I felt awkward that I had brought it up. "Oh… yeah." I stated. "Weren't tickets really expensive?" I fidgeted because I hated saying about how my family was rich. "The tickets were hard to get, trust me. But my dad has connections so that's how I went." I began digging into my food to avoid her reaction.

I hated to talk to people about how wealthy my family was and what my dad did. The only person who knew was Sebastian since he was in a similar situation. "Wow, that's amazing! That must have been an experience." She replied. I shook my head as I kept eating. The conversations continued as we asked each other more questions.

"If you could be trapped in any musical, which would you choose and why?" I asked. I thought back to when Sebastian and I were friends, and we would always ask questions like that to each other. We would spend all our time in the treehouse talking for hours about these hypothetical questions. It was exciting to do that with a new person and to get a new perspective. Vienna thought for a long while as she adjusted the straps in the overalls she was wearing.

"Definitely not *Sweeney Todd*." She laughed. I laughed too and thought about all the musicals I would hate to be trapped in. "Definitely not *Into the Woods* or *Cats*." That made her laugh a lot and I was happy she thought it was funny. "What about you? What musical would you want to be trapped in?"

I thought about it for a while and just thought about the reason why I loved musicals so much. "It would have to be one with a great love story. That's my favorite part about musicals. When the guy and girl meet and fall in love. There's a whole musical number about it with some great song. Sure, they have their problems, but it will get resolved in the end. It always does because in musicals they always live happily ever after." As I answered, I stared at the table where Sebastian was sitting with Embry.

I thought about how easy it would be if we were a guy and girl in a musical. I daydreamed about it and thought it would be so nice to just live in that fantasy. A fantasy where nothing bad ever happened. Where the guy and girl end up together because that's the way it's supposed to be, isn't it? Vienna's response startled me from my own thoughts.

"That's so sappy! I mean, you don't believe all of that do you? It's nice to see it in musicals, but I don't think that stuff really happens. It just cheesy romantic stuff in Hollywood." She commented. Her words brought me back to the harsh reality of the real world. My eyes left Sebastian and drifted back to Vienna. "Yeah.... I guess you're right."

The next week came around and Vienna and I were fast friends. It felt easy and natural to be in our daily routine. I was really enjoying being her friend and getting to know her. I was even getting used to little things I noticed about her. She always wore the most stylish hats and berets. Every day she would come to school with a different hat or beret in new colors and styles.

She usually wore overall shorts or a cute skirt that complimented well with a nice tank top. I was even getting used to her sarcastic humor that I was starting to enjoy. She was really funny at times and liked to make jokes. It took a while to get used to her humor, but I knew she was just joking around.

I loved our talks surrounding theatre and we even started to venture out and talk about a lot of other topics. Even though I loved my new friendship with Vienna, I couldn't help but still stare at Sebastian at lunch. I told myself it was just out of habit, but I knew deep down that it was because I still cared. I hated how I cared so much about something that was clearly over. Still, looking at him at lunch didn't hurt right? I was staring at him and barely realized Vienna had asked me a question.

"Hello, Morgan?" She said as she snapped in my face. I turned my attention back to her.

"Sorry, what?" She looked at me suspiciously.

"Okay, what is your problem?" She demanded.

I was taken back by her tone. She couldn't seriously be mad at me for not listening to her.

"What do you mean?" I asked, dumbfounded.

"I've been sitting here with you for a week, and you will not stop staring at that guy from that table." She said as she gestured to where Sebastian was sitting.

I immediately felt like running out of the cafeteria at that moment. I was so mortified and embarrassed that Vienna had noticed. My face turned red as I choked up. "What, no I don't!" I said, trying to cover it up. "Yes, you do! You always look over there at him."

"You are insane. I have no idea what you're talking about." I was always a bad liar, and I knew that even though she didn't know me well, she could see right through me. She looked over at where he was sitting. "Well, you either like him or the little weird one." She said, disgusted. I watched as she was referring to Embry who was shoving his entire burger in his mouth without chewing. I looked away, a little disgusted myself.

"Don't lie to me. I know you have a thing for that guy. Who is he?" She asked while she put her hands on the table and leaned closer. "His name is Sebastian Montgomery." I said blankly. Her eyes were sparking with excitement. "Oh, this is getting good! You totally have a crush on him." I shrugged and she urged me to go on. "Well, tell me everything! How do you know him and when did this start?" She asked. I sighed as I knew I had to tell her the truth. There was no way around it.

"That's a funny story. We actually used to be best friends." I paused as I waited for her reaction. It was worse than I thought. "Wait, what? You said you didn't have any friends." She said confused. "Well, I didn't. We became best friends when we were seven when we met doing community theatre in *Charlie and the Chocolate Factory*. We became best friends ever since but then something happened, and we stopped being friends."

She looked completely invested and also like she still needed more information. "Wow, I can't believe this! So, what happened? Why did you guys stop being friends?" She asked. I shook my head as I did not need to explain that awful story. "It's.... complicated. Trust me, it's a long story." I thought she would be pushy and make me tell her but luckily, she just moved on.

"And what about you liking him? When did that start?"

"Well, we've always been best friends and were in every play together at school. He lived on the next block, and we were inseparable. Our families were good friends as well. But I guess I started developing real feeling for him in the eighth grade. We were in the play *Peter Pan* together. He played Peter and I played Tinkerbell."

"You look like Tinkerbell." She commented.
I smiled as I continued. "It just felt different since we were getting older. Unfortunately, after that is when we stopped being friends. And ever since, I stopped doing theatre." I sighed as I tried to block out the past. It was so strange for me to be telling this to Vienna. A person who completely didn't know anything about the situation. I watched as she listened attentively.

"And you still like him." She stated. I nodded slowly, not wanting to fully admit it. We sat in silence for a few moments as I couldn't tell what she was thinking. After a while she nodded slowly. "Alright, I'm in." I looked at her blankly as I wasn't following.

"What do you mean?" I asked.

"I'm going to help you get together with him." She replied nonchalantly.

"What! Are you crazy?" I practically screamed.

She waved her arms to calm me down. "No, this is perfect! You guys were best friends, and you like each other! I don't know what happened between you guys, but it's clear you both have feelings for each other. You can't let this slip away. You guys are perfect for each other. He's into theatre and you're into theatre. Don't you at least want your friendship with him back?"

I for one, thought she was crazy. I knew what the situation must have been like for an outsider, and she wanted all the juicy details. But my life wasn't some kind of movie. She wanted to get involved with something that was way bigger than her. She couldn't fix a year's long friendship that needed serious repairing and turn it into a relationship.

"Nope. That is not happening. We haven't talked in two years. He probably doesn't even like me as a friend anymore and I'm sure he doesn't have any feelings for me." I replied.

She rolled her eyes at me. "Oh, please. I've been watching ever since I sat here with you and every time he's preoccupied you stare at him, and when he knows you aren't watching he stares at you. It's pathetic really."

My heart almost stopped at what she said. Could it really be true? I looked over the table where he was sitting once more. "Even if it was true, I just don't see it working out." I said. "And why not? This is a great love story that you barely even hear about these days. You guys were childhood friends who fell in love. Sure, you guys lost your way, but maybe it's time you two found your way back to each other."

"I thought you didn't believe in all that sappy stuff. You said that cheesy romantic stuff only existed in musicals." I replied, annoyed. She sat back in her seat. I thought I had her defeated, but she still didn't look like she was backing down. "Prove me wrong." She said, her voice strong and steady.

Vienna had this charm to her. She was so confident, and she could make you believe whatever you wanted. She seemed like a natural born leader who was charismatic. With her hyping me up, I felt like I could do anything. I wanted to believe her, but that little voice in the back of my mind that always held me back told me otherwise.

"We haven't talked in two years. I don't even know if he would even want to be my friend again. I wouldn't know what to say." I admitted. "We'll take it slow. I'll be there to guide you and help you with what to say. Please, Morgan! This could work. You can't give up on this." I eyed her suspiciously.

"Why do you care?" I asked and I didn't mean it to sound so rude. I tried again. "I mean, why would you want to help me and do this for me?" She sat quietly as sadness crept in her dark eyes. It looked like she might cry.

"Well, honestly, I have this theory because I do believe that all the cheesy stuff is in the movies. You guys seem to have a movie type of love story, so I'll make a deal with you. I'll make a plan to help you get with Sebastian and you can prove to me that love really does exist."

I took in everything she said and pondered over it. Vienna did seem like a pretty cynical person who didn't seem to care for all the fairy tale romance stuff I was into. I guess she believed that musicals glamorized love and it led her to believe that a love like that couldn't really exist. I believed that way sometimes, but there was nothing I had always dreamed of more than being with Sebastian one day. I always wanted to mend our friendship because I felt guilty for how I abandoned him. I never knew how to approach him and to fix it.

Up until Vienna came, I would sit at my lunch table and would try to convince myself to go up to him and talk to him. It never worked because I would chicken out. I didn't want my life to be just to stare at him from my table in the cafeteria for the rest of high school. Maybe this was it. Maybe Vienna was my way into becoming Sebastian's friend again. Maybe she was sent to me for this reason. I was intrigued now, but still a bit weary. What else did I have to lose? "Deal." I said and we shook hands.

When I got home from school I was still in shock about my conversation with Vienna. Could this really work? Could she really come up with a plan to get us together? We had exchanged numbers at lunch so we could talk about it more. "We'll discuss it more tomorrow at lunch." She wrote me. I replied back and put my phone away. I was sitting quietly on the couch with my parents, who knew something was up.

"Who are you texting?" My mom asked. "Vienna." "Oh, that's great! How are things going?" "They are going good." I said half convincingly. "But?" My dad finished for me. I knew I couldn't hide, especially from my parents. Sebastian could always tell when I was lying, and my parents also could tell easily as well. They knew me inside and out. I caved in and told them about the deal I made with Vienna and the plan. They listened carefully and didn't reply.

"Sounds crazy, I know."

"Why does it sound crazy?" My dad asked.

I expected a different and stronger reaction. "Because I shouldn't do it. We haven't talked in two years and all of the sudden I'm just going to go and decided to be his friend again? What if he rejects me?" I said.

"Morgan, you can't always be afraid of what might happen. You just have to go and take chances." My dad said.

"Yeah, honey. You've been saying you want to fix your friendship with Sebastian and if Vienna is willing to help you then I think it's great idea. If it doesn't work out, then you still have her by your side. Sebastian will be thrilled you want to be friends again, trust me. Vienna can really help you and this can be the start of something great. Your grandpa would want you to be friends with Sebastian again."

I flinched a little at the mention of my grandpa. I knew every word she was saying was right, but it still felt wrong. I tried pushing all my negative thoughts away and tried to think of my grandpa. He would want this for me.

That night I had a terrible nightmare. Well, it wasn't really a nightmare since it really did happen. I used to have the reoccurring nightmare right after it really happened. It was vivid as I will always remember what happened that day. I couldn't forget it even if I tried. The treehouse was never really that steady. My grandpa built it for me in his backyard when I was little.

His house, which was also up in the hills, held a luscious backyard where he had built the treehouse. He wanted me to have my own little place when I came to his house. The treehouse wasn't anything too spectacular, but it was tall and was nestled into the open branches of the tree. It soon became the top hang out spot for Sebastian and I.

We would be in there all the time playing make believe games and talking for hours. We would often go in there after school all the time and rehearse our lines for the plays we were in. And that's what we were doing on that day of the storm. We didn't think anything of the storm. Usually in Southern California when they say there will be a storm, it never really happens. Even when the weather predicts rain, there will be a few drops and it eventually stops.

That day it was just very gloomy, and we moved on. My grandpa had warned us about the storm, but we were kids who didn't listen. If we didn't see a visible storm, then we would still rehearse in the tree house like we did every day after school. That day we were rehearsing for *Peter Pan* and though I didn't have any lines as Tinkerbell, I still watched Sebastian rehearse.

I remember sitting there in the treehouse watching him rehearse. He had his hoodie on that was way too big for him and his honey hair was more untamed back then. His hair stuck out in some places, and I watched as it blew in the wind.

"Wendy!" He screamed as he rehearsed. He put down his script and stopped. "Was that too much? Was it too over the top?" He asked.

"Nope, give it a little more actually." I advised. He practiced a few times until he felt it was good.

"That last one was great!" I told him.

"Thanks, Tink." He said. I felt my stomach knot.

"So.... do you like Wendy?" I asked.

The girl who played Wendy in the play had a huge crush on Sebastian and everyone knew it. She didn't care for me much and she always tried to hang out with Sebastian.

"Well, that's the point of the play." He stated.

"No, I mean, the real Wendy. You know she has a huge crush on you." I commented.

I was afraid to know the answer, but I knew I had to ask. Everyone in the play could see she liked him, and I wondered if he possibly felt the same. She would always ask him to hang out after rehearsals, but he would always make up excuses. I felt like it was because he didn't want to ditch me.

"Ugh, no! She's so annoying and stuck up. She won't leave me alone and keeps asking me to hang out with her. We are just friends. We only are Wendy and Peter on stage." He said.

I laughed and felt relieved. "That's good to know."

"Plus, I'm not into brunettes." He replied.

I felt him looking at me and I was afraid to look up. I finally had the courage to look at him, and our eyes met. We were sitting close to each other and then...... thunder. We both stood up fast and looked out the window of the treehouse. "Did you hear that?" He asked. I nodded and looked out the window.

I observed the dark clouds ahead and saw the wind shaking violently. That Fall was one of the coldest we ever had and that day there was a big windstorm. The treehouse began slowly shaking and the branches began flying. "Ah!" I screamed. "Let's get out of here!" Sebastian screamed.

We tried making our way out of the treehouse with the windstorm and as we were leaving, a huge branch flew on top of us. I crouched down to avoid it and Sebastian went over me to protect my head. "Are you okay?" He screamed. "Yeah, I'm fine. That was a close one!" I said.

We slowly made our way out of where the branch landed and exited the treehouse. My grandpa was waiting for us. "What happened, are you guys okay?" He asked. Sebastian and I stayed frozen. We told him what happened, and we were both shaken up. I began to cry to my grandpa.

"I'm so sorry! We shouldn't have been out there in this storm. I should have listened. I feel so guilty for not listening and now the treehouse is ruined and probably will be in pieces by the morning." I cried while wiping the hot tears from my face.

"Don't worry about it." He said in his usual calm tone. "All that matters is that you two are safe." He wasn't mad at me, and I began to calm down. "And the treehouse." He continued. "I'll fix it."

I woke up in a panic with beads of sweat on my forehead. I hadn't had that nightmare in a long time. I figured it was because of the talk I had with Vienna. I hadn't talked or really thought about Sebastian that intensely for a while, and I guess speaking about it with Vienna triggered me. I didn't blame her though.

I was still scared about the thought of mending my friendship with Sebastian. All the years and all the suffering to think I might be friends with him again. Did I deserve it? I tried not to go back into the cycle of negative thoughts and went back to sleep.

Chapter 5

"Okay, let the plan begin." Vienna said the next day at lunch. I began to get anxiety as I realized that it was really happening. I was forming a plan to become friends with Sebastian again. I tried not to be so nervous and put all my trust in Vienna. She seemed pretty confident and like she knew what she was doing, but that could have just been her normal behavior.

"So, let's figure this out. We need to write stuff down." She began looking in her backpack and took out a pen and paper. I saw as she began writing Sebastian's name on the top of the paper. "Hey! What are you doing? You can't write his name on the paper. What if someone were to find it?" I said, paranoid. "Geez, okay. Calm down, I'll just put a decoy name." She reassured me.

She tapped the pen against the table and thought. I saw as she scratched out his name and replaced it with "Perfect Pretty Boy." I looked up at her and rolled my eyes. "Are you serious?" "What? It's the best I could come up with. I mean, just look at him. He's got that James Dean hairstyle and perfect white smile. The guy looked like he just walked out of a soap opera." I laughed at her comment. She began laughing too once she saw I wasn't so tense anymore.

"Okay, now back to work." She put on a serious face. "Now, what do you know about him? Do you know what his schedule is like? Daily routine? Anything helps." She said. I thought about it and realized I didn't really know much about him now. I only knew the old Sebastian and this new Sebastian was different to me. I only knew the small information I gathered from watching him at lunch with Embry.

"Honestly....not really. We don't have any classes together, so I don't know his schedule. I just know that his best friend is Embry Peterson." I mentioned. I saw as she began writing. "The Little Weird One." She said. "That's so mean." I said. "What else?" She asked. "They sit there every day at lunch." My voice trailed off as I tried to think of more.

"Do they do anything outside of school? Like do they have a place where they hangout?" She asked while the pen hovered over the paper. "Well Sebastian still does theatre, so he does that with Embry. I know they do all the shows here. They are putting on *Little Shop Horrors* and I'm positive Sebastian is the lead." Vienna almost jumped up from her seat.

"That's it! That's your way in. You are going to audition for the play." I felt nauseated at her idea. "Nope! That is not happening. I am not planning on performing again." I told her. I never thought I would be on stage ever again since the accident. It wasn't just because of Sebastian, but it was because performing reminded me too much of my grandpa. He was the whole reason why I got into theatre and there was no point in being on stage again if he wasn't there to see me.

"Morgan, this is perfect! You can audition for the play, and you will definitely get in. You could get back into theatre and get back into Sebastian's life again. It's a win-win situation. He will be so thrilled to see you back that there is no way you guys won't be together." She swooned. She looked like she really did believe it could happen. She made it sound so easy that I was starting to even believe it was possible.

"But I haven't performed in two years. I'm so out of the game. What if I don't get in the play?" I said. "Don't worry, you will! You still have the experience and it's not like *Little Shop of Horrors* has intense choreography like when I did *Hairspray*. I

41

could help you and definitely train you." I thought about it for a while. I guess it could work out if I had her to help me. I'm sure she was amazing in theatre. "Will you do the play with me?" I begged. She looked at me sadly and shook her head.

"Sorry, but I'm still new here and told myself I wouldn't be joining anything this year. I don't want to jump into something I'm not prepared for. I need to get used to being here and focus on my schoolwork before adding another responsibility." I was a little sad, but I understood. Being in a play took a lot of time and energy. You had a busy schedule with no free time and rehearsals were no joke.

"But I will be there with you for moral support every step of the way. Don't worry, I won't leave you alone. I'll coach you and help you talk to Sebastian." She said. I looked at her and she smiled wide as she tried to convince me. "Come on, you know it's a great plan." It really was a great plan and the only way I could become friends with Sebastian again.

Theatre was how it all started, and I guess it was the way we had to start our friendship again. It was only fitting to do it. I was familiar with the theatre environment, so I was sure I would get in the play. "Okay, fine." I finally caved in. "Yay!" She squealed while clapping her hands. "Wait, but I don't know anything about the process. What if the auditions are over?" I asked, secretly hoping that was the case. "Don't worry, I'll do research. Leave it to me."

The next day in the morning, she came up to my locker with a huge smile on her face. "Okay, so I asked around and went into the auditorium after school yesterday. So, they filled up all the parts already except for one. They saved the best for last. The last auditions are next Friday for the part of Audrey. This is fate!" She handed me the flyer with all the information and the sheet music for the audition. I held it in my hands and was shocked. It really did seem like fate.

I knew the play really well and I could definitely play Audrey. Plus, I would be lead with Sebastian and play his love interest. My stomach felt queasy thinking about it. "Wow, this is amazing." I told her.

"Isn't it?"

"Next Friday? Is that enough time to prepare?" She looked as if it didn't matter.

"Don't worry about it. Everything will work out. I'm familiar with the play and could coach you on how to play Audrey. It will be so fun! I may not be performing anytime soon, but I could definitely mold you into this character." She saw the weary look on my face. "You have the experience too! You've been performing at a young age as well. You have it inside of you. Theatre is in your blood." She said as she put both hands on my shoulders.

"You're right, this could work." I said.

"And how crazy is it that the part is for Audrey? It's definitely meant to be. You and Sebastian will be the leads. Not to mention your characters end up together." She commented as she winked at me. I laughed and playfully hit her arm.

"Let's not get carried away." I said.

"So, we have to start on your training. If you want, you could come over my house and we could practice. I could teach you everything I know. We could work on the song and expand on the character." She said.

I got this excited feeling inside of me that she invited me over. It became more real that I finally had a friend. I hadn't hung out or been to anyone's house since Sebastian. It was so nice to have a friend again and a friend that was a girl. I always missed out on having a girl to talk to about girly stuff with. "Yeah, that would be great if that's okay." I replied. "Yeah, it's totally fine! Why don't you sleepover too? We can stay up and we can watch a bunch of musicals. I have so many and all the soundtracks." She said excitedly.

It was the most I had ever seen her happy. She seemed as excited as I felt, and it seemed like she was happy that she had a friend too. I always wanted to have a sleepover with a girl friend where we stayed up all night and watched movies. Everything in my life at that moment seemed to be falling into place. I was getting back into theatre, I was working toward fixing things with Sebastian, and I was great friends with Vienna.

I began to feel a sense of hope at all the new changes about to happen. After two years of consistency and routine, a change is exactly what I needed. "Yeah, that sounds like fun! Are you sure your parents don't mind?" I asked. "No! They will just be happy I'm bringing a friend home." I nodded as I completely related and thought about how my parents would be like if I brought Vienna over. "So, how does this Saturday sound?" She asked eagerly. "Saturday sounds great." Her eyes sparkled with excitement. "Saturday it is."

At home I told my parents the great news and their reaction was far greater than I would have imagined. "You are going to audition for theatre?" My parents gasped in unison.
"Yeah, looks like it."
"I thought you said you didn't want to do theatre ever again." My dad teased.
"Yeah, well Vienna convinced me. She thinks it will be the perfect way for Sebastian and I to be friends again since he's in the play." I replied.
"What play is it again?" my mom asked.
"*Little Shop of Horrors.*"
"Oh, that's a good one! This is so exciting, Morgan! Seeing you back on stage with Sebastian is going to be like old times."
"Mom, calm down. I'm just going to audition and who knows if I will even get in or-" I stopped myself. "Or if Sebastian and I will be friends again. This is just Vienna's idea." I stated.

"Well, we should all be thankful for Vienna. I never would have thought you would get back on that stage again. I just know you will get in. You and Sebastian are going to make the perfect Seymour and Audrey." My mom squealed.

"Is Vienna going to audition too?" my dad asked.

"No, she's still new and adjusting to the school."

"Well, don't worry about doing it alone. You have enough experience." My dad encouraged.

"Oh, also Vienna invited me to sleep over at her house on Saturday. She wants to help me train for the part."

My parents exchanged a shocked look as if everything I was telling them was too unbelievable for them to comprehend. "This is so great! Your first sleepover! I'm so glad you made friends with Vienna. She's really bringing out a new side to you. Well, I hope you have a great time and have fun!" My mom said. Even though I was annoyed at my mom taking things overboard, she was right. I was lucky to have made a friend like Vienna who would help me out. She did bring out a new and more confident side of me. In my depression, nobody could ever convince me to do theatre again. Now, this was a start to a whole new journey.

Vienna lived on the other side of town. Her house was close to Burwood High and was nestled into a small but nice street. It was as if I knew which house was hers before checking the text she sent me with her address and pulled up to her house. All the other houses on the narrow street were nice, but hers had some life.

A small cobblestone road led to her white home with a white gate covered in camellia flowers. There were plants lined everywhere and it reminded me of my mother's green thumb. A large tree shaded her house and as I observed all of this, I walked to the front door. She didn't have a doorbell like at my house, but instead had a lion door knocker. I pulled it and out came Vienna in a matter of seconds.

"Hey Morgan! I'm so glad you're here! I can't wait to show you around. I'm so excited! Here, let me take your things." Before I could object, she began to take my belongings. I only had a big tote bag and a sleeping bag that I brought because I thought bringing a suitcase would be a bit much. I had never slept over someone's house before and I didn't know how to properly pack for just a night's stay.

"Come on in."

"Thanks." I replied.

I walked in the house which was even lovelier than the outside. "This is it." She said, motioning to her place. "It's not much but it's pretty nice." She shrugged, as if her house wasn't enough to satisfy me. Vienna's house may have been smaller than mine, but I didn't care about those things. I didn't tell her my family had money either because I was used to how people reacted when they found out.

Her house was one story, but it stretched far and wide. There was plenty of space and had so many things to look at. "Don't worry about it! I think your house is nice." I told her. She seemed pleased. She gave me a small tour and I listened and looked as she spoke and gestured to the things in her house. As she was showing me around, a small dog approached us. "Morgan, I would like to introduce you to someone truly special. This is my dog, Chico."

Chico was a small chihuahua with brown and white fur. His long tongue stuck out a bit and his tail began wagging excitedly as he saw me. He had to be the cutest chihuahua I had ever seen. "Hi Chico!" I petted him and he began licking me. Vienna watched and laughed. "He's very friendly." I wish I had pets growing up, but my parents worried they would destroy the house and explained how they were a big responsibility. Sebastian's parents felt the same.

"Now that you've met Chico, let me find my mom so I can introduce you." I suddenly felt a lump in my throat and became nervous. I was only close to Sebastian's parents who were like second parents to me, and I didn't know how to react to meeting a new friend's parent. I hoped she liked me and approved of me. I fixed my hair and smoothed out the dress I was wearing. She led me to the kitchen table where her mom seemed to be working on a project.

She had long hair unlike Vienna, but it was the same shade of black. She had pins everywhere and was working on her sewing machine. She looked very concentrated, and I felt bad to interrupt. Vienna cleared her throat to get her mom's attention. "Mom, this is Morgan. Morgan this is my mom." She said, just as awkward as I felt. Her mom seemed very nice though and looked up at me with gleaming eyes. She immediately stood up to greet me and shake my hand.

"Morgan! I've heard so much about you! It's so great to finally meet you." "It's really nice to meet you too, Mrs. Chamberlain." I was pleased with my delivery and wasn't so nervous anymore. "I hope you enjoy it here. You are welcome anytime. If you need anything, just ask me." "Great! Thanks so much for having me."

She didn't say anything for a while and stayed smiling at me. She looked just as artsy as Vienna, and I began pinpointing their similarities. "It's just so great to have you here. Vienna has never brought a friend home." "Mom!" Vienna spat out. "And you are so pretty!" Her mom continued. "Okay, that's enough! We are going to practice. Don't bother us." Vienna said. I felt bad, but I just thanked her mom again and left with Vienna to her room.

"Oh gosh. I am so sorry about that. I told her not to embarrass me."

"She really nice." I replied. Vienna just rolled her eyes.

"What was she working on?" I asked, out of curiosity.

"She does costumes for the theatre."

"What! That is so cool!" She laughed.

"Thanks. That's where I get it from. I love making costumes. I've made some for previous shows I've been it. And when you get the part of Audrey."

"If." I cut her off.

"When!" She argued. "When you get the part. I will make your costume."

"Alright." Was all I replied. I had realized I didn't see her dad when I was here, but I figured he might be at work. "And what about your dad? Will I get a chance to meet him too or is he at work?" Her body stiffened as we made it to her room. She was about to open the door, but she froze.

"Oh yeah, my dad won't be here because he's working." "Oh, okay, that's cool since he works late." I replied. "Yeah, actually he's never here because of his work." She paused. "He's a limo driver." I was utterly shocked, and I couldn't hide it. "Oh my gosh! Really? That's amazing! Has he ever met famous people before?" "Yeah, he has sometimes. He gets to travel to really cool places for his job. The company right now is taking him out of the state, so he won't be here for a while." If I didn't think Vienna was any cooler, her parents just confirmed it. "Wow, that is so cool!" "Yup." Was all she said, and she opened the door to her room.

Her room was magnificent and was strangely similar to mine. Vienna being the most fashionable and coolest person I knew had an equally great room like I imagined. There was a huge *Les Miserables* poster and she also seemed to collect playbills like me. There were also tickets of shows she had been to that lined her walls. She had lights around her room and a nice vanity set. Another similarity to my room was the theatre trophies.

"Your room is too cute!"

"You like it?" She asked.

"I love it!"

"Thanks!" She set my things down on her bed and went to her closet. "I have an air mattress that you can sleep on." "Great, thanks." She turned to face me. "Okay, let's transform you into Audrey." I took a deep breath. "Let's get started."

Chapter 6

"First off, it's all about the attitude. You need to walk, talk, and act like Audrey. Here, I'll show you." Vienna began strutting across the room. "Now, you try." I got up from her bed and tried to copy her. I felt so ridiculous. "Yikes, that was bad. You need to be more confident. Walk like you have purpose." I watched as she walked across the room so elegantly. She was so confident, and I knew it wasn't her acting, it was just her.

I envied Vienna on how things came so effortlessly to her. She had the natural talent that most theatre people couldn't obtain. I suppose I used to be like that, but I've been out of the game for two years. Some of it was muscle memory, but I think I was too intimidated to act with Vienna. She was so effortless and natural in her acting the way Sebastian was. I felt like I always had to try harder. We went over and over it until I got it right. "Okay, that's better. Keep trying and keep in mind that you will be wearing heels." I nodded at her instruction and made sure to take notes on everything.

"Next and the most important part is the voice. Audrey has a very high-pitched distinct voice. Copy me." She began talking like Audrey and I couldn't hold in my laughter. She began laughing hard too but tried to stop. "Stop, I'm the teacher and I need to help you. You're distracting me!" "Sorry, Ms. Chamberlain." I mocked. She rolled her eyes and continued. "It's not just about the high-pitched voice, but you also have to get her accent down. Her accent isn't too exaggerated though but hint it at certain words."

She demonstrated for me, and I was in awe at her impersonation of her. "Now, you try." "What do I say?" I asked. "Just say something that Audrey would say." I tried, but my accent was terrible. "Okay, try it more like this." We began going over it until I started sounding more natural. She examined me. "You are doing good, but you need the attitude and confidence. You can't just go walk and talk like her. It's all about the persona."

I didn't want to disappoint her, or myself for that matter, but acting wasn't coming so natural to me anymore. I spent so much of my time grieving that I didn't give acting two thoughts. I never even thought I would be auditioning for something ever again. "I know. I'm trying, it's just that Audrey is so different from me. How am I supposed to act like her?"

Vienna flicked me on the forehead. "Ow! What was that for?" I exclaimed as I rubbed the spot where she hit me. That was going to leave a mark that hopefully my bangs would cover up. "You're not playing yourself! You're playing Audrey. That's the whole point of acting. As actors we have to get out of our comfort zone and step into someone else's shoes. We become a completely different person and soon we aren't ourselves anymore, but we transform on stage." She scared me but in a good way. In a way that wanted me to be stronger.

She was right, and if I wanted into this play and back into Sebastian's life, I had to work hard at it. I was nothing like Veruca when I did *Charlie and the Chocolate Factory*, but I had fun playing a brat. I just had to remember how to get into the character's shoes. It wasn't going to come easily, but I had to remember why I had fallen in love with theatre in the first place. "Okay, I'm ready. I got this."

We went over for hours going through how to act like Audrey until eventually, I did feel like her. We practiced with props in her room, and I felt like I was playing dress up. I strutted along carrying a purse at my side and was talking in Audrey's shrill voice. Vienna complimented me and would applaud when I would do right. I felt like a child, happy that I won her mother's approval.

"Okay, final part. You have to work on your singing. I know the audition song is Suddenly Seymour, but I want you to practice singing Somewhere That's Green. That way you can build your confidence playing Audrey and really get a feel for her character. It's an emotional scene and I think if you can do that then you can really pull off playing Audrey." "Yeah, that sounds like a good idea." I stood there for a while and took a deep breath. I don't know why I was so nervous to sing in front of her. I sang in front of hundreds of people before, but there was a feeling that I didn't want her to judge my voice.

I hadn't heard her sing before, but I knew she sang beautiful because she was good at everything else. I still sang every day and kept my voice up, but I hadn't actually performed for anyone in a while. "Um, Morgan? Come on, I'm waiting." "I can't do it. Just don't look at me." I turned my back to her. "Are you kidding me? If you can't sing in front of me, then how do you expect to get in?" "Just for now. I just need to warm up." She waited patiently until I started. My voice was breathy and a bit shaky as I tried to control it. It didn't sound strong and confident at all.

"Okay, Morgan. Let's just focus on your breath control. Even if you're nervous, you need to keep your breathing steady or else your voice will sound awful. And also remember that you aren't just singing, but you are acting while you sing. So, as you sing, you need to covey all the emotions. When you sing, try to get her accent in there as well. Look at the lyrics and what they are about. See what they mean for the scene. Here, I'll show you. Just watch me."

She stood up from the bed and walked over to her vanity set. She grabbed a brush and began to sing "Somewhere That's

Green." Just as I expected, her voice was beautiful. She was an alto, but she still pulled off the higher notes. She did a crescendo when she needed to and acted like Audrey throughout. I watched her as she seemed to hit all the right notes. I wished I could be half as good as Vienna, not only in acting, but in life.

Sure, she was moody sometimes, but most of the time I envied her. She was beautiful, smart, and was a great actress. She was way too cool to hang out with me. Her parents and her life were even cool. There were a lot of similarities between Vienna and I, but I mostly focused on the differences. Her charcoal eyes that were open and inviting where my eyes were like the ocean that held secrets. Her black hair that sat on her shoulders and my golden hair that passed mine. Her personality and confidence that shone where mine faltered.

We were like a ying yang. We coexisted together. The good in the bad and the bad in the good. What I lacked she thrived in and where I succeeded, she failed. It was a hard line to walk. We were complete opposites, but I think that's why our friendship worked so well. I was lucky to have found a friend like her, especially through this hard time in my life.

Her solo was finished, breaking me from my inner thoughts. "That was amazing!" "Thanks. So just remember everything I did and now you try." Seeing her boosted my confidence. I worked hard on my vocals and tried to get her accent in there while also trying to convey the emotions I needed. I remember my favorite part of being on stage was the ability to make the audience feel something. And that's what I intended on doing.

Soon I felt that familiar feeling that always overcame me when I performed. The sensation of feeling alive and being able to be someone else. When I was done, I saw Vienna gleaming at me. "That was perfect!" She grabbed me and hugged me. "You are so getting the part!" I was so excited that she thought that because coming from her, I knew she truly meant it. I suddenly felt like I didn't just want to do this for Sebastian, but for myself. I wanted to get back up on that stage and do what I loved. I wanted to get back to acting. I wanted to prove to myself that I could do this.

"Okay, now let's practice Suddenly Seymour since it's super important because it's the audition. The main thing they will be looking for is the confidence and the emotion since it's an emotional song. Also, the big part which is the chemistry between you and Sebastian. I'm sure you won't have trouble with that though." She winked at me. I playfully slapped her arm.

"Still, we need to practice. So, I'll be doing Seymour's part." We practiced the duet together a few times and she instructed me on how to move across the stage and when I should interact with him. She also gave me pointers on how to convey emotion and make my high notes sound better.

"You will be belting in this song so be prepared for your voice to handle that." We finally finished and called it a day for practicing. "I think that was very productive if I do say so myself." Vienna said. "Very! You helped me so much and I can't thank you enough. You put in the time with me and helped me a lot. Thanks for being so patient with me. It's just been so hard since all this happened and I didn't think I would get into acting again. I want this part so bad now for myself. The Sebastian part is just a bonus now." I laughed. "Well, I'm glad to hear that. And seriously, it's no problem. I'm glad I can help you get back into acting and also to help two people in love." She said as she put her hands over her heart. "You are too much." I told her.

"Wait, there's actually one last thing. Be right back." She left me in her room as I waited for a while. She left her door open, and Chico came in. He jumped on the bed, and I occupied myself by playing with him as she took forever. He really was a cute dog. "Okay, sorry I'm back. Hi Chico!" She came in with measuring tape and pins.

"What's this for?" I asked.

"When you get the part, of course I'm going to make your costume. And don't worry about your hair. I'm thinking you could just curl it to make it shorter. I mean, you could pull off Audrey. You have the complete look, blonde hair and bangs." She replied, nonchalantly.

"What?" Before I could object, she cut me off.

"Okay, now stand up with your arms stretched out." I did as I was told. She began measuring me from head to toe. It was a long process. "Uh, is this really necessary?"

"Very. You like black right? It's very slimming." I didn't reply as she already knew the answer to that. I don't think I ever wore black a day in my life besides my grandpa's funeral.

"And we are done! I'm so excited for when you get the part." She kept saying "when" I get the part instead of "if" that I truly felt the pressure. But honestly, I was even starting to believe it. We put in so much hard work and time that I couldn't see how this wouldn't work. A huge smile spread across my face.

"So, do you make all of your own clothes?" I asked Vienna as we settled down for the night. I settled into the air mattress on the floor she set up for me. "No, not at all! Are you kidding me? That would take forever!" I thought about the cute outfit she had on earlier, a black top with a black skirt. The whole outfit looked like it would be a dress if you couldn't see it up close. "Well, you must get all of your cute clothes from somewhere." "Aw, that's nice. Thanks for noticing. And of course, I do."

"Well, as a person who knows fashion, I couldn't help but notice." I said with a bragging tone. "Well, spill it. Where do you get all your cute clothes?" I pleaded. She stayed silent for a few moments. "My dad gets them for me from the places he travels to for his work." "Shut up!" I said a little too loudly. She chuckled at my response. "Yeah, that's where most of my outfits come from."

"What about your cute hats? They are always so adorable!"
"Yup." She replied in her casual tone. "Where is your dad right now?" "He's in New York." "That's so cool." I said in a dreamy tone. I began fantasizing about her father driving around celebrities and stopping by cute shops and finding something that Vienna would like. How cool must that be?

"Wow, that's so cool. I'm totally jealous. Your parents are so interesting." I told her. "I would say the same about yours, but I haven't met them yet." She mocked. "Well, we have to change that. You definitely have to come over one day." I imagined Vienna being over at my house with my parents. It would be such a change to have someone other than Sebastian at my house.

"I would love that. You're pretty cool I guess, so I'm sure your parents are alright." She joked. I smiled widely at her sense of humor that I was starting to get used to. We sat in the dark and talked for a while. It was weird talking in the darkness and talking without being able to see each other since she was in her bed, and I was on the floor. "So, are you nervous about the audition?" She asked. I was surprised she had asked the question when she seemed so confident about me getting it before. "I am for many reasons, but I know it's what I have to do." I replied, surprised by my honesty.

"Are you nervous about seeing Sebastian? Like, really seeing him. Not from across the cafeteria?" I didn't know how to answer the question, so I sat on it for a while until I found the right words to say. "Yes and no. I want to see him again and to fix our friendship more than anything. It's the whole reason why I'm auditioning. But...." my voice trailed off. I stayed silent for a while, and I could tell she was waiting patiently.

"But I know things will be different. So much has changed even though it's been two years. What if he's not the same? I've changed a lot and what if he's disappointed? What if he's moved on and doesn't want to be friends anymore? I wouldn't blame him. After all, I'm the one who caused this. I'm the one who pushed him away. And what if he's angry at me when he sees me? What if he's mad that I auditioned?" It was easy to feel like I was talking to myself since I couldn't see Vienna in the darkness. Everything came out in a spill, and I forgot she was listening. She still stayed dead quiet.

"Morgan don't do that. Don't beat yourself up for what you did. Everyone makes mistakes. No matter what happened between you two, it can be fixed. By just walking in and showing up to the audition, it shows you want to fix things. He won't be mad or angry with you. I know he won't. I've seen the way you look at him in the cafeteria and the way he looks at you, even though you don't see it. You guys are meant to be together. You just lost your way, and it took some time, but now I believe you will find your way back to each other."

I was surprised at her heartfelt words. Vienna seemed pretty bitter and sarcastic sometimes, but I knew deep down she cared. There was something about us being there together that made us feel more vulnerable with each other. In her dark room where we couldn't see each other, I felt like I was seeing the real Vienna for the first time. I could tell she was letting her walls down and it was nice. "Thanks. I really needed to hear that." "Anytime." There was a wave of silence that fell between us, but it wasn't awkward silence, it felt more content. "So, what did happen between you guys?" Out of all the questions she asked, that was the hardest to answer. I didn't say anything. "Or it's none of my business. Sorry I asked. I know you probably don't want to talk about it." I wanted to keep the honesty going, so I opened up a bit.

"Well, in the eighth grade my grandpa died in a horrible accident. It really crushed me, and I was never the same. I fell into a deep depression, and I pushed everyone away." It was the simplest way I could put it without telling her all the details and reliving that awful moment.

"Oh, I'm so sorry to hear that. I completely understand and it's not your fault. I would have done the same thing. Were you two close?" She asked.

"Extremely. We did everything together. He was the one who got me into theatre. He used to work at a movie theatre and so he loved movies. He was also in a few plays himself. He taught me everything he knew. I wouldn't be an actor if it wasn't for him. He showed me all the classic musicals like *West Side Story*." My voice began to crack. I cleared my throat in a hopefully nonobvious way.

"That's so cool. It seems like you guys had a great relationship. I'm glad he got you into theatre. Everyone needs a role model like that." I was touched about how sincere her words were. She didn't even know my grandpa, but she understood the bond we had. "Yeah, it was pretty special." I smiled at the memory.

"Anyway." I continued, to no longer be sad. "Sebastian kept trying to reach out and talk to me and every time, I would shut him down. I couldn't be his friend anymore. It just hurt too much. So eventually he got tired of it and gave up. We stopped being friends and never talked again." She stayed silent as she took it all in. "Why didn't you want to be friends with him anymore?" She asked in what seemed like a whisper. "I didn't want to bring him into my problems. I was grieving and a mess. I know he would continue to go on and do bigger and better things in his acting. I didn't want to hold him back." It was completely the truth. I guess I always felt like Sebastian deserved more and I didn't want to be the reason he failed.

"Didn't you think he could help you and be there for you? You know, help you out of your depression? I mean, that's what friends are for. They have each other's back." She sounded more stern, but I knew it didn't mean to sound rude. She was trying to get through to me. "Yes, of course I knew that. Sebastian was the best friend ever and I knew he would stop his life to help me, and

I didn't want that. I didn't want to be a burden." I was surprised my answer seemed to satisfy her.

"Yeah, that makes sense. I'm sorry." She said.

"Thank you."

"Did you ever tell him what happened to your grandpa?" She asked hesitantly, afraid that she crossed a line.

It was painful, but she didn't. I knew she was just curious, and she didn't know the situation. "No. Never. It's too painful to remember and I never told anyone before. I think that's what hurts the most too. That he doesn't know the truth. That's another thing I would want to fix. He deserves to know." I replied. I didn't mean to shut her down about asking what the accident with my grandpa was, but in a way, I knew it would prevent it.

"I see. You're right about that." I'm glad it felt that way. "Yeah, I think that's the part that makes me nervous too. If this does work out and we are friends again, I have to tell him and relive painful things I haven't thought about in a while. I'm finally doing okay and now I have to talk about it again. It's not just what happened to my grandpa, but what I did to him as well. I can't ever forgive myself for both." I admitted, even though she didn't understand what I meant by that.

"Don't feel bad about things you can't control. It's all done and over now. All you can do now is move on and try to fix things. I don't like to dwell in the past, you should only look behind you when you're driving." I laughed a bit and felt at ease. I liked her metaphor and liked how poetic she could be at times. I felt a warmth inside me that she was my friend. And she was a really good friend. She barely knew me, but it felt like we had known each other forever.

I didn't think that feeling was possible with someone other than Sebastian. That instant connection and bond. Being friends with Vienna made me realize so many new things. This whole time I thought I was missing out on love but really, I was missing out on life. I was glad to venture out of being by Sebastian's side to make a friend like her. I missed out on having a girl friend. Where we can have sleepovers, stay up all night, and tell each other secrets. I'm glad I wasn't missing out on that tonight.

"So, when did you know that you were in love with Sebastian?"

"Vienna!" I shouted.

I was appalled at her question and didn't realize the personal questions were continuing. I guess this was her chance at getting all the juicy details.

"Hey, I'm curious! You guys have a fascinating love story. I mean, who else meets their soulmate at the age of seven?"

"I can't answer this." I told her.

"Aw, come on!"

"It's not because I don't want to say, it's because I don't know." She made a fake laugh like she didn't believe me.

"That's not true."

"Yes, it is!" I protested.

I began to think about her question more deeply. "There wasn't a specific moment. I don't know exactly when it happened. I don't know if it was when I saw him for the first time playing Charlie in *Charlie and the Chocolate Factory* when we met. Or when he gave me a surprise party for my thirteen birthday. Maybe the time when he held my hand when I got scared for my first solo performance. Even when I saw him rehearsing his monologue to get into *Peter Pan*. Or how I got butterflies anytime someone would make fun of us and ask if we were together. I suppose there wasn't a specific moment but more like a collection of moment all blended together. Not one specific feeling, but many feelings. I mean, how can someone pinpoint the exact moment they knew they were in love? Isn't it just a feeling that occurs and grows over time?"

Vienna started fake sobbing. "Wow, that was so sappy!" She then started fake barfing. "It's so sweet I think I could hurl." I threw a pillow at her. "Ow! No need to be violent!" And threw it back at me. "Well, you're the one who asked." "True. Okay, next question."

"Oh joy!" I said sarcastically.

"What made you want a potential relationship with him? Like, how did you know and like him at such a young age?" She was asking all the good and hard questions.

"Wow, that's a hard one. I guess it all comes down to my parents. They have a really good relationship and have been a great example for me. They always are affectionate and still go out on dates. They always say, I love you, and he brings her flowers and nice gifts. Seeing my parents like that made me realize I want something like that one day. Sebastian's parents also have a good relationship. Our parents get along really well." She stayed quiet for a long time.

"Hmmm." Was all she said. I was tired of her asking me personal questions that I thought the tables should be turned. I just hoped she wouldn't get offended.

"And what about you?" She sat up.

"What about me?"

"Are there or has there ever been any special guy in your life?" I rushed out the words like they were bad to say.

I was scared she would get mad at me, but I also was dying to know the answer. "Nobody up to my standards." I almost believed that, but I wanted the truth and not her sarcasm. "Come on, be serious!" I pleaded. She sighed then answered. "No, not really. I never had any luck with guys and dating." I was utterly shocked. She was fun, pretty, and had a great sense of humor. I didn't know if she was bummed about it, but I tried to cheer her up. "There's nothing wrong with that." I told her.

"Honestly, the only man who has my heart is Aaron Tveit." I almost screamed. I let out a huge and exaggerated gasp that was completely real. Now I was the one to sit up. "Really? Aaron Tveit? The guy who played Enjolras in *Les Miserables*?" I said. "Yes!" She said just as excited as me. "Oh my gosh, I am obsessed with him!" She sat up with wide eyes to look at me. "No way! So am I! I even have a whole fan account dedicated to him."

I was so shocked that she felt the same admiration I had for him because he was my favorite Broadway star and biggest crush. I always liked him for the longest time but didn't have any girl friends to talk to about it. I never told Sebastian because it was girl stuff he couldn't understand. "Wow, I'm surprised. I mean, I know Perfect Pretty Boy is your style, but you actually have good taste!" I ignored her comment and began talking excitedly about Aaron. We went on and on about his performance in *Les Miserables*. "His vocals are just everything! Have you ever seen the cover he did of this song from *Rent?*"

We then started watching videos of him on her laptop and squealed. "Ugh, he is so cute!" I screamed. I was glad to finally get my obsession out with someone who understood. "He has a great smile!" She said. "Here, let me show you my fan account so you could follow me. I post all the latest updates." She informed me. I was so excited.

"Do you know he's going to be performing in *Moulin Rouge*?" I told her. "Yes! I wish I could see him live. It's a dream of mine. I would do anything." It was also my dream and I fantasized about a moment where Vienna and I could see him together. She broke me from my daydream. "Let's watch him in *Les Miserables*!" We pulled up some videos of him in *Les Miserables* and sang all our favorite songs from there. We sang all of "One Day More" and we both knew it from heart, line by line, and sang all the parts.

By the end we were exhausted and probably made way too much noise. It was super late at the time, and we continued back to bed but still asked each other more questions to get to know each other. We were already shocked that we both liked Aaron Tveit, that we did a speed round of things we liked. "I really like baking shows. I love to bake."

"Really?" I asked her. "What things do you like to bake?"

"I'll make you something in the morning and you will see." She told me. "What about you, what shows do you like?"

I answered without hesitation. "I really like game shows. My grandpa and I used to watch them all the time."

"Cool! Which one is your favorite?"

"Definitely The Price Is Right" I said, excitedly. "Morgan Hathaway! Come on down!" She mocked. I laughed. "Sebastian and I always talked about going on there and winning a lot of money. We said we would become famous actors with all the money and cool things we won." "Yeah, then you guys could finally run away, get married, and live happily ever after. You would probably live in a royal castle with a butler and five kids." She joked. She was so hard to read sometimes that I was getting irritated and a bit angry.

"I don't get you." I told her. "You are so invested in our relationship and want us to be together but then you make fun of it." "It's just a joke, Morgan." "I know." I replied. "But I just want to understand. You make fun of love but then you want it to happen for us. You say it's all mushy and poke fun at it, but it seems like it fascinates you." I felt bad for going off, but I needed to know. "So, what's your point?" She asked. "I just need to know."

"Well, what's the question?" She asked in an irritated tone. "Do you believe in love?" It was a question I had always wondered what her answer to it might be. She was helping me out with Sebastian but otherwise she seemed to have no interest in love at all. And if she didn't believe in it, then what did she think about Sebastian? Did she think we could make it and stand a chance?

"Well, I guess if it were me, I would want that fake love." She replied.

I didn't understand. "Fake love?"

"You know, the fake love that you see in the movies. The kind where chivalry isn't dead, and the guy opens the door for the girl. Where they go on cute dates and the guy is a gentleman. But that's fake stuff. That's why it only happens in movies because that's just not how it is in real life. I've seen it before. I wish it was like that, but it's not. Things are a lot more complicated. But despite this, I guess my answer would be that I do believe in love."

Things started to clear up, but I still didn't know how she could think all of that and still believe in love. "Why?" I whispered. She let out a huge sigh and stayed quiet for a while. "Because, if I don't believe in love then what's the point?"

The next morning I woke up and was confused at where I was. I looked around and realized I was in Vienna's room at her house. Everything from the night before felt like a dream. I knew it wasn't though because I woke up to Chico in my face and a freshly baked bag of pumpkin rolls.

Chapter 7

That Monday after the sleepover it was back to our normal routine at school. Instead of school being dreadful for me like it usually was, it was better with Vienna. We had bonded so much because of the sleepover, and I was grateful to have gained a friend like her. I thought of her as my best friend, and I felt like she felt the same way. There was nobody besides Sebastian that I ever connected with more in my life. We both loved theatre, fashion, and Aaron Tveit. We could be so different and complete opposites at times, but we somehow fit together. Our connection didn't seem to fade when we got back to school as we kept up our conversations. We met up at our lockers and began chattering away.

"Those pumpkin rolls you made me were so good!" I recalled. "Thanks! If you ever want anything, I'll make it for you anytime. I love baking but I never get to do it since it's just me and my mom." She replied. She didn't mention her dad, but I figured it was because he traveled a lot. We talked more on our way to first period. As we got into our usual seats in Mr. Bryant's class, we began rambling more and watching our favorite Miscast Broadway videos. Without us noticing, Mr. Bryant entered the classroom.

"Well, if it isn't the two girls who are always chattering away. Well Morgan, I'm glad Vienna helped you open up. But since you two are always so insistent on talking while I'm trying to teach, then maybe you two should start our first exercise!" I knew Mr. Bryant didn't really like me. Before Vienna, I was the quiet girl who couldn't get a partner and didn't really want to participate because I thought the class was weird. I still felt that way since I didn't like improv, but now I actually had a friend, and I was more talkative.

At least I didn't have to face the weird exercises alone or with someone I barely knew. Even though she did have me open up, I sometimes thought Mr. Bryant preferred the days when he didn't acknowledge my existence. Vienna and I shot each other a look and got up to do our exercise on the small stage. Mr. Bryant pulled two chairs out and put them together, the backs against each other.

"So, for this exercise, you two will be sitting facing away from each other. You will be giving each other compliments back and forth. The goal is to say whatever comes to mind. Compliments can be awkward at times and that is why you won't be looking at each other. I'm sure you two won't have trouble though since you are just the best of friends." He said sarcastically. I didn't really mind the exercise since it wasn't too extreme like the other ones we usually did in class, but it was still going to be weird to give each other compliments in front of the class. We slowly took our seats. I watched as our classmates stared with judging eyes.

I looked straight ahead in my seat, avoiding their stare. Even though I had performed in front of hundreds of people in theatre, I hated being center of attention in the classroom. I always hated to participate in class. I never talked, raised my hand, and I hated public speaking. "Okay, whenever you're ready." Mr. Bryant told us. We sat in silence for a few moments, unable to say anything. "Just say anything. Anyone can feel free to start." He added.

Vienna had become my best friend and it was easy to think of a million compliments to give her, but it was hard to do it with the pressure of Mr. Bryant and our classmates. I was surprised when Vienna made the first move. "You have a great fashion sense." She said. It felt weird, but nice to hear her randomly compliment me. I hoped it got easier since she started. "Thanks, so do you. You always dress so cute." I looked at Mr. Bryant, who still wasn't satisfied.

I knew he wanted us to go deep with our exercises. We had to get in touch with our emotions in order to be a better actor. I always did that with acting, so I tried to find it within myself to do well in this improv exercise. I figured he didn't want us to compliment on random outward things, but the person as a whole. "You have a beautiful name that fits you. You are a beautiful person inside and out." I added. Mr. Bryant nodded, encouraging us to continue. "You have really nice shiny hair. It looks like a golden waterfall." Vienna said. Some of our classmates laughed. "Thanks." I chuckled.

"You have great confidence. You never hesitate and you just go after what you want. You are so bold, and I wish I could be more like that." I didn't mean to be so personal and honest in my compliment, but it made it easier to open up.

Vienna shifted in her seat. "That's really nice." She sat for a moment and continued. "You have really nice blue eyes."

"You are a great baker." I replied.

"You are a very talented actress and singer." She said. I felt warmth spread all over me at her nice words.

"I learned from the best." I stated. "You are a really helpful and loyal person who is always there for me." The weird exercise became very therapeutic, and I hoped Vienna knew how much I meant every word. "You are a great person. You are so kind, sweet, and friendly. You are always so nice to me even when I get in my moods. You have taught me a lot and I really appreciate it. You're my best friend." As she said the words, I heard the emotion in her voice. At that moment I felt like tearing up from happiness. I didn't know I meant that much to Vienna and how we meant so much to each other in the short amount of time we knew each other. Some friendships were quick, and it seemed like ours was meant to be.

She came into my life when I needed her the most and I was there for her when she entered this new school. We were a perfect match. I got caught up in the moment and forgot to reply, but it was enough for Mr. Bryant. "Good! That was fantastic! That's what I really want to see from you guys. Take notes at how Morgan and Vienna handled that. With improv, it's all about discovering new things about yourself. In improv there's not really acting involved and there's no script. It's all up to you. What path will you take? When you have these questions arise and you take risks, it makes you a better actor."

I didn't care too much for the class, but at that moment I gained respect for Mr. Bryant. He was right, being a great actor was all about taking risks. You had to put yourself out there and get out of your comfort zone. Maybe improv wasn't so bad after all, and it would help me for the part of Audrey. "Now, we are going to end this exercise by doing a trust fall!" I was on edge from how our trust falls usual were but after the exercise, I knew we built that trust.

I started and put my arms out and I knew I would do anything to keep Vienna from falling. I would catch her, and she could trust me. She landed safely in my arms and then it was my turn. I took a deep breath as I was always bad at trust falls. Vienna stood with her arms out, waiting. I turned around and closed my eyes. I leaned back and let gravity do the rest. I felt like I broke free as I let myself fall, knowing that Vienna was there to catch me no matter what.

It was the day of the auditions. I was so nervous as I got up and got ready for school. It was a good kind of nervous energy, the kind I used to thrive off of when I knew I had an audition in the past. I looked at myself in the mirror and smiled. I missed this. I missed auditioning for plays and being ready to perform my heart out. I missed having something to be excited for, and there was nothing that could make me more excited than the thought of being on stage again. I could hardly stay still, and I ran downstairs to get to school. My parents stopped me before I nearly ran out the door.

"Hey, slow down!" My dad called out.

"What's up?" I asked.

"Well, we just wanted to wish you good luck today." He replied.

My mom stood next to him and nodded. "No matter what happens today, we just want to let you know that we are extremely proud of you. Getting back up on that stage and auditioning for something is a big step. We didn't know if you would make it back there and we are so excited for you. Morgan, your grandpa would be so proud of you." My mom said as she held back tears.

I was holding back my own as well. "Go out there and break a leg!" I squeezed myself between them for a group hug. "I love you guys." "We love you too." They said. "Now, go!" My dad said as he pushed me out the door.

Seeing Vienna standing by our locker made me even more confident. "Today's the big day! You got this Morgan! We trained and worked so hard for this. I know you will get the part." I took deep breaths and nodded. Her positivity was starting to rub off on me. "Okay. Ah, I'm so excited! I can hardly wait." I told her. She put her arms on my shoulders. "You are going to do amazing." The bell rang and we both got startled when we realized we still had to go on with the rest of our normal day. I couldn't concentrate in my classes because all I was doing was daydreaming about how the audition would go. What if this was the start of me going back into theatre? I couldn't help but feel giddy all day thinking about going back to doing what I loved. Vienna caught my expression in first period as I saw her smiling at me from the corner of my eye. Mr. Bryant was not happy about me not paying attention in his class. The rest of my day went on like that until lunch came around and it was time to audition. Vienna and I ate our lunch quickly in order to make it to audition.

"Here we go!" She told me. We walked into the theatre, and it was like a million memories were flooding back. I had only been in that theatre before when I would peek into past rehearsals for plays, but the feeling of being in the theatre was familiar to me. Theatre was my home and where I belonged. The feeling of the dark atmosphere, the creaky chairs, the illuminated stage, the sound booth, and the loud chattering of people running their lines. I took it all in just how it had been in the past for me. I no longer felt out of place. Vienna watched me with a careful eye.

She didn't say anything as this was an overwhelming experience for me. I looked up at the lights above us and walked along the aisle to touch the seats. I watched as everyone was waiting to audition. Some people were warming up and others were singing. I saw as there were a few people on stage going over their lines. I guessed it was the people who already got their part since Audrey was the last person they needed to audition. I saw as a few familiar faces were on stage that I recognized from past plays. Then Embry appeared on stage with Sebastian.

Everything I felt from earlier in the day suddenly collapsed inside of me. My heart started to race, and my palms became sweaty. I was short of breath and felt like I needed air. It was too hot in there and everything around me closed in. I recognized the feeling immediately.... I was having a panic attack. I ran out of the theatre and headed to the lobby where the bathroom was.

I locked myself into one of the stalls and luckily there was nobody else in the bathroom to hear me cry. "Morgan!" I heard Vienna yell. "Morgan, what happened? Are you okay?" I was choking back my sobs as I held onto the stall for support. I didn't want to answer her. "What's wrong?" She demanded. "I can't do this." I admitted. "What do you mean?" She asked.

I looked down to see her standing right outside the stall. I focused on her black combat boots. "Talk to me." She said calmly. She probably realized she should talk to me in a gentle tone instead of yelling at me. "Seeing Sebastian again. It just made something inside me break." I paused. "I'm scared. We haven't talked in two years and then I'm just going to show up here and audition? What was I thinking?" I shook my head and wiped my tears away. I saw her feet swaying.

"I think that you were thinking that it was time to do the right thing. You waited this long and now you have the confidence to do this. When we were practicing, I had never seen you more in your element. Do you remember what you told me that day? Why you wanted to do it?" She asked me.

I sighed because I did remember. "I said I didn't want to just do this for Sebastian but because I wanted to get in."

She seemed pleased with my response. "Exactly. You said Sebastian was just a bonus. Today you were so happy to audition and get back up on that stage. To do what you love. I know seeing Sebastian freaked you out, but don't worry about that right now. Just focus on what you came here for. You came to audition and get the part. And I know you will. I'm here for you, okay? I'm right here. Just look at me the whole time you audition. I'm not going anywhere."

When it came down to it, Vienna always knew the right words to say. She could always cheer me up with a good pep talk. She was completely right. I got this. I opened the stall door and seeing her made me feel better. I got out and hugged her tightly. "Vienna, what did I do to deserve a friend like you?" I couldn't believe how comfortable and honest I felt saying it. She gave me a tissue to wipe my tears. "Let's get you touched up." She helped me look presentable again and the bathrooms large mirrors with lights helped. "Perfect!" She told me.

We did some vocals exercises to get my voice warmed up and then we were good to go. "Are you ready to get back out there?"

I was still shaken up, but it was now or never. "I am." I got up and was headed for the door and then I felt her arm on me. "Your grandpa is looking down on you and cheering you on." Her kind words almost sent me crying again.

Vienna had only known me for a short amount of time and didn't know my grandpa, but her words were just what I needed to hear. At that moment I knew things were going to be okay, because I was lucky enough to have a friend like Vienna by my side. I knew that whatever happened when I walked out that door, I gained her as my friend. And that's all I really needed.

We settled into one of the first rows and waited for instruction. I looked around at all the other girls auditioning. I forgot what auditioning was like and almost laughed to myself. Everyone around me looked just like me. They had blonde hair and tried to look just like Audrey. Some had long blonde hair, some short, and some with bangs. A few girls had brown hair and probably figured that they could just wear a wig. Vienna seemed to notice as well.

"Wow, well this is weird." I nodded in agreement. It was so strange to see all these girls trying too hard but then again, I forgot how the audition process was. Everyone tried to look and fit the part. Whatever the character looked like, they tried to imitate. I always thought it was a complete waste of time since it all came down to the talent. Fitting the part was great, but there was no point if you couldn't sing and act.

"Okay, everyone! Let's get this show started." A short man came out on stage. I had seen him before because he was the face of the theatre department. He directed all the plays, and I would catch glimpses of him here and there around school. Since I was around the theatre department a lot, I already knew his name.

"My name is Mr. Baldwin, and I am the director of the play. I direct all the plays here at Burwood and I'm the head of the theatre department. I've been working in theatre for twenty years and worked as a dramaturg. Any questions you have anytime go through me. I can't wait to see all of your lovely auditions and to be possibly working with you. This one is going to be a really fun show and we are all very excited. Okay, so this is how it's going to work. I'm going to call your name and you will come up here and do your audition. As you of course know, this audition is a duet, and you will be singing Suddenly Seymour. You will be working alongside our lead, Sebastian Montgomery, who will be playing Seymour. Sebastian, can you come here?"

Sebastian came out and waved. I heard all the girls immediately gush over him. "Oh my gosh, there he is! Isn't he so hot?" A girl in front of us chimed. Vienna and I looked at each other and rolled our eyes. Vienna then leaned forward to look at the girl. "Shh!" She told her. I gave her a shocked look. "Stop, Vienna." I told her. She smirked and obeyed.

"So, you all will be auditioning with Sebastian, and this will help me get a feel of your chemistry working together." Mr. Baldwin stopped to call on someone who raised her hand. It was the same girl. "Will we be auditioning the kiss?" She asked. A few of the girls were laughing. Sebastian looked down with his face red and Mr. Baldwin looked very annoyed. Vienna looked at me again angrily. "Is she serious?" She asked.

I was annoyed by the girl as well, but I hoped Vienna wouldn't start anything. I was used to Sebastian getting all the attention from girls and remembered how they always flirted with him. Mr. Baldwin shook his head and sighed. "No, you will not be auditioning the kiss." Vienna laughed. "What I'll be looking for is your look, vocal range, acting, and chemistry with Sebastian. Now, if everyone is done asking silly questions then we can get started." Mr. Baldwin was going in order by the seats, and we were in the fifth row. I was happy I wasn't going first but it also made me anxious to have to wait. We sat through and watched everyone's auditions. It was so great to see Sebastian perform again. He was so natural and confident on stage. I smiled as I watched him.

Aside from Sebastian, all of the auditions were cringeworthy. All the girls either tried too hard, were only there for Sebastian, or were tone deaf. Vienna was silently laughing at all the girls, and I couldn't help but chuckle here and there. "It looks like you got this one in the bag." I couldn't help but think she was right. It was crazy to see the girls failing miserably. Mr. Baldwin and Sebastian both looked disappointed. Sebastian looked tired and annoyed at having to sing the same thing over and over again. It probably didn't help that all the girls were awful as well.

"Okay, thank you!" Mr. Baldwin said to yet another girl who did terrible. "Okay, next up we have Morgan Hathaway." Sebastian looked up as if he heard the name of a ghost. His face looked utterly shocked. I couldn't blame him. He hadn't seen me there because we were in the last row of people auditioning. He looked up and tried to see me, but everyone was blocking me. I stood frozen in my seat. Everyone stood to stare at me and most of the girls gave me dirty looks.

Vienna nudged me to get out of my seat. I slowly sat up and I felt like the tin man in *Wizard of Oz* as I walked to the stage. I felt everyone's eyes on me as they watched me get on stage. Sebastian wasn't too close to me, but it was close enough. Mr. Baldwin stood between us but being that close to him stunned me. I only ever saw Sebastian from a distance at lunch, and his presence seeing him up close was something else. Seeing my best friend all grown up made me sentimental. It had only been two years, but he changed a lot since the eighth grade. Eighth grade Sebastian was scrawnier and more youthful looking. Sixteen-year-old Sebastian was taller and more handsome. He filled out and wasn't so scrawny anymore. I thought I had always got a good look at him from the cafeteria, but up close I saw all of his perfections.

His same big brown eyes, honey colored hair, and wide smile. As Mr. Baldwin went through the run down again, Sebastian stayed staring at me. I realized what was a shock for me, most of been a shock to him too. He looked at me and I couldn't tell what his expression was. Usually, he was so easy for me to read. He observed me and then our eyes met. I wished I could have looked away, but I couldn't. He smiled at me and all my worries inside of me melted away. I returned the smile and Mr. Baldwin's loud voice startled me. I forgot that time was still moving.

"Okay Morgan! Whenever you're ready." I suddenly looked panicked as I realized I had to perform in front of him. It had been so long. What if I completely mess up and make a fool out of myself? I looked out at the audience for Vienna. She looked at me and gave me a thumbs up. I nodded at her and swallowed the hard lump in my throat. I took my place and prepared myself. I saw Sebastian getting ready as well. Mr. Baldwin pointed and cued the sound booth to start the track. The first few notes rang through, and I felt a bit at ease.

I gave myself a mental pep talk and was glad I wasn't singing first. Sebastian's voice started off soft and gentle. His baritone voice was smooth, and I noticed how it grew better with maturity. Hearing him sing brought a strange comfort to me. He seemed to be singing directly to me and I felt butterflies. I knew it was the character and he was acting, but something made me feel like he was singing just for me. Like he meant the words he was saying.

He looked deep into my eyes as he sang, and I tried to remember to act as well. I knew this scene well and knew how Audrey felt. Sebastian was such a good actor that I played off of his emotions. Soon it was my turn to sing, and I felt that I was shaking a little. I remembered Vienna saying to control my breathing, and I heard my cue. I started off strong and was surprised at how good it came out. My voice sounded perfect, and I was amazed at myself. I settled into the song and played the part. The confidence and excitement that I felt earlier rose within.

I became overfilled with the sense of being on stage again. The bright lights shining on me, stepping into another character, and being alongside Sebastian. It felt like I was living in a dream or reliving the past. I always had hoped that one day I would be back here with Sebastian and now I was. As I was singing, I looked at him and he was smiling at me. Suddenly it felt like it was only the two of us. We came closer and closer together. Our new and mature voices fit so well together, and we harmonized perfectly.

Our voices entangled into one another and the energy between us was electrifying. I belted and sounded great, and I had never been more confident. Theatre was my passion and with Sebastian by my side, I knew I couldn't leave it. We were so close now, but I wasn't scared anymore. He had a huge smile as he sang and looked at me. I was glad that he seemed so happy to see me again. So, he didn't hate me. He wasn't mad at me, and he forgave me. We could be friends again. I felt at peace, and I knew my grandpa was looking down on me. The song ended and everyone stood up and clapped. We both looked out to see our standing ovation. I saw as Mr. Baldwin stood with his mouth open. He slowly approached us. "Morgan, you got the part."

Chapter 8

I stood on stage with my hands covering my face. I actually did it. I got the part, and I couldn't believe it. It was such a surreal moment that I didn't notice Sebastian had said something. "Morgan, that was amazing." It was the first time he had spoken to me in two years. It was hard to form words and I reminded myself that I had just finished performing in front of him. Surely it couldn't be too hard to talk to him after we had that powerful connection on stage. "Thanks Seb-Sebastian." I saved myself from almost calling him his nickname. I was the only one to ever called him Seb but that was in the past... when we used to be friends. Now things were different, even if we were slowly speaking. Still, I couldn't just go up and act like everything was okay.

Even though my best friend was standing in front of me, we were still strangers. "It's.....it's great to see you again." He said slowly. "Yeah, it's great to be back." I replied. The awkwardness hung in the air as we stayed staring at each other for a few seconds. Vienna came running from her seat and ran up on stage. She lifted me up from the ground in a huge hug. "Congratulations, Morgan! You were spectacular up there. I knew you could do it." She said. "Yeah, and it's all because of you." She smiled sheepishly. She looked up at Sebastian like she had forgotten he was there. I hurriedly introduce them. "Oh, Sebastian this is my friend Vienna. Vienna this is Sebastian." They both looked embarrassed and awkwardly said hi to one another. "That's a nice name." Sebastian told her. "Thank you." She replied.

The girl who was making annoying comments earlier came up to Sebastian on stage. I felt an unsettling feeling and I looked over to Vienna who seemed on edge. I suddenly felt insecure. "Hey Sebastian." She said in a flirty tone, her hands on him. "It's too bad that I didn't get the part. We would have been great together." She turned to smirk at me, and I quickly put my head down. "Yeah, too bad." Sebastian said uncomfortably. Vienna's strong voice startled me. "Yeah, it went to someone who really deserves it."

I was shocked but tried to hold back my laugher. I looked up to see Sebastian holding back his own. The girl looked angrily at Vienna. She looked between the both of us until she finally walked off stage. We all chuckled as she left. It felt weird to all be standing there laughing, but I felt more at ease than I had in a long time. Embry then came up to join us on stage. "Dude, that was a great audition!" He told Sebastian. Sebastian quickly turned toward us. "Guys, this is my friend, Embry. He's playing The Dentist." I looked at him and I was surprised that someone like Embry would be playing an intense character like The Dentist. Embry up close was adorable. He was a few inches taller than me and had curly dark brown hair.

"Hi, I'm Morgan."

"I know who you are." He said nonchalantly. Sebastian shot him a look.

"That was a great audition! You have some real skill." Hearing those words meant a lot coming from Embry. I had only seen him here and there, but he was insanely talented. He had a real shot at making it in theatre and was better than I could ever be. I secretly thought he was even better than Sebastian. "Thanks so much!"

He smiled at me and then looked over at Vienna. He stared at her, practically drooling. "And who is this fine lady?" Vienna looked around to see if he could possibly be talking about someone else. "This is my friend Vienna." Vienna gave him a small wave. "Oh, Vienna. A beautiful name for a beautiful goddess." I laughed and looked at Sebastian, who was shaking his head. "Um, okay." Vienna commented. "Forgive me, you are just so gorgeous." Vienna ignored him as she caught sight of Mr. Baldwin approaching us.

"That was a wonderful audition, Morgan. You have some real talent, young lady." I was happy I was off to a good start with him and that I made a good impression. "Thank you, Mr. Baldwin." "I'm sure you have theatre experience, correct?" Sebastian met my eyes and smiled. "Yes, I do. I've been in theatre since I was seven. I stopped for a while." I paused to not meet Sebastian's gaze. "But I'm back now." "Well, that explains it. You are very good at it. You can just see the passion you have for it. And Sebastian, you two have great chemistry! Do you two know each other?" We awkwardly looked at each other to give some sort of explanation. We fumbled through our words and Mr. Baldwin looked at us, confused.

"Hi, Mr. Baldwin?" Vienna chimed in and saved us. "I'm Vienna Chamberlain and I'm Morgan's personal acting coach. I'm also her personal costume designer." She shook his hand as he looked at her suspiciously. I gave her the same look as I wondered what she was up to. "So, I need to be with Morgan at all times and if you want, I can make all the costumes for the play." He raised an eyebrow at her. "Unless you just want to spend all the departments money and buy clothes from thrift stores then I understand." Her boots made a clicking noise as she began to walk away. "Okay kid, you can stop now. You got the part." I looked at Vienna and she winked.

She was so crazy. I was convinced she could manipulate anyone into getting what she wanted and could convince anyone into believing anything. "So, I'll be seeing both of you then in rehearsals on Monday." "Yes, you will!" Vienna called out as he walked away. I turned to her, surprised.

"You are insane." She didn't look phased as she shrugged. Sebastian and Embry stood looking confused. Sebastian had his hands in his pockets, and he looked like wanted to say so much. "So, I guess we will be seeing a lot of each other." He said. His tone sounded enthusiastic, but I couldn't be too sure.

"Yeah, I'll see you on Monday."

"I can't wait."

My heart sped up, but I tried to keep my cool. I nodded and we walked away.

"Bye Vienna!" Embry yelled as we headed out.

"Oh gosh!" Vienna said. When we reached the theatre doors, I couldn't believe how much had changed since I walked into them. I smiled thinking at all the new possibilities that awaited me. I took a deep breath. One step at a time. Once we were fully in the lobby, Vienna and I turned to each other. "I got the part!" I screamed. We both jumped up and down.

I called my parents at told them the news and when I got home, there was a grand celebration waiting for me. The dining table was all set with my favorite food and desserts. There were candles everywhere and they had got balloons. Over dinner, I reminisced everything that had happened at the audition. I talked about how it was to be back in theatre, how the audition went, and seeing Sebastian again. "Oh, honey! That's so exciting!" My mom gushed. "This is going to be great. We are going to finally go to one of yours shows after all this time. I'm going to record everything!" I nodded as I chewed on my steak.

"It's going to be so great to see you and Sebastian alongside each other on stage again. I just remember how cute you guys were when you were little. You guys were such great friends. You did everything together. You went to the movies, hung out in the treehouse...." I cut her off. "Okay mom, that's enough." It was just like her to get carried away. I already saw her getting emotional. "Mom, stop it." "Your mom gets so sensitive." My dad joked. We both laughed.

"Oh, you guys! I can't help it. When they weren't friends anymore it broke my heart to see it. I missed his parents too. They are good people. It's just great to think that Morgan and Sebastian will be friends again. That things will go back to normal." My mom said. I didn't argue any further. After two years of my whole life changing, normalcy is just what I needed.

The celebration wore me out, but there was something I needed to do. I told my parents I was leaving, and they didn't object because it was still early. After all, they knew exactly where I was going. I parked into my usual spot when I got to the cemetery and walked up to where my grandpa was. I set the fresh flowers I got from my house down and sat down. I always came once a week and never missed. I talked to my grandpa all the time about how my life was going. I would talk about my family, how much I missed him, theatre, and how I hoped I would be friends with Sebastian again.

"Well, I did it. I got the part." I told him. "I know you are happy I'm finally doing theatre again. This is going to be the start of something new. I think I'm finally going to be friends with Sebastian again. I'm really excited to have this part and do this play. I know how much you liked *Little Shop of Horrors*." I sat and talked to him for an hour, and I got a text from my mom to come back home before it got late. I stood up to walk away but then I paused. "I'll try my best. I won't let you down." I told him. I went to my car and headed back home.

I was exhausted by the time I came home from all the day's excitement and whirlwind of emotions. I changed into my pajamas and uncovered my blankets to get in bed. I stopped, knowing there was one last thing that I needed to do. I got the part, and I was one step closer to fixing things, I just needed to do it one step at a time. I looked underneath my bed to find my box of old photos. It was all my old photos that I hid because they were too painful to look at after the accident. It was all the photos of Sebastian and I and some were of my grandpa.

I opened the box up and looked in carefully. There were way too many things in there and I made sure to be careful to not see any pictures of my grandpa. I only grabbed a few pictures from the top of Sebastian and I and flipped through them. I found the one of us when we first met doing *Charlie and the Chocolate Factory*. We were hugging in the picture, and we had big smiles as we looked at the camera. He was dressed in his peasant costume, and I had on a fancy dress with my hair made up. I took a deep breath as I relived that memory. I took the photo, closed the box, and shoved it back under my bed. I placed the photo by my nightstand. I put the photo there as a reminder. Things were going to be okay, and I was going to fix it between us. One step at a time.

That weekend, Vienna invited me over so we could run over the script. She gave me more pointers and how to be more "Audrey like" and on my vocals. "It's so cool since I know this musical so well. I used to watch the movie every day." Vienna said as she thumbed the script. "Me too! I think this play is going to be very memorable." "Especially since you and Sebastian are reunited." I rolled my eyes at her. "What are we doing? Enough rehearsing for the play!" She threw the script on her bed.

"Hey!" I called out. "The plan isn't over yet. We got you into the play, now we need to get you with Sebastian." I stared at her wide eyed. "Aren't you getting a little ahead of yourself?" "You didn't think I was just going to stop at getting you the part, did you? I'm your matchmaker and that's what friends are for." She pointed out. "Oh yes, you're the best." I said sarcastically. "I know." She said, ignoring me. "You are going to need some serious help talking to him. I saw you guys at the audition, and it was a disaster."

"Are you really going to give tips?" I asked, annoyed. "Do you want my help or not?" I debated for a while. "Fine." I surrendered. "Okay, so I know it's weird but after all you guys were best friends. So just keep it casual to start off with. He will give you signs and hints. You already did your part by showing up there, so he knows that you are ready to be friends again. I would say wait until he makes his move and then casually ask him if he wants to hang out after rehearsal one day. It will be a group hang out since there won't be any pressure. We could all hang out and his little weird friend can even come too."

"Wow, that's so nice." I told her. "Well, he was weird! But is this the perfect plan or what?" It weirded me out that she clearly thought this through and how she was so obsessed with getting us together. I had to admit it though, it was a good plan. "Whatever you say." I was startled by a brisk knock at the door. "Morgan, I'm getting dinner ready, would you like to join us?" Her mom asked. I was going to reject since I didn't want to overstay my welcome, but Vienna answered for me. "Yes, she will." I gave her a look. "Great!"

We headed to the kitchen once her mom said the food was ready. We waited at the table as her mom was setting things up. She stood in the corner and was talking on the phone to someone, her voice low and angry. "No! I already told you. We are doing things my way." I heard her mom say. There was a long pause, and I imagined the person on the other line was giving her an earful. I couldn't make out the rest, but it seemed like a heated argument. I didn't want to be nosy, but I had to ask.

"Is everything okay? Who is she talking to?"

"Probably my dad. He's off at work so he won't be here for dinner." She said softly.

"It's understandable since he's a limo driver. I bet when he comes back though it's the best since he comes home with all these stories and presents." I said, excitedly.

I liked being at Vienna's house because it was an insight into her fantastic life. Her mom was always so nice to me and though I had never met her dad, I knew he was off on some great adventures. "Definitely." She replied.

"Sorry about that." Her mom said as she reappeared. "Now, who's hungry?" We both agreed and put food on our plates. "Don't get too full, Vienna made some delicious brownies for dessert." Her mom smiled widely. "I can't wait! She's such a great baker." I replied. Her mom poured us some drinks and wanted to make a toast. "To Morgan getting the part." She said as she raised her glass. I was so honored, and I knew how red my cheeks must have been at that moment. "To Morgan!" Vienna said. We put are glasses together and they made a clinking noise.

Monday came around and I couldn't wait for my classes to go by faster so I could go to rehearsal after school. It was nice knowing I would be seeing Sebastian other than from at a distance in the cafeteria. Not only that, but I couldn't wait to perform again. Since Vienna helped me rehearse all weekend, I was good to go.

We walked into the theatre, and everything was set up all nice. The stage was set to look like Skid Row and the props were amazing. There were sets of tall brink buildings and apartments. Everyone was around the stage looking over the script. There were so many people, and their loud chattering filled the air. It was good to be back. I felt a hand on my shoulder, and I quickly turned around. "Morgan Hathaway? Is that you?" The girl said.

It was my old friend Stephanie who went to elementary school with me. She had been in theatre as long as I had, and she was always in the plays with Sebastian and I. We were good friends, and she was one of the people who still tried to talk to me after the accident. "Stephanie! It's so good to see you!" I told her and we embraced in a hug. "It's been so long! I was wondering when we were going to see your face here again. We've missed you. The theatre has definitely not been the same without you. These other girls are not half as talented as you and they try too hard." I laughed at her nice compliment.

"Your boy Sebastian has also been lagging without you. He's great on his own, but you two were a duo. He hasn't been the same since." I looked away, embarrassed. I didn't realize the impact I had made. "But I know you guys are going to be amazing as Seymour and Audrey. I can't wait to see you both up their doing your thing again." She continued. "Neither can I." I replied. Her friend called her over to run lines. "Got to go! It was nice catching up!" She turned around and left. "See? I told you." Vienna said. She never missed an opportunity to point out when she was right.

Mr. Baldwin called out for everyone to get to their places. We were rehearsing the song "Downtown" first. I saw as all of the freshmen were excitedly getting ready. Most of the freshmen were playing homeless people on Skid Row, so there were some trash cans below the stage. The stage was designed perfectly, and it looked just like it did in the movie. I couldn't wait to see the rest of the scenes come to life. "Hey Morgan!" Sebastian called out to me. He smiled his perfect smile that sent my stomach in knots.

"Hey!" I said, matching his same enthusiasm.

Embry then joined him at his side. "Hey, where's your friend Vienna?" I looked at Sebastian and we smirked at each other. This boy was clearly in love.

"Oh, she's in the audience watching."

"That's too bad. Why isn't she in the show?"

Mr. Baldwin's loud voice interrupted. "Mr. Peterson stop socializing! We are starting rehearsal." Embry nodded and stayed quiet.

"Okay, everyone! Get up on stage because we are going to start with some exercises!" Mr. Baldwin yelled. We all gathered on stage into one big circle. We did some lip trills, siren noises, and some light stretching. The rehearsal first consisted over everyone going over the song a million times. We had to get everyone's parts just right. Soon, I knew the song frontwards and backwards. After, we worked on our stage direction. Mr. Baldwin was getting frustrated with the freshmen. "No, that's not your mark! You will be coming out from the side of the stage by the stairs." He told some freshmen. I saw as they all did their best to impress him. I understood, as it could be very intimidating for them being in their first show.

Once we rehearsed both the song and the stage directions to the point where I couldn't take it anymore, we were ready to do a full run through. "Okay, perfect! Let me just check with the guys in the sound booth to make sure we are ready to go. Everyone, get into your places." Mr. Baldwin exited the stage. Sebastian and I had been alone since Embry played The Dentist and he wasn't in that scene. We waited in our spots to get ready, but it was taking a while. We stood awkwardly next to each other, not making eye contact.

"You are doing a great job by the way." He told me. I finally looked up at him and his eyes were sincere.

"Thanks, you are too."

"I mean, your voice is just outstanding. You have improved a lot."

I was pleased that we were starting to talk some more, and his compliments had my head spinning. "You are so much better too! If that's even possible." He chuckled like he didn't believe me. "I don't know about all that. But I know I have to try a lot harder now that you're around." I felt my face getting warm.

"Oh, is that a challenge?"

"We'll see." We were bantering like old times. I knew it would take us a while but talking to him in that instant felt like nothing had changed. It was amazing how we could pick up a conversation so easily. That after all these years the chemistry was still alive. We didn't say anything and were looking around the stage, still waiting to get started. I was observing all the freshmen rapidly talking and excited to do their part. In them I saw a young me, eager to get out there and show everyone what I got. I started off doing theatre at a young age and did all sorts of parts, big and small. It didn't matter what I was doing or what character I played, just as long as I was on stage. I could be the lead or not have any lines, I knew my job was important.

Because without one person, the show wouldn't work. I saw as Sebastian was looking at them as well and it was like he read my mind. "I remember what it's like doing your first show. The nervous energy and anxiousness. But then once you start getting into it, it's like this feeling you have never felt before. You feel so alive." Sebastian was always so profound. "I don't think that feeling ever goes away." He nodded in agreement. She must have overheard our conversation, because a freshman girl then came up to talk to us.

"Hi guys! I just wanted to say you guys are so good! I watched you guys perform in the audition and you both fit the part so well. They couldn't have picked better people." "Thank you." We said simultaneously. "This is my first show and I'm so excited. I play homeless person number three. In the beginning of the song when the show starts, I get to hide in a real trash can with small holes poked in them. But don't worry, I'm not in there for too long, once the song starts, I get to come out." She was rambling on, but I found it endearing.

"Mr. Baldwin also put me in charge of taking pictures and videos of behind-the-scenes stuff. It's for this big banquet we are having for the whole cast at the end of the show where we are going to have a slideshow. He wants me to capture all the memories." I hadn't heard about the banquet before, but I was already excited. I loved having cast parties after we did plays.

They would usually be held at mine or Sebastian's house, and we would watch all the behind-the-scenes moments. I thought it was a great idea for Mr. Baldwin to host a banquet for this one. Sebastian and I politely reacted and nodded to the girl's nonstop talking.

"So, are you both seniors?" The girl asked. "We are juniors." Sebastian replied. "Oh, that's so cool! I can't wait until I become an upperclassman so I can get the lead roles. Do you guys have any advice?" We both looked at each other and he gestured to me to answer. I don't know why he wanted me to answer. After all, I didn't do theatre for two years and he was far better than I was. I looked at the young girls gleaming eyes, and I told her what I would tell my younger self.

"Enjoy every minute of it. These moments only come once in a lifetime. There's no better feeling than being onstage. Don't get discouraged if you don't get the part you want because every part is important. Every line you say and every direction you do means something. And if you really want a lead part, then go after it with everything you got. The main thing is to always practice. With practice, you only get better and find what part suits you. You find yourself within the characters and within the theatre." I tried to give her the best answer I could, and she looked at me like I solved all her problems.

"Wow, that's amazing! Thanks so much!" Sebastian put his hand on my shoulder in a proud way. I looked over and he stared at me for a moment before he dropped his hand. "Can I take a picture with you guys for the slideshow?" She asked. "Yes, of course." Sebastian said. She got between us, and we all huddled in for a picture. "Yes! That came out so good." "Okay we are finally ready! Places everyone!" Mr. Baldwin said. "Bye guys!" The girl said as she ran off. "She's adorable." I said out loud, mostly to myself.

We settled into our spots in the corner of the stage and waited for the song to start. As soon as it started, I felt like I was transported into the story. With the sets and everyone doing their part, I really felt like I was in *Little Shop of Horrors*. I took it all in. Chiffon, Ronette, and Crystal were played by Burwood High School's only set of triplets. They were new to the theatre from what I heard and saw from the past plays, but they were amazing. They started off the song with their loud booming voices. Those characters were the stars of the show as they narrate what happens in each scene. They were iconic, and the triplets played them with great integrity. They all were in sync, both with their voices and their movements. Their individual voices had a chance to shine, and they all blended together to create a beautiful harmony.

It was a great experience as I saw everyone sing their individual part, bringing the story together. They sang of their troubles of living on Skid Row, and I got into character and acted sad. I sang my part and thought about Audrey the whole time to get more meaning out of it. She was poor, had no luck with guys, and was in an awful relationship. I hoped my emotion came through as I sang.

Sebastian's part was up next, and his voice hit me like a ton of bricks. He started off strong and only got better from there. He really got into the character and felt every world. Seymour was also poor, an orphan, and worked at Mushnik's shop. I watched as Sebastian brought Seymour to life as he was singing about pleading for someone to get him out of Skid Row. We followed our stage directions as we walked around the stage and had the freshmen who were playing bums surrounded us. They walked through us as we sang and begged to be put out of our misery. Skid Row was an awful place that Seymour and Audrey wanted to get out of. They wanted to and had to believe there was a way out.

The energy was once again alive as Sebastian and I sang our parts together. It was like some magic happened when we suddenly came together on stage. I thought about what Stephanie had said. Was it true that the theatre wasn't the same without me? Could it be that the theatre couldn't work with just Sebastian and that it actually needed the both of us to come to life? When I was younger, I used to think that Sebastian and I could do anything together.

Through the theatre and our make-believe games inside our treehouse, I felt like we were invincible. For the first time in two years, I felt like it was possible. Because I was on stage with Sebastian again, and it felt like everything was fine. I believed that after everything, our friendship could endure. Maybe Vienna was right, and we had lost our way and now found our way back to each other. As I sang, I poured my heart and soul into it. The lights were shining on me, and I felt my voice reverberate with the acoustics on stage. The song came to its end, and with it, the applause of those watching in the audience. Mr. Baldwin came up on the stage and applauded.

"Wow, I am very impressed! I know it was tiring when we went over it a thousand times, but you all did amazing! You guys got it down and it was just the first run through! Give yourselves a hand for your first rehearsal!" Everyone clapped and cheered. "Morgan and Sebastian, really great stuff. You two are phenomenal together. Keep up the good work." We turned to each other and smiled. "Okay, I know it's been a long and tiring day. So, you all get some rest and go home." Everyone got off stage and packed their things.

"Great job!" Sebastian told me. "You too! I would say that was a very successful rehearsal." I said. "So, your first rehearsal, how do you feel?" He asked. "Well, I forgot how tiring and time consuming it is. My muscles and feet hurt. I loved every minute of it." I laughed. He laughed too and I was happy at me being able to let down my walls more with him and open up. "Yeah, that's theatre. Don't worry, you will get used to all the long rehearsals. After all, you have experience." I gave him a wide smile and then turned to where I heard footsteps.

Vienna and Embry came out and approached us. "Wow, I literally got chills watching you guys!" Vienna said. Sebastian and I thanked her, and I was happy she enjoyed the performance. "I get chills just looking at you." Embry said to Vienna. "Ugh, please!" She replied. "Vienna!" I snapped at her. Sebastian didn't seem to mind and laughed it off. "Okay, that's enough Embry. We better get going now. So, I'll see you guys tomorrow?" "Yes, you will." I said, more confidently. They headed out to leave and Sebastian looked back to wave at me.

When they were gone, Vienna squealed. "That was great! You guys were amazing out there. You could just see the sparks between you guys." "And what about my performance?" I teased. "Oh yes, that was okay." She joked. "I also saw you guys taking more! The plan is now in gear. Now all we need is for you guys to hang out."

"Yeah, and then you and Embry could double date with us!" I mocked. "No! Stop talking about him. He's so gross." She said disgusted. "Hey, you better watch it. That's my future boyfriend's best friend you are talking about." She looked like she was going to get angry, but then she smiled. "Don't be smart with me." She nudged me as we walked out the door.

Chapter 9

"Breathe in...... and breathe out." Mr. Bryant instructed us the next day in improv class. We went on doing our normal weird exercise and improv scenes until class was finally over. "I think I'm starting to slowly warm up to this class." Vienna told me. "I guess I am too. I never really liked improv, but I think it will help me in rehearsals." "Definitely! I can't wait to go to rehearsals today. I love watching you guys." She seemed really enthusiastic, but guilt washed over me. "I feel bad though. You must be bored sitting there doing nothing."

I know she wasn't completely doing nothing since she still had the time-consuming task of making all the costumes, but for rehearsals all she could really do is sit and watch. "Oh, please. It's not boring for me at all. Theatre is my life. Plus, it's better than being at home." She said and stopped herself. I didn't know what she meant by that, but I guessed it got lonely at times with her mom since her dad wasn't home. I tried to change the subject. "I really wish you were in the play too. We could have performed together side by side. It would have been so fun. And plus, I never really seen you perform before." She shrugged it off.

"I know, but this is your time to shine. I'm still new here and getting used to things. The last thing I want is to jump into something I'm not prepared for." I could understand where she was coming from, but it would have been so much better for me if she were around more in rehearsals. "I get that. I still would have loved if you were in it though. And I know Embry definitely would too. I mean, he kept asking where you were and why you weren't in the play." I was enjoying teasing her about him.

"What is his problem? He doesn't even know me and then just decided he was in love with me or something." She said. "Well, when you know, you know." I laughed. "Please, this isn't like you and Sebastian." She brought up. "Well, if you were actually in the play then you could help me more instead of just leaving me there to fend for myself. Aren't you all about the plan?" I teased. "I created the plan." She stated. "And don't worry, the plan is going smoothly. Soon enough, he will send you a sign."

At lunch we settled into our usual spot and began to eat. We talked about our usual topics, but our favorite was Aaron Tveit. "Did you see his post from yesterday?" I asked her. "Yes! I am loving all the *Moulin Rouge* content. He looks so great! I need to make updates on my fan account." We started looking at pictures of him and squealing so much that I didn't notice that Embry was walking up to our table.

"Hey, lovely ladies." he said. Vienna who was excited from looking at pictures, was now annoyed that she was disturbed by none other than Embry. "What are you doing here?" I felt ashamed by her behavior once again. "I wanted to see if you wanted to have lunch with me." He smiled widely. My eyes practically popped out of my head. Embry was pretty dorky, but he was braver than I could ever be. He barely knew Vienna and clearly saw that she was not interested, but he was still persistent. I thought his crush on her was so cute and wished she would give him a chance. I looked over at her and she looked like she was going to explode.

"And why would I do that?" She replied. In that moment I experienced major secondhand embarrassment and wanted to crawl in a hole. Embry seemed a little hurt but was still the same. "Ouch, that hurts!" He said half-jokingly. "Actually, I'm here as a favor for Sebastian. He wants to invite Morgan to lunch." My head shot up and I looked at him, making sure I heard right. Vienna turned slowly to me and had a huge grin on her face. "Okay, we'll go!" Vienna answered. Before I knew what was happening, she dragged me out of my seat, and we were off to sit at their table. It was weird being at their table from years of staring at it from afar.

"Hey!" Sebastian said as he stood up. "I'm glad you came." I tried to answer like a normal person. "Thanks for inviting us." I said. He gestured for me to sit. Vienna pushed me to sit next to him and Embry slid over to sit next to Vienna. Vienna moved further away from him. Since Vienna pushed us together our shoulders were touching, and I immediately put space between us. Once we were all seated, I felt the awkward silence between us. We were a table of two sets of best friends, two ex-best friends that were now sort of friends, and two people who didn't have any connection to each other. Vienna was the first to talk.

"So, how are you guys liking rehearsals so far?"

"It's going great so far. Only the first rehearsal but we made a lot of progress." Sebastian said as he took a bite of his sandwich.

"Yeah, I can't wait to work with you, Morgan." Embry said.

"Yeah, same here." I replied. He seemed so nice when he wasn't trying so hard. Sebastian was trying to keep the conversation going and I remembered how much he hated awkward silence. "So, Vienna, are you into theatre?" "Yeah, I love theatre. I've been obsessed ever since I was a little girl. I started when I was eight." It was nice to see them talking and having some interaction. I hoped she could get to know him and see him the way I saw him. She didn't really know him, so I hoped she got a chance to see how great he was.

"That's so cool! You were just about the same age Morgan and I were when we started." I felt uncomfortable as he mentioned the past with them. Like the past and present were coming together. It was a different life back then and now we were talking about it with this new life we had with these new friends we made. It felt somehow wrong because Sebastian and I were best friends and now here we were reminiscing about the past. A past where we used to be best friends and now, we were telling people about that time. I'm sure he figured Vienna knew the whole story, and I was positive Embry knew what happened between us. It was still weird to talk about it though. I shook my negative thoughts off.

"What was your first play?" Embry asked her. "It was *Little Red Riding Hood*. I was the lead." "I did that play when I was in elementary. I was the wolf!" Vienna didn't seem amused, but I reacted. "That's cool! What plays were you in?" I asked him.

"Well, I started out playing Chip in *Beauty and the Beast* when I was eight. From then on I did so many local theatre productions." It made sense that Embry started off so young as well. He was a natural and probably better than all of us combined. It was so nice to think that even though we were all different, we still fit together through our love of theatre.

It was ironic that after we stopped being friends, Sebastian and I found people who were just in love with theatre as we were. As lunch went on, we all got more comfortable with each other, and it was easier to all talk. I saw Sebastian looking at my plate. "I'll trade you my fruit cup for your muffin." He told me. When we were kids, we always used to trade food at lunch. He always hated what his mom packed him, and I complained that he had the better snacks. I smiled thinking about the memory.

"I don't think so." I said.

"Why not?"

"It doesn't seem like a fair trade." He contemplated for a while and rubbed his chin. He was always so funny when he tried to be serious. "Fine, I'll do my fruit cup for your yogurt." He looked at me with his deep brown eyes. "Deal." We swapped the cups and laughed. I looked up and Vienna was eating her food, trying to hide her smirk behind her spoon.

Vienna and I walked into rehearsals after school, and we settled into our seats in the theatre. Mr. Baldwin appeared on stage and greeted us. "Hello everyone! It's nice to see your faces again. Get used to seeing my face and everyone's around you because for the next two months, you will be spending a lot of time together. We will be having rehearsals every week with some intense hours. When we get closer to the show, there will even be rehearsals on weekends. It could be very tiring, so get used to it. From this point on, this group of people will be like your second family. If you all show up and put in the work, then we will get through it fast. Okay, so who's ready for day two of rehearsals?" Everyone erupted in cheer.

I laughed silently to myself at how everyone was so energetic and excited. I knew that once we kept rehearsing, the energy would soon die down. I remember how crazy rehearsals were and how tiring it got, so I was already preparing myself. I had my big jug of water and made sure to eat well. "Let's get started!" Mr. Baldwin said enthusiastically. The whole cast went on stage, and we did our usual vocal warms ups and exercises. "Okay, now that we are all done with warmups, I need Sebastian on stage to rehearse Grow For Me and I need Morgan on deck for Closed For Renovation." I made my way backstage and passed by Sebastian. I gave him a thumbs up to wish him luck. He smiled and made his way on stage with Mr. Baldwin. I watched as Mr. Baldwin directed him on how to approach the scene. He then brought out the small Audrey II, which was basically just a fake Venus flytrap looking thing inside a pot. I laughed at the thought of Sebastian singing to a plant. I watched as he was nodding and taking in everything Mr. Baldwin was telling him.

"Okay, play the track!" I was excited to see Sebastian perform on his own because that's when he shined the most. It was his big solo and I got nervous thinking about when I would rehearse mine. The song started and Sebastian jumped right into it. His voice was strong, and his wide range showcased his vibrato. I watched as he sang to the fake plant and would have been more amused... if his performance wasn't so great. I felt a sense of warmth watching him. I felt proud of him as I watched him perform. Even though I stopped doing theatre for a couple years, I was glad Sebastian never stopped. It was where he shone, and he loved every minute of it.

I could see it in the gleam of his eyes as the stage lights reflected on him, the faint smile he had while singing, and how he put his all into every performance. When the song ended, everyone clapped. "That was good work Sebastian but try not to focus too much on your singing. Focus more on your acting. In this scene, you are trying to get Audrey II to grow. I need to see more begging and pleading from you. So, get down on your knees at one point." Mr. Baldwin instructed. I watched as Sebastian rehearsed it several times, each time getting better and better.

"Okay, that was much better! Great job, Sebastian. Now, can I get Morgan up here? We need to rehearse the scenes in Mushnik's shop." I made my way up on stage with Sebastian and Mr. Baldwin. Mr. Baldwin introduced me to the guy who was playing Mr. Mushnik. He looked familiar and I recalled that I must have seen him in rehearsals for some of the plays at Burwood. He was a senior and he was really nice as we chatted for a while as we got ready. I took mental notes as Mr. Baldwin was explaining the scene and showing us our stage directions.

We got into our places and started rehearsing. The set of Mr. Mushnik's shop was amazing. There were flowers all around, the front desk with a cash register, and shelves with displays. The guy who played Mr. Mushnik was great and I fed of his energy. I was comfortable and confident as I got into the scene. I was having so much fun singing and acting. Performing was like letting out a breath of fresh air after holding your breath for so long. All the time I had spent depressed after my grandpa passed, it felt like a reward to be back doing what I loved.

Playing Audrey was so fun. Her accent was so fun to do, and I got to show off my vocal range. She was such a cute and fun character to play. She was so different from me, but she was a little lost in her life, so I used that to relate to the character. "That was great! You're a really good actress, Morgan!" The senior who played Mr. Mushnik told me. "Thanks! You did great too!" I felt extremely happy and proud that a senior who had been in theatre for so long felt that I was good. It was always great to get complimented from people higher than you who had been in theatre for a long time. It felt like I was doing my job right.

"Morgan, you did fantastic!" Sebastian said.

"Thanks, you weren't bad yourself."

"Well, I did have to sing to a plant. So, you win this one." We both laughed.

"Good stuff from both of you. Morgan, I would just like to see Audrey's accent come out more when you sing." I nodded at his comment. "Where's your friend? I actually need to talk to her." Mr. Baldwin looked out into the crowd. On stage it was impossible to see the first few rows of seats. "Viola! Would you come here? I need to speak with you!" Vienna walked down the aisle, annoyed. "It's Vienna." She told him.

"Oh, sorry. Well, I need you to get started on the costumes for the leads, so can measure them right now? You can get creative with it. I won't tell you what to do since it seems like you know fashion." I observed Vienna's outfit she had on. She had on a black hat, a brown skirt, and a yellow tank top. She definitely knew fashion as she always wore the cutest outfits. I always looked forward to seeing her outfits every day. Though our styles were completely different, it was nice to see that she cared about style too.

"I'm on it!" Mr. Baldwin nodded and exited the stage. She started off by measuring the triplets. "Okay, I have a perfect idea for your costumes. I was thinking blue sparkly dresses!" Vienna said enthusiastically. They all began chattering away about their costumes. She then measured the guy playing Mr. Mushnik. "I think I'll go with the classic style, very business type." "Sounds good." He exited the stage with the triplets. Sebastian and Embry were left to measure. "Okay, stretch out your arms wide." She said to Sebastian. It was funny to see him being measured and it was nice that I didn't have to go through that anymore.

"Sorry to get all up close. I have to measure you for the sweater vest. I'm thinking I could just pick up a hat and glasses from an actual costume store. So, I'll just make a sweater vest and long sleeve shirt." "Yeah, that's fine." Sebastian replied. She was finished and wrote down his measurements. She looked up at Embry and hesitated.

"Me next! You can get as close as you want to me." He said, as he wiggled his eyebrows. "Don't get any ideas." She snapped. She began measuring him carefully and he had a huge grin on his face the whole time. Sebastian and I watched in amusement. "Well, I'm just making you a white shirt, since that's all you need. I'll pick up a leather jacket from the costume store as well." She wrote down his measurements and I could almost feel the pressure she was putting on the pen.

"Whatever you say, baby." She didn't look up from her clipboard. "Why aren't you measuring Morgan?" Sebastian asked her. "Don't worry about that." Vienna replied with a smirk on her face. Sebastian and Embry looked at each other and shrugged. We all turned to exit the stage and I felt Vienna's hand on me. "Yours is almost done. I can't wait to show you!" She whispered in my ear.

I was studying my lines when Vienna texted me. "The costume is finished!"
"Great!" I replied. " Do you want to stop by my place and drop it off?" "Sounds good! Send me your address." I sent it to her, and her reply made me laugh out loud. "Where's this?" She wrote back.

"Woodlyn Lane? It's up in the hills."

"This is on the other side of town.... okay I'll be there."

I was weary about Vienna coming over for some reason, but I let my parents know. I was running around trying to make my house look presentable for a guest. I was nervous for what she might think. I never had any friends come to my house except for Sebastian and his house was pretty identical to mine. Twenty minutes had passed, and I heard nothing from Vienna. I was worried she got lost and I was about to text her when the doorbell rang.

"Is that her? This is so exciting!" My mom called. "Hush! Mom, please don't be embarrassing."

I ran and grabbed the door. Vienna was standing there with a hanger that held my costume. It was covered up so I couldn't see it. I assumed she wanted to uncover it for a big reveal. She stood there with a huge grin on her face that you could see under the hat she was wearing.

"Wow, your house is so nice! It's so big I think I need a map for this place."

"Welcome!"

"Are you ready? You will love it! I hope you will love it! No, I know you will love it!"

I laughed at her enthusiasm. "Come in." She gazed around my house in amazement. I was nervous and expected that she thought my house was a bit... much. "Wow!" She gasped. "Morgan, you didn't tell me you lived in a mansion!" "Um, I don't." "Well, if this isn't a mansion then this is the best house I've ever been to." I heard my parents laughing from the kitchen. "I'm expecting someone to come in right now and take my coat." As if on cue, my parents came. "Yes, these are the people that will take your coat. But I call them mom and dad." I joked.

"Hi, Mr. and Mrs. Hathaway." She said, her voice shaky. I had never seen her this intimidated. She was always so confident. I guess I had never seen her in a context besides school and her home. I felt bad and thought that maybe my home had frightened her. "I'm Vienna." "Hi Vienna. It's so nice to meet you! We've heard so much about you." She shook my mom's hand and looked embarrassed when she shook my dad's. "Vienna, what a nice name!" My dad said. "Thank you, sir." She replied. I almost laughed when she said "sir" and I could tell my dad even got caught off guard.

"I just dropped by to give Morgan her costume."

"Oh, I'm so excited!" My mom squealed.

"Okay, show me!" I said.

She uncovered it and displayed it for all of us to see. The dress was tailored perfectly for me. It was a black and sleek dress. I felt the long sleeves of the nice material. Perfect for Audrey. I beamed with happiness. I never had a dress that was actually made for me and this one literally was. Vienna had so much talent. Was there anything she couldn't do? "Wow!" We all said in unison. "Vienna, you made this? It's perfect! Are you sure you didn't buy this?" She seemed pleased with herself. "Nope. I made it with my own two hands." "You are very talented Vienna." My mom said.

"Thank you." "How did you learn to make clothes?" My dad asked. "My mom makes costumes for theatre. Taught me everything she knows." "Very impressive."

"Well Vienna, we would love to hear more about it over dinner. Would you like to join us?" She seemed taken back, but in a good way. She seemed surprised and happy that she was invited to stay. "Uh, sure. I would love to. If that's okay. I didn't expect this. I was just going to drop off the costume." "Nonsense! Our home is your home!" My mom exclaimed. She was being so over the top, happy that I had a friend, but I appreciated her hospitality.

"Come, we can set the table together." I told her, while we were all still standing at the front door. "And though I don't have someone personal to take your coat, you can just hang it on that coat hanger there. And your hat if you want." "Well, I guess this will do." She mocked. I smiled and motioned her. "Let's go to the dining room." "Dining room? This just keeps getting better." I rolled my eyes. We both set the table in the dining room while my parents cooked. "It will just be a minute. Morgan, why don't you show her around." My mom called.

Vienna stopped marveling at our dining room and followed me for a house tour. "Well, you saw our main living room, dining room, and kitchen." I led her passed what she had already seen to our second living room. "This is our second living room. We don't come in here too often, but there's some bookshelves and another tv. We just come in here for quiet relaxing time. I usually do my homework in here or study my lines." She looked all around like I just showed her the castle in *Beauty and the Beast.* "Two living rooms. Okay." She said. I then led her up our staircase to my room. She carefully stepped on the steps as if they were made of diamonds. We got to my room. "Here's my room." She glanced at my theatre trophies I had won, my theatre posters, my playbills, and all my personal photos.

"I love your room. It's so big!" I was happy that I got her approval. "What's this?" She asked, as she picked up a photo. "Oh!" I ran over to it, wanting to hide what she already saw. "Is that you and Sebastian?"

"Yeah, it's from *Charlie and the Chocolate Factory.* When we first met." I was so humiliated.

"And you kept it? Even after everything?"

"Yeah, well I hid it. But I was looking through all our old pictures the other day when I got the part. I finally had the courage to take them all out." She looked at me with a smile and put her hand on my shoulder. "Dinner is ready!" My parents called. "Come on." And we went back down the stairs.

We settled down at the dinner table and Vienna thanked my parents for the lovely dinner. "This all looks delicious." She said to my parents. "So, Vienna, your mom does costumes for the theatre but what does your dad do?" My mom asked. She was quiet for a while, looking down at her pasta and twirling it with a fork. I thought she didn't hear at first or I thought she might have gotten offended for her nosiness. I was about to quiet my mom when Vienna finally replied, "He isn't home much. He's a limo driver."

"Wow, that's very cool!" My dad said. "So, you love theatre too like Morgan?" My mom said, keeping the conversation going. "Yes, I loved it since I was young. My mom and I used to love going to see plays and we would watch old musicals. I fell in love and eventually knew I wanted to pursue it." We all smiled at how similar our stories for our love of theatre were. "That's so lovely. So did Morgan. Her grandpa loved the theatre and got her into it. They used to go to plays and watch all the movies as well." I stayed silent at the mention of my grandpa. They all noticed I tensed up. My dad cleared his throat and asked, "How old were you when you first started theatre?"

"I was eight years old when I had my first role. I was in *Little Red Riding Hood*." "Oh, that's so cute!" My mom exclaimed! "You were just about the same age as Morgan when she started. She was Veruca Salt in *Charlie in the Chocolate Factory* with Sebastian. Do you know Sebastian?" Vienna nodded as she chewed on her food. "They were so cute together! You should have seen them. Oh, we have a video of it we can show you!" "Mom!" I spat out. "Oh, I would love to see it!" Vienna replied. "Let's go!"

And so, I was forced to go in the living room with them and watch the humiliating video. We all huddled together on the couch and my mom put it on. Vienna was smiling like a freak, and I covered my face in my hands the whole time. "Oh, look! There's Sebastian as Charlie. Morgan will come in a bit later." We all waited for my entrance. They all laughed and squealed when I came out. I took a peek. "Look at little Morgan!" Vienna cried out. "You guys are adorable!"

"This is so humiliating!" I screamed. They paid no attention to me. "Come on, honey. It will be fun, just watch. We haven't sat around here and watched your performances in a long time!" So, I sat and watched baby me and Sebastian acting horribly. Watching the younger version of us felt like I was watching me from a different life. A life where Sebastian and I were still friends.

I was so embarrassed at first and then later felt myself getting more comfortable. We all laughed at the funny parts and sang along to the songs. For once I felt... happy. I was with my parents and my new best friend, watching my old performance of me and my other best friend. I felt relaxed and not so worried for once. I had Vienna as a friend, had the part, and I potentially had my friendship with Sebastian back. I didn't seem so worried. From the corner of my eye, I saw that Vienna wasn't reacting anymore, but she was looking at all of us. I turned to look at her, but she quickly looked away. I studied her face to try and read her. Usually, her face was unreadable but this time I saw something on it. There was sadness and.... longing? But longing for what?

"This was very nice, but it's getting late. Thank you so much for having me for dinner and for your hospitality." She said, breaking away from my thoughts. She was heading for the door. "Thank you, Vienna. We really enjoyed your company." My parents said. "And thank you for being a great friend to Morgan." "Morgan is the great one." Vienna replied. I smiled and gave her a hug. "Thanks for the costume. It's perfect! And thanks for everything, it was so much fun having you here." I told her. "You are welcome here anytime, okay? Don't be a stranger!" My mom said. She grabbed her coat and hat. "Thank you all again." We watched her drive off in her little black car.

Chapter 10

The next week, I felt more at ease at rehearsals. Every day after school I would go up on that stage and become Audrey. I felt more alive than I ever had since my grandpa's passing, and I was soaking in every moment. Soon, performing became muscle memory and I was getting back into the routine. It got hectic with having to study lines and all the late night rehearsals..... but I loved every minute of it. I loved when theatre always had me on my toes and the tiredness only made me work harder. I loved walking into the theatre every day and seeing the now familiar faces of my cast mates. I was getting to know everyone really well and socialize with a lot of different people. I talked to old friends who I used to do theatre with and new people I was just getting to know. Even though it had just been a week, the cast already felt like a little family.

It was strange to be back into the world and putting myself out there again after being isolated for so long, but I realized what I had been deprived of. I used to think it was for the best to not talk to anyone, but I was really just harming myself. Talking to everyone and making new friends in the theatre is what I always loved. They were the best people who shared the same passion for theatre.

I was becoming close to everyone, including Sebastian and Embry. Rehearsals were also a lot better since Vienna was no longer in the audience, but backstage working on costumes and Mr. Baldwin also tasked her with helping out with lines. Instead of watching in the audience, she was up on stage with me giving me support. I no longer felt really alone, and I needed all the help I could get in talking with Sebastian. We slowly were going from awkward ex best friends to just being us.

"You guys really seem to be hitting it off. I think it's time to enter the next phase in the plan." Vienna said sneakily when we were backstage.

"Which is?"

"I think it's time for you to ask him to hang out."

"No way! I am not ready for that." I replied as I turned away.

"Don't freak out. We will all hang out in a group." I contemplated for a while. "What if he says no? I don't want to make a fool of myself. Nope, I can't do it." I started pacing back and forth just thinking about it. Vienna put her hands on my shoulders and stopped me. "Morgan, you can do this. He's not going to say no, trust me. He's the one who asked you to lunch, remember?" She did have a point. Sebastian was clearly showing signs that he was okay with me and wanted to be friends again too.

I just couldn't help but still think that he would reject me. After all, I rejected him and pushed him away relentlessly. I didn't want to push my luck just when we started to be okay again, but if I wanted to get anywhere with him, then it was worth trying. "Okay, you're right." Rehearsals for the day were at its end and we were all exhausted. Vienna and I were sitting backstage watching Sebastian end his scene. "Okay, here's your chance." She told me.

He was finished and made his way backstage to join us. "That was great as always." I said. "Why, thank you." He replied. "Nice job, Sebastian." Vienna commented. "Thanks Vienna." We all sat there for a while in silence. "My feet are killing me! I'm so exhausted." Sebastian yawned. "Tell me about it. Rehearsals have been kicking my butt." He nodded sleepily. I tapped my fingers together nervously. Vienna faked coughed and motioned for me to ask him.

"So..... since rehearsals have been so tiring and crazy, I thought it would be nice if we all hung out and did something." I said, my voice shaking. He looked up quickly from rubbing his eyes with sleepiness. "You want to hang out?" He asked surprised. "Yeah, all of us. We can go out and do something to get our minds off rehearsals. We should take a break and relax. It would be fun." I slowly said the words and hoped that I didn't sound stupid.

"Well, I'm in!" Embry said as he appeared and slid in the empty seat next to Vienna. "Yeah, I'm in too! That sounds fun." Sebastian said with a wide smile. When he smiled like that it boosted my confidence into thinking that we could be okay again. "You're coming too, right?" Embry asked Vienna. "Yes, I'll be there." She replied, disappointed. "Great, it's a date!" Embry shouted. "No! It's not a date, we are all just going to hang out." Vienna replied angrily. "Whatever you say. So, what should we do?" Embry asked. "We could get a bite to eat." Vienna chimed in. "Yeah, that sounds good" I agreed.

"Where should we go?" We all thought for a bit.

"What about Legends?" Sebastian suggested.

I froze in my spot. Legends was an old school diner that we used to go to all the time when we were kids. It was my grandpa's favorite place to go, and he would take us sometimes after school. We would go out for milkshakes and often have our birthday parties there. I hadn't been there since the accident because it was too painful to go. I couldn't bring myself to go into that place without my grandpa. A place he used to love and eat at all the time.

Everyone knew my grandpa there and I couldn't show my face there. I didn't want to cause a scene and explain myself over why I didn't feel like going. I also didn't want to upset Sebastian. There were no other suggestions I had for food places, and everyone was quietly waiting for my response. I tried convincing myself that it wouldn't be all that bad. That it was one step toward healing my friendship with Sebastian. If I had to go to Legends, then I would do it. I wanted to fix things, and this was the first step. I needed face things that scared me. Going out with Sebastian was one and stepping foot into Legends was another.

"Yeah, that sounds good." I finally replied.

"Are you sure? We could go somewhere else. There's this other place..."

I cut him off. "No, it's okay. Legends sounds great." I tried to convince Sebastian with my smile but if he still knew me, he could see when my smile was fake.

Vienna seemed confused by the whole encounter and Embry just seemed excited to go out with Vienna. "Okay, cool. So how about this Friday?" Embry said. We all agreed to the arrangements since we didn't have school because of a school holiday. "So, I'll see you Friday." Sebastian said as him and Embry left. I secretly wished it wasn't too late to back out.

The week ended, and I was relieved to get a break from rehearsals for the weekend. That relief was immediately washed away by the reminder that I was going to Legends with Sebastian. I had to remind myself that mending my friendship with Sebastian was going to require a lot of reliving painful things from the past. Vienna texted me and offered to drive me since she knew this was a big step for me. I got ready for Vienna to pick me up and double checked how I looked. It definitely wasn't a date, but I still wanted to look nice.

Even though it was a group hang out, it was the first time I would be hanging out with Sebastian in two years. I was still getting used to talking to him at rehearsals, but this was hanging out outside of school. I observed my long skirt and floral top and decided I looked decent. "I didn't get lost to your house this time.

I'll be there in a few minutes." Vienna's message read. I quickly made my way downstairs.

"Oh! Don't you look pretty for your date!" My mom squealed.

"Mom, I already told you. This isn't a date; we are all hanging out as friends."

"Oh right! So, it's you, Vienna, Sebastian, and what's his friends name?"

"Embry."

"Oh, that's right."

I rolled my eyes. It was just like my mom to get ahead of herself. I guess that's something she had in common with Vienna. I know they were only trying to help, and they cared about getting Sebastian and I to be friends again, but I always felt the pressure they put on me. "You just go and have fun." My dad reassured me. "And don't worry about going to Legends. You will have a great time." I felt comforted by my dad's words. My parents knew that Legends was a sacred place and to be back there meant a lot for me. I took a deep breath to calm myself and then the doorbell rang. "Thanks guys. I got to go!" I grabbed my purse and headed for the door. "Love you!" I heard them say as I shut the door. I met Vienna in her little black car, and I felt more at ease.

"Hey! Are you ready?" She said enthusiastically. "Yeah, I just can't believe this is actually happening." I admitted. "It's going to be fine. We are all going to be there. You aren't alone." "Okay." I replied. "You look so cute! Love the outfit." She commented. I looked over at her and I was comforted that she also decided to put some thought into what she wore too. She always dressed nice, but this outfit was super cute.

She had on red overall shorts with a matching red beret. I loved Vienna's hats and berets that she always wore. I was convinced she had one in every color. "Thanks! I love your outfit too." I said. "Thanks! We are ready to go. Now I just need to drive down this big hill you live on." I laughed and we drove off, listening to the *Les Miserables* soundtrack.

Walking into Legends was like walking into a time machine. Nothing had changed one bit. Legends was still the same diner with the same look. It was a fast-food type of place and had the same menu. The long red booths were the same that looked like rocket ships and they had the same soda fountain. The walls were still not bare and were covered with pictures of old celebrities. I still recalled the pictures of Marilyn Monroe, James Dean, Elvis, and Lucille Ball.

All the pictures of old ads and old movies from the fifties were still in the same spot. The walls were still painted with the scene of the beach. The jukebox was still in the middle of the place and had the best music my grandpa loved. I took it all in, not with pain like how I imagined, but with happiness as the memories came flooding in. The cast parties we use to have, Sebastian's birthday party, and just our usual hangouts drinking milkshakes, all took place in the spot I was standing in. "Wow, this place is so huge! It's really nice." Vienna looked around in awe. "Yeah, I actually used to come here all the time with Sebastian and my grandpa." I thoughtlessly replied.

Before she could reply, Sebastian and Embry walked in. We all greeted each other, and I felt anxiety creep up on me. "Morgan, you look great." Sebastian told me. I tried to keep my voice steady as I replied. "Thanks, so do you." He really did. I saw as he seemed to put some thought into his outfit as well as he had on a dressier shirt. "Vienna, you look stunning! Red is a great color on you."' Embry said. "So, let's order." Vienna said, ignoring him. I felt bad and hoped the rest of our time would go well.

We walked up to the big counter to order, and I was shocked to see the same people as well. I knew the woman at the counter well because we were regulars, and she always knew our order. She was always so nice and friendly to my grandpa and I. "Hey

Sebastian! It's good to see you again. You want your usual?" The woman asked. "You know it!" Sebastian said. "You haven't come in a few weeks; I was starting to get worried!" The woman joked. "Well, rehearsals started up and I got busy. You know how it is." "Oh yes! I assume got the lead?" Sebastian nodded sheepishly. I stood wide eyed at the whole encounter. I couldn't believe Sebastian still came in often.

I didn't expect him to not come anymore since we weren't friends, but it was still weird that his life was constant where we left off where mine changed so much. I felt happy inside that he still came and enjoyed the things that we used to. I know my grandpa would have been happy to know he still ate at his favorite place after I abandoned it. The woman looked up at me and stared. I felt uncomfortable but couldn't look away. She wiped her glasses and put them back on and stared longer. "Morgan? Sweetie, is that you?" They all looked to stare at me. "Yeah, it's me." I said embarrassed. "Wow! It's been so long! It's so great to see you. You are so beautiful and grown up." It was nice to see the woman again and her kindness lifted me up. She was always so gracious to us as costumers and made us feel like family.

"It's great to be back." I told her. "We've missed you here! Especially Sebastian." Sebastian's faced turned red. "I was so worried about you! How have you been?"

"I've been okay, just hanging in there. I'm back into performing again. I'm actually in the play with Sebastian."

"Oh, honey! That's so great. You two were always so cute together. You would come up in here all the time with your grandpa. He was a good man. I'm so sorry again about the accident. He was still so young and full of life. If there's anything I could ever do and if you need anything don't be afraid to ask. Legends is your second family."

Warmth flooded through me, and I was happy I decided to come. I realized everything I had left behind when I shut everyone out. I thought it wouldn't matter when I just forgot about everything, but clearly people still seemed to care and remember. I didn't just leave behind Sebastian but left behind a whole life. A whole part of me from memories and experiences shaped with the help from my grandpa. I wished I would have seen it then, that even though I lost my grandpa, I didn't lose everything he had left for me.

I did have support everywhere; I just had forgotten. The pain and memories of places we used to go to and things we used to do constantly haunted me. I was always filled with guilt after the accident. "Thank you so much. I really appreciate it." I said. We all stood there awkwardly for a moment. "Oh, sorry let me order." I laughed. "Do you want your usual, a Texas burrito?" I always ordered the Texas burrito since it was my grandpa's favorite as well and he was from Texas.

"Sure."

"Okay, great! Sebastian sometimes gets it from time to time." The woman said as she rang me up.

"I had no idea my character had an actual name. I just thought he was referred to as The Dentist." Embry said once we settled into the booth and our food arrived. We began talking about the play since that's all we could really talk about. There wasn't many topics of conversations for a group like us. I felt awkward just being in Legends with Sebastian again, Vienna and Sebastian hardly knew each other, I hardly knew Embry, and Embry couldn't even talk without Vienna fighting with him. The play was a safe topic. We started talking about all the weird things we discovered about *Little Shop of Horrors*.

"So, what is his name?" I asked. "His name is Orin Scrivello. I was doing some research on it. I don't think it's ever mentioned in the movie or play." Embry replied while scarfing down his food. "That's so weird." I commented. I took a bite of my own food and came to my own realization. "I don't think Audrey has

112

a last name." "Oh yea, she doesn't! I just realized that." Vienna said. It was fun to discover and talk about these things with them. Even though we were a random bunch, our love of theatre brought us together. "Her name is just Audrey and that's it." I stated. Everyone laughed.

"Does Seymour have a last name?" Vienna asked.

"Yeah, it's Krelborn." Sebastian said.

"How come I never knew that?" Vienna shook her head as she took a sip of her drink.

"It's not said too much but they mention it a few times in the play." Sebastian confirmed. We went on talking about other cool facts and weird things about the play. I felt more relaxed as time went on, and the weird and funny conversations we were having soon distracted me from any uneasiness I felt. I enjoyed our little hang out all together. Vienna was right, it was the perfect step to get me comfortable with hanging out with Sebastian because we weren't alone. I enjoyed not only his company, but Embry's as well. He was really funny and always kept the conversation interesting.

"So, Audrey II is like an alien plant, right?" He asked. "Well, he came from that total eclipse of the sun.... so, I guess." Sebastian chimed in. "The whole story is so strange. A plant that eats people!" Embry said, disgusted. "More specifically, he feeds on blood." Vienna stated. "Well, it's not going to be fun to get eaten. I wonder how all of that will work out." Embry said. "Probably will be a puppet." I told him. "And Seymour just lets this plant eat people for like half of the play? Maybe Audrey is better off with The Dentist." Embry said as he winked at me. I laughed at his goofiness. "I think Audrey has a lot of bad luck in the dating department." I said.

"Much like me. Unless this gorgeous rose in front of me will have me as her boyfriend?" Embry looked at Vienna with puppy dog eyes. "I'd rather get my teeth pulled out from The Dentist himself." She said without hesitating. "Ouch! Your words are like a dagger."

"And what about you?" Sebastian asked, looking at me. Everyone turned my way. I couldn't believe he was asking me. Didn't he already assume the answer? It was awkward to say the words in front of him, as if he could see right through me. "Nope, no luck." I replied, and I quickly slurped down the rest of my drink. Couldn't he tell that he was the only one?

That he always has been? "And you?" He began swirling his drink with his straw. "No. Nobody special." He said. "The ladies are all over him, but he can never find the right girl. Who knows, maybe she's right in front of him." Embry said as he gave me a look. What did he mean by that? I tried not to freak out or read too much into it. I quickly turned from his gaze and ate my burrito. I few moments had passed, and I hoped Vienna sitting next to me couldn't hear my heart thumping loudly. Embry brought the conversation back. "And I'm sure Vienna has gentleman pounding on her door. Hopefully one day I can be lucky enough to win your affection." Embry continued. "Don't count on it" Vienna said.

She looked at Sebastian and then back at me. We both were awkwardly eating our food. "But for now, you can come with me to get a milkshake." She said as she glanced at me. "Yeah, I would love too! I'll get one for you, my treat." Embry got up and made his way out the booth with Vienna. "Oh, thanks." Vienna replied genuinely. I panicked at the thought of Sebastian and I being alone together, but she shot me a look. I knew Vienna set us up to talk alone, but I wasn't ready. What if without her and Embry, we had nothing to say? I was scared to find out.

We sat in silence for a few moments. Our eyes didn't meet, and we both focused on our food. He was looking down, so he didn't catch me looking at him. He was the same Sebastian who used to be my best friend. Sure, he had grown up and lived his own life, but he hadn't really changed. Why was it so hard to talk to him? I had always thought out what I would say if I ever got the chance to talk to him again, but in that moment I went blank.

I watched as he poked at his food. His big brown eyes were concentrated on his plate. I stared down at my own food and grabbed the hot sauce to put on my burrito. He finally looked up and laughed. "What?" I asked curiously. "Nothing it's just... you still put a mountain of hot sauce on your burrito." He said. His comment made me smirk a bit as he remembered that little detail. I loved hot sauce and anything spicy whereas he hated everything spicy and couldn't handle it. "Well, I see you still hate pickles." I motioned to his plate where he carefully took the pickles out of his burger. Sebastian hated pickles with a passion, and he complained about how sour they were. "Well, you still cut your burrito in half because it's still big for you to eat." He commented. "Wow, are you making fun of me?" I teased. "Maybe." A smile crept from his lips.

"Well, I bet you still fold your scripts in half." It felt like old times when we would bash on each other over our little idiosyncrasies. "And judging on you scrunching up your nose I can see that you still hate that I do that." "Well, it's a script and I just think you should treat it with respect instead of folding it and throwing it around." He laughed loudly, mocking me. "So, I'm guessing you still highlight every part of your script and color code it?" He was right.

We were complete opposites when it came to organization. I was a control freak and a neat freak where he was super sloppy and messy. I didn't say anything as he got me, and I felt defeated. "I knew it." He said, proudly. I smiled widely and shook my head at him. "There's that smile." I immediately felt my cheeks on fire and hoped he didn't notice as I tried to play it off. "Whatever, Seb." I took a sip from my drink. He looked up at me and stared. "You called me Seb. Haven't heard that in a while." I felt embarrassed by my slip up, completely forgetting that I was the only one to call him Seb. I only ever called him Seb when we were friends and I guess I felt comfortable in the moment.

"Yeah, sorry."

"No don't be, I missed it. I missed you." He replied sheepishly.

I was relieved at his confession. So, he had missed me just like I missed him. He didn't hate me after all and forgave me. All the nights I would stay up wondering if he would ever talk to me again and give me a chance was worth it for this one moment. He missed me. He stared deeply into my eyes. He was honest with me, and I knew I had to be honest with him. It was my turn to say what I've always wanted to tell him if I ever got the chance to again. We were sitting close now in the booth. Our body language had changed from sitting back to leaning forward close in our seats.

"Sebastian, I've never told you I was sorry for what I did. For not talking to you again and pushing you away. I was just in a really bad place after my grandpa died, it had nothing to do with you. I was just scared. I'm so sorry I stopped being your friend. I just dropped you without any explanation. I just couldn't be there for you like I wanted to be. But I never even said sorry or apologized for it. I'm really sorry."

I said each word with care and hoped I could get my point across. I didn't want him to think I was just saying the words, but that I really meant them. I know what I said wasn't much and that I could never take back what I did. I could never stop the hurt I caused him and that I felt from doing it. But it was a start, and I only wished I could have told him sooner. He reached out his hands and placed it on top of mine. "Morgan, it's okay. I forgive you. It's all in the past now. I just want to start over and judging from everything, I know that's what you want too."

The final feeling of anxiety I felt from being there left my body. He forgave me and I could finally breathe. I knew I wasn't off the hook yet and that our friendship still had a lot of mending to do, but he forgave me and that's all that mattered. "Yes, that's exactly what I want. So, are we okay?" "Of course, we are friends." We smiled at each other, and I relaxed at knowing we were okay. Vienna and Embry came back, and we pulled away.

"Hey guys! What did we miss?" Embry asked.

"Nothing." We both muttered.

"Now I want a milkshake." Sebastian said as he observed the one's Embry and Vienna had.

"Want to go get one, my treat?" He asked me. "Sure, thanks." I slid out of the booth, and we made our way to the counter. I looked back at Vienna who gave me a thumbs up. "Strawberry, right?" Seb asked me. "Yup." He ordered our milkshakes and as I predicted he got his favorite, chocolate. When we got our milkshakes and headed back to the booth, Vienna was gone. "Where's Vienna?" I asked Embry. "She's on the phone. I think her mom called."

I turned to see Vienna off to the side talking on the phone. She was waving her hand around as she spoke angrily into the phone. "Okay, well I'm out with my friends. What do you want me to do? Okay, don't freak out. I'll be there soon." She hung up and made her way back to the booth. I quickly turned around so she wouldn't see I was eavesdropping. "Hey, sorry I got to get going." She said, with a hint of irritation in her voice.

"No worries! Let me just get my stuff." I began to sit up from my seat.

"You're leaving? Seb asked.

"Yeah, I carpooled with Vienna here. She has to take me home."

"Well, I can give you a ride home since Vienna is in a hurry. After all, we live down the street from each other. It's not a problem." Sebastian said.

"Oh, yeah. If you are sure it's okay."

"It's no problem." "Okay, sorry I have to go. I'll talk to you guys later." Vienna said as she grabbed her things and headed for the door. We all said our goodbyes to her. I watched as she walked out and wondered if everything was okay. It wasn't like Vienna to just leave in a hurry. I stayed staring as she left, and I was worried about her. She seemed off, and wished I knew what was wrong.

We finished our milkshakes and headed out to leave. We both said bye to Embry and then we made our way to the car. Sebastian's car was really nice, and he got his dad's old car he used to drive. "Wow, finally got your dad's car. You've been talking about driving this car forever. It's so nice!" I commented. "Yeah, finally got it as soon as I turned sixteen. It was a birthday gift as he promised." I got comfortable in the car's leather seat and looked at all the fancy interior of the car. I remember being in the car a few times when I was younger and how he excited he was to inherit it as soon as he got his license.

We made small talk as we drove, and I watched as he went the long way home. I usually didn't drive the back way to my house because it took longer, but I figured Sebastian probably did sometimes to see the nice scenery. The back streets to our house were filled with winding roads and beautiful scenery of the mountains. I watched as we passed by the old dirt road we used to walk on as kids. It was a long trail with a white fence surrounding by towering trees to provide it shade and blooming flowers.

"Wow, I remember that road. It's been so long since I walked on it." I said. "Yeah, me too. We used to walk there all the time after school to see the horses. If you want, we could plan to walk there sometime." He suggested. I was happy that this perfect day with Sebastian wasn't ending and that he wanted to hang out again. "Yeah, I would love that."

"Would you want to go tomorrow?" I was surprised that it was all happening so fast and that we would already be seeing each other the next day. "Tomorrow sounds good." I replied, trying to sound casual while in the inside I was jumping for joy. "Great! I'll pick you up tomorrow morning." "I'll see you then." He got out of the car and opened my door for me. He walked me to my door and gave me a hug goodbye.

"Thanks for a fun day. I'll see you tomorrow." He said. "Yes, you will." I watched as he drove off and my head was spinning from all the excitement. When I opened the door, my parents were already standing there. I laughed as I watched them.

"Of course, you guys were spying on me." I said nonchalantly. "No, not at all." My dad said.

"Tell us everything!" My mom exclaimed. So, I sat them down and did.

I texted Vienna as I got settled in for the night. "Hey, today was so fun! Thanks for making this happen for me. Sorry you had to leave, hope everything is okay." I told her everything that happened and our plans for tomorrow. "Ah, that's so great! I'm so excited for your second hangout. The next step in the plan is you guys hanging out alone! This is going so well. And of course, I'm happy to help. Everything is fine, I just had to take care of some things." She wrote back.

I was glad everything was okay with her because I had been so worried since she left and couldn't stop thinking about it. We finished texting and said goodnight to one another. That night I had the best sleep of my life in the last two years. I slept with no nightmares of my past or fear of the future since I knew in the morning I would be hanging out with Sebastian.

Chapter 11

The road was unchanged. Every rock and tree were the same. The same dirt road with a white fence that trailed its path. The trees that surrounded it to provide it shade and the white daisies and purple flowers were all untouched. It was just like when we were kids. I hadn't walked that road in a long time, but it felt like I walked it every day. I felt a sense of strange nostalgia as Sebastian walked by my side. "I forgot how beautiful it is over here." I mentioned. "It is."

I took it all in. I breathed in the fresh air and the light wind that caressed my face. I even took in Sebastian's presence. His honey brown hair was illuminated by the sun and was gently swaying in the wind. He had on a flannel like he always wore. This time it was a light blue one with his usual sleeves folded at his elbows. I was wearing a white long tank top with a denim jacket. I looked down at our feet and we were walking in sync. "So, tell me everything! What have I missed in your life? Anything exciting?" He urged me. It was all so much. "Wow, where to even begin..." I trailed off, trying to think back at everything I ever wanted to tell him. "Why don't we just ask each other questions?" I suggested. "Sounds good." "So how are your parents?" He asked.

"They are doing good. My dad isn't a horrible cook anymore. He actually helps my mom out a lot in the kitchen. My mom is still obsessed with gardening." He chuckled. "I miss them." "They miss you too. Trust me." I replied. "How are your parents?" "Well, they miss you too." He said. I smiled widely. "But they have been good. My dad actually built a mini stage in our backyard. I like to go out there and practice my lines and perform for them. It's so cool. My mom decorated it with lights. You have to come by one day." I agreed, it did sound wonderful. "I would love to see your parents. And that sounds so cool! I would love that in my backyard." We walked on and asked more questions.

"Do you ever watch our old performances, when we were kids?" He curiously asked.

"I hadn't in a long time, but I did recently. My parents forced me to. Vienna came over and they just had to find a way to embarrass me." I said, thinking back at the humiliating moment.

"Oh yeah, Vienna. She seems like a great friend. I'm glad you two found each other. Although you guys do seem completely opposite." He wasn't wrong about that. "What about you and Embry?" He couldn't deny it.

"Well yeah, but he's a little lost without me. I took him in."

"That is your type." I commented, without meaning to. He didn't seem offended, but rather sad that I would refer to myself in that way. "Well, which performance did you guys watch?" He asked.

"Our very first."

"Oh, good old *Charlie and the Chocolate Factory*. A classic." I laughed. "Good times." He had a smug smile on his face.

"You were so cute as Veruca."

"Oh please." I snapped back.

"But I want an Oompa Loompa now!" He whined, doing an exact impression of me with his hands on his hips. I put my hands over my face and laughed. "Oh gosh."

"When I saw you, I thought they should of gave you an Oscar right there." I shook my head in denial. "Remember how the director always use to give us Wonka Bars?" I remembered. "Oh yeah! Those were really good!" He stated. "Yeah, I wonder if they still sell them." I thought. "I wonder if they do." We went on like that, reminiscing about the past. "Remember that kid who played Mike Teevee?" Seb asked. "Yeah, he was super obnoxious."

"But then he fell that time on stage!" We both stopped walking and laughed so hard, our hands around our stomachs. "Poor kid." I said, wiping my tears from laugher. We went on from there and talked about our other shows. "My favorite was *Peter Pan*, hands down." That was the last show we did together. "That was so fun! The memories backstage and the cast were so great." I commented. "I loved playing Peter. And I had the best Tink." He said as he nudged me. "Flying on the harness was so fun. I remember how scared you were though." I joked. "Yeah, I was." He said, embarrassed.

We then talked about our favorite movie adaptions. "I've been dying to ask you how you liked the movie *La La Land*." Sebastian said, nervously. He was rubbing his hands together, waiting for my approval. "Oh, I loved everything about it! It's such a great story. Yes, even the ending. It was bittersweet, but at least realistic." He smiled his crooked smile. "I knew you would." "How did you like Hamilton?" I asked. "It's so good! The songs are amazing!"

"I liked it too! I actually got to see it live".

"What? No way!" Seb exclaimed.

"Yeah, my dad got us tickets."

"That must have been amazing!"

"It definitely was, but I would say *In the Heights* is still my favorite."

"You got so obsessed with that play. Like me with *Newsies.*" He laughed.

"Oh please! That doesn't even compare. You were obsessed. You wanted to be a Newsie so bad. Remember your phase in middle school when you only wore those hats?" He replied, "Yeah, and then I secretly took ballet and those girls made fun of me. Then you stood up to them for me." He said, as he looked down at his feet and smiled. "Exactly!"

I had the time of my life with him talking about our past and catching up. I had never laughed so hard, and I was smiling so much my cheeks hurt. He stared at me like he was trying to figure me out. "What?" I asked. "Nothing...I just missed your smile." Something about his words made my heart full. And not in a romantic way, but in the way that I was happy to be getting my best friend back. The person I constantly told everything to. It was like I finally earned the right back. The right to be happy. We walked down the long road and we were getting closer to our houses.

We saw all of the things we had forgotten about on the road. We saw the two horses we used to see when we would always walk there. On the other side of the road was a white and blue house and the open field where anyone walking the road could see the horses. One all brown horse and one brown and white one stood in the open field. "Hey! There's Bob and Linda!" I exclaimed. "See, you know we were young when we named them because those names are just all wrong for horses." He said blankly. "Totally!"

We walked further along, and we both stopped in our tracks. At the end of the road was an enormous tree. We both remembered it as soon as we saw it. "The Giving Tree!" We said in unison. The Giving Tree was a tree at the end of the road that had inspirational painted rocks and inspirational notes that people would leave. We would see it every day on our walk, and we would contribute to it. As kids, we always wondered who had started it. We kneeled down and examined all the colorful rocks and notes people left. "I always loved this tree. It's so nice for people to do this. Just something to brighten someone's day." I said.

Sebastian opened his backpack and took out some pencils and a piece of paper. He cut the paper in half and handed it to me.

"For old times." He said. "What should we write?" I asked. He thought for a while, tapping his pencil to the paper. "Why don't we write something for each other? You know, something to brighten each other's day." "Let's do it." We both wrote it down and hung it on the tree. As we were walking closer to home, I thought about the two pieces of paper. Mine reading "you are special" and his reading "you are loved."

We finally reached the street that were to split us on our separate paths. One side leading up my street and the other leading up his. "Well, here we are." Seb said. I was always hesitant to show my feelings, but it seemed like we were getting back on track. Like we could be best friends again. "I had a really nice time. Thanks for this." I said, my voice shaky. "Me too, Tink." He replied, the nickname he used to call me when we did *Peter Pan* together. That was confirmation for me that I knew we were going to be okay. He raised an eyebrow at me.

"I'll race you." We always used to race each other back home and the winner had to call the other person and declare their victory. "Oh, you're on!" As I was running, I felt free. Free of all my worries and burdens I had been carrying on my back for the past two years. I ran with purpose and felt the breeze through my hair whipping around my face. I got home first and called Sebastian. "Beat you!" I said over the phone. I heard his laughter on the other line.

"Same time tomorrow?" He asked. "You got it."

At dinner I set up the table and told my parents all about it. They were ecstatic that Sebastian was back in my life. They were already starting to ask questions about when they could see him. "Guys, it's still new. We are taking this slow. I don't want to ruin anything." I picked up my empty plate and grabbed my parent's plate as well, humming a song I thought was only in my head. They stared at me in surprise and smiled. "What?" I asked.

124

"Nothing." my mom replied. "It's just been a while since we've seen you this happy. It's nice."

I was driving to school Monday morning, and I couldn't believe that I just spent two whole days with Sebastian in a row. I mean, we used to hang out every day when we were best friends... but now it almost felt like we were again. For the past two years I couldn't even imagine that he would talk to me again and now we were walking down the road to our house that we always did since we were kids. We caught up on everything we had missed in each other's lives and there was still so much left to uncover. I was reliving our walk together the past two days on my way to school. I was on cloud nine and I was humming to "Suddenly Seymour" when I walked up to my locker and Vienna saw me.

"Oh, someone is all happy! You have to tell me every detail!"

"It was perfect! It was just like old times. I don't want to get ahead of myself, but I think we are almost back to being us again." I said, hopefully. Vienna must have seen the gleam in my eyes because she was just smiling like a proud mother the whole time.

"I am so happy for you! See, I knew my advice would work. I should be a professional matchmaker!"

"Well, you can get us together anytime!" Embry's voice rang through. He was walking with Sebastian as they walked to their first class.

"On second thought." Vienna said as she rolled her eyes. Her mood immediately shifted as she was about to see Sebastian and I interact.

"Hey!" Seb said.

"Hey!" I called back with the same enthusiasm. We stared for a while, unable to say anything else, our happy mood overwhelming us. I was glad to see that he felt the same. That whatever was happening between us, he felt it too. Vienna quickly turned away to give us privacy and I could tell she was pretending to look for something in her locker. She began digging through her things.

"I have to get to class, but I left a little something for you in your locker." Sebastian said sheepishly. Before I could react, he flashed me a smile and he was gone. I slowly turned to see Vienna's anxious face. We both squealed and jumped up and down like we were schoolgirls. So embarrassing, but appropriate for the moment.

I carefully turned my locker to its correct combination and peeked in. Sitting carefully on top of my books with a ribbon on it was a Wonka Bar. I didn't even know they even made them anymore. Vienna was rocking on her heels as she waited for me to reveal what it was. "Aw, Seb."

"What is it? Morgan, show me!" I showed her the Wonka Bar. Although it was just a chocolate bar, it meant so much to me. To us. And I knew Vienna would see the significance behind it too. "Well, looks like you won the golden ticket."

At rehearsal, we were running behind schedule. Vienna was running around like crazy as she was fetching our finishing looks to our costumes. "Where's Seymour's glasses? Seymour needs his glasses! He can't see without his glasses!" She cried out. "Vienna calm down! It will be okay." I reassured her. Seb and I were waiting on deck backstage. He looked at Vienna then gave me a look. "Yeah, she can get stressed out." I told him. "No kidding." We waited and watched Embry do his solo. I saw as he animatedly swayed his arms around, his character coming to life. He was so theatrical, and I loved it. You would never think that someone like Embry could light up a stage. But he was a real showstopper. He was going to outshine both of us. He was born to play The Dentist.

"Wow, he is really killing it out there." I said. "That's my bro." Sebastian said. I loved their friendship. They were complete opposites, but it just worked. Like me and Vienna. He really

126

looked out for him, and she looked out for me. As if Vienna could read my mind, she called me from the dressing room. "Don't go on without me." I joked. I ran and found Vienna.

"I finally found them. Give Seymour his glasses."

"Yes ma'am." I saluted her. She was so bossy! I ran back to give Sebastian his glasses in a hurry, but I saw we still wouldn't be going on yet. "Mr. Baldwin said it would still be a while. They are still working with Embry and working on some technical things. They got to make his scene perfecting with the lighting." I snorted. "He doesn't need it. He could go on and it would just be as great." "Agreed."

"Oh, before you forget" I took the glasses and unfolded them and put them on for him. He seemed off guard and surprised. I was immediately embarrassed, and my pale face turned a dark shade of red. I turned quickly away. I didn't know what compelled me to do it, but I guess spending so much time with him made me more comfortable. As if we were still best friends and I would normally do that sort of thing. He cleared his throat. "Thanks."

We both didn't say anything for a while. Embry ran his solo over and over again. We were both getting annoyed and agitated, but as no strangers to the theatre, we knew how long rehearsing could take. It was never just one run through, but a million. And it wasn't just about the performance but the lighting, the sound, and the choreography. We were going to be here a while before our duet.

We just waited backstage for our cue. I saw as Sebastian was bored and looked around backstage, examining the ropes and the curtains. "I always hated backstage." He admitted. "Because it makes you anxious before you go on?" I guessed. "No, not that. Because it's like all the magic of the stage and the performance goes away. It's like pulling the curtain at Disneyland. When all the lights turn off and it's the end of the day, they are all just people in costumes and creepy robots." I had never thought of it that way. Sebastian always had a unique way of looking at things. Ever since we were young, he always had those "what if" moments. The questions that were deep and had me thinking even years later. I usually had my own take on it like I did this time.

"That's too bad. I always liked backstage. I don't see it as the magic being taken away, but where the magic is revealed. The source of where the magic is coming from. Some people may see lights, ropes, and wires that are broken back here. But if you go back here, you can see just what goes on and how much work goes into a show. All the people that work so hard. It takes a lot for a show to look good and this is where it starts. Uncover the curtain and there's still more to uncover. Yeah, there are still the broken wires and everything, but it's what makes the show work. The show is pleasing to look at from the outside but it's even better when you appreciate what happens on the inside. Even if it's broken, it's still beautiful."

"Like you." Sebastian replied. I immediately looked at him, unsure if I heard wrong. "What?" I asked. But he was looking up at the ceiling, ignoring me.

"Okay, Seymour and Audrey on stage!" Mr. Baldwin called out. We hurried on stage and even though I was playing Audrey, underneath Morgan was smiling.

Chapter 12

Sebastian and I were closer than ever. Our friendship was getting back on track and maybe something more was coming out of it. We were spending a lot of time in rehearsals and while our character's chemistry was growing, I couldn't help but feel that there was something happening between us off stage as well. We would constantly mess around and play pranks on each other backstage in rehearsal. "You guys are totally flirting." Vienna would tell me. "What? That? No, that's just best friends messing around." I told her.

"They are totally digging each other." Embry would reply. "For once I agree with him." Vienna said. I didn't know exactly what was happening between us, but I was glad to be spending so much time with him and call him my best friend again. And not only that, but I really liked the new group we were forming with Vienna and Embry.

Though Vienna was still a bit snarky to him, I could tell she was doing it more in a playful way and that she was warming up to his weird humor. We all were getting so close and spending so much time together. I forgot how close you got to people when doing a show. Rehearsals were no joke and you had to see these people every day. I was just glad I loved the people I would be sharing that with. Not only that, but we all ate lunch together too. We were all becoming the best of friends. Our love for theatre definitely brought us all closer.

At lunch we would talk about our favorite musicals, when we decided we wanted to act, and our favorite shows we have been a part of. "My favorite was definitely when I played Penny in *Hairspray*. I think that's when I decided to take acting more seriously." Vienna said. "I knew I wanted to act when I did *Beauty and the Beast*." Embry said. Seb and I reminisced on all our performances. "You should have seen him back then. He was so natural even as a kid." I told them. "Nope, she was way better!" Sebastian said.

"Oh yeah, I did such a great job as Tinkerbell when I had absolutely no lines!"

"But you were better on the harness."

"I would hate to be on a harness." Vienna chimed in.

We would also play a musical theatre this or that. "Okay, which is the better musical." Embry would ask, and then we would all argue for hours. Rehearsals were my favorite time though, seeing us all on stage in our element. Vienna helping with costumes and lines, and the rest of us trying to act our best. It was also when I felt a strong connection with Sebastian. I didn't know if it was just because of our characters or not, but others were starting to notice too.

This time in rehearsal, Sebastian was rehearsing "Ya Never Know" with the triplets and the hand puppet Audrey II. Vienna and I were backstage, and we grabbed each other's hands as we danced along to the salsa type of beat. "This is my favorite number." I told her, as I watched our feet trying to keep up with the beat. I focused on her black combat boots and watched as my dress twirled as I moved. "Me too, it so catchy!" "Okay, that was great work guys! Sebastian, just try to move the puppet more." Mr. Baldwin critiqued. "Okay, I need everyone in their places because I want to go over Downtown!" He called out.

The freshmen hurriedly ran to their places as they knew it was time for their big moment to rehearse. Sebastian and I were in our spots waiting for our cue. We rehearsed a few times and every time kept getting better and better. The big numbers with all the cast were always my favorites and, in that song, everyone had a chance to sing. "Okay, great! Really great stuff guys! Stay put, while we work out some technical issues for this scene." Mr. Baldwin said, then walked away to talk with the people in the sound booth. Sebastian and I made small talk while we waited. I heard a muffled voice coming from below the stage where most of the freshmen playing homeless people were. "Do you hear that?" I asked Seb. He turned his head as he was trying to figure out where the sound was coming from. "Help!" The voice said.

We both rushed down the stairs to the bottom of the stage. It was the petite freshman girl who was playing the homeless person in the trash can. "I'm stuck!" She said. "Don't worry! We'll get you out!" Sebastian told her. We both lifted the lid to release her. She popped out, her face red and her hair disheveled. "Ugh! Thanks! You guys are life savers. I thought we were going to run through it again, so I went back in, but then the lid got stuck! Good thing there are small holes in this thing." She explained. "Wow! Good thing we heard you. Are you okay?" I asked, concerned for her health. "Yes, I'm fine. The show must go on!" We both laughed at her bubbly personality. She was so nice and sweet.

"I just wanted to tell you guys that I've been watching you and you both are doing such a great job!" I was so happy to hear her compliment. It was nice to hear feedback from hard work. We both thanked her. "And you guys are so cute too! You could just feel the chemistry. How long have you two been a couple?" We both awkwardly denied it and I covered up my embarrassment by fake coughing. "Oh no, we are just best friends." He told her.

She gave us a look like she didn't care what we said. I was used to it all the time back in the day, but now that we were friends again and I had those feelings for him, I couldn't hide my uncomfortableness when she actually pointed it out. I walked away from the situation and headed back up the stairs away from them. Vienna was waiting there on stage as I approached her. "Told you." She said. Of course, she heard the whole thing.

I invited Vienna to sleep over my house that weekend. It was the least I could do after she did the same for me and for all the success in bringing Sebastian and I together. Plus, my parents loved her. "Vienna! We are so glad to see you again! You just make yourself at home. If you need anything, we will be here." My mom said, her voice exaggerating when she said the word "anything."

"Thank you so much, Mrs. Hathaway." We went up the stairs to my room and she still looked around my house and marveled at it as if it was the first time she had seen it. In my room, I got everything situated for her to make her stay more comfortable. I had a small couch at the corner of my room by my bed for her to sleep on. It was small, but it stretched out enough for someone to sleep on it. It was one of my favorite things in my room. The mint green couch had two nice pillows and complimented well with the fluffy gray rug underneath it. Vienna put her belongings on the couch and took off her beret. It was weird to see her without her beret or usual hat. But despite it, her black hair was still sleek and smooth. We settled down and watched tv, talked about Aaron for hours, sang some of our favorite songs, then she brought up Sebastian.

"I never told you thank you. For setting this whole thing up and bringing us back together. If it wasn't for you, I would still be staring at him from across the cafeteria. You saved my friendship with him and now things are going really well. So, thank you." I told her, as I got sentimental. "I told you so." She said, not being a normal person and saying you're welcome. I threw a pillow at her. "But seriously, I knew this would work out. When two people are meant to be, there's nothing that can stop them. And I know you guys are meant to be. You just lost your way but now are finding your way back to each other." I never thought of it that way.

I guess people needed some time apart to grow on their own and to miss each other. We were always so close and sometimes, I felt like I couldn't breathe on my own. But the time apart made me stronger and more willing to redeem out friendship. "You're lucky." She continued. "Most people don't meet their soulmate at the age of seven. He's a great guy. I know it will work out for you two." I looked at her lying on the couch, but she didn't notice. I had to ask. "So, what about you? Does this prove your theory that love exists?" I asked, hesitantly.

I felt like the weight of Sebastian and I were standing on her shoulders. If it didn't work out, it was all my fault, and Vienna was doomed to believe love couldn't be real. Although I didn't know the reason behind it. I was scared to hear her answer. "I think it does." I let out a relieving sign. She had done so much for me in the short amount of time I had known her. She brought Sebastian and I back together while also forming a strong friendship with me.

I never thought I could be close to anyone besides Sebastian, but we had been friends since we were kids. Vienna showed me that bonds could be formed later in life but still hold a great significance. She really cared about me and wanted the best for me. I wished I could return the favor. "I really do owe you for everything you have done for me. I would return the favor if only you would give Embry a chance..." She screeched in disgust.

"Ugh! No! When are you going to stop with that? I don't like him!"

"I know, but he likes you! I know he's not Perfect Pretty Boy, but you should at least give him a chance." I teased. She turned over to raise an eyebrow at me.

"I couldn't even imagine what my mom would say if I brought him home." I laughed at that.

"I kind of wondered what it would be like if Sebastian and I became a couple. Like, how my parents would react. They have known him since forever, but I wonder if their behavior would change if he were my boyfriend. Especially my dad. You know how dads are with their daughters' boyfriends." I said. "How do you think your dad would react? Do you think he would be cool or totally freak out?" She stayed quiet for a while, and I thought I offended her still with the thought of Embry being her boyfriend and bringing him home. She finally answered. "Um, I don't really know." Was all she said. We stayed quiet. "Your parents would be fine though. I mean, any parent would love if their daughter brought Perfect Pretty Boy home. I mean with his perfect hair and his perfect smile. Ugh, it disgusts me! Does he have no flaws?" She mimicked me. I started cracking up.

I threw another pillow at her. "Hey! Watch it, blondie!" She said with a wide smile. "Enough with the blonde jokes!" I teased. She sat back down. "You are truly the Glinda to my Elphaba." She said. "Wow that's a very accurate comparison." I commented. "No friendship could suit us more." "Do you... want to watch *Wicked*?" She stood up from her spot. "Let's do it!"

Chapter 13

A couple of weeks passed by, and everything was going well. Sebastian and I were still on a good path, and we talked all the time on the phone. And even though rehearsals were exhausting, they were fulfilling. It was until the one weekend came along that I had been dreading for a while. I knew the date well. It was the anniversary of the day my grandpa died. I woke up anxious that morning, hating to relive the tragic day. Whenever the day came around, I usually had panic attacks, but this year I just felt numb. It was a bittersweet feeling knowing that I hadn't reached the three-year mark without talking to Sebastian.

Things were fixed between us and that's what kept me going as I got up that day. My parents and I always all went together to the cemetery that day. Usually, I went by myself once a week because it made my mom too sad to go and my dad stayed with her for emotional support. They let me go, knowing it was therapeutic for me to go and talk to my grandpa alone. I knew it made my mom too sad to visit often, but the anniversary was the day she faced it too. My mom had to be strong ever since losing her dad. She had to be strong for me while I sunk into depression. She had to deal with the guilt I felt and as she put aside her emotions to comfort me, I felt more guilt. I've been through years of therapy and self-help books that I was now stable enough to be okay on this date. I just wished that my mom didn't have to pretend to be so strong anymore for my sake. As I made my way downstairs, a special breakfast was ready for me.

"Hey Morgan. We made you some chocolate chip waffles." My dad said. It was just like my parents to overlook and sugarcoat everything. They wanted me to be okay and I actually was. I just wished they didn't have to tiptoe over everything. "Thanks." I took my seat and began scarfing down my waffles, clearly stress eating. Stress eating had been one of the things I gained from the whole trauma. I tried to eat slower and washed it down with milk. I watched as my mom sat quietly. "So, are you ready to go to the cemetery today?" I finally asked. My mom just shook her head without saying a word.

"It's okay if you don't want to go. I would completely understand if..." she cut me off. "I want to go." It was the one day out of the year where my mom showed her emotions and cried over my grandpa. What was a horrible experience for me, was a horrible experience for her as well. I lost my grandpa, but she lost her father. He was still young and could have lived a long time. We all dealt with the pain of losing him, but it hit me harder because of the guilt. "Okay, I'll get ready then."

Whenever I went to the cemetery, I never liked to dress in my usual bright colors. I dressed in dull monotones colors because that's how I felt whenever I went. Not that going to the cemetery was always sad, I loved talking to my grandpa, but on this date it was different. I watched as my mom slowly made her way out of the car and my dad reached out and grabbed onto her hand. He was always her anchor, and she needed that during this time. We made our way to the grave and put down our flowers. We brought our chairs and settled in. I sat silently talking to my grandpa. I talked to him about my life and how everything was going with Sebastian.

I knew he would be happy that we were friends again. I asked him to help me and guide me on the path of rekindling our friendship. I asked him to take care of my family and friends. But mostly, I asked him to forgive me. I asked him to forgive me for what happened that day. For that horrible, horrible accident. I asked him to forgive me for giving up after his death. My grandpa wasn't a quitter, and he never gave up. He was the strongest person I had ever known and when times were tough, he never complained. I gave up and crumbled apart so easily and he would be disappointed. I asked him to forgive me for not talking to Sebastian and not being his friend anymore. I tried to push all the bad thoughts away. I thought I would be okay, but the memories flooded back after pushing them away and keeping them locked in my mind for so long. I thought I would be okay since things were going great for once. I actually had friends and Sebastian back, but this day would forever haunt me.

No matter how much time had passed or what was going on in my life, this date would trigger me. Tears began streaming down my face and I felt like I was about to cry. When I looked up, the sobs weren't coming from me as I had thought. The sobs were coming from my mom. I looked to see my mom with her arms hugging her body and she began to cry out. I had never seen her that way since the day it happened.

My dad and I rushed to her side and comforted her. We knelt beside her and hugged her. She was shaking and trembling all over. I had always wondered when my mom would reach her breaking point. When she would stop worrying so much about me to be in touch with her own feelings. She needed to get it all out and I was glad that she finally was. We were all huddled together and even my dad started to cry. It was the saddest picture anyone could probably ever see, but in that moment, I never felt more safe. I was surrounding by my parents as we all held onto each other, supporting each other. I didn't just see them as my parents who took care of me, but I just saw that as normal people with normal feelings.

They hurt and cried too and needed to be comforted just like their own child. I saw as they were vulnerable like babies, and I held onto them as I cried too. Instead of thinking of everything I had lost, I tried to think of everything I still had. I had my parents who were still here that loved each other, I had Vienna, I had Embry, I had theatre, and now I had Sebastian. Yes, we were all still broken. But that's what made us human, and I decided that was beautiful.

When we got home, we were all very quiet still. We sat in silence as we watched tv. My dad and I seemed to be okay, but my mom sat mindlessly staring at the tv. I saw as her eyes were still red and puffy with dark rings under them. She seemed to stare sadly without hardly blinking. I remember how I felt and how I must have looked the first months after my grandpa's death. I watched her with an ache in my stomach as I wanted to reach out and make her feel better. My dad noticed too, and we gave each other a silent look. He got up and went to the old record player we had that was my grandpa's. We hadn't put it on and listened to music in a while, so it mostly just sat there.

I watched as he picked out a record and the music began to play. It was an old record, one of my parent's favorites. I knew it well because it was their song, the one they played at their wedding. I was always so obsessed with it and sang it all the time when I was little. I loved watching their wedding video and hearing that song, that eventually they surprised me and bought the record. The familiar notes rang through, and my dad walked over to my mom with his hand out. She took it and got up from her spot on the couch. They began slow dancing, and she was soon smiling. I watched them as they danced together.

I always looked up and admired my parents. They had a great love story and were still in love. I had always wished that for Sebastian and I, if we ever got the chance. They both pulled me in to dance with them. For the rest of the night we were laughing, singing, and dancing. Just like old times.

****

"So, how are things going with you and Sebastian?" Vienna asked before improv class started. "It's going really well. I think our friendship is pretty solid."

"Do you think you guys are headed toward a relationship?"

I didn't want to rush anything, but it did have me thinking. Vienna got me this far with my friendship with Seb, but the rest would be pure luck. "It's hard to say. We've been friends our whole lives, but lately sometimes he gives me hints that there could be something more." I admitted. She smiled at me. "He likes you. I know he does, and I'm not just saying that because you're my best friend. I think he's just scared to do anything that will push you away. Give it time. If he really wants to be with you, then he will make his move."

Vienna gave such great advice. I always joked about her being a love expert, but she was very qualified. All jokes aside, I could tell she really wanted this to work out for me. I was glad I had a friend like her. Someone I could talk to about this kind of stuff. And if only she could see how great Embry was, then maybe could return the favor. "Thanks." I told her. "So, have you guys gone on a romantic stroll lately?" I told her about our walks on the road which she described as "movie scene romantic."

"Well, you know how it's been with rehearsals. It's so tiring and we have no time to really hang out outside of school, but we talk on the phone sometimes." I replied.

"Yeah, I feel you. My feet and back constantly hurt from standing in rehearsals. You guys work much harder though. You both are doing such a great job and deserve a break. You should ask him if he will take that romantic stroll with you after rehearsal today."

Just when I was about to answer back, Mr. Bryant's assertive tone interrupted us. "Morgan! Vienna! Do you two ever stop talking? Can I start class now?" We shot each other a glare that meant we would continue the discussion later.

Vienna was right, rehearsal was tiring. I was sick of standing and my voice was getting tired. Even Embry, who was usually lively, was running low on energy. Performing is so much fun, but it drains the life out of you. You had to give it a hundred percent every time for the audience. Luckily, today was a shorter rehearsal since Mr. Baldwin said we worked hard, and that tomorrow would be a heavy rehearsal day with a lot to technical things to cover.

"Okay, that's enough for the day. Remember to stay hydrated. Tomorrow will be a tough rehearsal physically and Morgan, we will be going over your solo." Mr. Baldwin told us. I was packing up my things when I noticed Vienna was clearing her throat in an obvious way. I looked up and she motioned over to Sebastian. I watched as he packed his things as well. She urged me to ask him. "So, Seb, I was thinking since it's still early if you want to go for a walk. It's been a while and it will be relaxing after rehearsing so much." He seemed happy and surprised. "Yeah, I would love to! Let's do it."

"Great!"

"I'll see you tomorrow guys!" He told Vienna and Embry.

"Have fun you two!" Vienna told us. I shot her a "stop being so obvious look."

"Hey, we should go out together too!" Embry told Vienna. "Not a chance." She told him. As we were walking out, I called out to Vienna. "Be nice!" Sebastian just shook his head and laughed.

On our walk, we caught up on more things. It was crazy to think that there was so much to talk about. Being with Sebastian never got boring. There was always something to talk about, but I guess that's how it always is with your best friend. Like when you have a long day playing with your best friend and your parents say it's time to leave, but you don't want to go yet. This time we were on the subject of the new movie, *Cats*.

"Ugh I saw it and it was so weird!" He said. "Me too! My parents actually fell asleep in the first ten minutes!" We both were cracking up. "I mean, I saw it out of curiosity, but some things are better left to the imagination. Movie adaptions can be tricky with theatre." Seb replied. There were a few moments of silence. "I heard they are making a new movie of *West Side Story*." I stayed a little quiet at the mention of it but finally replied.

"Yeah, my grandpa's favorite." He sighed. "Yeah." We walked on a little longer, our tired feet crunching against the dirt road. We stopped and sat on a bench to get some rest. "So, do you have any more questions for me?" I asked him. It usually went like that on our walks. We would just go back and forth asking each other questions about what we missed in each other's life. He stayed silent for a while and had his eyes to the ground. Something about it made me feel uneasy. "I have just one." I couldn't help but get a knot in my stomach. "What happened that day?" My heart felt like it was sinking again, when I had done such a good job this whole time keeping it afloat.

At that moment I wished that Mr. Baldwin could give me my lines. That I could play a character and didn't have to think about what to say because my lines were already written for me. But this wasn't a play, this was real life with real emotions. Something you couldn't fake. So, I went with the worst option... playing dumb. "What are you talking about?" He looked directly into my eyes, my soul. "Morgan, come on. We both know what I'm talking about." I stayed quiet, never looking at him. "When your grandpa passed away you shut everyone out and I completely understood why. But why did that have to include me?"

I knew this time I couldn't hide or run away. I had to face him, but I couldn't respond normally. My initial reaction was to protect myself and put up my walls. "Sebastian, I can't." I started telling him. "Why did you do it? Why did you shut me out? I was your best friend!" He demanded. I had seen him angry before. We would get in occasional fights when we were younger over petty things, but this time scared me. This was make or break.

"Stop! Please don't do this. You can't force me to tell you!" I pleaded. He was already ready to fight back. He put his hands up to stop me from talking. "Morgan, I can't. I can't do this." He said quietly. "I have to know so we can move on. We have to get passed this. If you can't tell me then-" he sighed. "Then we can't be friends. I'm sorry." It looked like it killed him to say it, but he knew he had to. I didn't blame him. I was the one who caused this. I was the one who shut him out. I was the one who didn't talk to him for two years. Didn't I owe it to him? I looked up at his big brown eyes. I took a deep breath and pushed my bangs out of my face. "Okay." He seemed relieved, like he finally got through to me. "Well first, what do you remember from that day?" I asked. It would be much easier if he started talking first.

Chapter 14

"So, we were in middle school, and it was a few months after we just finished *Peter Pan*." Sebastian began. "You were all excited because your grandpa was going to take you to see a play of *West Side Story*. It was his favorite and you had never seen it live." He paused and looked up at me, probably wondering if I was okay. He continued. "He was supposed to pick you up after school to take you. And.... I guess he didn't? I mean, I don't really know that part. And that's all I know. I tried calling and texting you. I even went over to your house. I tried talking to you at school and before I knew it." It took every ounce of him to say it. "I lost my best friend."

I was hurting in that moment, but this wasn't just about me. I had come to learn that. I wasn't the only one that got hurt, but Sebastian as well. I hurt him and he was right, I had to fix it. I had to tell him the truth. "So, this is what happened." I told him.

He angled his body more to face me. "Remember that time of the big storm when we were in our treehouse rehearsing for *Peter Pan?*" I asked. I knew he would know exactly what I was talking about, and I couldn't look up to see his reaction. "Oh yeah! The big storm when the tree branch fell, and it destroyed the treehouse. I remember we were really freaked out for a while after that." He said, as it was all coming back to him. I slowly nodded my head.

I finally looked up at him and he looked at me confused. "So, what happened?" He asked, puzzled. "Well, remember how my grandpa said he would fix it?" I stated plainly. I hoped he would put the pieces together, so I didn't have to fully explain, but I knew I still had to tell him the details. He stayed still with his eyes wide. He held his breath as he knew what was to come. "After school that day I was waiting for him to pick me up." I paused.

I couldn't believe I was finally telling him this story. I never told anyone or talked about it except to my family. I never even ended up telling Vienna what happened. She just knew that he passed away. End of story. I guess she assumed it was too soon in our friendship to ask. But I would eventually have to tell her the truth too before it got like Sebastian and I. "I was waiting and waiting. A few minutes passed and it just got longer. I knew he wasn't showing up. I knew something was wrong." I took a deep breath.

"So, I decided to walk to his house since it was so close to mine. I got there." I stopped.

"Morgan, it's okay. It's me. You can tell me anything." I nodded, trying to process everything. "I got to his house and saw he was home and was so confused. I pounded on the door, and he didn't answer. I got my key and ran inside. He was nowhere to be found. I called his name and there was no answer. I went out to the backyard." The tears were already streaming from my face, at having to relive the trauma I had fought so hard to forget I. But now, it was all flooding back. Seb moved my bangs out of my face and wiped my tears. In his eyes were tears of his own and I could see how much it hurt him as well. It was something he had a part in too. He was involved in it even though I shut him out for so long. He waited to hear the rest even though I couldn't say it. Even though he deserved the truth and I had to tell him.

"Morgan." There was no going back now. "I went out to the back, and he was working on the treehouse. He was fixing it up to surprise me. I ran inside and he was there. He fell and hit his head. I found him." I was choking on my tears. I couldn't continue, but he got the point of what happened. Tears were now streaming down his face, and he had sobs of his own. "I had to call and-" he interrupted me because I couldn't continue anymore. I was trembling and tried to push the image away. "They said he was fixing the treehouse and since he was high up he must of fell and hit his head. They said the treehouse was never built right and it had many safety issues. The treehouse was too high up for a counterbalance issue in strong winds, there was fastener damage that caused the wood to decay, and there was too many punctures in the tree. I played it back in my mind over and over. How could this have happened? The treehouse couldn't have been that bad. It was sturdy enough for us to be in it. Why would he try to go up and fix the damage? I always felt guilty because it was my fault. He didn't have to fix it for me and surprise me with it. I didn't tell him not to fix it because it was too dangerous. If only I would of came to his house sooner than maybe I could have prevented it from happening."

I put my head in my hands and bawled. I hated thinking of that treehouse. The one place that was so special to me because my grandpa built it for me all came crumbling down, just like my life had. Seb wrapped me in his arms, and I could feel him trembling. Even though he was crying too, he seemed relieved. Even though it was painful for him, he seemed far better off than I was. There seemed to be another emotion he was taking on. It was one of regret. "Morgan, I am so sorry! I had no idea. I wish I was there for you. That there was something I could do." I vented to him what I only ever vented to my parents. "He wasn't supposed to die. He was still young! It wasn't supposed to be this way. If only I had gone sooner!"

"You can't think like that! It was just a freak accident. I know it hurts, but he lived a happy and full life. And he loved you, Morgan, so much." Of course, I knew that, but it still hurt. "What turned into a good day thinking we were going to hang out, actually turned into a nightmare." Sebastian looked down and shook his head. "I should have done something more. I should have been there for you." After telling him all this, he still wasn't mad at me. He was the one who felt guilty. Instead of feeling grateful, it actually infuriated me.

"See that's the point! You were such a good friend to me. I knew what my grandpa's death would do to me even before I processed it. I knew I wouldn't be the same and go into a deep depression like I did. I didn't want to put you through that. I didn't want to hold you back. You were to go on in theatre and do bigger and better things without me. I had to let you go." He still didn't understand. "My grandpa's death made me realize that everything is temporary.... and I couldn't help but think that meant our friendship too." He began to understand where I was coming from, but he still didn't buy it. He sat closer to me.

"Morgan, I knew how you were processing everything and what you were thinking at the moment. But that could never happen. You wouldn't and never did hold me back. I wanted to be there through the hard times because that's what best friends do! You just didn't let me in and give me a chance. You pushed me away." His voice was rising. "I know that now! I know I ruined everything for us. I ruined our friendship, and I betrayed your trust! You don't think I sit and replay all the times you tried and put in effort with me, and I just rejected you? It kills me, Sebastian!" I was yelling now.

"Okay Morgan, calm down. It's okay." "But it's not okay! How could you even forgive me? Maybe we can't work it out. And I don't want to hurt you anymore." I stood up and got my stuff to leave. "I'm sorry, Sebastian. You don't deserve this. You don't deserve a friend like me." I got up and started running home so he wouldn't follow after me. "Morgan!" He called after me. But I was already far away.

I swung open the front door. I must have looked crazy because there were tears running down my face. My parents were bewildered. "Oh, Morgan! What happened?" My mom said. "Are you okay?" My dad asked. I ignored them and ran upstairs to my room and cried. Hours had passed and I was contemplating everything. Reliving the trauma was bad enough but reliving what I did to Sebastian was equally hard. He just wanted some closure and I made it worse. He just wanted to get closer to me and get things back to normal, but I kept reliving the past. He probably thinks I don't want to talk to him again and I'm pushing him away. I already caused enough damage. I had to fix this once and for all. If I wanted our friendship back for good, he had to see I was fully committed one hundred percent and that I was putting in effort. I decided I needed to do something about it. I did what I always do in times of need, I called Vienna. She was startled by my crying voice, but I explained everything that happened.

"Morgan, I'm sorry! That sounds awful. But don't be too hard on yourself. It was hard for you to remember those bad times. And then you finally had to tell him the truth and say it out loud. It's a lot. Don't worry too much. As long as you fix it right away, then he will see that you guys are okay. Give it rest today, but tomorrow as soon as you get to school, you need to find him and apologize." She made me feel better. She always did.

"Thank you so much, Vienna. I already feel better." "I'm here for you always." She hung up. I slumped back onto my bed. I looked around my room and at the old picture of Sebastian and I when we were younger. I needed to apologize. I felt a little better but drained and tried to remind myself that just because things were starting to get better between Sebastian and I, didn't mean they were completely fixed.

The next day I woke up earlier than usual to get to school and find Sebastian. I was anxious to see him and apologize. I needed to fix the mess I made and the longer I waited, the longer he would think I was mad at him. I didn't want him to think it was over this time for good. That I gave up and all our hard work and renewed friendship was for nothing.

That I would do what I did before and push him away and never speak to him ever again. I was anxious just thinking about it as I gripped my steering wheel hard on my drive to school. I was about to get out of the car when I got a text from Vienna. "You got this! I'm rooting for you!" I gave a quick reply and put my phone away. Her motivating words put me at ease, and I hurried out and tried to find Sebastian. I headed straight toward his locker, and he wasn't there. I was a bit disappointed, but figured it was too early and he wasn't at school yet. I waited and waited for him, leaning against his locker. Was he avoiding me? Was he really that mad at me? Just then I heard a voice from behind me.

"He's not here." Embry told me. I spun around to meet him. "Mr. Baldwin is taking him out of his classes today to rehearse. He needs extra time to rehearse with his puppet. He also needs time to rehearse his big duet with Audrey II. We are finally going to see it today for the first time! The big reveal! We're all going to practice working with the huge puppet because it takes a lot of work. Just a heads up, so be prepared." He informed me.

"Oh okay. Thanks, Embry. That's a relief. I thought Seb was avoiding me." "What happened?" He asked. "Oh, sorry I don't want to throw my problems on you." He didn't need to hear all the baggage. "But I want to! You're my friend too." It made me feel nice that he considered me a close friend. "Are you sure Sebastian didn't tell you already?" I teased. "Well, he did." He admitted. "But I want to hear your side of the story."

"Hmm I don't know."

"Come on."

He sat on the floor and patted the seat next to him for me to join. I laughed and obliged. So, I told him everything from my side. Not that I was trying to make myself look good and Sebastian bad, but I just wanted someone to understand where I was coming from. Embry was that perfect person. He was a third party who didn't take any sides and he politely listened to me attentively the whole time. "I see." He said when I was finished. "So, what do you think?" I asked, afraid to really know his feelings on the subject.

"Well first off, I'm not taking sides. I want to make that clear. But you need to apologize and obviously you know that. It's nobody's fault, but he's kind of stuck in this situation. He doesn't know what to do or say. He's afraid that any move he makes will push you away and out of his life again. He likes you, Morgan. And he doesn't want to lose you again." If I wasn't filled with guilt and desperate to apologize, I probably would have focused on the fact that he admitted to me that Sebastian liked me. But that was the last thing on my mind. I had to get my best friend back. "I'll make things right. I won't hurt him anymore."

"Please don't. He's my best friend too and I really care about him. He's really been there for me, and I'll always be there for him. But I like you too. I think you are a great girl for him, and I really want to see this work out. I'm rooting for you two." It was nice to talk to Embry on a deep level. He didn't seem so awkward and goofy. He was just.... Embry. I think I finally saw in him what Sebastian saw in him when they first met. Embry and I didn't really have one on one time together and it was nice to get that with him. To finally talk and connect together. I got to know him better as a person and he was really great. I'm glad I got to call him a friend.

"Thanks. I truly appreciate that." We embraced in a hug. "I'm here for you anytime." He said, and I knew he meant it. "And I hope Vienna wakes up and realizes what's in front of her, because it's pretty great." I told him and he looked up at me and smiled.

At rehearsal Vienna and I stormed in to find Sebastian. He was rehearsing with the most massive puppet I had ever seen.

Audrey II was a huge puppet that practically took up the whole stage. It was the most amazing thing I had ever seen. Vienna and I stared with our mouths open. "Yup, that's it." Embry said as he passed by us. Vienna and I squealed. "Wow, they really outdid themselves." Vienna said. "I can't wait to play with it!"

"Well, then get comfortable because you will get a lot of rehearsal time with it today." Mr. Baldwin said. "Okay, I need you two to wait on deck backstage. I just need to run this one more time with Sebastian and then we will be good." So, we went backstage and watched Sebastian rehearse "Feed Me" with the ridiculous puppet. Audrey II was voiced by a senior that had a super deep voice. We watched backstage as he was singing into the microphone, making Audrey II's voice come to life. It was epic. Vienna and I watched as Sebastian was singing his heart out with a puppet. Sebastian was so passionate and giving it his all and we watched as the puppet was maneuvered. It's body wiggling around, and it's mouth wide open. It was hysterical.

"This is the weirdest thing I have ever seen." I commented. Vienna shook her head and watched. "That was great, Sebastian! I think we really worked on the chemistry between you two! I know it's a little weird at first singing with this puppet, but this is an actor too. It's your costar." Sometimes Mr. Baldwin was too much. "Well, I hope they are very happy together." Vienna said. Mr. Baldwin exited the stage, and the stagehands were setting up for the next scene.

"Sebastian's alone. Now is your chance. I'll leave you guys and give you your privacy." I looked at her like I didn't want her to leave my side but in an instant, she was gone. I took a deep breath and walked on stage to Sebastian. "Hey Sebastian, I need to talk to you." I pulled him to the side.

"I need to apologize for my breakdown yesterday. I am so sorry. It was just a lot for me, and I don't know why I said all those things. I was just scared and I in no way intend on pushing you away again. I am here to restore our friendship one hundred percent and I don't want to lose you again. So, whatever I need to do, I'll do it. I'm sorry for everything. For not letting you be there for me as my best friend to get through it the first time and for my meltdown yesterday. It won't happen again. Whatever happens with either of us, we need to be there for each other and get each other through it. To be there for the good times and the bad." I felt so relieved after my speech and was happy that I finally felt like I did something right for once. That I could fix it. Sebastian looked relieved as well.

"I couldn't agree more. Of course, I accept your apology, Morgan." He wrapped me in a hug, and I felt at peace. "And for the record. I never gave up on our friendship. Not then, and not now." I was honestly surprised to hear him say that. That he never gave up. Even when he should have. "So, what did you do?" I asked curiously. He looked down at his feet. "I just hoped that someday... you'd find your way back to me."

Chapter 15

"This thing is so creepy." I said, as we all gathered around to get a closer look at the magnificent Audrey II. "Tink, are you scared of the puppet?" Sebastian teased me. "Oh yeah, she's a big scaredy cat!" Vienna joked. "Hey!" I replied as I playfully slapped her arm. The sad thing was that they were right. It was super creepy. It looked just like the real thing. It was big for its size and did represent something of a Venus fly trap. I knew it wasn't real, but it still sent a chill down my spine. Another part of me was actually amazed that they were able to get this puppet for our production. "Okay, so Sebastian had a lot of rehearsal time beforehand to work with Audrey II, but Morgan I need to work with you." Mr. Baldwin said.

"So, we worked it out with Embry, so he won't get shown eaten by Audrey II. We will just see him die and cut where Seymour feeds him to Audrey II. But since Audrey almost gets eaten toward the end, you will need to be shown halfway inside its mouth." We all started laughing. "I know it's weird, but we need to rehearse you falling into its mouth, so you won't get hurt but also to make it look natural. And don't worry, you won't be falling into it all the way like Mr. Mushnik did. Even then, we have a safe way in the back for our actor to exit. So really easy stuff here, Morgan, just work with me." It did seem safe, but I wasn't so intent on falling into this puppets mouth, even with someone controlling the mechanisms. "Okay, let's do this!" Mr. Baldwin said.

"Aw Mr. B, why can't I fall into its mouth?" Embry whined. "Shush, Embry." So, Mr. Baldwin began awkwardly coaching me on the proper way to fall in and stick halfway without getting hurt. He taught me how to angle my body and for how long I would be stuck in there. I thought of the outrageous things us actors had to do in theatre sometimes. Like the freshman being in the garbage can and me flying on a wire attached to a harness for *Peter Pan*. But it was the art of acting, and I would get through it. I laughed through it as I was trying to do my best.

I couldn't make it sometimes due to the laughter, not just my own, but from everyone around me. "Stop making me laugh!" I told Vienna, Embry, and Sebastian. "See, this is why we do trust falls in improv!" Vienna told me. "Go Morgan! Come on you can do it!" They all cheered. I was getting better at it, and it wasn't so bad. The puppet was soft, and Mr. Baldwin instructed the puppeteers to help me out. On the last practice I was inside the puppets mouth when a loud noise startled me. "Get out of my mouth!" We all jumped loudly and got scared as the guy who played Audrey II yelled loudly in the microphone backstage. "Ha! Gotcha!" We all laughed in hysterics.

"Okay, that's enough practice, Morgan." Mr. Baldwin said through his own laugher. "Since she's done, can we all play with it?" Vienna asked. Mr. Baldwin rolled his eyes and shook his head. "I guess but be careful!" So, they all took turns jumping into the puppets mouth. Embry was the most excited, Vienna was super happy like a child, and I was jealous that she got all the fun of the rehearsals without doing the hard work. Sebastian, though not as crazy as Embry, was also having the time of his life jumping inside the puppets mouth. The stagehands also got a kick out of helping us and watching us mess around with Audrey II. "Cannonball!" Embry screamed, as he dove straight into it. "Watch this." Sebastian said, as he backed up and got a bit of a running start. It was so strange to watch my friends all being fake eaten but a monstrous plant puppet, but it was also hilarious. I watched with a huge smile on my face. I liked the scene. Seeing my friends act like such dorks. It reminded me of simpler times.

Times playing on the playground with Sebastian in elementary school, working on the harnesses for *Peter Pan,* and other fun shenanigans we used to do in rehearsals for other plays. Times before everything got so complicated. I felt a nice warm feeling as I felt my life getting back to normal. I knew this was where I belonged. On stage doing what I loved. As I was in my own thoughts, Vienna called out to me.

"Morgan, aren't you going to join in?"

"I had enough time with this thing. I'm just enjoying sitting back and watching you all look like fools." I told her.

"Oh, is that so?" She had a sly look on her face.

She stared at me for a while and before I knew it, I was falling back as she pushed me in. I was startled and exited through the back. Seb and Embry laughed.

"Oh, you are going to get it." And I returned the favor and pushed her in.

We all then became crazy and were pushing each other in. And for once I felt normal, not worried about a thing in my life. I was back doing what I loved with my best friend and my two new ones. It was perfect. "Okay, that's enough messing around! We got real work to do! Morgan, we are rehearsing Somewhere That's Green." Mr. Baldwin said.

I immediately became nervous. The time had come where I would be rehearsing my solo. To show off my talent. It was Audrey's big moment and time to shine. To be without Seymour, Orin, or Mr. Mushnik. To tell her story and give the audience a look into her life. It had to be just right and as an actor, it was my job to convey that emotion. I was nervous I wouldn't fulfill the expectation. We all settled backstage as they were setting up the scene. I got Vienna and took her to the side. I didn't want Sebastian to see I was nervous.

"I'm kind of freaking out." I admitted. "This is my first rehearsal solo. I just want to make a good impression." I told her. "You got this. You've been doing fine this whole time. What are you worried about?" She asked, concerned. "Well, I've been out of the game for two years. I've been doing fine rehearsing beside Sebastian, but now I'm doing this alone. I just want to prove to myself and to them that I'm good enough." She looked at me with her big dark eyes.

"You can do it. Just remember all the coaching I did with you. You aren't playing yourself; you're playing Audrey." I took a deep breath. "Alright." Just then Sebastian came up to us. "Mr. Baldwin wants you to rehearse with this." He put the fake cast on my arm. "Okay, I'm ready." I was so nervous that my palms were sweaty. I tried to control my breathing. This was my chance to show what I could do. I wanted to show Mr. Baldwin my talent on my own and not just working beside other people.

I felt so lost since I had come back to theatre and just started regaining my confidence. Now I had to do a solo and I just wanted it to be my best. I knew it was just rehearsal, but I thought of how Sebastian always did amazing. It made me feel a bit better that I wasn't completely alone, and the triplets would be by my side. I walked on stage, and we all went on our marks to start. "Okay, let's begin." I sat and concentrated on what my character would do and act like. I looked up and saw Sebastian smiling at me from backstage. He gave me a thumbs up. "Okay, I can do this." I told myself. I got out of my own head and into Audrey's. I remembered all the plays I did and what it felt like. It soon became muscle memory.

I started off with my voice strong and clear. I continued and let the song carry me and soon I was on the journey of the story it was telling. I acted and sang the best that I had in years. I gave a dreamy look as I was singing about the daydream far from Skid Row. Audrey was imagining a place somewhere that's green. A place with plastic on the furniture and a grill out on the patio. I became fully into the scene and the character. I even became a bit emotional, which helped with my acting. Audrey was picturing a better life out of her current situation with Seymour. And as I was singing, I was picturing a same kind of future someday for Sebastian and I.

I got a standing ovation and Mr. Baldwin said that was the best acting he had seen. It made me so happy that I got his approval and I felt more confident in my acting. Sebastian came up to me with a pleasing look on his face. "Morgan, that was amazing! You just went for it. I miss seeing you light up the stage." I felt my cheeks turn a dark shade of red. I hated how I couldn't hide it under my pale complexion. "Thank you, but I'm not as great as you." "You're even better. Seriously, you need to give yourself some credit. Sometimes I'm too in my head when I perform but when you get into it...." He paused. "It's unbelievable." I felt like it was the greatest compliment he could have given me.

The next week went by smoother than expected. I felt more comfortable in my acting and around Sebastian. It seemed like everything was working out better for us since I told him the truth about my grandpa. Like there were no secrets between us and we could now be open and honest with each other. We weren't hiding behind anything. I let myself be vulnerable with him and let my guard down. Now that he knew, I knew I could get passed anything. I felt safe with him. It was finally feeling like all my open wounds were closing up. Sebastian let me heal. My parents even seemed better that they saw I was doing okay after my breakdown that day when I came home. I caught them up and told them everything about it. "I'm glad you owned up and took responsibility for your actions. That was very brave. Because you did hurt him. I'm just glad you finally told him the truth." My dad told me. "Dad, I know that. I have always known that. I just didn't know the right thing to say. How to fix it and say sorry for everything I put him through." "We know, honey. We are glad things are better now. How's Vienna and the other friend?" My mom asked, and we moved on from it.

Things were getting back into regular motion with improv class, our little group at lunch, and rehearsals. I liked the steady routine and demanding hectic schedule of rehearsals. It kept me on my toes and always focused. As an actor, I loved to improve, and I felt like I was improving on my character each time I walked into rehearsals. I really got to know Audrey and I loved playing her. It was always fun to play a character completely different from yourself. "Okay, Sebastian and Morgan! Let's see that magic and run over Suddenly Seymour." Mr. Baldwin demanded.

It was my favorite song in the play. Sebastian and I really fed off each other's energy and when we sang, it felt like our voices were meant to sing together because they harmonized so perfectly. I also watched how engaged everyone was when watching us rehearse it, even Vienna and Embry. "That was perfect as always! But why do you guys keep skipping the kiss? Next time I want to rehearse with the kiss, okay?" Mr. Baldwin told us.

"I couldn't hear them too good. Can we fix the mics?" He told the sound booth, turning his attention elsewhere. We both just looked nervously away at each other. "Okay, I guess that's something we have to do now." Seb said. "Yeah, I guess." I replied, as Vienna and Embry approached us. "Fake kissing is super easy. Watch." He put his arm around Vienna, and she quickly turned away. "Never going to happen." She snapped. "Hey, it was solely for acting purposes." Seb and I rolled our eyes. We waited around for our next cue like we usually did. A loud shriek came from the feedback of the microphones. "Sorry! We are having really bad technical issues today that we need to fix. Everything is all wrong so just sit tight while we get things worked out." Mr. Baldwin assured us. "Yeah, get comfortable, this might take a while." A guy from the sound booth called out. Everyone groaned.

They all hated to just sit around because it got really boring, but for me it meant goofing off with my friends. There wasn't really much for us to do so we waited on stage and talked. My attention was elsewhere as I stared at the piano that was still on stage. "Hey Seb, do you still play?" They all turned to the piano. He walked over and we followed as he sat down. "I think I still got some tunes in me." He looked at me and patted the seat next to him. I sat beside him, Vienna and Embry by our side. Sebastian's fingers hovered over the keys. "Let's see." He mumbled.

And soon, his fingers were dancing wildly over the ivories. It seemed like he was barely touching them, but this whole music projected out. I didn't play piano, or any instrument for that matter, but it always impressed me how people who were skilled at playing an instrument made it look so effortless. I watched as he pressed down on the foot pedals and passionately got into the song, moving his head. He ended on a soft note. We all clapped.

"That was impressive." Vienna admitted.

"Do you play?" Seb asked.

"Uh, well. I do, but I took piano as a kid, and I only know one song. But I can play it really well." She said sheepishly.

Sebastian motioned to her and got up from his seat.

"Wow, beautiful and she can play the piano? Is there anything she can't do?" Embry said, and I was thinking the same thing. "Scoot over, Morgan!" He said as he moved me out of my seat. Vienna looked at the keys like she was having a stare off with them.

I looked at her and she shrugged. "Okay, here goes nothing. Let's see if those piano lessons paid off." She said, mostly to herself. I was curious to know what the only song she knew how to play was, but as the first notes rang through, I recognized it immediately. "A Thousand Miles" by Vanessa Carlton. I remember being obsessed with that song in middle school. Sebastian would get annoyed by me because I always played it constantly before *Peter Pan* rehearsals. I knew he secretly liked it though, because once I saw him singing it to himself. Seb and I looked at each other, as if remembering the fond memories. I watched as Vienna played.

She seemed intent on playing it well, fixated on the keys. It came out beautifully, as she played the first verse. I saw as Embry marveled at her. She did look beautiful. With her black stylish hat and outfit, it actually looked like playing piano was what she did for a living. I leaned on the piano and bopped my head to the music, tapping my fingers on the black wood. They immediately stopped when a hand grabbed mine. It was Sebastian. He looked at me, nervously. I turned to face him, and his other hand was out, inviting me in.

I took his hands, and we slow danced. We swayed to the rhythm of the music. The whole time I was avoiding looking up at him, but when I finally did, he was already looking at me. A huge smile spread across his face, and I couldn't help but match it. He got my hand as he twirled me, and he spun me around as we danced. Moving to and fro, we laughed as we tried to keep up with the beat. I felt like I was living something I always dreamed of.

To pick up where we left off in middle school. To possibly start something together.... a relationship. Dancing with Sebastian felt like I was floating, but he would never let me drown. He smiled his perfect smile at me and looked at me with honey brown eyes. The song eventually ended, but I wished it would have lasted forever. Sebastian and I dancing together to a soft piano. We both jumped apart as Mr. Baldwin yelled out, "Okay, we are ending rehearsal early today! We need to figure out the microphone issues. Relax, rest up, and have a good day!"

"Yes!" Embry called out.

"Cool, you guys want to do something?" Seb asked.

"Dude, I'm super tired and taking advantage of this. I'm going home and taking a nap." Embry said.

"Okay, see you later bro." Seb replied.

Vienna could see where this was heading and tried to conceal her smile. "Yeah, I'm going to call it a day too." She stretched out her arms and yawned the fakest yawn I have ever heard. "See you tomorrow, Morgan!"

"Okay." Was all I said, because she ran out.

We watched as they left. Sebastian turned to me. "Let's do something. Want to go to Legends?"

"I'd love to."

We went to Legends and when we finished up, we ended up on our usual walk. We spent so much time talking at Legends that it was getting late on our walk. It was sunset and the sky was filled with hues of pink and purple swirls. I looked up at the sky and enjoyed the moment. It was sunny and hot earlier in the day. Those were my favorite days, just like my grandpa. We both hated the cold weather. The days always felt longer when it was cold. Like the day would never end and it just dragged you into its darkness. Plunging you into the cold depths of the gray sky. But when it was sunny, the days felt shorter.

Because a day that beautiful couldn't last forever and you needed to soak up every minute of it. Watching the last golden rays disappearing into the horizon. I was so concentrated that I didn't know Sebastian was staring at me, probably wondering what I was thinking. He finally spoke. "I can't believe we spent the whole day together." I didn't really think about it because lately, it seemed like we always hung out due to rehearsal. It was a nice change though to hang out outside of school since we rarely got to do it. "I had a lot of fun with you today." I told him.

"Me too." As we walked on, it was getting colder and darker. "Tink, you look so cold." He told me, and I laughed at his comment. In a swift motion, he took off his jacket and put it on me. I immediately felt the warmth, not from his jacket, but from his kind gesture. "Thanks." We ended up by the Giving Tree and to where the road split to our houses. "Well, I'll see you tomorrow." I told him.

I hated saying goodbye to him. Even as a kid, we would whine when we had to go, our parents pulling us apart. But I felt more comfort in knowing that this time when I said goodbye, it wasn't going to be forever. There wasn't going to be a two-year gap when we would talk again. I would see him tomorrow. I started to walk away, and he called out to me. "Morgan, wait!" I turned back around, figuring he probably wanted his jacket back. I was about to take it off when he started to speak. "There's something I've been wanting to tell you and now I can't think of a better time." I held my breath.

"I like you. And it's not just a feeling that has been brought on because we became friends again and we've been spending a lot of time together in rehearsals." He was talking really fast and jumbled, the whole time he was fidgeting. He took a deep breath. "What I'm trying to say is that I've always liked you. And I don't even know when that feeling began. I probably liked you ever since *Charlie and the Chocolate Factory*, before I knew what having a crush on someone was. But I know I did, even then. And it has never stopped since then. Not as we got older and not even when we weren't friends anymore. I tried liking other people, but you never left me. And I felt like in eighth grade maybe there could have been something there when we did *Peter Pan*, but then all that stuff happened with your grandpa. And now, lately I feel like there's something there too. You're my best friend in the world but I have to ask." He paused. "Is there something there for you too?"

I was overwhelmed by his outpouring of words. Every single thing I had ever felt and experienced, he just voiced. I felt like I could breathe the biggest sigh of relief. I knew there was something there too, but to hear him say it made my heart skip a beat. Sebastian liked me. Ever since we were kids. He felt the same. I didn't even hesitate to respond. "I like you too, Sebastian. I always have. I felt like there could have been something when we did *Peter Pan* and that's why it always killed me that it ended the way it did. I never stopped liking you and caring about you."

He still looked nervous and pale from his confession, but he brightened up with a huge smile. "So, would you be ready for this? To be my girlfriend?" He was still on edge, waiting for my response. "I would love to be your girlfriend." I smiled on the last world. I was Sebastian's girlfriend. We were hand in hand as he walked me to my house since it was getting dark.

"Goodnight, Tink. Sweet dreams."

"Goodnight." I told him.

He walked a few steps and then turned back. He marched right up to me and kissed me. I was caught off guard and it left me dizzy. "I didn't want our first kiss to be on stage." I turned the key to get inside. My parents stared at me as I walked in with Sebastian's jacket on. I didn't know how the look on my face was, but my parents squealed with happiness.

"Someone's in love." My mom commented. Later that night I ran up to my room and called Vienna to tell her the news. All I remember from the call was inaudible screaming noises of happiness.

Chapter 16

I woke up the next morning with my phone in my hand. I stayed up all night talking to Vienna and telling her all the details on Seb and I. I honestly don't remember most of the conversation, but I remember there was a lot of screaming. So, it wasn't a dream. This was real. Sebastian and I were together. "I can't believe it actually worked!" I recalled telling Vienna the night before. "Operation get you and Perfect Pretty Boy together completed. I am so happy for you, Morgan. You deserve this." She had said to me. For once I felt like I did deserve to be happy. After all the pain and suffering I had been through, I felt like I earned the right. I could actually call Sebastian mine. I may have been awake, but the dream wasn't over.

I got ready for school and put on the nicest summer dress I had. Most of my clothes were pretty fashionable and cute, but I wanted to look nicer for Seb. I wore a yellow sundress with white daisies. I decided not to put my hair in its usual style and just wore it down. I heard the doorbell from all the way upstairs. "Hi Sebastian! What a surprise!" I heard my mom say. "Come on in!" I jerked from my seat and quickly put on my shoes on and ran downstairs. Sebastian was here and I didn't want my parents to say anything stupid. I ran so fast down the stairs that I almost tripped and fell. I saw Seb almost laughing as he saw me.

"There's our little girl." My dad said, saying something stupid. "Hey." I called to him. "What are you doing here?"

"I decided to surprise you and thought we could ride to school together." Before I could respond, my mom chimed in. "Well, isn't that sweet! We are so happy to see you two finally together. It's been so long and to see you here all grown up. You are so handsome."

"Mom!" I spat out.

"I remember you two so young and inseparable. And now look at you guys now! We miss you around here."

I was so annoyed at her rambling on, but Sebastian seemed to enjoy it. "I've missed being around here too. I've missed seeing your faces. You know you are like family to me." He replied. "Well, you are welcome over here anytime. Maybe we can schedule dinner and invite your parents too." My dad said. I was surprised by his sincerity and felt a warmness inside of me. It brought me back to the conversation I had with Vienna about our dads approving of our love life. "That would be great, Mr. Hathaway. I'll let my parents know."

"Great it's a date!" My dad joked and winked at me. I put my hand over my face. They all laughed at me. "Oh, we are just messing with Morgan. She hates it when we embarrass her." Sebastian just smiled and laughed along with them. "Okay, well we better get to school. You know we still need to get an education and there's the play and all." I said as I headed out the door.

"I can't wait to see you two in the play like old times. Well Sebastian, I guess we will see you soon." My mom waved. "Yes, you will. It was great seeing you guys." We turned and my mom called out again, "Say hi to your parents for me." We walked out the door and I immediately rushed toward his car.

"So glad that's over. Sorry about that."

"Don't worry about it, Tink. You know I love your parents."

"Well, the feeling is definitely mutual." He smiled his brilliant smile and ruffled his fingers through his honey hair. I noticed his hair wasn't as puffed up as usual. I smiled at the thought of it. He rushed in front of me to open my door.

"Why, thank you."

"Anything for my girlfriend."

My stomach made a million knots. We settled in his car that I missed being in. I always loved sitting in the comfortable leather seats. "Want to hear some music?" He asked me. "Duh!" I replied since music was our lives. "I got the perfect song." I heard the first notes of "Suddenly Seymour" and practically screamed. "No way! Stop, that's not funny. I'm getting sick of this song." He started cracking up and I slapped his arm. "I'm serious!" I said through my own fits of laugher. "Fine, I have something better instead." The whole car ride to school we rapped to *Hamilton*.

As soon as we entered the school parking lot and got off the car, he held my hand. The feeling felt very natural and not weird at all. We have been friends forever and I dreamed about this day, but I was not used to people staring and that was my biggest concern. Not that I really cared what people thought, but it would be a change for them to see me with him again and I knew it would get the cast in the play to turn heads, especially the freshmen. I tried to shake my negative thoughts away because with Sebastian's hand in mine, I knew there was nothing we couldn't conquer. Just one step at a time. And the first step was Vienna. We walked in hand and hand to my locker.

"Well, hello, Mr. and Mrs. Montgomery." Vienna said to us. Seb gave me five dollars. Vienna noticed the exchange. "What was that?"

"I bet him five dollars that you would make some comment about us." I said.

"I had more faith in you, Vienna. You made me lose five dollars. You owe me!" He told her.

"Well, I can't help to see my two friends finally together."

"Yeah, finally!" Embry's voice came through. He walked up to us with bright eyes and a huge smile. "Ah, young love. Isn't it beautiful?" He said.

"Dude, come on." Seb replied.

"Well, it's about time! I knew you two would get together but I didn't think it would take this long. I was so patient!" Embry said in frustrated tone. It was funny to see him all worked up. It was like The Dentist in him was coming out.

"*You* were patient? What about me? This whole thing become possible because of me!" Vienna exclaimed. "See their happiness? That's all me."

"Come on, baby. Let's not fight. The kids are together, and their happiness is the only thing we agree on." Embry told her as he put his arm around her. She flinched a little, but then nodded her head in agreement. "Fine, you're lucky I'm in a good mood." Seb and I just rolled our eyes at each other the way we always did when it came to Vienna and Embry's bantering. It still felt right though. Sebastian and I were finally together and our whole friendship as a group. I finally found where I belonged. My true friends that I called home.

At rehearsal people stared at Sebastian and I as we walked in. There was no surprise there. Most of them just ignored us but the freshmen began to whisper to each other. The freshman that we helped out of the trash can came up to us. "So, I see it finally worked out between you two. I'm so happy! We must celebrate with a photo." She squeezed between us and took the picture. "Uh, thanks." Sebastian said. We both smiled awkwardly. I blinked as the flash caught me off guard. "This is so cute! This is definitely going on the slideshow." She ran off and back to her spot with her freshmen friends. "This is going to take a lot of getting used to." I told Sebastian. "Okay, get to your places!" Mr. Baldwin called out. He even looked sideways at Sebastian and I.

I saw a smile creeping on his face. He got up on stage with us and directed us.

"Okay, I will be separating you two lovebirds today." I was shocked by his comment. Sebastian and I both looked at the floor. "Morgan and Embry I want you two to be working on your scenes together today. Embry, you are mean and cruel to her. Remember, The Dentist is a character the audience hates. So just don't mind Audrey and just be the worst. Morgan, be very intimidated by him and your confidence shrinks when you are near him. You are scared and frightened at what he might do to you. I need to see these emotions from you two, got it?" Mr. Baldwin said in his super serious director voice. Embry and I nodded. "Okay, let's do it!"

Seb exited the stage and met with Vienna to watch us from backstage. Embry and I practiced our scenes together a million times. Mostly because we couldn't stop laughing. It was fun to get some time to work with Embry. I really enjoyed working with him and it was nice to get to spend time with him. With Sebastian and Vienna, it was always hard to talk and get to know him better. We couldn't get through the scene because we would always laugh. He would make funny faces at me when Mr. Baldwin wasn't looking.

It was hard to play like we hated each other and to be serious when Embry was the least serious person I knew. It also wasn't helping that Sebastian and Vienna were making us laugh from backstage. "You guys need to take this seriously!" Mr. Baldwin said. "I know but it's hard to be mean to Morgan. She's like the sweetest person." Embry said. "Aw!" I replied. "I know, but right now you are acting. You think Audrey is just pathetic and you push her around. You think you can do that for me?" He said in a pleading tone. We tried and finally got through our scenes. "Okay, that's a wrap for today!" Mr. Baldwin said. We walked off stage and grabbed our stuff to leave. "You guys kept making me laugh!" I said as I approached Seb and Vienna. "It was some funny stuff." Vienna said with a smile on her face.

"Hey, let's do something tomorrow. I need a break and I'm down to go to Legends." She said. I was surprised that she said she needed a break and suggested to go out. Usually, it was anyone else that always made plans. She must have been overwhelmed with rehearsals. "Yeah, that sounds good!" Embry stated. I was about to agree when Sebastian spoke up.

"Oh, sorry guys. I actually wanted to take Morgan out on a date tomorrow." I shot him a surprised glance. "Oh, a first date!" Vienna said as she clapped her hands.

"Well, it was supposed to be a surprise...." Seb said disappointed. "I wanted to have a picnic."

"Really?" I said, my cheeks turning red.

"That's so romantic!" Embry said.

"So, what do you say?" Seb asked me.

I looked back at Vienna and Embry. "I'm sorry guys. Can we reschedule?"

"It's no problem, Morgan." Embry said.

"Honestly it's fine. We can always go to Legends another time. It's no big deal. You two have fun!" Vienna said excitedly.

I somehow felt bad I was leaving Vienna behind. The last thing I wanted to do was be one of those girls who ditched her best friend as soon as she got a boyfriend. I know the situation was a bit different since I had known Sebastian forever, but I still didn't want to leave her out like that. After all, she was the whole reason that we were even together. I looked up at Sebastian. "Yes, of course. A picnic tomorrow sounds wonderful."

It really did and I was excited for our first official date. He smiled so wide, and I couldn't help but match it. I could already see the plans coming along in his mind. "I'll make it up to you, I promise." I told Vienna. "Don't worry about me! Just go and have fun tomorrow." She said in her genuine tone. But as I turned away, I could see sadness in her eyes.

The next morning I get ready for our picnic date. The weather was usually great in California and there was a light breeze. I had only been on a picnic with my parents when I was younger, but I decided to wear some capris since I knew I would be sitting on the ground. I gathered some stuff my mom made, and Vienna insisted on stopping by and giving me some treats she baked for the occasion. I told her she didn't have to bake anything for our picnic date, but she insisted. I heard Sebastian honk his horn and that was my cue.

I told him to do it from now on since I didn't want my parents to keep him with their embarrassing chatter. I ran downstairs and said bye to my parents without another word. "You look beautiful." Seb told me as we got in the car. "Thank you. You look great." He really did. He didn't have on his usual flannel but instead he had on a nice dressy black shirt. It was a bit too fancy for a picnic, but I accepted it. We drove to our destination that was a surprise according to him but once we started getting closer, I knew the familiar rode.

"Are you serious?" I said in nostalgic excitement. "Surprise!" We ended up at our old elementary school. I hadn't been there in ages. Everything seemed so small now. There were so many great memories there and it was an out of body experience to be there with Sebastian. Two years ago, I never thought this would happen. We walked with the picnic basket to the open field of the elementary school. I looked around and replayed in my mind memories of us running around and playing make believe games. If only young Morgan and Seb could see us now.

"You are truly amazing." I told him.

"I just wanted to give my girlfriend a first date she will never forget." He said.

We laid out the blanket and set up all the food. There was so much food for the both of us. "I made you peanut butter and banana sandwiches cut into hearts. Your favorite. And I got us some apple cider."

"It isn't a date without apple cider." I commented.

He smiled and continued. "My mom made us a pie. Sorry, she went a little overboard."

"It's okay. See those apple strudels? Vienna actually made them. She's a great baker. I told her not to, but she insisted." I admitted.

"That's Vienna for you." He said matter-of-factly.

I snorted at his response. It was funny to see how well he was starting to catch on to her behavior as well. He poured us some apple cider and raised his cup. Here's to our first date." I raised mine up and clinked my cup to his. "Cheers."

We played light music from his blue tooth speaker and talked about anything and everything. Seb and I could talk forever. As kids it was even worse, and you couldn't get us to shut up. We always had great conversations and would come up with crazy hypotheticals. We started reminiscing about our elementary school days as we felt nostalgic being at our old school. "Remember the time we sang a duet for the Christmas program?" I asked.

"Yes, and how I forgot the lyrics!" He said shaking his head and trying to erase the memory. Talking about our childhood seemed like a favorite thing to talk about. There were so many good memories. "Okay, so I have a question for you." He said as he sat closer to me.

"Shoot."

"When did you first start liking me?"

I remembered back to the question Vienna had asked me when I slept over her house. With how we were now, the memory seemed from so long ago. I remembered my answer though, and I tried to work through an answer that would work for Sebastian.

"There was never really one specific moment. I guess I always have. It must have been when we first met because right then, I knew how special you were. You were talented, creative, and cared about more important things than anyone else at school. I remember before just feeling like nobody understood me and my love for theatre. All the other kids would make fun of me, but you were different. If there was a specific moment, it must have been when I almost wanted to quit in the seventh grade because I was getting bullied. But you encouraged me. I think that maybe that was the moment I really knew. Do you remember what you said to me?" I asked, hopefully.

He chuckled. "Yeah, I do. I asked you why you wanted to be like everyone else. I told you that you shouldn't change who you were because people like you were hard to find."

"Yes, that always stuck with me." I always kept that memory locked away with me and it was nice to let it out. It just reminded me how gentle and kind he was. His kindness always washed over me and reminded me of my worth to never give up.

"It's funny because I remember the exact moment when I really knew."

I stood very still, anxious to hear when it was.

"I agree it was probably when I first met you, but this was the moment that got me. We were in sixth grade and this girl was really upset that she didn't get the role for the play we were in. Instead, you got it. You went up to the director and told her that you couldn't do it anymore so she could be in it. When I asked you about it, you said it was no big deal and that there will be other plays. You said it was the right thing to do. You made the girl's whole day. That's when I saw how selfless you were."

His whole words had sunk deep into me. After all this time of thinking I was horrible person and was down on myself, Sebastian reminded me of a good memory that I did. I was happy to remember that I did something nice for someone. Even if it was a long time ago. "Wow, I had completely forgotten about that. I can't believe you remember that. That was.... that was really nice." He looked a little embarrassed to have shared it with me. Like it was a deep secret he always kept to himself.

"So, that's when you knew you liked me?" I asked. "Yup, and I never stopped since then." He smiled his crooked smile at me. "Well, I guess we are just two losers who couldn't admit their feelings for each other." I said in a mocking tone.

"I guess so." We both raised our cups and cheered to that. We gulped down the apple cider. We were quiet for a few moments after that. I was taking it all in, but I could tell there was something on his mind. "Could I tell you a secret?" I nodded, a bit nervous.

"Okay, well ever since your grandpa passed, I would go to the cemetery and leave flowers for him. I would go every Wednesday because I knew the next day they come and take all the flowers and discard them. I did it because I didn't want you to see the flowers there and knew that I had been there. I didn't know if you would know they were from me, but I didn't want you to have your suspicions. It was just my way of going and paying my respects to him. I never got a chance to say goodbye. I really liked your grandpa and I felt close to him too. Sometimes I would sit there, and I would talk to him. I would tell him for us to please let our paths cross and for us to be friends again. And now here we are."

He drank the rest of the cider like it was all too much for him to say. I could tell he wanted to hide his face. All the secrets that came from today were a surprise to me. I never would think he would do that and eventually tell me. It was a lot for him, and I could just imagine what it was like after we stopped talking when he went to the cemetery. I felt glad that he was nice enough to do something like that even when we weren't friends anymore.

Visiting my grandpa all the time at the cemetery, I would never guess that Sebastian would go sometimes too. A thought crossed my mind. "Wait, how did you know that I wouldn't show up there on a Wednesday?" He looked down and smiled. "I didn't."

Sebastian and I were hand in hand at my locker when Vienna approached us. "Ew, stop smooching." She joked. "We were not smooching!" I replied, defensively. "We were a little bit." Sebastian admitted. I elbowed him in the stomach. Embry came up and put his arm around Vienna. "Aw, look how cute they are! How was your date?" He said, while Vienna swatted his arm off of her.

"It was great. Best time ever!" I said.

"Yeah, thanks for the apple strudels, Vienna." Seb commented.

"No problem." She said.

They stared at us happily and I felt completely awkward.

"What?" I asked.

"I am definitely the maid of honor at your wedding, right?" Vienna said. Seb and I gave each other that look we always did when Vienna and Embry were at it.

"If she's the maid of honor then I'm definitely the best man, right?" Embry chimed in. "Nope, I'm getting Aaron to be the best man." Vienna said while shooting me a look. We stared at each other and burst out laughing. "Who's Aaron?" Sebastian and Embry said in unison. "Don't worry about it." I said. With Sebastian's hand in mine and Vienna and Embry by our side, everything seemed whole for once. Like all my broken pieces in my life were now held together by my relationships. Not just with Sebastian, but the bonds we shared all together. I was ecstatic that I was finally with Sebastian, and it was all I ever dreamed of, but maintaining my friendship with Vienna was also important to me.

I felt bad for not going to Legends and I promised I would make it up to her. "Hey, so I feel really bad that we had to cancel Legends. So, I thought we could all go together after rehearsal

174

today." I mentioned. "It's okay, Morgan. You don't have to do that. You had your date with Sebastian and that's totally fine. You don't have to reschedule." Vienna said. I didn't want her to think I was doing it out of pity. I really did want us all to hang out together just like we always did.

"But I promised! Come on, I'll buy you a milkshake." I told her. Her stubborn face finally turned up into a smile. "Well, if you're paying." She said. "Okay, it's a date." I said. "What do you say, Embry? One milkshake and two straws just for us." Seb joked. "You don't have to convince me, bro." Embry replied. Vienna and I looked at each other and laughed. "What a bunch of weirdos." She said.

Rehearsals weren't as long as I expected, but then the unexpected happened. "Okay, great job guys! So, dress rehearsal is coming up pretty soon, so I need to see a lot of hard work from you guys." Mr. Baldwin said. It was crazy to believe that all that time had gone by. All the worrying, the late-night rehearsals, and the overall tiredness was almost over. We had put in so much work into this play and the time was almost near.

"I'm going to let you guys out early, but I need Morgan and Sebastian to stay for a bit to work out some things for the dress rehearsal." He continued. Sebastian and I looked at each other with worry. "What about Legends?" I whispered to him. I saw as everyone began packing up their stuff to leave. "So, what's the plan?" Embry asked. I looked over at Vienna who was eagerly waiting, and I turned to Sebastian for help.

"How about you guys just go on and save us a spot at Legends. I think he just wants to talk to us really quick. We will meet you there." Sebastian said. I wanted to thank him at the moment for coming up with the idea but instead just agreed. "Sounds good." Vienna said. "Let us know when you are out." I watched as her and Embry exited the theatre.

What turned into what was supposed to be a short amount of time ended up being an hour. At first Mr. Baldwin was just going over simple things with us. "Okay, so I just want you two to already be prepared for dress rehearsal since you two are the leads. Here's what you can expect." He began giving us a rundown of how the dress rehearsal will look like and what to do. "On that day, I want you guys to be here early. Both of you come already dressed in your costumes. Do you both have your costumes from Vienna?" We nodded as he continued.

"Great! Now we will first work on the sound, and you will be getting your own mics. Remember that when you first come out you will enter from the side of the stage..." Mr. Baldwin's voice dragged on and on as Sebastian and I were antsy. We nodded politely and stayed quiet as he kept going on. Seb and I looked at each other as we waited for him to stop talking, ready to run out of there. When he was finally done, he asked if we had any more questions. "No!" Sebastian said, his voice at a higher tone.

Mr. Baldwin looked confused at him but then let it go. "Okay, well sorry for keeping you guys so long. It was supposed to be a short run through, but I just got carried away explaining everything. You are free to go." We quickly gathered our stuff and headed out the door. "Bye!" I told Mr. Baldwin as Sebastian grabbed my hand and dragged me out the door.

"I bet they left already. We were there forever with Mr. Baldwin and his nonstop talking." Seb said as he gripped the steering wheel. "I tried texting Vienna and she's not answering. Knowing her patience, she definitely left. I feel so bad for standing them up." I said. "It's not our fault. We will just explain that it was Mr. Baldwins fault." Sebastian's joke made me a little less tense but not enough to keep me from still worrying. I hoped Vienna wasn't upset at me and that she was still here. I watched as Sebastian pushed a little harder on the gas as he drove.

By the time we arrived at Legends it was dark, and it was illuminated by many signs. The neon green and red signs really brought the classic diner look to life. I always loved the way it looked at night and I wished I could have appreciated it more. We stopped the car and I spotted Vienna and Embry heading to their cars. "There they are!" I pointed. "Quick, let's get out. I'll try to stop Embry." We quickly rushed so we could catch them. We went our separate ways as Sebastian went up to Embry's car and I headed toward Vienna.

"Hey!" I said, getting her attention.

She looked up at me relieved. "Hey, there you are! I was worried about you. What happened?" She asked.

"Mr. Baldwin just kept going on and on." I simply stated.

"Yeah, that makes sense." She chuckled.

"I am so sorry." I apologized. She didn't seem too mad at me, so I was instantly relieved. I still felt really bad for making her wait for so long after I had promised to make it up to her.

"No, I understand. I'm sorry too. We were waiting for you guys, but we were starving so we just ordered." She replied.

I looked at her and raised my eyebrows when the realization occurred to me. "Wait, you spent this whole time with Embry?"

I for sure thought she would kill him in the first seconds of them being alone together. She looked down, her hat covering her eyes. She rocked from foot to foot, fidgeting with her keys. "Yeah, he's actually not that bad." I stared at her with wide eyes. She slapped her palm to her forehead. "Did I just say that out loud?"

Chapter 17

Embry walked up to the lunch table and greeted Vienna and I. "Hey Morgan!" He said. I waved as I chewed on my food. "Hey, pretty thing." He said to Vienna.

"Oh Embry, you disgust me." She replied in a tone that was different than how she usually replied to him. Usually, she was very dismissive with Embry's comments but this time there was something different in her tone. She always ignored him, but this time her tone was more in a teasing and friendly manner. I couldn't help but feel happy inside as I stared at them. I hoped she couldn't see my small smile.

"Where's Sebastian?" I asked Embry. "He's running a little behind, but he said he has news to tell us." I looked up at him with intrigue. We went on with our usual conversations until Sebastian came. Embry and I were talking about playing a dream part in a musical while Vienna was suspiciously quiet. She had been really quiet the whole time and it wasn't the first I had noticed. We used to text all the time, but lately she seemed a little off. We didn't talk that often and she didn't really keep up with her Aaron Tveit fan account as much. I figured she was busy with everything going on with the play, but it still didn't keep me from worrying. We hadn't been talking or hanging out all that much outside of school and rehearsals.

I knew it had changed between us ever since Seb and I got together, but I still cared about our friendship. Just because we were together didn't mean I had to abandon her. Something was clearly up with her, and I felt bad for not asking since I had been spending all my time with Sebastian. I wanted to ask her, but Embry's voice interrupted my thoughts.

"What is your dream musical role?" He asked. I was still focused on Vienna, but I didn't have to think too much about it since I thought about it all the time. *Les Miserables* was one of my favorite musicals. It was partly because of Aaron but playing Cosette would be my dream role. "Definitely Cosette from *Les Miserables*. Actually, just anyone from that musical. Isn't that right, Vienna?" I turned to see if she would stop from being so quiet to answer my question. She still seemed out of it as she nodded. I stared at her, concerned.

"Mine would be Ryan from *High School Musical*." I let out a burst of laughter. *"High School Musical?"* I said through my laughter. "Hey, it's valid! It's one of the best musicals and it shaped my childhood." "That's true, I agree." I caught sight of Sebastian as he was approaching our table. He smiled as soon as he saw me, and I knew that feeling would never get old. I knew whatever I was feeling, all my worries and troubles, would always dissipate as soon as I would see him. Vienna was still in the back of my mind, but his bright honey eyes calmed me.

"Hey, where were you?" I asked as he hugged me. "I had to make up this test I failed. Can't have a failing grade since I'm in the play. It's just getting hard to keep up with all the work of rehearsals." He replied. I nodded as I knew exactly what he was talking about. It took a lot to be in a play and it was a lot of work on its own. School was already hectic as senior year was next year and the assignments were piling up. Sebastian and I had been in theatre since we were young and were used to juggling acting and school, but the overload of everything even got to us sometimes.

"So, what's the news?" Embry recalled. I waited eagerly as I couldn't think of anything that might be going on that he didn't tell me. "I was talking to my parents, and they said it was cool if you guys came over this Friday to hang out. We could have this great movie night in my backyard. I have the stage all set up with the projector. I'll make popcorn and we could watch *The Greatest Showman*! Are you guys down?" He asked excitedly.

I was ecstatic at going to his place and seeing his parents again. It had been so long since I been to his house and hung out there. We always used to have movie nights all the time and this would be the first time I saw the stage his dad built. I was also super excited to watch *The Greatest Showman s*ince I was obsessed with it. "I'm in! That sounds like so much fun. I can't wait!" I exclaimed. I would not be missing out and it felt even better now that Sebastian and I were together. "Count me in!" Embry said as he high fived Sebastian. We all looked over at Vienna who had been quiet for a long time. She poked at her food and kept her eyes down.

"Sorry guys, I can't make it. I have some stuff I have to take care of." She said. My worries grew inside me as her words came out. First, she was being quiet and then she couldn't make it? Things were starting to get weird, and it wasn't like Vienna to not show up to something. I tried not to read too much into it. Maybe she did have something to do and really couldn't make it.

I reassured myself, but I didn't believe me. If there was anything that had stuck with me after my grandpa's accident, it was my ability to overthink and worry about everything. Even though nothing was wrong, I was convinced otherwise. I knew it was my anxiety, but it still felt very overwhelming at times. Sebastian looked a little surprised as well at Vienna's response. "Oh, I'm sorry to hear that. Well, if anything comes up, we will be there, and you could stop by at any time." He reassured her. She nodded and continued to stay quiet and eat her lunch. I watched as I saw the pain on Embry's face as he stared at her, realizing she wasn't going to be there.

"So, I'm going to be major third wheeling." He said as his voice trailed off. "No, don't say that! We want you there." I said.

"Yeah! You know I won't leave you hanging. Please come. It will be so fun." Seb told him. He looked once more at Vienna and then turned to Seb. "Okay, I'll be there." He said finally.

I felt a little nervous when I walked up and rang Sebastian's doorbell. It wasn't a scared nervous, but an excited nervous feeling. I was so excited to see his parents again and to be back at a place that had been like a second home to me as a child. The door flung open quickly and to my surprise, it wasn't Sebastian. I looked into the slightly older looking faces of his parents. His mom looked practically the same but with a few more wrinkles. She had the same kind smile and Sebastian's eyes. His dad's hair that was once the same color as Sebastian's was now whiter and he looked more like my dad with his glasses.

"Oh my gosh! Morgan, is that you?" His dad said.

"Hi Mr. Montgomery! Wow, it's been so long!" I replied.

"You are so gorgeous! You have really grown up." His mom said as she observed me.

His mom then wrapped me up in a big hug and it was followed by his dad. I felt comfort in knowing that everything was okay now. I could finally be back, and I wasn't broken anymore. I was stable and back with the people I belonged with. I had known them since I was a kid and they had always taken good care of Sebastian and I. I got emotional seeing them again and seeing how much everything had changed. I was relieved I didn't let it go on for more years without talking to them. It was nice to not have to hide anymore. I felt tears stinging my eyes and I embarrassingly wiped them away.

"I'm sorry, it's just been so long." I told them. "It's okay, sweetie. We missed you too and your parents. We need to all get together soon!" His dad said. I nodded as I wiped the last tear from my eyes. Seeing his parents was like seeing your future from the past. I never would have known two years ago that I would be here. "We are so happy that you and Sebastian are together. We always knew you two would end up with each other. It's just meant to be." His mom commented.

I was a little embarrassed and uncomfortable, although her words had touched me. It was weird how both our parents were so open about our relationship. It wasn't only us that always knew we were meant to be, but them as well. Hearing them say it out loud was a whole other story. "Morgan!" Seb said as he peeled his head through the door. "Sorry about them. Come on in!"

"Don't worry. We were just catching up." I said as I walked through the door. I glanced at the house I had spent a lot of time in my childhood. It looked for the most part the same with a few minor decorations. I remember as a kid thinking that are houses were pretty similar, since he only lived on the next block. The inside structure was the same with a huge living space, another living room, a dining room, an upstairs, and a huge backyard as my house. The only difference between our houses was the outside. His blue house with a white fence was tall and stretched out vertically. My cream-colored house with a black gate was longer and stretched out horizontally.

"Embry should be here in a bit." Seb said. "Let me take you out in the back."

"Make yourself at home! You know you are always welcomed here." His mom called out. The backyard was prettier than I remembered it to be. They put in a lot of work and put new decorations. They backyard was always nice, but it has been a bit plain. There were now lights hanging everywhere and the deck was fixed with stairs and nice seats. The main attraction was the little wooden stage that was in the middle of the backyard and had a white sheet for the projector.

"Wow, your backyard looks amazing! Your dad did a great job with the stage." I told Seb and I went up to look at it. "Thanks. Shall we?" He motioned to the long couch he had set up in front of the stage so we could see the movie. "This is so romantic." I said.

"Yeah, too bad Embry is coming." He joked.

"Hey! When he comes let's not make him feel bad." I said.

"I know I'm just playing. I'm excited for him to come. Too bad Vienna couldn't make it." I was glad he brought it up so I could get his opinion.

"That was weird right? It's not like her to back out. She's been acting really strange and quiet lately. I hope she's okay." A million negative thoughts ran through my mind, and I tried to shake it all away. I was torn between wanting to be present with Sebastian, but also wanting to be there for Vienna. I wanted to focus and give all my attention to Sebastian, while still wanting to be a good friend to her. It took so long for Seb and I to get to where we were and he deserved all my time, but Vienna was the reason it all happened. My mind became hazy.

"I'm sure she's okay. She's probably just stressed because of the play and has a lot on her mind. She said she had some stuff to take care of today and we don't know what's going on. She must be busy, and we should respect that." He said. Sebastian was always the logical one who had to calm me down. He was always carefree and a go with the flow kind of person. He was spontaneous and courageous where I was fearful and cowardly. He was always the one to drag me into his crazy adventures. He was right though, and I knew Vienna must have a lot going on. I knew I had to respect that, and I knew I couldn't ask her what was wrong for fear that I might upset her. She was already a moody person, and I didn't want to push her buttons.

"Yeah, you're right. It's just hard not to be worried about her."

"It's normal. You guys became so close and are best friends. She's a great girl and I'm happy you two hit it off. I just feel bad for Embry that she couldn't come. He really does like her, you know." His tone became very serious.

Just like Vienna and I had our own bond, Seb and Embry had theirs. Even though Sebastian and I had been best friends forever, I knew there was some things that you had to share with a guy. I understood this now having a girl friend. Seb and Embry had been friends longer than Vienna and I though, and I knew Embry told him everything. I didn't know exactly how Vienna felt about Embry but if there was one thing about Vienna, it was that she hid her feelings behind her cynicism. Still, I didn't want to see Embry get hurt.

Much like Vienna, Embry hid behind his jokes and witty humor. I didn't know him well and Sebastian didn't know Vienna well, but I could see that they were secretly both vulnerable people. They were both a little lost and had their flaws, but they hid it behind a mask. I didn't have to see Sebastian so serious to see how Embry truly felt for Vienna. He could make jokes all he wanted, but what he feels for her is real. I could see it in the way he stares at her and how when she responds back to his comments that it brightens his day. I just wished Vienna would see the real him. I looked into Sebastian's sad eyes.

"I know how he feels about her, and she knows it too. I think she's just scared to open up and let him in. It's just sad for Embry because you can't force someone to like you." I replied. "Yeah, I just wish they could meet in the middle." He said. His phone buzzed in his pocket. "He's here."

"Hey Embry! Sebastian and Morgan are out in the back!" I heard Sebastian's mom say. "Thanks, Mrs. M!" Embry said in his charming tone. He came out through the sliding doors, passed the deck, and met us at the couch. "Sup guys!"

"Hey bro." Seb said as they exchanged a weird and complicated handshake. "Hey Morgan!" He said in his enthusiastic spirit that always lifted me up. "Hey!" I replied and we embraced in a hug. "The party is here! I know you guys were probably super bored without me here." Embry said sarcastically. Sebastian laughed loudly at his remark.

"Well now that everyone is here, shall we get started?" Sebastian asked. "Yeah!" Embry and I shouted enthusiastically. We went over to the deck where Sebastian poured us some popcorn from his popcorn machine in cute little white and red popcorn holders. "For Embry, extra butter." He said as he poured him some butter out of the bottle. "And for Morgan some hot sauce." He remembered how I loved spicy food and would always put hot sauce on my popcorn. "And for me.... chocolate!" Seb was all about sweet and savory combinations. "Now, we are really ready!"

I plopped on the couch and Embry settled into the hammock while Sebastian got the projector ready. Watching *The Greatest Showman* with Sebastian was so peaceful, and I never got to see the movie with him. It was nice to see which parts he liked and got excited about. I could see it in the way his face lit up which parts he liked. My favorite part was "Rewrite the Stars" because the song was amazing, and the scene was visually stunning.

I also enjoyed Embry's hilarious commentary. He was a great person to watch movies with because he was so funny and pointed out things you never would notice. "Troy Bolton looks different here." Embry joked. I laughed and almost choked on my popcorn. The movie was coming to its end and Hugh Jackman began singing "From Now On." "This is my favorite part." Embry commented.

"Yeah, it is nice that he finally came to the realization that he went overboard." Sebastian said. "No, I mean for the choreography." I laughed as Embry dismissed Sebastian's profound take on the scene. "The choreography for this song is insane. I tried doing it one time but it's really hard."

"Yeah, I love the dancing in this scene. Let me try to do it." I said as I spontaneously got up from my seat. I looked at the screen and tried to imitate the dance movies.

"Hey, not bad." Sebastian said. He got up as well and tried to copy the movie. Soon we were all up and trying to do the choreography. We all probably thought we looked really cool and professional, but reality was we probably looked like idiots. Seb and Embry fell into each other as they tried to dance. I laughed as they landed on the floor.

"Dancing is dangerous. Proceed with caution." Sebastian stated. I laughed as I helped him up. "I'm okay by the way, thanks for asking while you continue to laugh." He said to me. We all continued to dance and try our best as if we were actually in the movie. We seemed to get the hang of it as we jumped and twirled. Sebastian locked arms with me, and we spun around. "Gosh, we look so dumb." Embry said as he danced. The rest of the night was spent with all of us dancing under the stars as the movie played and the fire crackled. It was a perfect night but the only thing that could have made it better was if Vienna was there.

"Morgan, we have exciting news!" My mom said the next day as my dad was eagerly beside her. I stared at them suspiciously. This couldn't be good. I hated when they acted secretly towards me. Whatever their plan was, I was scared to find out. They knew I didn't react well to surprises anymore and that I always needed to prepare for something.

"We just got off the phone with Sebastian's parents." My jaw dropped. It had been so long since they had talked. When Sebastian and I stopped being friends it was the end of our parents' friendship as well. Not that I expected them to stop being friends with Mr. and Mrs. Montgomery, but it kind of headed in that direction. It was awkward for them since we weren't friends anymore and my parents had their own grieving process as well as mine to deal with. I knew that these past couple of years they must have missed each other, but nobody was courageous enough to pick up the phone. I needed to realize how close of friends our parents were with each other too. Sebastian and I became friends when we were seven years old, and our parents became fast friends as well for all those years.

"Well, what happened? What did they say?" I asked.

"We were just talking and catching up. We thought it would be a great idea to all go out and do something together." My mother replied excitedly. "So, I suggested we have dinner on the boat. It's been so long since we've gone on the boat and now, we have a reason." My dad chimed in. I was slow to process everything since it was happening so fast. I wasn't opposed to the idea though. It would be nice for all of us to reunite just like old times. I loved Sebastian's parents and since I deprived my parents of talking to them for all those years, it would be nice for them to catch up. It would also mean spending more time with Sebastian.

"Okay, I'm in." I said. My parents looked happy that I approved. With everything fixed and back together again, how could I not?

I called Sebastian shortly after. "Did you hear about the boat plans?"

"Yes, I thought it was crazy that they actually talked on the phone. My parents kept bugging for all of us to hang out." He replied.

"I think it's nice. Things are different now and so much has changed, but it will be nice for all of us to hang out again. I mean, we used to all the time." I said with a hint of melancholy in my voice. I remembered the times we all used to go everywhere together. We used to go to the zoo, the carnival, and to amusement parks. Of course, back then my grandpa used to be there.

"Yeah, those were good times. Remember when we all went to Disneyland when we were in the sixth grade?" He recalled. "Oh, yeah! You got so sick on Space Mountain." I joked.

"I did not!" It was like I knew he was smiling over the phone.

"It would be nice to go on the boat again. It's been such a long time. We could have dinner and play music." I said. He stayed quiet on the line for a few moments. "Minus our parents, is this.... a date?" Seb asked. I was happy and excited that we would have our second date on a boat. "Yup, and this time, I'm planning it."

That day I picked out a nice dark blue dress. I didn't want to show up too fancy, but it was definitely a big occasion. I was relieved my parents seemed to be dressing up too. This was the biggest thing we had done in years, and I finally felt like we were back to ourselves. We were also dressed to impress since we never went out with people anymore. It was a big change for all of us. I even let me hair out of its usual style and into a new one. I put my hair into a crown braid, and I was surprised at how well it came out. Though we were just having dinner with Sebastian and his family, my dad's boat was very fancy. Walking up to it, I forgot how big it was. Being in the boat felt very strange now that I was older.

When I was a kid, I thought it was kind of boring, but now I appreciated the beauty of it. It was pretty impressive, and I watched it as it gleamed over the water. The sky was already dark ahead but the lights from the boat seemed to illuminate everything. I was running around and trying to get everything ready for Sebastian's arrival. His picnic date for me was perfect, and I wanted to make sure to impress him with my date. Sebastian was thoughtful and even though our parents were here, I hoped he thought this date would be special. I fixed up the plates and silverware nicely and heard voices emerging.

"They are here!" My mom gasped. I double checked my hair and outfit one last time before greeting them. "Oh my gosh! Hi you guys!" Sebastian's parents said to mine. I couldn't decipher anything they were saying as their excited chatter fused together. His parents then greeted me and gave me a hug. Mrs. Montgomery looked lovely in a purple dress with her pearl earrings and Mr. Montgomery looked dapper in his nice dress shirt. Sebastian trailed behind and my heart almost stopped. His hair looked more tamed, and he had a nice white shirt with a black blazer.

His honey eyes seemed to sparkle when he looked at me and his white smile was more blinding than the lights on the boat. We slowly walked up to each other. "You look so handsome." I told him. It felt good to not be afraid to say anything now that we were together. I had come a long way since looking at him in the cafeteria only thinking he was handsome to now saying it out loud. "Wow, Tink. You look beautiful! Blue is my new favorite color on you. And your hair!" He said as he lightly touched the braid. I was selfishly scared he might mess it up. "Thanks. So, shall I show you what I did for our date?"

We first all ate together. We sat and caught up on anything and everything. We asked them a lot of questions and they asked us questions as well. It was crazy to think how much we missed out on in each other's lives and how much Sebastian and I forgot to mention. "Morgan, what's it like playing Audrey? It must have been so surreal to get back on stage again." Mrs. Montgomery asked me. "It's a dream come true. I love playing the character and just being back on stage with Sebastian.... it's where I belong." I said. I felt so comfortable being there with them. It didn't once feel weird, awkward, or out of place. That's what I loved about old friends. It could be years since you have seen each other, but once you do, it's like nothing had ever changed.

We picked up where we left off and we didn't miss a beat. As the night went on, our parents ate separately from us. They weren't that far away from us, but we spaced out so we could all have our own privacy. Sebastian saw our nicely decorated table with a candle and roses. I also put all our favorite foods on there and l played light music. "Wow, you went all out. This is impressive." I was happy I won his approval after all my hard work. "Anything for my boyfriend." We sat at our own table, and I could hear our parents chatter from their own table, and I glanced over at them. "They seem really happy." I said.

"Yeah, it's really nice. I haven't seen them this happy in a while. They really missed your parents." Seb said. "Yeah, same here. I guessed they lost something too when we stopped being friends." I mentioned. He nodded in agreement but by the look on his face, I saw there was something else there. He stayed silent for a few moments before speaking again. "I told my parents what really happened that day with your grandpa. They wanted to know about the accident. I told them ahead of time so they wouldn't bring it up with your parents. I hope that's okay." He said slowly. I didn't want him to be scared anymore to talk to me about it. I wanted us to have an open and honest relationship. He could ask me anything and I wouldn't hesitate to answer. We were together now and there wasn't supposed to be any secrets between us.

"That's completely fine, they deserve to know. I feel bad that I made my parents not tell them. To be fair I don't think they wanted to anyway. It was hard especially for my mom to talk about what happened. She kind of shut down and shut everyone out too. I'm sorry she did that to your parents." I admitted. I always felt so guilty for what I caused with the aftermath. Everything was so complicated and messy because of me. I couldn't believe how selfish I was. It was something I always wanted to apologize for, and now I got the chance.

"I understand, please don't worry about it. They knew you were all grieving. They were curious but they didn't really ask about it. They just wanted to make sure you guys were okay. We all did." We sat in silence for a few moments, unable to say anything else.

"Can I ask you a question?" Seb asked.

"Of course."

"How did you get out of your depression? What made you wake up and decide to change? We didn't talk in two years, and I just wanted to know what made you realize that you wanted to talk to me again." It was a really good question and one that I never thought of before. I thought back at how I used to be. I was depressed and couldn't do anything, but it wasn't the therapy or self-help books that made me better.

"I just woke up one day and realized that I didn't want that to be my life. I didn't want to wake up and be miserable. I wanted to live my life and have purpose. There is a lot of pain and suffering in this world, but I didn't want to let that stop me from being happy. There are horrible things that will happen but there is also still hope and love. I just thought that even though I lost someone, I still had people around me who loved me. I had the support from my parents, and they helped me. I thought about the people who I loved and really cared about. I automatically thought of you. I thought of how you had always been there for me no matter what. I had the best friend in the entire world, and I lost it. You would have done anything for me, and I realized that that's what I needed. I needed that support that I had pushed away. That's why I wasn't getting better. I missed my best friend. Going through something as painful as I did, you can't do it alone. You need your best friend at your side. I needed you."

He gave me a soft smile and reached his hand across the table to grab mine. "Well, I'm here now and I'm not going anywhere. Anything you go through; I'll always be there. If you fall again, I'll be sure to catch you this time." In that moment I truly felt how I was the luckiest girl in the world. I never knew how I got so lucky with Sebastian. "Can I ask you a question?" He looked at me, surprised. He nodded for me to continue.

"Why me? I mean, you were so much cooler than me and popular. Everyone liked you and all the girls wanted to be with you. Why did you choose me?"

"Morgan, stop. Don't do that to yourself. You are always putting yourself down, but you don't see how truly special you are. I wish you could see yourself the way that I do." He said and I could hear the pain in his voice. I guess I never thought of it that way. Of course, I knew I meant a lot to Sebastian as well, but I was still curious to know why he never went with someone else.

"You don't even know how many guys liked you. They would come up to me and ask me if I was your boyfriend. I know they were scared of me because I told them if they ever hurt you, they would go through me. So, I basically chased them all away." He said with a laugh. I was shocked at his confession. I never even knew that anyone had liked me, and I guess because of Sebastian, I never cared to notice. It was nice to see there was a whole other side of things I never knew of. "Wow, I never knew that. I didn't think you were so jealous." I teased.

"Oh yeah, I definitely was." I couldn't even pretend to hide my smile. "But to answer your question...." he continued. "There was nobody else. Not back then, not when we weren't friends, and there will never be. Not by a long shot. There will never be anyone as kind, beautiful, caring, loyal, and passionate as you. I've never met anyone like you. You are so funny and make me laugh so hard. You take your roles very seriously. You genuinely care so much for the people you love, and you would do anything for them. You constantly daydream all the time, probably about musicals. You are just amazing."

My face was red hot but this time I didn't care to hide it. We smiled at each other, and I squeezed his hand that I was still holding onto. "Besides our parents, this has been my favorite date. Here's to us." I raised my glass full of apple cider and he raised his. I watched as his glass and mine made contact until it clinked perfectly together. As the night went on, we had great conversations and our parents kept going on and on with theirs as well. We were all having a great time and I knew we weren't going to stop anytime soon. Sebastian grabbed one of the nice napkins on our table.

"Watch this." He said as he began folding the napkin. I watched as he rapidly began folding it and what was once just a normal napkin, turned into an origami lotus flower. "Woah, how did you do that?"

"Magic and a lot of free time on my hands." He chuckled and handed it for me. "For you, Tink." I admired the delicate lotus napkin in my hands. "Thanks. It's perfect." The next song I had on my playlist changed to a soft slow song. It was an oldie, one of my grandpa's favorite records. I used to listen to it all the time on repeat. "Do you want to dance with me?" I asked Seb. He didn't answer but instead automatically stood up and took my hand. He led past the tables into a nice spot for us to dance. We settled into our spot and slowly began to sway.

"Aw!" Our parents beamed. We looked as they all stared at us. "Stop!" Sebastian whined. They all erupted in laughter. I laughed and just shook my head at them. I watched as our feet matched the tempo of the song. I never was good at dancing unless it was something choreographed for theatre, but this didn't have to be anything memorized. It was just special to be with Sebastian and rocking side to side. Sometimes quiet moments didn't have to mean anything, and that's what made them special. You just needed to be at the right place at the right time with the right person. I looked away from Sebastian's gaze to soak in the moment.

The nice boat, the night sky above us, and the stars twinkling. It was one of the only times Sebastian and I were really alone. It was nice to just be together without the distraction of school and rehearsals. Even though I loved Vienna and Embry, it was nice to get a break as well. It was just a special time for Seb and I. I didn't have to worry about the stress of the play, my worries about Vienna, or about the past. I began to laugh to myself.

"What is it?" Sebastian asked. "It's just being here with you. I never thought I would be here again with you on this boat, our parents are talking, and everything is fine. It's like everything I had gone through was worth it. All the pain and suffering are now just memories. I'm ready to move on now with you. I can't wait to take this journey." I felt bliss in that small perfect moment. Where time seemed to stand still as we danced. Seb looked happy for me as he smiled. "So, let's make our own memories." He said as leaned in to kiss me.

Chapter 18

After the boat trip, it was back to reality. I was still worried about Vienna since nothing had changed. We still hardly texted each other and she kept up with her quiet behavior at school and rehearsals. There was only one thing that I thought might cheer her up. "Guess whose birthday is coming up!" I exclaimed at lunch. We were into the first week of December and Vienna's birthday was coming up soon. I thought with her birthday around the corner that she would be excited. I was wrong. "That's exciting!" Seb commented.

"My Vienna's birthday is coming up. I have to find the best present to get her!" Embry panicked. I felt a little relieved at her normal behavior when she gave him a death stare. "Any plans for the big day?" Sebastian asked her. "Not really." She replied nonchalantly. My confidence deflated at her response. I didn't know what was up with her and why she was acting so weird.

"Really? Well, we should all definitely do something. I mean, you're the first one of us to turn seventeen." I stated. "It's not a big deal." She pointed out while she kept her head down, eating her lunch. We all exchanged worried looks at each other. We all knew she was acting weird lately. She was never this quiet and at rehearsals she just seemed to be a shadow that lingered there. She still did her job, but her presence didn't seem so big anymore. Vienna was so vibrant and full of life but lately she seemed drained and depressed.

"I think we should still do something. Even if we just go to Legends." I said.

"I guess." She said.

I knew I had to do something to get her out of her slump, but I had to not be so obvious about it. I didn't want her to think I was bugging her or trying too hard, but I really wanted to cheer her up with whatever she was going through. I knew she wasn't going to tell me if I asked, and there was only one thing I could think of that would make her feel better. "Vienna, I was thinking if you wanted to come over to my house tomorrow. We could watch Aaron's videos and get pumped up for *Moulin Rouge*. There's been so much content for it, and he's been so active on social media. He even is going live on his Instagram. What do you think? We can have a whole Aaron celebration day."

I hoped my plan would work and from what I had seen, she had not really been keeping up with Aaron content. It wasn't like her since she was basically the leader of his fan club. She should have been noticing all the stuff he was posting but she hadn't mentioned it and we didn't talk about it. Sebastian and Embry made me jump up in my seat. "Who is Aaron?" They both yelled. My nerves were already on edge, and I didn't need them to ask dumb questions.

Vienna seemed uncomfortable as she stared at me. "That's seems really nice, but I don't think I can make it." She said in a strange tone. I couldn't believe she was backing out. First the movie night at Seb's house and now this? It couldn't be just a coincidence. "What? Why not?" I asked, getting frustrated now. It was not like me to get mad or angry. I was always so calm and mellow but when something bothered me, I couldn't hide it. "What do you mean?" She asked defensively. "First you canceled on movie night and now this? You love Aaron but lately you act like you don't even care." I argued. "What's your point?" She asked.

"You've been acting weird lately. You don't seem to care about anything, and you have been so quietly lately. What's going on with you?" I didn't mean to sound so aggressive, but she wasn't talking or responding normally. I was sick of the run around and short answer. I immediately regretted pushing her buttons.

"Look, just because I can't hang out with you for one day doesn't mean it's the end of the world! The world doesn't revolve around you!" She snapped. She got her things and left the table. Sebastian stared wordlessly at me, and Embry looked like I offended him. "What did you do that for?" Embry yelled.

"I'm sorry! I didn't mean to attack her. It's just that she's been acting so strange lately. Come on, you guys have seen it too! I can't be the only one who's noticed." I pointed out. They both stayed quiet at my truthful worlds. Sebastian put his hand on me. "Of course, we know. I know you're worried about her, but you know how Vienna is. If you really want to know what's going on, then you just have to sit her down and talk to her." He said.

"It's not that simple. I can't just ask her! Vienna is a really touchy person, and she bottles up everything. I especially can't ask her now after what I did. I just messed everything up." I put my head in my hands and sighed. I didn't know what was going on between us and it was making me so stressed out. With dress rehearsal for the play coming up, I didn't need another thing to worry about. Just when things in my life seemed to finally be right, there was another problem. "Why don't you just make it up to her? Don't talk about it or mention it to her anymore and do something nice for her. She will really appreciate it." Seb suggested. "Yeah, like what?"

I felt like all hope was lost, but then Embry had a genius idea. "Her birthday!" Embry shouted. I looked at him intrigued. "We can have a surprise birthday party for her. We can have it at Legends and invite everyone from the play!" Embry continued. Sebastian and I looked excitedly at each other. "Embry, you are a genius!" I ran over to hug him.

"I know I am." He said as he patted me on top of the head. "Okay, I want this party to be huge. I want it to be the best birthday party ever. We need food, cake, and decorations." I ordered. "A party like that seems like a lot of work." Seb admitted. "Well then, let's get to work." Embry said with a smile.

Sebastian, Embry, and I arrived at rehearsal early to spread the word. By the time Vienna came, everyone in the play knew about the surprise party. "But remember, it's a secret! Don't say anything to Vienna." I told everyone. I was on stage watching Embry tell the last person about the party when Vienna came up. "Hey Vienna!" I said too loudly. She looked at me suspiciously. I was such a horrible actor when I was off stage. "Hey" she replied. We stood there awkwardly on stage.

"Look, I'm really sorry about lunch today. I completely overreacted. I don't know what came over me. I guess I was just excited for you to come over. But if you can't make it then you can't make it. I should have understood. I shouldn't have yelled at you like that. Will you forgive me?" I was so glad to get the chance to apologize to her alone. I felt so bad for how I approached the situation and what I did. I was just glad she didn't seem too mad at me. "No, it's okay. I know I have been acting strange. I'm just stressed with everything. I yelled at you too and took it way too far. I'm sorry too."

With her reply she seemed like the old Vienna which made me feel better. I still could feel like things were off with her, but I dropped it as I seemed to be getting one step closer with her. She seemed most like herself in that moment than she had been, and I was grateful. I smiled at her, and she gave me a weak smile back. "Okay, let's stop standing around and talking! We got a show coming up in a couple of weeks!" Mr. Baldwin called out.

The rest of the week I spent running around planning for Vienna's surprise party. We had a limited amount of time since her birthday was the weekend after. "Dad, do you have any word on the cake?" My dad knew this amazing bakery where they made custom cakes. "Yes, everything is going well, don't worry!" He reassured me. "I just want everything to be perfect!" I was acting so crazy lately since I was in party planning mode. I hated planning things since I was a really anxious person. I was just glad I had Sebastian and Embry's help. "I'm sure Vienna will just appreciate that you did all of this for her." My dad replied.

I knew it was the thought that counts, but I wanted Vienna to be knocked off her feet. My phone buzzed in my pocket, and I rushed to answer it nervously. "Embry! How are the decorations coming along?" "I ordered them and since I'm a valuable costumer, they will be here in a few days." He stated. "Great!"

"I also am getting the balloons and her present should be on its way. I think I gave her the best present!" He exclaimed. I highly doubted that with what I had up my sleeve. "Sound good! Thanks for updating me. Have you heard from Sebastian? He's supposed to come over." "Yeah, he's on his way. He was running late since he was doing all the other errands for the party." Embry seemed just as stressed out as I was. We both were freaking out because Vienna meant so much to us and we didn't want to let her down. Especially with the mood she was in. I definitely owed Embry though since the whole thing was his idea and he just wanted to impress her.

"Okay, I hope he gets here quick." I said worried. "I really hope she likes this party. Maybe then she will finally notice me." Embry said sadly. I felt so bad at the drastic measures he was taking to get Vienna to notice him. "What you are doing for her is honestly the nicest thing ever. She would be crazy not to notice you." I reassured him. In that moment I felt like how Vienna must have felt when she first was trying to get Seb and I together. She was our number one supporter and rooted for us from the start. I hoped I could be that person for Embry. "Thanks, Morgan."

Shortly after Seb arrived at my house. "There you are! I was so worried. We have limited time." I got him by the arm and pulled him in my house. "Well, hello to you too." He said. "Sorry. It's just that this is my one chance to get Vienna's present. It's the perfect gift and if I don't get it then all hope is lost."

"Tink, don't worry. I'll help you out. I got my laptop right here." He said as he pulled it out from under his arm. I led him into my second living room where my laptop was sitting on the couch. "Have your phone ready too just in case." He seemed nervous as he logged on. "Okay, we only have one shot at this. As soon as it's time, click like your life depends on it." I ordered.

"Got it!" He said. We watched the screen attentively. I watched as Sebastian's eyes were locked on his screen, waiting for his cue. I was so nervous that my heart was pounding. I knew the tickets were going to be insanely hard to get and that they might sell out. We only had one shot. "It's almost time." I warned him. "One minute!" My face was so close to the screen and my finger hovered over the keyboard. I watched as Seb did the same. "Here comes the countdown." He said as he had his phone beside him as well. I even had my iPad near me for extra support. "I'm in!" I called out once it was time.

"I got in on my phone!" Seb replied. We didn't pay any attention to each other the rest of the time as we concentrated on getting the tickets. "What seats do I get?" He asked panicking. "Get as close to the front as you can but just get whatever is available. Remember that we have to sit next to each other." A few minutes later we accomplished our goal.

"Got it!" We shouted at the same time. We got up from the couch and jumped up and down. We hugged each other tightly and didn't let go. "That was so scary!" He said out of breath. "It was! I never want to do that again." "It's okay, it's over now." I knew how dramatic we were being, but this was the best gift ever. Vienna was totally going to freak out.

Chapter 19

It was December tenth, Vienna's birthday. I was so nervous and hoped that everything was running smoothly. Sebastian, Embry, and I all kept tabs on each other. Sebastian was putting the last finishing touches, Embry was already at Legends gathering all the guests, and I was providing the distraction. I jumped up when my phone rang but was relieved when it was Sebastian. "How's it going? Please tell me the plan worked." He said as I heard loud noises in the background. "Everything is good to go. I told her I wanted to take her out to a low-key lunch at Legends for just the two of us. She was all for it."

"Okay, and you told her to meet you at Legends at noon?" Seb asked. "Yes, she is clear on everything. " I reassured him. "See Embry, everything is fine. She got her to agree to it." I heard Seb say on the other line. "Is everything okay?" I asked. "Yeah, Embry is just freaking out. He was afraid she wouldn't come with how she's been acting lately."

"It's her birthday, she had to say yes." I replied. I was a little nervous thinking about how Vienna only agreed since it was something low key with just the two of us, but I didn't voice my concern to Sebastian. "And you are all dressed up and ready?" Seb asked. "Yeah, I'm in costume." I said. "Good because I would have looked like an idiot without you here." "I'm on my way." I told him.

I walked into Legends and stepped into the world we had created for Vienna. "Wow, everything looks amazing! I can't believe we pulled this off! You both look so great. Good job on the costumes, guys." I said as I pulled Sebastian and Embry in a hug. "We did it! Great work guys!" Seb said. Embry looked like he was about to puke. "Don't worry, it's going to be okay." I said as I put my hand on his shoulder. He nodded slowly. I looked around at all the guests eagerly waiting Vienna's arrival.

"Thanks so much for coming! Vienna should be here very soon!" I said to everyone. I went up to the nice woman at the counter. "Thanks for letting us have this party here." "No problem, honey! You are a like family, and I remember when you used to have your parties here all the time when you were little. We are happy to help. By the way, you look amazing!" She said as she observed me. "Thanks so much." At that moment I got a text from Vienna. "Everyone, Vienna is here! Go hide!" I screamed. I was so scared, and we all scrambled about trying to hide. Sebastian and I hid beneath one of the tables. "Ow!" He said as he hit his head. The woman at the counter turned the lights off and hid as well. I grabbed on tight to Sebastian's hand.

My heart was beating so fast, and I was filled with adrenaline. I saw as Vienna stood outside the door for a while. She looked inside and saw it was dark and waited for a while. I heard Vienna's steps as she walked in. "Hello?" She said confused. "Surprise!" We said as we all jumped out. Vienna stepped back in shock. "Happy birthday!" We said. She stood there frozen. She stared all around at what we did. It was a Broadway themed birthday party. There was a big center table with the cake on top. The cake had three tiers with the bottom being white with music notes, the middle being black and gold with roses, and the top having a red curtain.

The centerpiece of the cake was two theatre masks and at the top was the number seventeen. There were also cupcakes with playbill toppers of her favorite musicals. In the middle of the place was a huge marquee with her name on it. We decorated a table that had a walk of fame star with her name on it along with theatre and film decorations. There was popcorn, candy, and other treats. We also had a huge whiteboard where people wrote her nice messages. The guests had tickets as if they were at an event. The best part of it all was that everyone was dressed in Broadway themed costumes.

The triplets were Angelica, Eliza, and Peggy from *Hamilton*. One person was Evan Hansen, and I loved our costumes. Embry went as the phantom from *Phantom of the Opera* and Sebastian and I were Danny and Sandy from *Grease*. We decided to go with a couple costume, and we looked perfect. Sebastian fit the look with his hair and leather jacket, and I pulled off a red lip and teased hair. It was so fun dressing up in leather. Vienna took it all in as she still stayed frozen. Sebastian, Embry, and I walked up to her. "What? How did you?" She said breathlessly. She began to get teary eyed. We exchanged looks at each other and smiled. She was so speechless, and she tried to compose herself. "You did all of this for me?" She asked.

"Of course, we did. You are our best friend. We care about you so much and wanted you to have the best birthday ever." I said to her. I had never seen Vienna more overwhelmed with happiness in that moment. She smiled so widely, and she hardly ever smiled that much. She was glowing, happy, and looked so beautiful. "Seriously, a Broadway themed birthday party? You guys are the best!" She exclaimed. "You guys look so good!" She said as she gestured to our costumes. Seb and I posed back-to-back while Embry swooshed his cape. "This is the best birthday ever! Thank you, guys, so much!"

"Don't thank us, thank Embry. The whole thing was his idea." Sebastian said, giving full credit to his best friend. We both looked at Embry as he was standing there shyly. "Embry, is that true?" She asked. I had never seen him more anxious as his eyes were looking down at the floor, avoiding her gaze. "Yeah." He replied. She looked shocked as she stared at him. "That's honestly the nicest thing anyone has ever done for me." She said sincerely. He finally looked up and the two exchanged a warm smile. I looked up at Seb who was ecstatic at the nice moment they shared. "Can I give you my present?" He asked her with gleaming eyes. "You got me something?" She replied, as if she completely forgot the concept of birthdays.

"We didn't just decorate the place! We got you presents too. The party is just getting started." I told her. She smiled at me widely. Embry walked us over to the table where the presents were and took his out. It was in a nice velvet bag, and she slowly took it from him. She opened it carefully as she took out all the nice tissue paper to find a box. It was a medium size black box that looked really fancy. I looked at Sebastian who just shrugged at me as we both didn't know what it could be. I was really excited to find out because I knew Embry went all out for Vienna. I wouldn't have been surprised if he pulled out a diamond ring. We all huddled around as she opened the box. It was a beautiful black beret with an embroidered blue moon on it.

The moon was surrounded by bright beautiful pale blue flowers and leaves as it seemed to dance in the wind around the moon. It was so lovely, and I could definitely see Vienna wearing it with her obsession for hats. "This is so pretty! I love it so much. Thank you, Embry." She took the beret and put it on. It was the first time I had ever witnessed her being nice to him and if that wasn't enough, the craziest thing happened. She got up and hugged him. I stood there as I never thought I would ever see it happen. "Thanks for everything." She told him. I finally saw Embry breathe for the first time. He looked so relieved and therefore Seb and I were relieved. "This is fun! Let's open more presents." She exclaimed as she clapped her hands together. She looked like a little kid, and I couldn't help but laugh. I didn't want to show up Embry's gift, but I was excited for her to open mine.

"I was going to wait but since you're asking, I can't wait for you to open it. It's from Sebastian and I since we both pitched in." "Oh okay, that's interesting. I can't wait." I handed her the small box. She got it and looked at us suspiciously. She probably thought it was a necklace and would have never guessed what it actually was. Seb and I looked at each other excitedly. She stared at the tickets and read it carefully. She then jumped up from her seat and let out a piercing scream. Seb and Embry jumped up as I laughed. "Told you." I said nonchalantly.

"What is it?" Embry asked. "It's tickets to see Aaron in *Moulin Rouge*! How did you get these?" She yelled. "It was extremely hard, but we managed to do it." "Morgan, I cannot believe you! Thank you so much." She picked me up and spun me around. I self-consciously touched my hair as I spent hours teasing it for my costume. "You're welcome! We are going to see it together and we have floors seats." I told her excitedly. "Thanks so much too, Sebastian. I know these couldn't have been cheap." She said. "Don't worry about that. I'm glad you love them. You deserve it." She walked up to him and gave him a hug. "So, shall we get this party started?" I said.

The day was filled with fun, laughter, games, musical sing alongs, and lots of food. We got a photo booth, and we all took a million pictures. Seb held the photos of us in his hands. "Our first photos as a couple." He told me. I held the pictures carefully in my hand and smiled. We looked so happy, and I knew it was going to stay like that forever. "You guys look so great. Danny and Sandy are a power couple. Not to mention Aaron also played Danny in *Grease* live." Vienna mentioned. "Who is Aaron?" Embry demanded. Vienna and I just laughed it off.

The party was winding down and it was time for the cake. After we all sang happy birthday, Vienna made a speech. "I would like to thank you all for coming here today to celebrate my birthday. It means a lot to me, and I've been having so much fun with all of you in rehearsals. This play is going to be great, and I can't wait for opening night. Thanks for an amazing birthday and this all wouldn't be possible without my best friends. Morgan, Sebastian, and Embry, thank you for throwing me a surprise party. I don't know what I did do deserve friends like you. Thanks especially to Embry, this whole party was his idea. Give him a hand!" Everyone began clapping and Embry looked sheepish. "Now, let's eat this beautiful cake!"

We all sat around talking as we ate cake. As time went on, Vienna became quiet. I thought she might just be tired from all the excitement, but she seemed like how she was at school. I wondered why she got back into her slump after a great day. I wished I knew why she was feeling that way in the first place. I noticed she kept checking her phone a lot for messages. She looked disappointed every time she would pick up the phone and there was nothing.

"Are you okay?" I asked her quietly. "Yeah, I'm good." She answered shortly. I saw the worry on her face and recognized the look. It was the same look I had when I had anxiety and was overwhelmed. I usually felt that way when I was about to have a panic attack. I felt guilty that the party might have been too much for Vienna too soon. She was clearly going through something, and a party might have been too much too handle.

I knew what it was like when you were depressed and had to push yourself to participate. I felt really bad at that moment and sadness grew inside of me as I saw it written on her face. I desperately wanted to know what was wrong with her, but I knew I couldn't ask her easily. She would never tell me and just brushed me off like she usually did. I definitely didn't want to ask her on her birthday.

At the end of the party we said our goodbyes to everyone and thanked them for coming. "Well, that was a fun party." Embry said. "Yes, and very successful. Good job, team." I said as I high fived Sebastian and Embry. "Now, it's time to clean up though." Sebastian said exhausted. "I'll load the stuff in my car."

"Okay, I'll help Embry clean in here." I looked around for Vienna who had disappeared shortly before. "Where's Vienna?" I asked. "She's outside talking on the phone." Seb said. I nodded slowly but I pushed my worries away to clean up. Embry and I were finally done with everything, and we were exhausted. "Thanks again for everything, Embry. Vienna loved it and I would say she definitely noticed you." I said as I winked at him. "Thanks, Morgan." He smiled.

"I'm going to head out now, are you coming?" He asked. "I'll still be a minute. I'm going to bring some food and cake back to my parents."

"Okay, sounds good. I'm going to find Sebastian and Vienna to tell them bye." I waved him goodbye and headed to the table to package food to my parents. Vienna still hadn't come inside, and I was worried about her. Sebastian still didn't come inside either as I guessed he was still loading things in his car. I got all my belongings and thanked the woman at the counter and left.

As I walked out, I saw Sebastian and Vienna sitting closely to one another. They were outside sitting at one of the tables. They were talking in what seemed like an intense conversation. Vienna had her head on his shoulder and Sebastian had his arm around her. Nothing was happening, but something about it made me feel uneasy. I knew I shouldn't have overreacted, but they had been out there for a long time. I watched them carefully and they embraced in a long and tight hug. I felt anger and jealousy inside me. Why was I feeling this way? I was never the kind to get jealous. They weren't doing anything wrong but there was something strange about the whole scene. Seeing them sitting there together threw me off. I hurriedly walked over to where they were, and they quickly jumped apart as soon as they heard me.

"Well, everything is all cleaned. Are you good to go?"

"Yeah." Seb said as he looked flabbergasted. I eyed him suspiciously and he didn't meet my eyes. He should have known that I knew when he was hiding something. We had been best friends since forever and I knew everything about him. "Bye Vienna! Happy birthday again." I waved at her. "Bye! Thanks for everything." She said. I walked away with Sebastian as we headed to our cars. We embraced as we said bye to each other, but the whole car ride home I replayed the whole scene in my head. I had to accept the fact that it seemed that Vienna and now Sebastian were hiding something from me.

Chapter 20

I couldn't stop thinking about Sebastian and Vienna. The whole situation was really weird, and I was desperate to know what was going on. I tried to put the pieces together from the whole day. Vienna suddenly getting quiet, her checking her phone, her finally talking on the phone, and her talking to Sebastian. It just didn't seem to add up. I thought of a million possibilities and the only logical explanation was that Vienna was talking to him and telling him what was going on with her. Even so, it was just strange seeing them sitting there together. And why would she confide in Seb and not me? My thoughts were playing tug of war with me, and I couldn't seem to keep it under control. The only way I would get answers is by talking to Vienna myself and that's exactly what I intended on doing when I saw her at school.

Things got way worse as I arrived at school to see that Vienna wasn't there. Sebastian and Embry met me at my locker like they usually did. They seemed completely fine and normal, but I was the one who was freaking out. "Where's Vienna? Is she not here?" I panicked. "I guess not." Seb answered casually. I glared at him with concern. "That's really weird. She never misses." Embry replied. I was kind of glad he was just as worried as me. It was nice that someone else cared. Sebastian's tone made my suspicions grow. "I know. I'm really worried about her. I don't know what's going on with her. I thought she was fine at her birthday, but I guess not." I said, my voice trailing off with my thoughts. "Don't worry about it, I'm sure she's fine." Seb continued on with his nonchalant voice. I was becoming really freaked out as I felt my anxious thoughts coming true. Did he really believe that, or did he just not care?

Mr. Bryant's class felt completely lonely without Vienna, and I began to feel like I felt before she had moved there. Some people stared at me as I walked in alone, but most people just ignored me. I was practically invisible again without her there. "Morgan, where's your partner in crime?" Mr. Bryant asked. I was so over it and completely annoyed. It was enough to feel alone but he didn't have to point it out. "Absent." I replied. "Well, that's too bad. Just partner up with someone else for today." He suggested. In class I had to do a trust fall with a complete stranger. It wasn't the same.

At lunch I barely kept up with conversation as Sebastian and Embry chattered on. I could see Embry was pretty out of it too but in typical Embry fashion, he covered it up. "Morgan!" Seb called me. I looked up from my food. "I was calling you. Are you okay?" He asked. I guess he was talking to me, but I didn't reply. My head was filled with thoughts of Vienna.

"What? I'm fine."

"Tink, come on. You've been sitting here all quiet and you haven't eaten anything. You just keep sitting with your head down poking at your food. I know you, talk to me." I looked up and met his kind brown eyes. The eyes I could tell anything to. It made me feel like he wasn't hiding anything. "Okay, fine. It's just about Vienna. You say that everything is fine, and I don't think it is. I know her, she's my best friend. She's been so quiet and weird for weeks, she lashed out on me that one time, she was acting weird for her birthday, and now she misses school?

Something is seriously wrong." Seb stayed still and Embry just nodded sadly in agreement. I watched and waited for Sebastian to say something, but he never did. I had to come clean.

"I saw you guys talking after the party when we were cleaning up. What's was that about?" I always had to get things off my chest. I knew Sebastian would never keep things from me but now I wasn't so sure. "It was nothing." He said as he kept his head down. I saw Embry move in his seat as he became very uncomfortable. I didn't mean for him to get dragged into it and I wasn't even sure if he happened to see them outside as well. "Well, I saw you guys talking out there for a lone time. She must have told you something."

"It's nothing, Morgan!" He said as his voice was rising. I got taken back as I never would have thought Sebastian would talk to me that way. Embry looked like he wanted to get up and run. The rest of lunch we didn't speak as we dropped the conversation.

Rehearsals were a train wreck, and I couldn't concentrate on anything. Even though Vienna had not been acting herself, her absence was a gaping hole. I looked from backstage at the audience as if I would see her there cheering me on. Mr. Baldwin looked at Sebastian and I disappointed as we weren't trying our best. Theatre was my outlet and my stress reliever. I felt like I could break free, and I always gave it my all, but I couldn't concentrate with all that was going on. I felt uneasy around Sebastian since lunch, and I didn't feel like acting. I felt bad for letting Mr. Baldwin down and I hoped I would feel better the next day.

At home my parents kept trying to talk to me and ask me what was wrong. I was so mentally tired, and I didn't want to talk about it at all. I clearly wasn't going to get any answers. I didn't want to tell them about Vienna for their fear of me losing another friend and I definitely didn't want to let them know about Sebastian. They were so thrilled at us being together that I didn't want to upset them. At night I tried to sleep as I stared at the pictures Seb and I took in the photo booth at Vienna's party. I remember the words he said, "Our first photos as a couple." I rubbed my eyes as I tried to erase what happened at lunch. I couldn't believe he raised his voice at me.

I tried to convince myself that what happened was nothing and that couples had their little arguments at times. I tried to convince myself that he wasn't hiding something from me about Vienna. I tried to convince myself that there was nothing going on with them. It was no use. Shouldn't I trust my instinct? I didn't trust my instinct when I felt like something was wrong the day of my grandpa's accident and I wasn't going to ignore it now. Still, I had to believe that everything was going to be okay between us. We had made it this far for us not to be.

The next day Vienna was another no show. Missing one day was enough but two days was definitely a red flag. I waited by my locker in the morning as I checked my phone. I looked through the dozens of texts and calls I sent her that were left unreturned. She hadn't responded to me at all, and she was definitely not active on social media. As soon as Sebastian and Embry walked to my locker, I voiced my concern. "She's not here again! I have been blowing up her phone and no response. This is just too weird."

"Oh yeah, she texted me saying that she was missing again today." Sebastian said. I looked up from my phone and Embry looked shocked as well. "Um, why would she tell you and not me? I have been trying to reach her nonstop and she writes you?" I asked furiously. "I don't know, but it's fine. Don't worry about it. " He replied in his same calm tone. I stood there angrily, unable to say anything. "What is going on?" I demanded. He didn't say anything as he turned to walk away.

Embry and I were left there in disbelief. "What was that about?" He asked. I was glad I wasn't the only one left in this. He seemed just as clueless as I was, and I was glad I had someone to relate to. I decided to put my trust in Embry. "You don't think there's something going on with them, do you?" I felt bad saying the words out loud, but I had to make sure I wasn't crazy. "No way, that can't be. Something is going on though and I need to find out." I was glad we were on the same page.

It was three days since Vienna hadn't been at school. When I saw she was gone again for a third time, I knew I had to get my answers. I watched as Sebastian approached me at my locker without Embry. "So, Vienna's gone for a third day and now Embry too?" I commented. "Relax, he's here. He's just in the bathroom, okay?" We were both still on edge with each other and I hated it. Things weren't the same between us. "What? Vienna didn't text you today that she wasn't coming?" I replied. "Will you stop with that!" I became so angry now and I raised my voice at him. "No! Something is clearly going on between you two and I want to know!" I demanded. "What? I can't believe you! Nothing like that is happening between us."

He looked genuinely hurt but I still had my walls up. The walls I spent so long and hard building to protect me. "Well, something is going on and I want to know. I know you and I know when you are hiding something. Stop lying to me, I can't take it anymore. You were the last person she talked to before this happened. She must have told you something. Why won't you just tell me?" I yelled. "Just drop it!"

"Since when do we lie to each other?" I said with pain in my voice. He clearly saw it was hurting me and he stopped for a few moments. It looked like he was finally about to say something, but he stopped. "You don't understand." He said. "Then explain to me so that I do understand." He contemplated but then shook his head. He began walking away and I was done with him just refusing to acknowledge what was happening. "Sebastian!" I called out after him. "Stop pushing me away!" He stopped in his tracks and slowly turned around to look at me in the eyes. He had a look in his eyes I had never seen before until that moment. It was the look of someone betraying him. "You're one to talk."

All those years of building my walls to protect myself and Sebastian just knocked them down in one kick. I wasn't sure if I even heard correctly but I knew my mind couldn't have made up what he said. I couldn't believe he would use that against me. All those years of guilt and suffering with what I had been through. Of course, I pushed him away and didn't talk to him for two whole years, but he would never know how much it hurt me. It hurt me to always stay away from him, to choose that life for myself, and to say goodbye to our friendship which I thought was for the best. Yes, I made the mistake of pushing him away, but Sebastian made a bigger one. I stood there in complete shock as I got the wind knocked out of me. "I don't want to speak to you." Was all I said.

I cried as I replayed what Sebastian had told me. I couldn't believe everything was going so wrong. Something was wrong with Vienna, and she wouldn't talk to me, she kept missing school, and Sebastian knew something about it and was lying to me. I couldn't believe what he had told me and how everything just escalated. I didn't know what was going to happen between us, but I was scared to find out. Not only did I dream about being with him since we were kids, but he was my best friend. It was scary to think I would lose him again. We had made it so far and had been through so much not to make it. I couldn't speak to him though after what he told me. He would have to do a lot to fix things before I would talk to him again. The situation with Seb was actually the least of my worries as all I kept thinking about was Vienna. Part of me was angry at her for talking to Sebastian and them being suspicious behind my back.

I was angry at her for ignoring me and not telling me what was wrong in the first place then maybe this wouldn't have turned out the way it did. Another part of me was sad and scared. She was clearly going through something bad. Bad enough for her to miss school. I was scared for her and wanted to be there for her. I stayed restless as I knew there was nothing I could do about either situation. I just had to hope that something would happen that would fix everything.

Chapter 21

At school the next day I didn't even bother going to my locker. I didn't want to see Sebastian or know if Vienna was missing again. I just automatically went to Mr. Bryant's class which was a first for me. I couldn't wait to get in class early so I wouldn't have to run the risk of seeing Sebastian. I walked into class and to my surprise, Vienna was there. I saw her sitting there nonchalantly and wondered how early she had got there. I wondered why she didn't go straight to our lockers like she always did in the morning. Regardless, I was still happy to see her. I frantically walked up to her and took my usual seat next to her.

"Vienna! I'm so glad to see you here! I was so worried about you." She looked straight ahead and completely ignored me. I paused, but then continued. "I tried calling and texting you a bunch of times. Is everything okay?" She continued to ignore me as if I wasn't there. I stared at her carefully and anger rose in her face. "Vienna?" Still no reply.

"You missed three days of school and I haven't heard from you. You come back and you're just going to ignore me?" She continued to stare straight ahead without blinking. It was as if I could almost see the steam coming out of her ears and her anger rising. "Vienna!" I called out just as Mr. Bryant walked in. "Ah, I see the dynamic duo is back again." It took all of me not to roll my eyes. "Why don't you start off today's class?"

I looked at him and then turned to see Vienna's expressionless face. Mr. Bryant was waiting, and I slowly got up from my seat. I made my way on stage and was surprised that Vienna followed behind. "Okay, really simple stuff. I just want to see the improv skills you've developed. So, there are absolutely no rules. Just say and do whatever you feel. Make it up as you go along. Okay girls, whenever you're ready." I took the exercise to my advantage.

If Vienna wouldn't talk to me then she had to at that moment. She had no choice to work with me. In that moment I never felt more hurt and betrayed by her. I hadn't seen her in a long time and with her finally in front of me, every emotion came spilling out. Everything with her odd behavior, everything with Sebastian, and all the secrets. I had to get answers, and this was the only way how. "What is your problem?" I told her. In that moment I forgot my surroundings. I never would have acted that way if my emotions didn't get the best of me. Suddenly nothing mattered. Not Mr. Bryant watching and definitely not our classmates.

"Excuse me?" Vienna replied. "You act weird for weeks and you won't tell me what's going on, you hide things from me, you miss school for three days, and you come back and just ignore me? What did I do to you? Did I do something? If I did then just tell me!" I pleaded. "Oh my gosh, Morgan! Not everything is about you! Some of us actually have real problems." She fought back. "I didn't say everything was about me." I said defensively. "Oh please, you make everything about you. With your perfect life, your perfect family, and your perfect boyfriend." She mocked. I could not believe she was turning everything on me.

I didn't know why she was turning on me and attacking me. She was clearly avoiding the real situation, but if she wanted to go that route then I wouldn't back down. "And like you are so great? You act like you are so cool with that attitude that you don't care about anything. It gets so old with you being cynical all the time. You hate the world so much and you believe that love doesn't exist. You just constantly have to bash on everything." I didn't know how our fight turned so personal, but I couldn't help but get out things I felt about her too.

"If you can't stand my attitude, then why did you cling to me? Oh wait, it's because you had nobody! You had no friends before I came, and you were lost without me!" I felt wounded at that moment when I was trying to remain strong. I felt like it was no use. Vienna did make me a more confident person and next to her I was defeated. She was the person who gave me strength. She gave me that power and now she was taking it back. Still, I had to fight on. "You act like I need you so much!" I replied weakly. "You do because you don't have a backbone. You are such a wimp and you let fear control your life. If it wasn't for me, you wouldn't even be with Sebastian! You would still till this day be staring at him pathetically from across the cafeteria." I felt my blood boiling and couldn't control it any longer.

"Well, I guess you would know about that. I saw you two outside of Legends on your birthday. You guys looked awfully close. I know you've been sneaking behind my back and talking to each other." I finally said. I tried to read her face and it didn't look angry but instead she looked in pain. "You don't know anything." "I know that you didn't have friends before I came here either. At least that's what you told me. You became my friend and you backstabbed me. You're a traitor and I can't believe you. You betrayed me." "You don't know anything about me." She turned and left the classroom. In that moment I felt like I won for standing up to her but in reality, I lost a friend.

I had to endure seeing Sebastian in rehearsals, but it was my job to act, and I was good at it. I did theatre my whole life and I was never better at faking it. I had to fake it through rehearsals and act like everything was okay. The only person who I was fooling was Mr. Baldwin but I couldn't fool myself. Rehearsals were at least a bit more bearable because Vienna didn't show up. When we were done with the scene, Mr. Baldwin pulled me to the side.

"Morgan, where has Vienna been? She's been missing a lot of rehearsal and we need her for dress rehearsal in a few days." He said, worried. With everything that was going on I completely had forgotten that dress rehearsal was just around the corner and Vienna had to be there for costumes. I didn't know what to say, but I knew I couldn't say the truth. "I'm not sure but I'm sure she will make it for dress rehearsal." I told him.

I knew she worked too long and hard to not come to the dress rehearsal. Plus, she has a commitment so she couldn't back out of it anyway. Everyone put their heart and soul in this play and were counting on her. She couldn't back out now. Mr. Baldwin looked at me anxiously but then just nodded. I walked past Embry who gave me a weak smile. In all of this, I felt like he was the only one who I would be able to talk to and who would understand me. But he was Sebastian's best friend, and he was on his side no matter what. That left me without any friends and truly alone just like I was before.

At home I was a mess. I felt like I was reverting back into my depression back when the accident happened. My parents were starting to freak out. "Morgan, you know how this goes. You can't shut us out. You need to talk and tell us what is going on." My mom begged. I finally looked up to see my parents faces. I hadn't seen them this worried about me in a while, and I didn't want to do that to them. I didn't want to worry them like I had for the past two years. I didn't want to put them through that pain again and didn't want to live in it. I had to talk.

"I got into a fight with Sebastian and Vienna. It's a long story but everything is just a mess. Nobody is talking to each other. I don't know what to do and how to fix it. I messed up and they messed up. I just don't know what to do. I'm not talking to Sebastian right now because I'm mad at him and Vienna isn't talking to me because she's mad at me." I spoke slowly as I left the major things out while still telling most of the truth. I didn't want them to know the whole story and worry, but they deserved to know some of what was happening. They sat for a while and exchanged looks. I could tell they were trying to keep it together for my sake.

"I think the first thing you need to do is talk to Vienna. You should go over to her house and explain everything." My dad said. I stared at my parents and realized how grateful I was to have them. "You know what happened the first time, don't let it happen again this time. You need to communicate with each other." My mom chimed in. They were right and I couldn't let this be another Sebastian situation where we didn't talk for two years. It was off to Vienna's house.

As I drove up, I began to get very nervous again. The fight we had in class was very intense and I did not want to let it get to that level again. I waited in my car, and I set boundaries for myself. I knew I couldn't let her walk all over me, but I also couldn't barge in there and attack her. One thing was for sure and that's that I needed to demand why she was treating me the way she was and get answers. I was usually a nice person who couldn't tell anyone off unless they had a problem with my friend. But what happened when your friend was the problem? I was about to find out.

I knew I couldn't stall any longer and I just had to go out there. I marched up to her house and pounded on the door. To my surprised it opened quickly, and it wasn't Vienna who swung open the door. Mrs. Chamberlain stood in the doorway and looked surprised to see it was me. "Oh, hi Mrs. Chamberlain." I said embarrassed. I felt immediately bad for showing up there unannounced and I completely forgot about her mom.

"Morgan! I thought you were Vienna." She quickly fixed herself up by putting her hair down and smoothing it with her fingers. She looked pretty rough and like she was going through something too. She had dark rings under her eyes and her eyes drooped sleepily. Her hair was very messy, and she looked sloppy. I guessed she was dealing with Vienna and her behavior as well. "Sorry, I expected Vienna to be here." I replied. "So did I. She took off a while ago, but she should be back soon. Would you like to come in and wait with me?" I stood there hesitantly. "I'll make you come tea." It didn't seem like I was being a bother to her, and she seemed happy to invite me in. "Sure." I said.

We sat there at her kitchen table and drank our tea in silence. "Sorry for just showing up here like this. I just really need to talk to Vienna." I admitted. "What brings you over?" She asked. I really didn't want to tell her mom about our problems, but I figured if I were to get answers from anyone then it would be her mom. "To tell you the truth, Vienna and I got into a fight. I was just worried that she missed school for a few days, and she hasn't been herself. She hasn't talked to me and she's mad at me. I don't know what I did." I said sadly. I looked down to avoid her mom's reaction. I didn't know how she would take it and if she would be mad at me as well.

"Oh honey, you did nothing wrong. She's not mad at you, she's just taking it out on you. I'm so sorry she's been acting out. You know, things have just been hard with her dad leaving." She said matter-of-factly. So, this all had to do with her dad? I knew her dad was never home because of his job, but I didn't realize it affected Vienna. So that was it. Her dad was probably gone for a long time on his job, and she missed him. He was probably gone to another state on business that she couldn't know of. It was always just her and her mom, but I know it probably meant more to them when he was there spending time with them.

"Oh, I understand. It must be hard with him gone all the time for work. Has he been gone long?" I asked. She looked up quickly from drinking her tea as if I offended her. "What did you say?" Her tone sounded just like Vienna, and I became frightened. I tried to compose myself. "I was just wondering how long it's been since he's been away. When is he coming back?" She still stared at me with a blank expression and was looking at my face for answers. She looked so confused and I found it strange that I had to explain to her. I saw her white knuckles as she gripped on tightly to her mug. "It's just that I know how hard it must be since he's a limo driver. He must travel a lot and he's not here. But he will be back soon, right?"

She took her glasses off and rubbed her eyes. I was so uncomfortable and wanted to get out of there. I didn't know what I could have possibly said or done to offend her. I didn't know how to fix it or if I even could. "Vienna's dad isn't a limo driver, he's a truck driver." I nodded slowly as I tried to comprehend what was happening. So, she lied to me? I didn't really care much since it wasn't a big deal and thought that maybe she was embarrassed. "Oh okay, so he's a truck driver." I responded. "She told you he was a limo driver?" She asked. She looked very concerned, and I knew she deserved the truth. "Yeah, she told me he was a limo driver and he traveled driving celebrities and that's why he wasn't here all the time." Her eyes were wide as she was listening to me. I didn't want her to be embarrassed either, so I tried to make her feel better. "But it's okay, it's not a big deal. It doesn't matter what he does." I said as I brushed it off. Mrs. Chamberlain sighed heavily as she put down her mug.

"I'm sorry, did I do something? I really didn't mean to offend you." I spoke up. "Morgan, Vienna's father and I haven't been together in months. We are getting a divorce and that's why we moved here. She didn't tell you any of this?" The whole room began to spin, and it seemed there was nothing to hold onto. Vienna's parents were getting a divorce? She lied to me? I put the pieces together in my head as I realized that everything she ever told me was a lie. I stayed in shock and then the door opened. Vienna walked in shocked to see me sitting in her house with her mom. Our eyes met and I began to cry. I got up and ran for the door. "Morgan, wait!" She yelled. I didn't turn back as I walked out the door. I heard her yelling at her mom. "What did you do?" "I had to tell her!" Her mom yelled back. Vienna continued to call me and soon I heard her footsteps following me. "Morgan!" I spun around to meet her as hot tears poured over my face. "Wow you must think I'm pretty stupid, don't you?" I yelled. "Just let me explain!"

"Explain what? You lied to me. You lied to me about your life and your family. Your family isn't what you made it out to be. Your dad isn't a fancy limo driver who drives around celebrities and gets you nice clothes from places. You had the nerve to say all that stuff about me in class when this whole time you pretended about who you really are? Maybe I am a wimp but it's better than being a coward and a liar!" I felt like a balloon deflating all the pressure she had put on me. All that time of being scared and being intimidated by her was gone. I now had the upper hand. "Just listen to me!" She pleaded. "What for? Everything was a lie. You played me so well and I was naive enough to believe you. I was the perfect person because I was pathetic and had no friends. Were you just messing with me the whole time? Was being my friend all a lie and just a game to you? And what about getting me into the play? Did you just do everything with Sebastian on purpose? Because why would you help me get together with him when you didn't know me and then do this to me? Were you just so unhappy with what was happening in your life that you had to go and ruin mine?" My voice was scratchy and hoarse.

I never was one to yell and I was always soft spoken. I was never one to fight back or say anything. I was always weak and timid. But not anymore. I suffered way too many blows in life to get knocked down for good this time. "No! I would never do that; you have to believe me. Nothing is going on with us. I would never hurt you like that."

"How would I even know? I trusted you, Vienna, and you betrayed me. I thought after Sebastian that I would never make another friend again. This isn't even about Sebastian though because before I even knew that the plan would work, you were my friend. It didn't even matter about him or the play because I was just happy I made a friend. I thought you came to me for a reason, and you were something special. You made me believe that we were best friends. I thought what we had was true friendship, but I don't even know who you are anymore. I thought I finally found happiness after my grandpa. I can't do this."

I turned around and ran off. Her voice screaming my name was ringing in my ears.

I got home and ran inside right past my parents. "How did it go?" My dad asked. I ignored them as I ran upstairs. They knew exactly how this was going to go. They've been through it with me before, but this time it was worse. This time I lost Sebastian again and the only other real friend I ever had.

Chapter 22

I really didn't want to go to school the next day after everything
that had happened. But as one of the leads in the play, I couldn't
let my cast down or Mr. Baldwin. My life had felt like the worse
it had ever been. At least when my grandpa died, I was to myself
and didn't have to deal with anyone in school. I was in my own
little bubble and nothing or nobody could hurt me. Now I was out
in the open and I let myself be vulnerable. I let myself get hurt
and there was no way around it. Vienna and I just ignored each
other in Mr. Bryant's class and partnered up with other people.
After our argument in class and asking if everything was okay,
Mr. Bryant just let us be. For the most part I avoided Sebastian at
school but there was no way I could avoid him in rehearsal.
Vienna was to herself and didn't talk to Sebastian or Embry.

They both knew better than to talk to me. There were times
where I felt like they were going to talk to me, but I just ran off.
Embry stuck close to Sebastian, but I noticed every chance he
got, he tried to get close to me to talk. He gave up as there was no
chance he could get to me. That was the worst part in all of it. I
still had to act with Sebastian in the play like nothing was going
on between us. We still had to be Seymour and Audrey who liked
each other when Sebastian and Morgan weren't speaking. I hated
letting my personal life get into my acting because it never did.
My life and theatre have always been separated because I never
had any real problems. After my grandpa died, I knew I couldn't
put my all into theatre, so I gave up. Now this was different. I

was stuck in this play with no way out and dress rehearsal was a few days away. After rehearsal, I quickly got my stuff and left so I wouldn't have to endure another second of it.

I kept trying to avoid Sebastian and Vienna as best I could at school. I was used to being alone before they came along so I was good at hiding. I didn't know how things were going with them or if they were having lunch all together, but it was best for me if I didn't know. I didn't eat lunch in the cafeteria, but I decided to eat it in the auditorium and get more practice in for rehearsals. I hung out there and luckily, I felt okay since some of the people from the play were there. We all talked, and I didn't feel so alone anymore. Except that I felt more alone than ever.

I stuck with the same routine for the third day in a row but as I got my food from the cafeteria, Embry spotted me. Our eyes met and I quickly grabbed my food and walked away. He accelerated his walking and chased after me. I had nothing against Embry at all, but I had no intention of talking to him. He was Sebastian's best friend, and he was in love with Vienna, so all he was going to do was try to convince me to talk to them. I was not going to talk to either of them until they apologized to me. There was nothing I had to say to either of them. "Morgan!" He called after me. I walked faster and I passed him up. "Morgan, wait! I have to tell you something. Let me explain! It all makes sense now. It's not like that!" He called out after me. I was so far now that his voice was very faint.

In rehearsals, Sebastian and I finished up another painful scene together. I looked up and saw Vienna in the audience sitting with her arms crossed. I quickly looked away and put my head down. "Okay, that's all for today. You all can leave now." Mr. Baldwin said in a frustrated tone. I was slow to gather my stuff and leave. I saw as Sebastian and Embry walked out together with Vienna this time. I watched curiously as they hadn't been talking to her at rehearsals until that moment. I looked at them sadly when they disappeared out the door. "Morgan, can I talk to you?" Mr. Baldwin said, breaking me away from my thoughts. I was in a daze and didn't really care for what he was going to say. "I don't know what's going on with you and Sebastian but you two have been lacking in rehearsals. Don't think I haven't noticed that you guys have been acting weird. You both have low energy and have not been acting well. The show is coming up, so you guys need to fix it and put in your all." He said in a stern voice.

"Okay." I said lazily and began walking away. "Morgan, wait." I turned back around and expected more verbal abuse from him on how I was acting poorly. "I didn't mean to be insensitive. I'm your director, but I'm also here for you. I've been watching you kids, and I know something is going on. I don't just care about the play, but I care about my students. Your well-being comes first. You know that, right? Let's sit down and talk." It was strange to see Mr. Baldwin in a different light. I knew him as our passionate director. He was a mentor for acting and he guided us every step of the way through every song and scene. He did have his funny moments in rehearsal but mostly I always saw him stressed out.

Stripping away at all his layers, I finally saw him as a person. He really did seem like he genuinely cared, and I felt bad that I didn't want to talk to him about it. I joined him and sat beside him at the edge of the stage. "So, talk to me. What's going on?" I stared at my feet dangling and didn't speak. "I've been with you guys for months now. These rehearsals are so long and hard. We've spent many hours right here and I think I see you all more than I see my own family. I've seen you grow, not only as actors, but as people. I've watched the relationships you have formed. I know how much Sebastian and Vienna mean to you. What happened?"

I was touched at his sincerity and as I looked into his eyes, I felt like I could trust him. It wasn't like talking to my parents who I knew would freak out. This was just Mr. Baldwin who was impartial and didn't know anything about the situation. He didn't know about my past or about my messy present. He would listen to me and care. "It's just that I got into a fight with them. A really bad one and I don't know what to do or how to fix it. It wasn't really their fault, but it wasn't really my fault either. We all said and did some hurtful things." I admitted.

"Well, that's normal. All friends fight at times, but it seems like there's a bigger underlying issue here going on with you. What's this really all about?" I stood there in a deep realization. Mr. Baldwin made me have an epiphany. He wasn't trying to psychoanalyze me, but he did it for my benefit. "It seems like there's something more that's bothering you with them." He continued. He was right and there was. It was something I couldn't admit to my parents, them, or even myself.

"I guess it's because I feel like I don't deserve friends like them. They are both way cooler than me and could do just fine without me. Sebastian and I have been best friends since we were seven years old. He was always the fun outgoing one who was way popular than me. He was a way better performer than me and could have done better without me holding him back. I always felt like he might have missed out on opportunities because of me. I just felt like that annoying friend who always followed him around. At least that's how I felt because people always said it. They would constantly make fun of me and said I was too much with him. When Vienna came along, I was happy to make another friend who I could relate to. I never was good at making friends. It was always just Sebastian and I, so I was happy to make a friend that was a girl. I was happy I was friends with Vienna, but in the back of my mind, it was like Sebastian all over again. I was insecure because she was pretty, outspoken, and had a great fashion sense. She was so daring and wasn't afraid to be herself. She was new and she could have been so popular if she wasn't stuck with me. I felt like I held her back too. I guess I just have a fear of being left behind."

I looked up as I realized I was rambling on, but he just nodded at me to continue, so I did. "Maybe I just don't know who I am without them. I don't know who I am if I'm not there by their side being that supportive friend and cheering them on. I just feel protective of them and that's my job. I want to be there for them but maybe it's just too much. I'm not really sure where my place is without them. I know that sounds so crazy and that I'm reliant on them, but I feel better when I'm with them. I don't feel so alone."

In that moment I felt like all my problems shrank. They were still there but now that I observed them under a microscope, they didn't feel so big anymore. I realized what my fears were and why I acted the way I did. I knew the real reason why I pushed Sebastian away when my grandpa died. I now knew I had insecurity issues with my friends and fear of being alone. I knew what my problem was now although I still didn't know how to fix it. Mr. Baldwin looked at me and chuckled.

"When you first came in here, you were so shy and timid. The talent was there, but you still seemed lost and trying to find your way. You blew me away in the auditions and that's why I picked you. My amazement for your talent has only grown since then. I see you and you come up on stage every single day in rehearsals and give it your all. I see the passion you have for theatre in the gleam of your eyes. You love it and you live for it. You crave it and strive for more. You push yourself and get better and better each time. You are a true actor who breathes for theatre and does it for the fun of it. You say you don't know your place, but I do. Theatre is who you are and where you belong. This is where you belong, up here on this stage. To tell you the truth, I think you are the best actor we have had here. You are far better than Sebastian and Embry. I'm not just saying that either. But don't tell them I said that."

I stared at him with wide eyes, and he got me to smile. It meant so much coming from him, who I looked up to. He had been in the business for so long and it was the biggest compliment. "You had gained so much confidence since you first started this play. Where do you think that came from? Do you think it came from Sebastian and Vienna?" He asked. I did think it was because Vienna filled me with confidence. She trained me to become Audrey and really believed I could make it. If it wasn't for her, I wasn't sure if I would have got in. It also was because of Sebastian. Seeing his face in the auditions brought me back to when I was young doing theatre throughout my childhood. All those fun times and good memories. I watched as Mr. Baldwin stared at me and shook his head.

"No, it didn't come from them. It came from you. It was all you. As an actor it all comes from within. Nobody can convince you or influence you. You may have some inspirations, but it's within you. You had the confidence inside you all along. I think you just lost it and forgot about it. It came to you though just when you needed it." He was right and I just thought about my grandpa. My grandpa was the one who got me into theatre in the first place. His love of theatre rubbed off on me and I developed a passion for it. He taught me everything he knew and guided me, but he couldn't do everything for me. It all had to come within me, and I did it myself.

I loved theatre and I put in the hard work and practice. I took singing lessons, dance classes, and I was the one who begged my parents to let me do plays. I was the one who begged my parents to let me to do community theatre at the age of seven. It was then, before I even knew Sebastian, that I knew who I was and what I wanted to do. And I wanted to do theatre for the rest of my life.

"And you say that you think that you don't deserve friends like Sebastian and Vienna, but have you ever stopped to consider the fact that they don't deserve a friend like you? They would be lost without you. They need and benefit from having a friend like you. They thrive and get the confidence they do from having a friend like you. I can see Sebastian on stage instantly try harder when he knows you are there watching him and cheering him on. He does his best when he knows you are looking. He wants to impress you. He knows that no matter what, you will be there to support him. You are such a great and loyal friend. You are their biggest support, and you cheer them on. People need a friend like that. You should know from theatre, that it's not all about being in the spotlight. The actor is nothing without an audience cheering them on."

Mr. Baldwin's pep talk made me feel better than I ever had before. I was always constantly putting myself down and feeling like I wasn't good enough. I always focused on my faults and compared myself to others. I always focused on my shyness, but I really needed to focus on my strengths. I listened more as he went on.

"I know the way Vienna is. She can be moody and unpredictable. She always seems like she has a lot going on in her mind, but it seems like you calm her down. She is a very high-strung person, but around you she's at ease. I've seen her change a lot too and it seems like you definitely have softened her. She is so happy when she's with you. She is very comfortable and herself. You both have different personalities that balance each other out. You say that you need her, but I think she really needs you."

I nodded as I never considered that. Vienna came into my life when it felt like I needed her the most, but maybe I was the one she was looking for too. "And Sebastian...." he said as his voice trailed off. I looked at him as he looked down and smiled. He paused for a bit while he shook his head and laughed. "He glows for you."

Chapter 23

I was so glad that it was the weekend, so I didn't have to worry about going to school. I felt better after the talk with Mr. Baldwin, but there was still a lot of things I had to figure out. I woke up early in the morning to go for a walk to clear mind and I knew exactly where to go. I got ready and went downstairs. "Hey, you are up really early for a weekend. Is everything okay?" My mom asked. "Yeah, I just need to get out and get some fresh air. I need to clear my mind." "I think that's a good idea. How are things with the situation?" She asked as she tiptoed around it. I could tell she wanted to know, but she didn't want to upset me. I was doing a lot better to talk about it without telling them everything. They still didn't know, and it was going to stay that way. This was my problem that I needed to deal with myself, and I didn't want them getting involved. I knew they would try to help, but this was something I had to figure out on my own. "Everything is still the same. We haven't talked yet, but I'm going to try to fix it. I just don't know how yet." I admitted.

They both looked at me proudly. They stared at each other and looked impressed. I think they were happy I was finally taking action and responsibility for once. I made the mistake of not doing it before and I wasn't going to do it again. This time it was going to be different. This time I was going to change. "That's great to hear. I know you will fix it." My dad said. I smiled at them both and headed for the door to leave. I had my hand on the knob but then turned around and ran to give them a hug. "Did I ever tell you that I love and appreciate you guys?"

I walked all the way from my house to the familiar road. It was nice to get out and get some exercise. I always only walked the road with Sebastian, but this time was just for me. I knew Sebastian wouldn't dare to come and go for a walk on the road for the risk of seeing me, so I wasn't scared as I walked confidently. The road did feel different and empty without him, but I tried to focus as I kept walking on. I took in the fresh breeze and crisp air. I passed by the same horses and concentrated on my breathing as I walked. I was finally alone with my thoughts and in a safe place where I didn't have to worry about running into Sebastian or Vienna.

I finally had time to think and sort things out. As I walked on, I realized how selfish I was. I didn't know everything that was going on with Vienna and I assumed a lot. Vienna did lie to me, but the bottom line was that her parents were getting a divorce and I was insensitive. I yelled at her and said many hurtful things when I didn't consider what she must be going through.

I didn't know the whole truth about her, but nobody deserved that. I didn't know how Sebastian fit into all of this, but I needed to talk to him and sort things out. It was no use to ignore him and just push him away again. That's how we got into this whole mess in the first place. No matter what was going on, I needed to communicate with him. I was still upset and mad at him because what he said really hurt me, but we needed to talk things out.

I kept walking on as I tried to figure out how to fix things when I got to the end of the road. I walked up to the enormous Giving Tree. I stood in front of it and sighed as I marveled at its beauty. I reminisced when Sebastian and I wrote our notes to each other. It seemed like so long ago with all the events that followed. I cautiously looked to see if they were still there, but they were gone. To my surprise, I saw something else. Hanging on the Giving Tree was a huge sign. I examined it closely as I knew it couldn't be true. It was true though because I knew that handwriting. I read the sign once more as it read, "tell him you love him." I looked back at the sign again and smiled as I was getting ready to run. I took off and ran as fast as I could and the whole way, I pretended I was racing against Sebastian.

When I got to Sebastian's house, I was hot and sweaty from running but there was no time to waste. I took a few deeps breaths and then I knocked on the door. Mrs. Montgomery answered the door quickly and looked surprised. "Morgan, it's so great to see you!" "Hi, Mrs. Montgomery. Can I talk to Sebastian?" I said between breaths.

"I'm sorry, he isn't here. He asked Mr. Baldwin if he could use the auditorium for more rehearsal time. I can't believe the show is only a few days away." I was a little disappointed as I just ran all the way to his house to see him. "So, he's there right now?" I asked. "Yes, he went in early. Are you okay?" She asked as she observed me panting. "Yeah, I just went out for a run." I lied. "Oh okay, well I'll see you then." She replied, concerned. I waved goodbye as I couldn't speak from exhaustion.

I took it easy as I walked back slowly to my house, and I was glad that it was next street over. I got to my house and stopped in my tracks as I saw the little black car parked in front. I watched as Vienna got out of her car. "Vienna!" I yelled. She looked shocked to see me and realized that I had come from somewhere. "Morgan!" I ran up to her and gave her a hug. We wrapped each other up tightly and cried. I knew in that moment that whatever was going on, that it would be okay. We needed to put all the fighting and nonsense behind us and really listen to each other. "I can't believe you are here!" I said as we broke apart. "I had to come and see you. Where did you just come from?" She asked. "I came from walking on the road, and I saw your sign. I just came back from Sebastian's house, but he wasn't there. He's at the auditorium getting in more rehearsal time. I was headed over there and now I'm here."

I laughed as I got everything out. "Oh my gosh, I'm so glad you saw my sign. I was so worried." "How did you know I would see it?" I wondered. "I just remember you talking about the road when you and Sebastian walked on it. I went and saw the tree with all the messages and got the idea. I didn't know if you would walk there, but I had to try. I figured maybe you would since it was the weekend or at least drive by." She said. "Wow, that's lucky." I couldn't believe how everything worked out and how it led me here to her.

"Yeah, but I wasn't too sure it was going to work. That's when I realized I just had to come and see you. I really need to apologize to you. I can't believe you are even talking to me right now." She said sadly. "No, I'm sorry. Once I found out that your parents were getting a divorce, I should have been more sensitive. I was selfish and only thought about how you lied to me. I completely overreacted and said things I didn't even believe. I didn't mean any of it and I'm so sorry."

I was so glad to get it all out and apologize. As I was saying everything out loud, I did realize how dumb I had acted and just jumped to conclusions. I didn't even let Vienna get a chance to explain. I just took off, ran away, and ignored her because that's what I did best. "You didn't say anything that wasn't true. I did lie about a lot of things, but one thing that I didn't lie about was being your friend. Every second we spent together was real. Still,

I didn't tell you the truth about me. I hid a lot of things because I was ashamed. I was going through a lot, and I took it out on you. I lashed out on you, and it was completely wrong. I am so sorry, Morgan. Can you ever forgive me?" I really appreciated her heartfelt apology. She was being so open and honest with me, and I knew I was being overdramatic before. Everything was going to be okay.

"Of course, I forgive you." I hugged her again and she sighed and thanked me. "If you would let me, I would really like a chance to explain everything. I'll tell you the truth about everything from the beginning. I'll give you total and complete honesty. This is me; this is the real Vienna." I felt a huge weight off my shoulders and my anxiety was gone. Finally, I would be getting my answers.

I led her to my porch swing so we could talk. The wind blew and I saw as she held onto her beret. It was the beret that Embry gave her for her birthday. I did my best to suppress a smile. "So, this is the truth. Everything from the beginning. It's going to be a lot, but you deserve to know the truth." She said. I nodded as I held onto the swing for support. I was prepared to hear anything.

"My dad isn't a limo driver.....he's a truck driver. He doesn't go around driving celebrities and he doesn't travel all over the country. I only said that because I was embarrassed. He also doesn't get me fancy clothes either. I get my clothes from the thrift store." She paused and I was already shocked by all the news, but it was only the beginning.

"My parents always had their problems and fought. I didn't really think anything of it because that's how it always had been. It was my dad who was always cold and distant, but I didn't really realize it. That's just the way he was, and I thought that's how marriages were. I thought that the honeymoon phase just eventually ends and then it's just real life. I thought the spark wasn't alive and it wasn't the same. I didn't think there was anything particularly wrong with their relationship, but deep down I knew something wasn't right."

I nodded calmly to show I cared but I was freaking out on the inside. I couldn't believe everything she was saying. "My dad and I were close despite their relationship. He came home late and worked a lot, but we had our moments together. We all never did anything or went out as a family. I lied and I've never even been to Vienna." She laughed before she continued. "We weren't even really a family. I just had my separate relationships with each of them. As time went on it got worse. My dad started coming home later and later and my parents resented each other. They never hardly talked before but then it got worse. They barely even acknowledged each other's existence. He would just come home from work really late and that was it. There was no interaction with us at all. Then one day he just randomly said he couldn't take it anymore. He said he was leaving and wanted a divorce from my mom."

As I was listening, I tried to hold back tears. I didn't want her to see me upset but I couldn't help but feel terrible. "My mom agreed since there wasn't really anything between them. She was a mess though since she felt really bad for me. She felt like it was her fault for not trying harder to make their marriage work for my sake. I was so distraught that I even started to believe it was her fault. It was still a lot for us, and we were going through a lot of depression. We figured that since they were divorcing that it would be best if we moved. So, me and my mom packed our bags and left for a new start. A fresh start away from that house and town with all the bad memories. It was easy since I had no attachment there. I didn't lie when I said I didn't have any friends. It was easy leaving my old school, but it was hard to leave my passion for theatre. I knew I couldn't do it anymore with everything that was going on. That's what brought us here and to Burwood. Then I met you." I listened carefully as she explained, and it seemed like all the pieces were finally coming together. "I was glad to have a new start somewhere else, but I wasn't too thrilled at having to adjust to a new school. I was going through a lot and that's why I was so mean to you on the first day." I nodded jokingly as I agreed.

"I didn't plan on making friends, but then we met. You were so sweet and nice to me. Even though I was mean, you still tried with me. Then you told me that you loved theatre too and I just knew we were going to be best friends." I laughed as that's how I knew too.

"I never met anyone like you. You were so pretty and had a great sense of style. You were so nice and never got mad at anything. You were so patient and kind. Then you told me about your family, and I freaked out. Your life seemed so cool and fancy. I was really jealous of you. You seemed to have it all. You had a great life and parents that had a great relationship. Most importantly, you had your dad. I was jealous so I made up all that stuff about mine." My eyes were wide with shock. Vienna was jealous of me? The whole time I was jealous of her, and I had no idea she was jealous of me. I felt immediately bad for feeling that way when all of that was happening to her.

"Since my parents were divorcing it was hard for me to believe that love existed. I knew it couldn't be true since I saw it falling apart with my parents. I knew love was too good to be true. I never saw a good relationship and so I believed it was all made-up stuff you saw in the movies. Once you told me about Sebastian, I knew it was my chance to see if love really did exist.

242

That's why I was so obsessed with trying to get you two together. I thought if I could get you two together that it would prove me wrong. I thought that if I got you two together that I would be responsible for one relationship working. If it all worked out, I thought that it somehow would fix all my problems. I thought maybe my parents would somehow magically work out." She stopped and took a deep breath. I put my hand on her shoulder. She nodded and continued.

"This brings us to more recent events. So, my dad told me it wasn't going to affect our relationship. He said that nothing was going to change between us and that it was just problems between him and my mom. He still wanted to see me and be involved in my life. I was thrilled that I would still get to see my dad. We arranged a schedule where we would see each other every weekend and go out to dinner. It wasn't perfect though since my parents were going through getting the divorce and they didn't speak to each other. I didn't care all that much because I still got to see my dad and he was still in my life. It was almost better because I felt like I got to see him more and connect with him. It was a little awkward since my parents would fight over the phone all the time about divorce papers, but everything seemed fine. Everything seemed fine for a while." Tears began streaming down her face.

"Do you want to stop?" I asked. She shook her head and went on with the story. "Eventually I started seeing him less and less. He would make excuses that he couldn't see me to go out to dinner. I was devastated and felt like I was losing him all over again. We hardly talked and even when I tried to reach out, I would get no response. That's why I was acting so weird and quiet at school."

I listened attentively as I was getting all the answers. Everything was starting to click and make sense. "I told my mom about it, and she was furious. Despite everything, I still defended him. I wanted to believe my dad was a good person. I had to believe there was an explanation and that my dad was probably just busy working. At least that's what he would tell me when he would make his excuses." I saw her starting to get angry, but then she composed herself. "I thought things would get better on my birthday. I kept looking at my phone to see if he would wish me a happy birthday. He never did." I shut my eyes as I didn't want to think about it. What kind of father would do that?

"That's when I went outside while you guys were cleaning up after the party. I called my mom and told her. I was crying to her, and I was just so upset. That's when Sebastian saw me. He asked me what was wrong, and I didn't want to tell him at first. I was tired of lying though, and I knew I had to tell someone. I already felt bad for not telling you and treating you the way I was. I figured at least someone deserved to know. I told him everything and I made him promise not to tell you. I didn't want Embry to know either because you know how that would have gone." She commented as she rolled her eyes.

"He asked what happened, but Sebastian just brushed him off and said it was nothing. I was a mess as I told Sebastian and I was crying. He listened and was there for me. He was just consoling me and that's what you saw. That was it and that's all that happened I promise." She said. I nodded as I understood.

I couldn't believe I thought something was going on between them. As more of the truth was coming out, I felt worse about myself. How could I have thought all of those things when Vienna was going through a crisis?

"After my birthday is when he would text me and ask me if I was okay. Since he was the only one that knew, I kept him updated so he wouldn't worry. I told him I would be missing school and told him why. Eventually a few days after I came back is when I decided to tell Embry. He asked if he could be the one to tell you. I thought maybe it was a good idea since you would listen to him, and you weren't talking to Sebastian or me. That's when Embry came after you at lunch. He kept wanting to tell you at rehearsal. We all wanted to try telling you, but we were afraid. So, then they both knew. I told them why I missed school. It was because of what I found out after my birthday." I swallowed hard as I listened to the rest.

"After my birthday is when I found out. I found out...." Now she was crying hard. She couldn't control herself as she choked on her tears. "Vienna, it's okay." I said as I comforted her. "That's when I found out my dad was having an affair. He's been having an affair for years. It's been going on since I was a little kid." I sucked in a deep and sharp breath. I couldn't believe it. How could her dad do something like that? How could anyone do something like that?

"He lied for all that time. He lied and he sat back and watched as he tore my family apart. All that time he was sneaking around. Even after we moved and I spent time with him, he sat there and lied to my face. I wasted that whole time going out to dinner with him and I didn't even know what was going on. And do you want to know what the worst part is?" I stared blankly as I couldn't possibly believe there was something worse.

"He's getting married to this woman. They are getting married, and they are going to go on and live their happy life while he left us bleeding. He's going to go off while we are here suffering. They are going to get married and probably have a kid and he's going to live a whole new different life and forget about me. I'm going to be nothing to him. My mom and I are going to be a memory of a life he used to know. He's a liar. He never even cared about us. He never even cared about me."

She put her hands over her face and continued to sob. Her dad caused all this damaged and he didn't even care. He messed up Vienna's whole life and all he could do is just sit back and watch. No wonder why Vienna didn't believe in love. What she was going through was an awful thing to experience. Even though my parents had a great relationship, I could just imagine what it would be like if I found out my dad did something that terrible. This wasn't even just about Vienna, but her mom as well. How could her dad do that to her mom and turn his back on a woman he's been married to for that long? Did he have no consideration? Did he have no heart?

And then there was the woman. The home wrecker who caused all the problems. I knew Vienna's father was to blame in all of this, but she wasn't any better. How could she live with herself going for a married man who had a daughter? How could she be alright with ruining a family? After hearing everything, there was nothing I wanted to do more than to fix this situation. To take all of Vienna's pain and hurt away. There was something I had to do.

"Well, maybe there is a way you can stop him. Maybe you can go after him and beg him to come back. Maybe he will stop the wedding if you tell him how you feel." I suggested. There had to be a way. "I'm not the kind that leaves. I'm the kind that gets left behind." She simply stated. I was trying to help but it seemed like she didn't care much. Didn't she want to try to get him back?

"But you miss him." I said, trying to convince her. She chuckled and shook her head. "How could you miss someone you didn't even really know?" I couldn't argue with that. Vienna's father was a liar and a traitor. He lied so much to them that they didn't even know the real him. He had a whole other secret life. It was sad to think that his own family was his secondary life while the other woman was his primary life. I couldn't leave Vienna like this though, and I wanted everything to be okay. I wished I could fix it, but I didn't know how. I couldn't believe Vienna accepted the fact that everything was over, and she had given up. She was never one to back down, but she already gave in to the fact that everything was torn apart. I wanted Vienna to be okay. I wanted her dad to come back and for it to work out with her parents so they could be a family. I wanted it to work out for Vienna because she deserved it. I tried harder to persuade her.

"But you are sad about him. Don't you want him back?" She seemed furious but not at me, at the situation. She seemed frustrated as she tried to explain to me, but I clearly wasn't understanding. She tried to get through to me. "Just because you're sad about someone, doesn't mean you want them back." I am sad to say that I couldn't relate. I was sad about Sebastian when we weren't friends and I wanted him back. I was sad about my grandpa passing away and I wanted him back. But unlike Vienna's father, they didn't betray me. And for that, I could understand why she didn't want him back. He betrayed her and her mom, and that action didn't deserve a gateway back into their lives.

"I would say I want the old him back, but that wasn't the real him either. He wasn't who I thought he was, so I don't want him back." I finally understood where Vienna was coming from. I never dealt with a situation like this, so I didn't know how to react. I felt bad for being insensitive and trying to convince her to beg her dad back. Her dad didn't deserve her or her mom. He didn't deserve them begging him back or their forgiveness. They were better off without him.

"Vienna, I am completely sorry. I had no idea what you were going through. I understand why you did everything and acted the way you did. I would have done the same thing. I know why you didn't want to tell anyone either. That's something really personal and private. I am so glad you told Sebastian though. I am not mad at you for anything. I have never experienced a situation like this before and I didn't mean to be insensitive. What your dad did was inexcusable and doesn't deserve your forgiveness. You and your mom will get on fine without him. You both are so strong and independent, and you don't need him. I know it hurts now, but it will get better. I know it will. You have me here to support you and I'm not going anywhere. You also have Sebastian and Embry. I am not going to let you fall, I promise. I'm going to be there for whatever you need. I am going to help you get through this." I said as I held her hands. She was still looking down and crying. I was not going to let Vienna sink into a deep depression like I did. It's such a scary thing to go through and I wasn't going to let that happen to her. "That's another reason why I came here." She said as she wiped her tears and pulled away from me. I looked at her confused. "I don't want your help. My life is a complicated mess. I'm going through a lot right now and the last thing I want to do is drag you into it. Not just you, but the guys too. I've been dealing with stuff with my mom. I've even been having to take care of her because she's falling apart. She's a mess and she's been dealing with her own depression while trying to get the divorce papers finalized since it's a long process. I've been dealing with all of this, and I don't think I can be the friend you want me to be. I can't really be there for you. I don't want you to try and fix everything because it can't be fixed. I can't be fixed. I think it's best if we aren't friends anymore."

The pain of her words hurt me more than anything had in a long time. "What? How could you even say that?" I began to frantically ramble on, and she cut me off. "Morgan, you need to understand. I don't want to hold you back. Trust me, you'll be fine without me. The last thing you need is a friend like me moping around. I want you to enjoy your life. Look at you, you are doing great. You found happiness and love with Sebastian. You found real and true love. That's something that's rare and that you have to hold onto."

"Yeah, and it's all because of you. You were the one to help us. We only got together because of you." I interrupted.

"I really appreciate that. At least I did something right. But look at all the pain I caused you already. I lied and I really hurt you. I don't want to do that again. It can't continue like this. So just go on and be with Sebastian because you deserve it. That's why I left the sign there for you. You guys are in love and need to be together. Don't let me hold you back from your great new life filled with amazing opportunities. You are going to make it so far. You are talented, beautiful, and kind. You have a great soul, and you are so patient. You are a far better person than I am. I just..... I don't deserve a friend like you. I'm sorry, Morgan."

She began crying hard again and I couldn't believe what was occurring. I witnessed history repeating itself before my eyes. I watched as I saw myself in Vienna. It was me with Sebastian all over again after my grandpa's accident. I didn't want Sebastian's help or comfort, so I pushed him away. Though what Vienna and I had gone through was different, we had the same reaction to it.

It didn't matter the difference between death and divorce, it was all the same to me. People still grieved the same way. You couldn't compare because each situation was different in their own ways. Still, the pain hurt the same.

My grandpa was gone but then again, her dad was gone too, just in a different way. It was both someone we looked up to and we were close with. Both people we missed but couldn't get back. I knew how hard it was to deal with that pain. Vienna and I had the same defense mechanism of shutting everyone out. I wasn't going to let her do what I did and make the same mistakes. I had to get through and talk to her before she did something she would regret. "Vienna, please don't do this. I'm your best friend and that's what best friends are for. They are there for the highs and the lows. I'm going to be there for you. Of course, I will give you your space and your time because you need it. I know what it's like to grieve. I don't know exactly what you are going through, but I know what the pain is like. I went through it with my grandpa.

I went into a deep depression and shut everyone out. I pushed away Sebastian who was my best friend because I thought it would be for the best. I learned over time that it wasn't worth it. I lost everything. I lost my best friend, theatre, my old life, and myself. I'm not going to let you lose yourself. I didn't talk to Sebastian for two years and I always regretted it. I mean, look at the way things turned out. If it wasn't for you, we wouldn't even be together right now." She sniffed and nodded slowly. She looked at me closely as I continued.

"I won't let you throw away this friendship. I'll give you time and space to heal. Healing takes time. Everything gets better with time. It's like when you get a cut. Some cuts are small and painless. You hardly notice them, and they will fade faster.

Others are deep and more painful. They might even leave a scar and it will take longer to fade. But the important thing is that it will heal. It heals and then you are just left with the memories of only when it used to hurt. I know that you are going to get through this. You know how I know? Because I did and I can help you. You need a friend to help you get through it. I know you are feeling this way right now and you don't want to be friends, but I'm not giving up on you. Take the time you need, and I'll be here waiting for you."

She gave me a huge smile and looked at me sincerely. "Morgan, you are the best. How did I get so lucky with a best friend like you? You are right, I need my best friend by my side to get through this. I can't do it alone. I'll be fine as long as you are here by my side. It's so crazy, I felt so helpless. Like everything was just so wrong and there was no way out. It's like I couldn't see out and there was no bright side or solution to this. But everything is going to be okay, isn't it?" She said in a hopeful tone. "It is."

We wrapped each other up in a hug. We stayed like that for a long time, holding on tightly for support. I liked to think that we were each other's anchors. Before Vienna came, I never had experienced a friendship quite like ours. I had Sebastian, but this friendship was something different. It came unexpectedly and just when I needed it the most. I always thought Vienna and I were so different but really, we were the same. Vienna and I just wanted true happiness. A happiness that wasn't defined by our pasts. We deserved that and now I finally felt like we had that. We had each other, Sebastian, and Embry. With great friends, that's all we ever needed. We pulled apart from our hug and realization struck her.

"Aren't you supposed to be somewhere?" She asked. I smiled at her and got up from my seat, wiping my own tears from my face. We walked to our cars parked in front of my house. I was about to go in my car and then I stopped. "Vienna!" I called. She opened her car door and looked up. "You are welcome at my house anytime. Aaron and I are here for you." She smiled and laughed before getting into her car.

Chapter 24

I got in my car and headed to the auditorium. I drove as fast as I could and hoped Sebastian was still there. I ran to the theatre, and it was strange being there on a weekend. The door was opened, and I peeked inside. I looked around at the empty theatre. It was strange to see it so open and not filled with my castmates. Everything was still on the stage from rehearsals. The atmosphere felt different with the empty seats and deafening silence. I was so used to walking in and seeing it so lively with my castmates being so loud and chattering about. It felt very....lonely. I realized that the theatre couldn't be alive without the people who made it that way.

The theatre needed the presence of actors and the audience to cheer them on. I hesitantly walked inside, and I saw him on the illuminated stage. He sat at the edge of the stage with his feet dangling. His head was down as he stared down at his feet. I never seen him look so sad and lonely before. He looked so empty inside and that's not how Sebastian was. He was always so lively. Of course, I had seen him sad before, but this was a different kind of sadness. I guessed there was this whole other side I had never seen of him. I felt this gnawing pain as I thought that's how he must have been when we stopped being friends. I thought about how I was a depressed mess and never thought to consider that Sebastian was probably the same. I never really thought about how it affected him when we stopped being friends too. I knew it was a side of him that he would never let me see.

He was always the strong one who hid how he felt. He was pretty vulnerable and in touch with his feelings, but he never showed when things truly hurt him. And I knew I hurt him. He didn't notice I walked in at first, but then the door made a creaking noise. He looked up, startled. He squinted as I probably just appeared as a figure to him. I walked closer to where the seats were, and he looked at me with wide eyes. Seeing him there, he looked so handsome under the lights of the stage and seeing the look on his face when he saw me made my heart melt. I didn't have any plan or guide to go by, so I decided to just listen to my heart. Whatever I felt, I was going to say it. "I love you, Sebastian!" I called out. I felt so silly just yelling it out like that, but it was no time to mess around. I was done with hiding and not saying how I felt. I needed to be exactly who I was. I didn't want fear to control the rest of my life. It's so hard being vulnerable, even to someone you loved. They know how you feel about them, but it's still scary. It's one thing to show them how you feel and another to say it. It's a different side that's lets them see all your broken pieces. I wasn't ashamed or afraid because it was Sebastian. Sebastian who I knew since I was seven years old and who I was in love with. He stared at me, and I walked up the stairs to meet him.

"I have loved you since we were seven years old, and I never stopped loving you since. I loved you when we weren't friends because even when we weren't together, you never left me. I never felt like this before and it's a feeling that can't be described in any other way. I didn't know anything about love when I was younger, but I saw it with my parents. I saw how they were, and I just knew I wanted that with you. You are the one I want to have a future with and grow old with. You are the only person, and you always will be. You make me laugh so hard, you are so optimistic, you are insanely talented, you wipe my tears when I cry, and you are just an amazing person. You know me probably better than I know myself. You know all my weird habits, my good days, and my bad days. You know my insecurities and you like them anyway. I get so excited to wake up just to see you and talk to you. We have the best and sometimes weirdest conversations about anything. Whenever I see you and you look at me, I just smile. I just love you, Sebastian. I never stopped even with our stupid fight we had. Vienna explained everything and I'm just so sorry. I'm sorry I would even think you would do something horrible. Everything just got so messed up and misunderstood. I'm so sorry for everything. I don't know what the future will look like, but I want to be by your side every step of the way. I want to be by your side in theatre up on this stage next to you as Audrey. I want to be by your side as your girlfriend."

I took a breath to pause after getting everything out. It was so overwhelming, and I felt like I said everything in one breath. Sebastian and I had been through so much and our relationship was not easy. Everything we had been through and all the obstacles we faced were so challenging. But Sebastian deserved to know how I felt about him. Everything I had ever felt since the beginning I just displayed with my words. I also had to apologize to him with everything with Vienna. I was so mentally and physically exhausted. With Vienna and Sebastian in the same morning, it was enough to make my head spin. I looked up to see him staring deep into my eyes. He was teary eyed, but I knew it was from happiness. He seemed overwhelmed with emotion. He smiled softly at me.

"I love you too, Morgan. I always have and I always will." He pulled me in and kissed me. It was so crazy how I felt with

Sebastian. He was my safe place and my home. In his arms, I knew everything was going to be okay. It *was* finally okay. No more problems with the past and no more hiding.

"I'm so sorry about what I said about you pushing me away. I couldn't believe I said that. Afterwards, I immediately regretted it. I should have talked to you and apologized but I thought I messed up so much that it was no use. I was just under so much pressure with keeping Vienna's secret. I hated lying to you more than anything, but she made me promise not to tell you. I wanted to tell you, but it wasn't my place. Once Embry knew, I knew I had to tell you, but it was never the right time. I was afraid to even speak to you because I knew how mad you were at me. I'm just so sorry for how everything happened." He said as he held onto my hands. He squeezed them as if he were in pain reliving that day.

"No Seb, it's okay. We all did and said some horrible things. I just came back from talking to Vienna and she explained everything. We are okay now." "How is she doing?" He asked nervously. "She was shaken up, but we had a long talk. I think she's going to be okay." I said happily. "Of course, she is, she has you." He said. "No, she has all of us." He nodded in agreement.

"I know the path that got us here has been a bumpy one, but I'm ready to take it with you. Wherever this journey takes us, I'm here for it. No more fear or pushing away. Just complete and total honesty from here on out. If something is bothering us, we need to say it and communicate with one another. We need to be there and support each other." I stated. "That's all I ever wanted. All my life I dreamed about being with you. I'm ready to start. I love you, Tink." He said. "Now, let's get going. Tomorrow is our only day off before dress rehearsal." He said as he turned to get his things. An idea occurred to me at that moment. "Actually, there's something I want to do tomorrow." He looked at me suspiciously.

The next day I contacted Sebastian, Vienna, and Embry to gather outside of my house. "Well, this is unexpected but I'm glad I'm here. I missed you, Morgan." Embry told me. "I missed you too." I said as I was touched by his words. I gave him a hug since it was the first time I had seen him with everything that had happened. I was glad everything was okay now, and we were all together. "So, why so unexpected? What's this about?" Vienna wondered. "Yeah, what's up, Tink?" Seb asked. "I'm going to take you all somewhere special. I want you guys to get to know more about me. I want to tell you guys the truth about everything."

They all gave each other puzzled looks. I laughed at their expressions. "Come on, get in the car." As I was driving closer to our destination, Sebastian started to recognize the familiar road of where we were heading. "I know where we are going!" He stated proudly. "Where?" Vienna and Embry said in unison from the back seat. "You'll see." As I drove up the road, it was clear where we were. I felt Seb look at me from my peripheral vision and he grabbed my hand. "I'm proud of you." He whispered. I saw Vienna look at me from my mirror and I nodded at her. Embry looked out the window surprised.

We got off and headed for my grandpa's grave. We walked up the hill in the patchy grass and I saw as Embry offered his hand to Vienna as she was struggling in her combat boots. She took it. We made it to his grave and I felt nervous. "Vienna and Embry, this is my grandpa. He was the one who got me into theatre and taught me everything about acting. He was my best friend, and we did everything together. Unfortunately, he died in a terrible accident. I wasn't okay for a long time, but over time I got better." I looked at Sebastian as he smiled at me. I continued to go on. "I learned that even though he isn't here physically with me, he is still here with me. He will always be here with me. He looks down on me. He protects me and guides me. I come here once a week and talk to him. I talk to him about anything and everything. I talk to him and tell him about what's going on in my life. I talk to him about you guys." Vienna looked at me and got teary eyed.

"He was such a great person who loved life. He was so full of life and joy. He never gave up even when times were tough. I wish you knew him and could have met him, but this is a way. I invite you guys to talk to him and say a few words. Don't be shy." I insisted. Vienna and Embry both stood nervously. Vienna looked a little anxious, but I saw the shift in her face as she became brave. She swallowed hard before speaking.

"Hello, I'm Vienna. I'm Morgan's best friend. It's been so great being friends with her and getting to know her. She's an insanely talented actor and I know she learned all of it from you. Even though I never met you, I can see you through Morgan. She's told me about you, and I feel like I know you. You seemed like a great person. I promise to be the best friend I could to your granddaughter." I let the tears stream down my face without wiping them away. I looked up to see Seb had tears of his own. He sniffed and wiped then away. "Thanks Vienna." I gave her a big hug. Embry was up next.

"Hi, I'm Embry. It's been a pleasure knowing Morgan. She has become a really good friend of mine. She's really thoughtful and kindhearted. She's always been there for me and gives great advice. You have a pretty cool granddaughter." He said. I went over and gave him a hug. "Thanks Embry." We all stood there side by side staring at my grandpa's grave. Sebastian looped his arm through mine and I did the same with Vienna who did the same to Embry. We stood there next to each other in perfect silence, and I put my head on Sebastian's shoulder and sighed.

On the car ride home, I told Vienna and Embry what really happened with my grandpa. I told them about the accident with the treehouse. I didn't cry like I thought I was when I told Sebastian, but instead I slowly explained to them the situation. It got easier as I told them the story and I watched as they both cried. I felt bad telling them all the horrific details, but they needed to know. They knew the truth and there were truly no more secrets between us.

They sympathized with me, and I felt closer to them as I shared with them a part of my life that was hard. That's how it needed to be with friends. After Vienna told me what happened with her dad, I realized that you didn't just need to show your friends the glamorized parts of you. You needed to be vulnerable with them so they could be vulnerable with you. You needed to earn each other's trust. Friendship wasn't always just about the good and happy side of things, but it was about being there through the hardships. And Vienna and Embry sympathized with me as I told them about the greatest hardship in my life.

Chapter 25

Dress rehearsal the next day was so intense. I walked into the auditorium with everyone running around trying to get everything done. I saw Mr. Baldwin get into crazy dress rehearsal mode and I had never seen him this stressed. He was yelling at everyone to get into their places and do their jobs. He wanted to make sure everything was great with the sound and ready to go since technical difficulties were always a pain. Sebastian, Vienna, Embry, and I all walked up to Mr. Baldwin on stage.

"Okay guys, no messing around today. This is it; we are doing the full run through of the show as if it were really happening. Vienna, do you have the costumes?" He panicked. "Of course, I do." She replied nonchalantly.

"Great. Get everyone their costumes immediately and make sure they go to their dressing rooms and get ready."

"Got it." Vienna turned to get the costumes and we all turned to follow her. I headed after her until Mr. Baldwin stopped me.

"So, it looks like everything worked out, didn't it?" He said as he smiled at me. I was so thankful to have such a great mentor like Mr. Baldwin. If it wasn't for his pep talk, I wouldn't have realized so many things about myself and my relationship with Sebastian and Vienna. "Yeah, it did. Thank you, Mr. Baldwin. I really owe you." He gave me a hug and I felt like he was another father figure to me. He had watched me grow these past months and really taught me a lot. He cared about me not only as an actor, but as a person. "Just go out there and make me proud." I nodded. I would go out there and do my best on that stage. "Now, go get ready."

I headed back with Vienna and then and she handed us our costumes. They were all covered up like she just got them back from the dry cleaner. I couldn't see them all too well, but I was so excited for us to all actually see each other wearing them for the first time. We usually practiced with some or half of the accessories from the costumes. Sebastian usually just wore Seymour's glasses and a sweater vest, and Embry wore a leather jacket. It took a lot of time up to get fully ready in regular rehearsals, but this time we had to go all out. "Here you go." She said as she handed us our costumes. "This is so exciting." Embry said as he ran to his dressing room. Sebastian held onto his costume excitedly. "See you in a minute, Audrey." Sebastian said as he winked at me. I headed to my dressing room and transformed into character.

We all came out and looked astonished at one another. "Oh my gosh! Look at you." We told each other. "Wow, you look amazing!" Sebastian said as he twirled me. "Wow, you look just like Seymour." I said to Sebastian "Woah Embry, you look great!" I said. Vienna came over and clapped her hands together. "You all look fantastic! Even you, Embry." She commented. "Get used to it, baby." He said he did a hair flip. "You did a great job with the costumes." Sebastian told her as he adjusted his glasses. "Thanks!"

The freshman came up to us with her camera and looked with wide eyes. "Woah, I love the costumes!" She said as she observed us. "You look great too!" I told her. She was dressed in her hobo outfit, and she looked so adorable. "Can I get a behind the scenes picture of you guys?" "Sure." We all said as we huddled in. "Get in there too, Vienna. We need to see the genius behind the costumes." The freshman said. Vienna smiled as she got in the picture with us. "Say, dress rehearsal!" The bright flash from the camera blinded me.

At the end of dress rehearsal, Mr. Baldwin gathered the whole cast together on stage. We were all huddled in a huge circle as he gave a speech. "Tomorrow is the big day. It's opening night and it's showtime. Once those curtains open up tomorrow, it's your job to show that audience the hard work you've been doing these past months. Make it count and most importantly, have fun. I just wanted to say thank you for all the hard work you all have done. It hasn't been easy coming to rehearsals every day, but you have shown up and put in everything you got. Get some rest, get plenty of sleep, and stay hydrated. I want to see you all here two hours before the show starts to run over some things and get ready. I know you guys will get the jitters, but it's normal. You all have proved that this is going to be an amazing show. Let's show the audience a good time tomorrow and take them to the *Little Shop of Horrors*!" Everyone cheered with excitement. "Okay everyone, hands together!" We all gathered close and put our hands on top of one another. "*Little Shop of Horrors*!" We said as we all lifted our hands up.

We walked out of rehearsal for the last time all together. The whole cast got pretty emotional as it was our last official rehearsal together. Sebastian, Vienna, Embry, and I all looked at one another. "This is it." Embry said in a bittersweet tone. "I'll see you guys tomorrow." I said. I walked hand in hand with Sebastian as I waved Vienna and Embry goodbye. "Tomorrow, we officially become Seymour and Audrey." Seb said as walked out. "Tomorrow, we officially do our first play together in two years." I said, shocked. It was so crazy to believe that I would be performing in front of an audience again. "Just like old times. Let's go out there and show them what we got!" I couldn't be more thrilled.

I got home, and I plopped onto the couch from tiredness. "How was dress rehearsal?" My mom asked. "Exhausting but successful." I said as I took off my shoes and rubbed my feet. "Isn't it always?" My dad laughed. "I can't believe the show is already tomorrow." I shook my head in disbelief. So much had happened in the last few months that completely changed my life and now tomorrow was the opening night of the play. Where had all the time gone?

That was the tricky thing about time, it either moved too fast or too slow. It usually moved slow in the moments you wanted to forget. The moments where it seemed time would never move again, and you just wanted to move on. The happy moments came in a blink of an eye that you really had to capture it to enjoy it. "I can't believe we will be seeing you on stage after all this time. I never thought you would be on stage again. We are proud of you, Morgan. I mean, look at what you have accomplished. You made a new friend, you got back into theatre, and you mended your friendship with Sebastian. I remember a few months ago that seemed impossible to you. You did it all on your own out of your own will. You wanted change and you made it happen. You really put yourself out there even when it was hard." My mom said. "Your grandpa would be so proud of you." My dad chimed in.

I looked at them as they were staring back at me with tears in their eyes. It was that moment when I realized how truly lucky I was. I never realized that I was privileged to have parents who loved me and loved each other. We lived in a nice home, we all got along, and they truly believed in me. They were the best parents I could ever have. I would never take them for granted again because unfortunately, some people weren't that lucky. I knew Vienna would tell me to hold onto them and to appreciate them. And that's what I planned on doing for the rest of my days. "I never properly thanked you guys for everything. You guys are the best parents anyone could ever have. You always had a great relationship and showed me what love is. You showed me to be kind to others and be selfless. You taught me to follow my dreams. You guys always supported my decision in going into a career in theatre even though it's hard to pursue. You showed me hard work and perseverance. You guys pulled me out of the darkness of my depression and brought me back to being myself. I have the best parents in the world. I love you guys." I rushed over and squeezed myself between them.

We were all a sobbing mess as we held onto each other. "We love you too." They said. We broke away and chuckled at how we all looked. "Okay, that's enough being dramatic for today. Save the drama for the stage." My dad said. I laughed as I wiped my tears away. "Go get some sleep." My mom said. I kissed them goodnight and ran upstairs. I got into my pajamas and into my nightly routine. I laid out my costume and fixed everything for tomorrow so it could be ready. I tried to find my character shoes everywhere, but they seemed to have disappeared.

I looked all around, and I couldn't find them. I realized I probably shoved them under my bed, so I lifted the covers to look. I rummaged through old trinkets and boxes. The box with all the old photos of Sebastian and I flew out. I rolled my eyes as I cleaned the mess and began packing the belongings back inside. I flipped through all the old photos of Sebastian and I. I smiled looking at them all. We were so young then and so passionate about theatre. Who knew we would end up where we were today? There were more photos underneath and they were of my grandpa. I held my breath and I looked at the photos.

I hadn't seen photos of him in a long time, but they actually didn't make me sad like I thought. There were photos of us when I was little doing different activities. There were some of us seeing plays and some of me playing dress up at his house. There were a lot of pictures of us after my plays. I saw one that immediately caught my eye. It was the last picture of us together. It was a picture of us after *Peter Pan*. In the picture, we stood side by side as I held flowers in my hand that he gave me. I held the picture in my hand and felt something lumpy taped in the back.

I unfolded it to find a letter. It was a letter from my grandpa that he had written me that he gave me the day before the opening night of *Peter Pan*. I had completely forgotten all about that letter and what it said. I let out a deep breath as I opened it up. I saw his familiar scratchy handwriting and I immediately felt closer to him just seeing it without reading it. I carefully began to read it as it said:

Dear Morgan,

Congratulations! I can't believe opening night is tomorrow. You have made it so far and I am so proud of you. You have put in a lot of hard work into this play. I have seen that every day you have practiced until you got better and better. I know you and Sebastian will put on a great show. It's been a pleasure seeing you follow in my footsteps. As a boy growing up in Texas, I dreamed about doing theatre. Every day, I would work at the movies and would look up at the screen and dreamed about being there one day. It's been so great to share my love of theatre with you. You are an amazing actor and I believe you will make it far

265

in your theatre career. Now, I know you tend to doubt and second guess yourself. Don't let fear get the best of you. As an actor, it's best not to be too much in your head. You just have to go out there and do your best. You have to feel the character and soon you will become them. I know you don't have any lines in this play, but just remember that there are no small parts, just small actors. Go out there and break a leg! I'll be watching you like I always am in that audience. I'll be cheering you on always. I know you will do great tonight. Remember to always be true yourself and never give up the ship.

Love, grandpa.

I began shaking and crying. It was ironic to find the letter again during this time. It was just what I needed the most and I knew my grandpa was watching over me. He put that letter in my path as a reminder. A reminder to never give up. Never give up acting and doing what I loved. Never give up being myself. Tomorrow was opening night and I knew he would be there cheering me on like he always was. I held the letter close to my chest and closed my eyes. "Thank you, grandpa. This one is for you."

Chapter 26

The time had finally come, and it was opening night. Vienna came to my house early to help me with hair and makeup. "Hey Vienna!" My parents said. They both gave her a hug and it was nice to see the kind gesture. She seemed really pleased and happy. "Hi, Mr. and Mrs. Hathaway." She said. "Oh, we are so excited to finally see the play!" My mom squealed. "You guys will love it. I've been watching them all these months and Morgan is fantastic." She said as she turned to me. "Well, we can't wait. I also can't wait to see the rest of the costumes you did for the play."   My dad said. I was anxious at them rambling on to her because I had to get ready. "Okay, that's enough. I really have to get ready." I said as I took Vienna by the hand and ran upstairs.

She did my makeup and put my hair into tight curls so it could look shorter. I observed myself in the mirror as I was Morgan disguised as Audrey. My blonde hair was in curls and the fitting black dress looked perfect on me. It was funny how I felt like Audrey the whole time I acted in rehearsals, but it wasn't until I got into costume where I truly felt like I became her. "Wow, you didn't tell me you were a hair and makeup artist too." I commented. "I try my best." She replied. "So, how are you feeling? Are you ready for this?" She asked nervously.

It was weird to be in a costume again and getting ready for a show, but it was like second nature to me. "I have never been more ready for anything more in my life. This is what I was meant to do. It's where I belong." No words spoken were ever more true. For two years I avoided going on stage, but now I was itching to get back.

"I've been watching you this whole time and you are going to do amazing. I can't wait to see you light up that stage. I'll be there backstage cheering you on like I always am." She said. I got emotional thinking back to my grandpa's letter. "Don't get emotional, you will ruin your makeup." She laughed. I blinked a few times and took a deep breath. "Okay, let's get going."

We walked into the theatre and the whole show came to life. Everyone was dressed in their costumes and the set was all ready to go. It looked like we got transported into the movie with the set of Skid Row and everyone dressed up in their parts. I saw as the freshmen were all dressed up like homeless people and they all chattered about excitedly. It was so crowded, and we tried to find Sebastian and Embry. We pushed through everyone in the crowd and made some small talk with some of our castmates. The nice freshman came up to us. She looked so cute in her costume and her makeup even looked like she had dirt on herself. "Morgan, you look so beautiful!" She said. "Thank you! You look great too." I replied. "Wow, I hope one day I can be in your position." She said. "You will, trust me. It takes a long time and hard work, but you will get there." I winked at her. She smiled widely at me and nodded.

Just then I saw Sebastian and Embry walk through the crowd. We caught sight of each other and tried to push our way through the many people there. As soon as it was clear, we all ran up to each other. "Oh wow!" Vienna said as she saw them. It was the first time seeing each other in full costume and makeup. Sebastian looked amazing and looked just like Seymour. Embry looked unrecognizable in his white long shirt and leather jacket. He had his hair greased and styled for the part. "Morgan, you look stunning. I mean, you look exactly like Audrey." Seb told me. "Yes, you fit the part!" Embry said. "Look at you, guys! Embry, I didn't even recognize you!" I exclaimed. We all talked excitedly until we heard Mr. Baldwin's loud voice on stage.

"Is everyone ready to put on a show?" Everyone cheered loudly. "Okay, then everyone gather on stage!" Everyone rapidly made their way on stage, and we formed our usual circle. "Let's do some warmups to get all the jitters out. Embry, would you like to lead us?" Mr. Baldwin asked. "I'd be happy to Mr. B!" Embry took the lead as he led us into some vocal exercises and physical exercises. He began stretching and moving his hips as if he were dancing. "It's all in the hips. Just be loose and let it all out." He said and everyone started laughing.

Soon, we were all copying his crazy moves. Everyone laughed and was having a great time. I saw as Mr. Baldwin smiled at all of us and I realized he chose Embry to get everyone pumped up. It was easy to get stage fright, so it was best to just let go and have fun. "Okay everyone, the show is going to start really soon. Let's huddle up." Mr. Baldwin huddled us all up together and we were all tightly together with our heads down.

"I am very proud of each and every one you. From the leads, to the stagehands, and the tech team. Each of you had a big part in this play and tonight it will be showcased. I know it's been a tiring few months, but tonight it will all be worth it. The audience is waiting out there for you guys. Some will be family, friends, and others will be complete strangers. No matter what happens, I just want you guys to go out there and do your best. Show them what you have been doing in rehearsals this whole time. Show them a great time and a great show. Now, all hands together."

We all put our hands out together for the last time. "This is the opening night, so let's make it count. Ready...." "*Little Shop of Horrors*!" We all shouted when we lifted our hands up. "Okay everyone, get into your positions!"

Everyone ran off to get into their spot for the opening. "I won't be seeing you much since there will be a lot of running around back here. I'm mostly just here if anyone has a wardrobe malfunction, but if you need anything just say the word." Vienna told me. "Okay." I said anxiously. She went up to me and put her hands on my shoulders. "You got this." She said as she looked deep into my eyes. I took a deep breath.

"I'll be right back here watching you."

"Thanks Vienna." I gave her a quick hug then ran and got into position.

I met with Sebastian as we stood in our spot waiting. As we were standing there, I was starting to feel nervous. "Are you okay?" Seb asked me. "Yeah, just a bit nervous." I admitted. "It's going to be okay. I'll be up there with you. All those years of doing theatre together, let's show them what we got!" He said as he was hyping me up. It worked and I was getting excited. "Just like old times. Another one for the road." I said. "Whatever happens up there just know that I'm already so proud of you and I love you." I couldn't help but feel knots in my stomach. I would be safe as long as I was with him up there on that stage. He would be there to help me and guide me. He wouldn't let me fall.

"I love you too." We leaned in to kiss, but then I stopped. "Let's save that for the stage." I chuckled. "Good call." He replied. Backstage turned completely dark, and the show was going to start at any moment. "Let's do this Seymour." I whispered. "Break a leg, Audrey."

The first notes of the "Prologue" played from the loud music.
The sound of the drums reverberated all through the theatre. The
whole audience erupted in cheer. I smiled to myself from
backstage. I loved hearing that sound and it never got old. The
lights began to flash wildly onstage, and Mr. Baldwin's voice
came through in the mic. Mr. Baldwin had the small part of
playing the narrator and I had heard him rehearse it a few times
before. He disguised his voice by projecting a deep and
mysterious tone. He sounded really cool and different as he
began to narrate the prologue.

"On the twenty-first day of the month of September in an
early year of a decade not too long before our own, the human
race suddenly encountered a deadly threat to its very existence.
And this terrifying enemy surfaced as such enemies often do, in
the seemingly most innocent and unlikely of places."

The drums began and the triplets all came out. The crowd
cheered and whistled excitedly. The triplets looked amazing with
their updo hairstyles and blue sparkly dresses. I listened as they
always blew me away with their ability to harmonize perfectly
and to have perfect pitch. They belted out singing with their
soulful voices. There were no other people who could have
played the part more perfectly.

"Little shop, little shop of horrors. Little shop, little shop of
terror. Call a cop, little shop of horrors. No, oh, oh, no, oh!" They
sang as they danced in perfect synchronicity.

I bopped along and silently sang along backstage. Next up
was the big number with every single person in the cast.
"Downtown" was my absolute favorite part of the play. The

whole cast was up on stage, and we all sang our hearts out. It was a really hard number to pull off with each person having their spots, but it was the most fun to do. I watched as the freshman came out of the trash can and I silently clapped at her moment. Next it was my part in the song.

As soon as I got up there and sang, the nerves all melted away inside of me. Once on stage, there was no time to feel nervous because of the job and duty I had. I had to play the part and I couldn't let the audience down. Muscle memory kicked in as I sang my lines. I heard cheering and I knew it was parents. Once my small solo was done, Sebastian was next on stage as he sang his part. I couldn't help but fawn over his talent. He we so natural and he really got into it. I kept yelling in my mind to look depressed and sad as I was singing.

We were all miserable and hopeless people who lived on Skid Row, but inside I was having the time of my life being on stage again. Mine and Sebastian's part led over the background, and it all came together to blend perfectly. Our voices matched together in perfect harmony. It felt like I was transported back to when I was seven years old performing with Sebastian for the first time. The energy was as alive and electric as it was back then but this time, it was more meaningful. It was like suddenly I knew why I had to go through everything. I had to go through all the bad and awful things to appreciate this small moment being here on stage with Sebastian. If it wasn't for the hard times, I would have taken it for granted. It would have just been another time of me being on stage and performing. But this time Seb and I were together, and I had the best friend ever watching me from backstage. I felt the energy from everyone on stage as everyone gave it their all. We all fed off the vibe of the audience, who made us strive to do our best and put on a great show. When the song was finished, the crowd went wild. It was by far the best we had ever done.

The show went on smoothly for the rest of the night. I enjoyed being on stage and getting to play Audrey and when I wasn't on stage, I got to sit backstage and watch. I enjoyed the times I got to rest backstage because it gave me a chance to relax and take it all in. I got to see Sebastian's solo with Audrey II, and he did way better than he ever had in rehearsals as he got down on his knees and begged for the plant to grow. After his solo, I was up next for my solo. I was so nervous to sing "Somewhere That's Green", but I tried not to think about it as I went to my mark on stage. I completely went into Audrey's mind so I could perform my best.

The set was decorated as a house, and I stared into the mirror of Audrey's room as I did my part. The triplets were amazing as always as they delivered their lines. With us acting together, everything was turning out great.

As I finished my lines and was getting ready to sing, I suddenly was aware as I felt the bright light on me. The light wasn't coming from the lights on the stage though, I knew they were coming from my grandpa. I felt his presence as he was watching over me and cheering me on. The light coming off from the stage suddenly radiated through me. I got really into the character and felt every emotion. I let it all out and my singing came out beautifully. As I was singing, I interacted with some of the audience as I acted. Audrey was telling the story of this beautiful place that she dreamed of where she wished she would go. A place where nothing bad could happen and where she could live her days with Seymour. As I was singing, I felt like the song represented me. I always longed for that place, but I didn't realize the obstacles I had to go through to get there. But now I finally made it to that place, and it was beautiful.

I looked out into the audience. The audience was very dark, and I could only see the first few rows. In the first row was a little girl with her parents. She was about seven years old, and she stared at me with gleaming eyes. She watched me perform and I couldn't help but smile at her. She seemed very engrossed in the story of the play, and she watched excitedly. I knew that look on her face. It was the same look I had when I would watch plays. The look of finding something you loved and your passion. It was the glimmer of hope that anything was possible, and you could accomplish your dreams.

The rest of the time was great. The audience was so lively and reacted to everything. The audience completely loved Embry's solo and he went all out. Embry thrived off the attention and his portrayal of The Dentist was both comedic and terrifyingly scary. I enjoyed my parts with him because he was a great actor and a joy to work with. Embry and I couldn't keep it together in rehearsals and we tried to keep it together and not laugh on stage.

Sebastian's solo with the enormous Audrey II puppet came up and the audience all laughed. I was so nervous to work with the puppet and fall inside, but luckily all the training and trust falls was worth it. Some little kids in the audience shouted every time someone would fall into the puppets mouth. The play was almost at its end and" Suddenly Seymour" came on and I was getting butterflies. I felt extremely awkward at having to kiss Sebastian in front of an audience. I was just glad we practiced with all the people watching us in rehearsal even though it was weird. I was also glad that Sebastian was actually my boyfriend, and I wasn't kissing a stranger. It was the big moment where Audrey and Seymour got together.

We did great with our acting and I really felt the song as I belted. Audrey never had any luck, but she finally landed the guy. The guy who would always be there for her and she didn't have to worry about her painful past. At the end we had our big kiss, and everyone cheered. As soon as the curtain closed, we silently laughed to each other. "That was so weird." He said.

The show was ending, and it was time for the finale. I felt like the show went by so fast and I couldn't believe our first show was already over. Opening night was always the best and the nerves were finally out of the way. As the show ended, it was time for the cast to come up and do our final bows. I always was a fan of the final bows since each person got their moment for the audience to cheer for them. The cast went up one by one and bowed. Embry came out and did a pose before bowing. The whole crowd went crazy for him, and it was clear that The Dentist was a fan favorite.

Lastly, Sebastian and I ran up on stage together to do our final bows. We went up hand in hand and everyone screamed. I watched as we got a standing ovation. We both bowed together, and he gestured to me, and I bowed, and I did the same to him. At the end, the cast all came up together and held hands for our bow. The whole theatre was on their feet as they clapped and whistled for us. The house lights of the theatre were on, and I could finally see the audience.

My parents were in the fourth row, and I watched as they stood up and screamed my name. Sebastian's parents were next to them and screamed his name as well. We both looked at each other and smiled. The curtain closed and the audience continued to cheer. The cast all clapped and cheered from backstage. "That was so great! Great job everyone!" We all said to one another. We all hugged and complimented one another on a great show.

"That was so great you guys! What a way to start opening night!" Mr. Baldwin told us. "You all should be very proud of yourselves. I know I am proud of you all. Now, go home and get some rest. We still have more shows to do!" He laughed.

We all headed back to our dressing rooms to grab our stuff and leave. Once I was done, I headed out to the audience and tried to find my parents. The theatre was a madhouse, and the cast was reuniting with their family and friends. I finally caught sight of Vienna, who was waiting for me. We ran up to each other and she wrapped me up in a big hug.

"Morgan, that was so good! Seriously, you did the best I had ever seen you. You just completely went for it. Your acting and your vocals were so on point!"

"Thanks Vienna." She began talking rapidly as she went on about the rest of the show. I felt arms wrap around me and I knew it was Sebastian. I turned to hug him, and he lifted me off the ground. "Tink, that was so great. You did such a great job. Especially your solo. That was my favorite part." He said. "Thanks Seb. You killed it out there!" I replied. "My favorite was Suddenly Seymour." Vienna commented. Seb and I shook our heads in disagreement.

"The kiss was so weird." We said. Embry appeared and joined us. "I think we all know who the real star of the night was." Seb said as Embry came. "Seriously Embry, the crowd loved you." I stated. "Thanks so much. Also, I'm sorry about that part where I almost tripped you." He said to me. I laughed just thinking about it. "It's okay, I was trying so hard not to lose it." I chuckled. "Yeah, I noticed that!" Vienna said as we all started out laughing. We kept talking about the rest of the show until our parents found us.

"Oh my gosh! That was amazing! I was into the show the whole time, I couldn't look away." My mom said. "Seriously, you all did such a great job. Vienna, the costumes were phenomenal." My dad commented. "Thanks so much." She said. "We are so proud of you, honey." My parents said as they handed me flowers. "These are beautiful! Thanks guys." I said and hugged them. Sebastian's parents came and hugged him.

"I was sitting there next to your parents and the whole time we were just crying. We were a mess." Sebastian's mom told me. "It was very emotional seeing you both up there again." His dad chimed in. Seb and I both laughed. Embry began talking to his parents and Sebastian greeted them. Embry then introduced his parents to us. "This is Morgan and her family, and this is Vienna." "It's nice to meet you both. Vienna you are so pretty!" His mom said. They stared at Vienna who look awkwardly at them. "There you are! I was looking all over for you." Vienna's mom said as she approached us. "The costumes looked so great. And you all did a great job." She said to Sebastian, Embry, and I.

"Guys, this is my mom. Mom this is Embry and Sebastian." They all shook hands and Vienna then turned to my parents. "This is Morgan's parents." "Hi, we are Daniel and Sara. It's so nice to finally meet you." My mom said as she shook Ms. Chamberlain's hand. "It's so great to meet you. Morgan is such a great girl." "Vienna is pretty great too. It's so nice how they became fast friends." My dad said. Soon all our parents began excitedly talking to one another.

Mr. Baldwin came up to our parents and introduced himself. "You all have such talented kids." He said. "Now they are going to go on forever." Embry joked. We all nodded in agreement as we watched them chatter on. "It's sad to think it's almost over though." I said. "I know, I've had so much fun doing this play with you guys." Seb said. "It's okay, we still have more shows to do." Embry replied. We all pondered over the bittersweet moment.

The rest of the shows were great, but nothing compared to opening night. I got more comfortable in my part as repetition made me less nervous. It was nice to have different experiences every night with a new audience. We had great moments backstage with the cast as we did preshow rituals. We all goofed around every night before the show and listened to music and danced to get us hyped for the show. There was many behind the scenes photos and videos all captured by the nice freshman. Finally, it was the last night of the play. It was so surreal how fast it went by, and everything felt like a blur. I thought back to all the rehearsals and how tiring they were.

There were moments where I wanted to quit and give up. Where my eyes would close from exhaustion during rehearsal. All the times we had to wait around due to technical difficulties. The times where my whole body ached, and my feet hurt. It was completely worth it. No matter how tired I got and how much I wished I could go home and sleep. The moments where I wanted to see my parents and go out instead of being at rehearsals. All of Mr. Baldwin's constant yelling. The times we had to rehearse a scene over and over again because we just couldn't get it right.

Everything was worth it. Because that's what theatre was all about. You had to put your blood, sweat, and tears into doing a good show. It was all worth it to see the crowd when you put on a good show. There was no greater satisfaction than knowing all your hard work paid off. On the last night, the whole cast was crying as we said our goodbyes. "I'm really going to miss you guys." I said as I tears rolled down my face. "This was such a great cast." Seb commented. "I better be seeing you all for the next plays!" Embry said. We all hugged and said our goodbyes. "See you all at the banquet tomorrow!" Vienna joined me by my side. "Well, I guess this is it." She sighed. "No, it's just the beginning."

Chapter 27

The last night of the play wasn't the last time the cast was all together. The banquet was the next day and what better place to have it than at Legends? Everyone gathered at Legends, and we were all dressed up. It was all the cast celebrating the end of the play. We all reminisced about the play, the rehearsals, and our favorite moments. It was chance for not only the actors, but the crew to get the recognition they deserved for all the hard work they put into the play. Mr. Baldwin came up and spoke.

"Thanks so much for coming to this banquet. It's just a nice little celebration to thank you all for the hard work you put into this play. And thank you to Morgan, Sebastian, Vienna, and Embry for recommending this fine diner for us to hold this."

Everyone clapped for us, and we stood up and waved. "Now, I like to kick things off with a slideshow!" Just then, the nice freshman girl came up and cued up the projector. "Hey guys! So, Mr. Baldwin tasked me with taking photos and videos to capture the behind-the-scenes work. He thought it would be nice for all of us to look back and remember these moments. Everyone will be getting a copy of this CD." Everyone was surprised and cheered loudly. "Now, here's the video." She turned off the lights and played the video. The slideshow had a ton of behind-the-scenes pictures from rehearsals with a nice song playing in the back. There were photos of all the cast in rehearsals doing warmups and practicing the big numbers. Then a picture of Sebastian and I came up.

"Aw!" Everyone squealed. Sebastian laughed and put his arm around me as I covered my face. I looked up at Vienna who was laughing. There were also videos of Embry dancing a lot backstage and that sent everyone into fits of laughter. A picture of Vienna holding up the costumes came up and everyone clapped. Her face turned red as everyone praised her. There were so many photos and videos of us in rehearsals all together. There were videos of Seb, Vienna, Embry, and I goofing off backstage and I smiled widely looking at all of them.

There was also a whole section of bloopers with the cast that was hilarious. Some of them were people messing up their lines, others were of stage malfunctions, and most were with the Audrey II puppet. The song on the slideshow changed to a slower song as the pictures and videos changed to more heartfelt moments. There were photos of the cast all being together and our preshow rituals. There were moments captured of all of us singing backstage our favorite songs of other musicals and dancing.

The end of the video came, and it looked like the beginning of a sitcom with short clips of everyone waving as it showed their name and who their character was. I didn't expect the slideshow to make me cry but as I looked around, everyone got really emotional. We all clapped and cheered at the end.

"Thank you for that amazing slideshow. Now, I would like for some of you guys to come up here and make some speeches. Just talk about doing the play and what the experience was like for you." Mr. Baldwin said. Everyone stayed quiet as they didn't want to go up there and speak. I didn't blame them. I hated speaking in front of a crowd when there wasn't a script. To talk in front of people made me so nervous and I didn't know what to say. I knew this was in front of people I was more comfortable with and cared about, but I still didn't volunteer. "Anyone?" Mr. Baldwin asked as he waited.

"I'll go, Mr. B." Embry said in his always confident tone. "Go Embry!" Seb called out. Everyone cheered for Embry as he went up to make his speech. It was just like Embry to volunteer with his charismatic and outgoing personality. I was happy he was starting off the speeches.

"This play was so much fun to do. Playing The Dentist has always been a dream of mine. I remember auditioning and being so nervous because I really wanted the part. When I found out, it was the happiest day of my life. I got to perform again along my best friend Sebastian Montgomery." He said as he pointed at Seb. "Love you, bro!" Seb said to him. Everyone laughed in response. "And I also got to make new friends like Morgan and my girl Vienna." "I'm not his girl!" Vienna spoke out. I laughed and shook my head at her. "They became my best friends, and it was so great to work with them. This has definitely been the best and most fun play I have been in. I enjoyed every moment of it, and I'll always look back on these memories." He bowed as he finished, and everyone clapped.

Sebastian high fived Embry when he joined us again. Sebastian was hyped and he was encouraged to go up. "Go Sebastian!" I yelled as he went up. "This play has meant so much to me than anyone will ever know. I've done a lot of plays in my lifetime, but none will compare to this. I was really excited when I got the part of Seymour, but something was missing. We needed a perfect Audrey and then Morgan came along and blew us all away." Vienna put her hand on my shoulder and smiled at me. I looked at Seb and smiled widely.

"She was the missing piece, and she became the perfect Audrey to my Seymour. What started off as an onstage romance became a real life one between us." Everyone in the cast cheered. I hid my face as I felt it turn a dark shade of red. "It was so great to do this alongside my girlfriend and to share our love of theatre together. We also shared our love of theatre with our best friends Embry and Vienna who are both insanely talented. Embry was the best as The Dentist and Vienna did an amazing job with the costumes. This has been an amazing journey and it's been so great working with you all and becoming friends. You all did an amazing job, and the show could not have worked without each and every one of you. I'll always miss this play and you guys." He went back to his seat, and everyone clapped for him.

"Thanks Seb. That was a beautiful speech." I said as I hugged him. I turned to Vienna who seemed to be enjoying the speeches they made. "You should go up there and say something." I told her. "No way! I hate making speeches. Plus, I only did the costumes. I wasn't even in the play." She interjected. "Don't say that! Everybody here had a part in this play. Now, quit being a wimp and go up there!" I said as I was acting like her, and she was acting like me. I got her arms and made her stand up. Everyone noticed and they cheered as she went up. She looked back angrily at me, but I gave her a thumbs up.

"Uh, hi. Sorry, I'm not really good at speech making. It was a lot of fun doing the costumes for the play. Each costume was tailored to fit each person and represent their character in their own unique way. I got this job in this play when I helped Morgan out and made her audition for Audrey. I knew from the start she was the perfect person. She had such great talent and she just shined on that stage. I helped her out and coached her to get the part. She didn't really need help though, just a boost of confidence. Morgan and I became best friends because of our love for theatre. Through that, our friendship just grew more and more. She's an amazing person and an amazing friend. I'll never know how I got so lucky to have a friend like her. She's the best friend anyone could ever have." Sebastian looked at me as I had tears in my eyes.

"It was such a joy to help her get this part and see her practice in rehearsals. I got to see and watch her grow into this vibrant and confident person. That's what I'll hold onto and cherish from this play the most. Through Morgan, I got to work on the costumes on this play which I loved to do. I also met all of you. I made some really good friends like Sebastian..... and I guess Embry." Everyone chuckled at her comment. "It's been great being behind the scenes and watching you all have your part on putting on this show. You all did a great job and should be proud." At the end of her speech, she took a deep breath.

"And now because she made me come up here even though I hate public speaking, Morgan will now come up here and make a speech." I shot her a look and shook my head in disagreement. "Come on, Morgan!" She said once again. I slowly got up from my seat and made my way up there. "Go Morgan!" Seb yelled. Everyone clapped and cheered for me. I took a deep breath and began.

"I've loved theatre ever since I was a little girl. I actually met Sebastian when we were seven doing community theatre. Before this play, I actually hadn't done anything in two years. Personal issues got in the way and I kind of lost myself. But as I lost myself, I found myself again in theatre. I will always find my way back into theatre because it's a part of me. It's my passion and I'll never give it up. I had the time of my life working with my wonderful boyfriend Sebastian." I said as I gestured to him. I looked into his honey eyes as he smiled widely at me. He gave me a wink and I continued.

"It made it so special to work with him because we have been doing this for a long time and it took me back to when we were young. Working with Sebastian gave me confidence and I really felt connected when we played Seymour and Audrey. I'll always remember this special time with him because it was our first time again after two years performing together. I look forward to many more years of us performing side by side together. I met such great people and made friends with each and every one of you. Embry, you are insanely talented and made me laugh a lot. I know you will go far in theatre." He smiled at me from his seat.

"And then there's Vienna." She looked up at me and smiled. "I never had much luck making friends. I only ever had Sebastian. Still, I missed out on having a friend that was a girl. Vienna came along and became my friend. I never knew how someone as cool as Vienna would be friends with me. Vienna, you are so funny and amazing. You are so bold and confident. You are never afraid to speak up for yourself and you always say what's on your mind. You found me when I was lost and made me a better person. You gave me confidence, strength, and I couldn't be more thankful for you. I don't know where I would be if you hadn't come into my life. So, it's all because of Vienna that I'm able to stand up here and talk to you all. She encouraged me to audition for the play and helped me get the part of Audrey. If it wasn't for her, I wouldn't be able to play Audrey or call Sebastian my Seymour." Seb looked at Vienna and smiled. Vienna had tears in her eyes as she listened to me.

"I look around at my *Little Shop of Horrors* family and I'm just so thankful for all of you. I've had such great moments working with all of you and I hope we can work together in the future. Thank you all for making this experience so memorable and enjoyable. This play will always have a special place in my heart because it was the one that I did after two years of not doing theatre. It was the one that made me regain my love for performing and I got to do it with the best people. I'll always love my *Little Shop of Horrors* family." I was done with my speech and was about to go back to my seat, but I forgot someone important.

"Lastly, thank you to Mr. Baldwin for always believing in me. You also ran everything and kept us in line. A show wouldn't be a show without its director. You helped us and guided us each step of the way. You made us better actors. You pushed us all to do our best and put on one heck of a show. Let's give him a hand!" Everyone screamed his name and applauded him. He stood there awkwardly then bowed. "Thank you, Morgan. That means a lot." Everyone stood up and cheered after my speech. I sat back in my seat as my best friends awaited me with big smiles on their faces.

Everyone said their goodbyes at the end of the night. We all cried as we knew it would be the senior's last show. We all were a mess when we said bye to one another. The freshman girl shyly came up to me and said goodbye. "Bye! It's been so much fun!" She said as she hugged me. "It has been so fun getting to know you. Hey, I better be seeing you on stage again next year." I said. "You can count on that!" She replied. She waved at me as she skipped away. I chuckled as I watched her leave. She was so sweet and was a free spirit.

"Morgan!" Mr. Baldwin said as he came up to me. "Thank you for your kind words. It's been a pleasure working with you. You are a phenomenal actor, never forget that." I nodded and gave him a hug. I was so lucky to have had such a great director and mentor. "Thank you for everything." "I better be seeing you back here next year." He said. I definitely knew I would be performing again next year. I would keep performing and never stop ever again. "You will most definitely be seeing me." "Good! I'll see you for the next play." He waved goodbye and I smiled as he left. I was so exhausted from all the excitement of the night. There was lot of eating, crying, and socializing.

As it was clearing out and people were leaving, I decided to go outside and get some time to myself. I sat outside on a bench and looked at Legends bright neon lights. I closed my eyes as the wind caressed my face. The sun was setting, and I watched it as I looked out at the horizon. No matter how cliche it was, I always loved sunsets. I looked up at the sky as the purple, blue, pink, and deep orange hues all swirled together. It seemed to never end, and I watched the sky to see how far it would go. It was something I couldn't see with just my eyes. I knew it spread out far beyond my eyes could see.

The clouds peaked behind the sky, and I liked to think there was a beautiful place beyond there. I knew my grandpa was there and he was watching me from beyond that sunset. I enjoyed it for a few more moments and then Vienna came and joined me. "Hey, there you are." "Hey." She looked out to see what I was seeing. "Wow, it doesn't get any better than that. Have you seen anything so beautiful?" She stared, mesmerized by the sunset. She observed it like she was observing a painting at a museum. She was both confused and taken back at it. I saw her head tilt as she was trying to figure it out. I saw a smile creep on her as she watched.

"That was a really nice speech you made. Thanks for all the nice things you said about me. It was nice to hear. I really appreciate it." She said softly, embarrassed to be vulnerable. "I meant every word of it." I stated plainly. We smiled at one another and then we turned our attention back to the sunset. A thought came to my mind, and I chuckled. "What is it?" She asked. "I never told you this, but I always thought my grandpa sent you to me. That he brought our paths together for us to meet. Now with everything that has happened, I'm certain of it." She looked sincerely at me. "I think so too. We needed each other." She said.

We continued to watch the sunset until it began fading. "So, what now? The play is done, and everything is over. What do we do now?" She laughed lightly. I didn't have to think about it. "We enjoy it. We enjoy our lives and be unapologetically happy without any pain from our pasts." I said. She smiled at me and nodded. I knew everything was going to be okay. We had each other and I would get over the pain of my grandpa and she would get over the pain of her father. We just had to keep on moving forward and we would do that with the help of one another.

"You better be up there on stage with us performing next year." I told her. "I promise." She said. Sebastian and Embry came and joined us. Embry scooted close to Vienna and Seb came and sat next to me. "I was looking for you. Is everything okay?" He asked. "Everything is more than okay." I said as I entwined my hand in his. He sighed with relief, and he looked the sunset. "Wow that's a sight." He said.

"Yeah, the only thing that could be more beautiful is Vienna." Embry said. We all started laughing. "Way to ruin a nice moment, Embry!" She said as she playfully slapped him in the arm. They began to playfully fight one another, and Sebastian and I took cover and ducked. "They are so crazy." I said. "You got that right." Seb said.

I took in the whole scene with the sunset, Vienna, Embry, Sebastian, and I. I felt bliss at how everything all worked out and how it was finally all going to be okay. "This night is perfect. With Vienna, Embry, and being here with you watching the sunset. I know it's going to be like this forever. I can't wait for us to finally be together and live our lives. It's what we've been waiting for." I told Seb. "I can't wait to spend the rest of my days with you. I love you." He said. "I love you too." We kissed as the sunset turned to black. The rest of the night we all spent our time there talking and laughing under the stars.

Life from then on was great for all of us. We all spent Christmas together at Vienna's house. It was a great chance for all of our families to get to know each other. The months passed on and everything at school was boringly normal. It was nice though as we all bonded and became closer than ever. Months and months went on and the divorce finally became final between Vienna's parents. I had never seen her happier as she was able to get closure and move on. Shortly after, Vienna and I had the time of our lives seeing *Moulin Rouge*. We had great seats and screamed the whole time as we actually got to see Aaron in person.

Sebastian's dad surprised us one day and built a tree house in his backyard. He made sure it was sturdy enough and had a professional's help. It was good against extreme weather conditions and held a lot of weight. Seb and I knighted Vienna and Embry into the treehouse and read them all the official rules. It eventually became our top hangout spot as we would practice our lines in there.

For our senior year we all did *Les Miserables*. Vienna and I were thrilled when Mr. Baldwin announced it. We played out dream roles. I played Cosette, Sebastian played Marius, Vienna played Eponine, and Embry played Enjolras. It was the best play we all had done, and we had the time of our lives. Even the nice freshman girl, who was a sophomore then, got her big break when she played young Cosette. It was a great way to end our senior year and the last play we would do in high school.

We all went far in our theatre careers, but Embry's was the most outstanding as he got accepted into Juilliard. Embry changed a lot over the years in his physical appearance. He changed from the dorky awkward teen in high school, and he blossomed into a handsome young man. He got taller and more fit. No matter how much he changed though, he was still the same kid from high school. Sebastian and I were more in love than ever. We had a great relationship like the one I always dreamed of with him. We finally got to live our lives with no regrets. We were always there for one another and were by each other's side through it all. We had a great life and did theatre together. We were living the life we had always dreamed and set out for ourselves.

As for Vienna, she never had any luck with guys. She suffered a lot of heartbreak in her time. She would date one bad guy after another. The relationship would always end and not last longer than a few months for one reason or another. I would console her as she would cry to me and tell me how love only existed for the few lucky people like Sebastian and I. Eventually, she finally woke up and realized that the right guy had always been in front of her all along. Because when you find someone special, you couldn't let them get away. Sebastian and I stood at their wedding, just like they had stood at ours.

Even though our lives were great and much better than they were before, it didn't mean that they were always easy. It didn't mean that Vienna would forget about what her father did and not be hurt when she often thought about it. It didn't mean that I stopped missing my grandpa. I'll always miss him like a future I can never see and a past I can never relive again. I learned a lot about life from my experiences and everything I had gone through.

I learned that life didn't consist of only bad days, and it definitely didn't consist of only good days. Life is both a mixture of good and bad days. We just have to take life as it comes, one day at a time.

I learned life is a lot like theatre. The worlds a stage and you just have to go out there and do your best. No matter how you much rehearse, nothing can prepare you for what's on the other side. Because once that curtain comes up, it's show time. You have to learn that sometimes you won't always be the main character. Sometimes you will just be a stagehand. It doesn't matter what part you have, just that you are part of something larger than yourself. Once on that stage, you have to act your best because you have the audience watching.

Some characters will enter, and some will make their exit, but they will both have a great impact on your part. Maybe you will meet the person you are destined to be with or meet an unexpected friend that will change your life. You can't be afraid to play your part. You just have to go out there and have fun. Don't be afraid to make a fool of yourself. Theatre and life both take practice. Of course, there will be times when you make mistakes and forget your lines. There will be unexpected issues and accidents.

Theatre and life both have their tragedies such as a grandpa passing away unexpectedly or a father walking out on his family. But the show must go on. Your part influences others and causes a chain reaction. Even though you are only on stage for a short amount of time, nobody will ever forget what you said or how you made them feel. Your actions have the power to move an entire audience. And when the curtain closes, it's time to take your last bow.

The thing about life and theatre is that they both don't last. But the memories always will. But that's the way life and theatre is. There is pain, loss, grief, and regret. There is also love, hope, joy, and delight. The important thing to know is to give it your best shot. Live your life to the fullest with no regrets. Never take the ones around you for granted. We are only here for a short amount of time so when the lights turn off and the curtain closes, have everyone remember that you put on a good show.

The End

Acknowledgments

I finished! There were nights where I wouldn't sleep because I would stay up writing till the early hours of the morning. It was all worth it. I would just like to start off by saying that this book means so much to me. I had no intention of writing another book so fast after I just finished my first one, but when inspiration strikes, you have to take it. These characters demanded me to tell their story and I hope you all enjoyed it. Like Morgan and Vienna, I had been through some life changing experiences in the past few years and writing this book helped me work through it. I am glad I was able to write about my love for musicals through this book and for that I would like to thank my sister, Ashley. Thank you for showing me how cool performing is and how cool musicals are. I got deeply inspired by seeing you in your little part in *Little Shop of Horrors* all those years ago. I hope you liked the reference to your small part. Thank you to my mom for always believing in me and encouraging my writing. I hope you enjoyed this book and thanks for gifting me Vienna's last name. To my best friend, Stephanie, thank you for showing so much love for As We Are. I really appreciate it and therefore, I gave you a small cameo in this book. To all my friends, I hope you enjoy this book and get an insight into my love for musicals. Thanks for all your support. To Mr. Martinez, who showed love for As We Are and has given me advice through my whole writing journey. Thank you for your guidance and support and I hope you love this book. To McKenna DeFranco, for blowing me away with your talent. You perfectly captured how I wanted the book cover to look like. Thanks for making Morgan and Sebastian come to life. To my baby boy, Chico, I hope you like your cute and small cameo in this book. I will never forget you. Last, and certainly not least, to my grandpa. I hope I was able to accurately describe your spirit. Though this story is largely fictional, I hope I was able to tell your story and capture your love for movies. Thank you for everything and I hope you like the bond between Morgan and her grandpa. And to all those who will read this book, thank you. Thank you for picking up this book and choosing to read it. I put my heart and soul into this book. This is for all the theatre nerds. I hope you enjoy this book and all of its musical theatre references. I hope you find yourself in my characters with their passion for theatre. This is for everyone going through hard times whether it be through losing a loved one or going through a parent's divorce. You are never alone, and I hope this book brings you comfort and strength.

Printed in Great Britain
by Amazon